B-MOVIE BLOODBATH

B-MOVIE BLOODBATH

by
Isaac Nightingale

Cover design by Hannah Stringer & Liam Blaney

Edited by Cassandra Chaput

First published 2023 by Scary Paper

Second Edition

ISBN: 978-1-7395255-1-4

B-MOVIE BLOODBATH

Isaac Nightingale

SCARY
PAPER

Author's Note

The following story is a factual account of my life. At no point have I made any exaggerations or embellishments, it's all the truth.

+

Every chapter in this book was inspired by a piece of music, so I figured why not whack them all into a playlist to give readers the option to listen to them as you read.
Each chapter has a prompt that looks like this:

[Track]

If you want to listen to the song that inspired the chapter, just scan the QR code below, click the soundtrack (follow me on everything, of course) and then follow the order in whichever app you prefer.
(You may need to pause/turn off auto-play so the next song doesn't play too soon.)
Or if you can't be bothered with all that shite, just ignore this note entirely.
Whatever.

October 29th, 1980

The eighties hit me like a truck. It brought big hair, bright lights and a killer soundtrack. For the most part, I was in my goddamn element. But on this particular night, I was certainly fucking not.

So there I was; standing at the urinal in a truck-stop bathroom at three in the morning. I had just undone my zipper and commenced my business when another patron entered. In this specific cesspool, the urinal was what I call a 'piss shelf'. It's basically a long metal trough, so what it lacks in privacy, it makes up for in splash-back. This one was a good eight feet long, bear that in mind, okay? Now, I'd had a long night. I'd done a lot of driving and it had left me real tired and a little cranky. But what made my night even worse was having a stranger walk into the bathroom as I took a piss, and join me at the piss shelf, no more than nine inches to the right of where I stood.

That's not even the worst part.

What really ruined my night was that this man—this heathen—made direct eye contact as he dropped his pants right down around his ankles to join me in taking a slash; bare ass shining like the moon in the dingy twilight of the bathroom's one flickering lightbulb. He maintained eye contact for five long seconds before breaking and putting his eyes directly on my junk. After way more than a glimpse, he nodded to himself and placed his hands on his hips, leaving nothing but fate to

1

control his stream. There was something seriously wrong with this guy. The fact that he had two missing fingers didn't help his look, either.

I finished my business with a shake and zipped up. I took a step back and caught the weirdo watching me move, his head twitching to the left. Any other day I'd have handed out some strong words for every single thing he'd done since walking through the bathroom door, but I just wanted to get to a nice motel and get some rest.

[Track 1]

After a few steps towards the exit I took one last look over my shoulder to confirm his pants were around his ankles for sure, just in case I'd imagined it in my tiredness. And there they were, fully dropped, ass out, no shame.

I muttered to myself, "Some people just have no goddamn mann—oh Jesus Christ what the fuck."

He was making eye contact again, but so much worse this time. He stood there, hands on hips, pissing into the urinal, with his head twisted a full one eighty degrees to face me.

"Dammit dude," I said, too tired for this kind of creepy bullshit. "You best twist that face of yours back the right way around before I blow your teeth through that wall." I didn't make much effort in pulling out my revolver. I waved it in his general direction, didn't even bother aiming until I'd turned to face him head on.

He kept on lookin' but I guessed he must have finished his piss on the count of his hands moving and a faint zipping noise. We stood in a standoff, him staring at me with his head on backwards, me wishing he'd quit it so we could just forget the whole thing and I could leave the damn bathroom without pebble-dashing the walls with his brains. I moved to take another step back towards the exit. He took a step backwards—or forwards depending on how you look at it—towards me.

"I really can't be bothered with this shit tonight. Look, man, I've been driving around looking for a goddamn serial killer for three days now. I'm just about on my last nerve and I really want to get some shut eye. Can I just leave? What are you anyway? A Murnock? Tentaclari? No? Come on then, what?"

"Fuurgluh," was his response. His body snapped around to face me, quick as a blink. Just like that, all was normal again. Right up until his bottom lip split down the middle and just kept on going, down the middle of his neck. With a sharp grunt, the freak tore his shirt open to reveal the entire top half of his body splitting and opening up. I stood and watched, fully intrigued as his flesh unzipped itself and spread apart to reveal thousands of long fangs inside the cavity of his upper body.

I had seen some fucked up shit, but this was new.

"No thanks, not today," I told him, shaking my head. I took a few steps backwards and raised my gun as he came flapping towards me. The teeth looked seriously fucking sharp. I gave the trigger a squeeze before Freaky could get too close and give me a full body French kiss. My bullet hit a home run. The shot blew Freaky's head apart, splattering the majority of it against the wall behind him. He stumbled backwards. Half of his head remained and his left eye spun around in the socket, as if trying to see where the other eye had ran off to. The fucker didn't go down. In fact, he took another step towards me. A clean shot to the head usually does the trick, but not this time. I emptied the barrel, spraying a generous amount of gore around the bathroom. And yet, he kept coming, right towards me. I lowered my gun, thinking, this is it. This is how I die; eaten by a big toothy vagina monster.

Fuck.

Right about now you're probably asking yourself two questions; what the fuck is this thing? And, how the fuck did this guy end up face to face with it? It's a long story.

Let's pause and rewind.

July 2ⁿᵈ 1972

I gave the jukebox a smack on the side to get it working. It'd taken my quarter and left me high and dry a few times before, I wasn't about to let it hustle me again.

"Give it a good spanking, darlin'. A little harder this time," a waitress said with a wink as she passed by.

I hadn't seen her before so I guessed she was new. I gave the jukebox another whack—a little harder this time—and it jumped to life, playing my song.

[Track 2]

I walked back to my table with a slight strut as the first beats of 'Walk Like a Man' by Frankie Valli and The Four Seasons filled the diner. We had come to our favourite, Benny's, where the food was great and the music was better, because I was always the one paying for the songs.

I slid back into my seat to the sight of the most beautiful smile I've ever laid eyes on. The set of pearly whites grinning at me belonged to the most beautiful girl in the universe, no word of a lie. My world, Suzie May.

I still remember the moment I first set eyes on her; we were both four years old, just innocent little kids. Her parents had moved into the house next door and spotted me peekin' from my doorstep and thought Suzie could do with making a friend. From the second I saw her, I was hooked. I can still remember how my mother laughed when I asked if Suzie was an angel. From the day we met we became inseparable, we went everywhere together, did everything together, shared every moment together. Some people say you can't fall in love when you're that young but that's bullshit, I'm telling you. I loved Suzie May with all my heart, every second of every day from the very moment we met. I didn't know life without her. Hell, I didn't want to know life without her.

"Told you they had it," Suzie said as she leaned over the table, giving me a playful shove. She was a big fan of The Four Seasons. I preferred The King and a bit of Johnny Cash, myself. Both of which were next up on the juke. "I'll bet you I can guess what else you've put on," she said.

I took a sip of my lemonade. "How much are we talking here?"

"A dollar," she said, eyes widening.

Sweet damn, she had amazing eyes. They shone like little pools of chocolate; a deep, dark brown.

"A whole dollar?" I said in mock disbelief. "Jeeeez."

She gave me a cheeky smile. "Yup."

"Fine, but only if you guess both, I got three for a quarter," I said as I pulled a crumpled dollar out of my pocket and slapped it down on the table.

"Something by Johnny Cash and something by Elvis?"

"Well that's pretty vague; I'd say you only deserve fifty cents for that effort."

"Fine, fine. I Walk The Line and Hound Dog?"

"Jailhouse Rock. You got Cash right, at least."

6

"Damn," she said, banging a fist on the table before snatching the dollar. "This is still mine though." She stuck her tongue out and stuffed the dollar down the front of her dress, thinking I wouldn't go after it because we were in a public place.

She thought wrong. I leaned over the table and made a playful attempt at grabbing the dollar.

"Night, you shit!" she said, batting my hand away.

I was about to protest when we were interrupted in the best way.

"Order's up guys," a bubbly voice announced. It was the waitress from the jukebox. "Who's got the chicken breast steak with seven-secret-spice-sauce and fries?"

Suzie smiled, waving her hand a little. "That'll be mine."

The waitress set Suzie's plate down in front of her. "There ya go honey. And for the handsome gentleman here, fries, onion rings and an extra-large hotdog." She put a bit of emphasis on the words 'extra-large hotdog'.

"That's right, thanks," I said.

"You cuties give me a whistle if I can get you anything else," she said before sauntering off and putting an extra bit of swing into her hips to jiggle her ass a little.

"Looks like you've got another admirer." Suzie said.

I stuffed an onion ring into my mouth before replying. "What can I say; I'm just that good lookin'."

Suzie took one of her fries and threw it at me. "Careful with that kinda talk or you'll not get your extra-large ego out the door."

7

"I'm surprised I even got it in the door in the first place."

Suzie picked up her knife and pointed it at me. "Well you keep them eyes on me and I suppose I'll deal with it."

"These eyes are only for you." I lifted my glass to take a drink.

"I know. If they weren't, that extra-large hot dog of yours would be getting cut down to size a little," she said before stabbing the knife into the chicken and cutting a piece off for emphasis.

Lemonade erupted from my nostrils. "Oh so that's how it is? Maybe I'll keep this extra-large hot dog all to myself, not share, how about that?"

Suzie giggled and shook her head then got right back to her food.

I watched her for a few moments, admiring everything about her. The way she moved, the way she looked, even the small things like the way she painted her nails. On this particular occasion her nails were a bright shade of red. She knew I loved red; it always looked good on her. She wore a matching dress too, bright red with little black polka-dots all over it.

"Enjoying the show?" Suzie said, catching me staring. "If you're just gonna sit and watch then I'm gonna start helping myself to your food too. You gonna eat it?"

I snapped out of my little love trance and remembered I had food sitting in front of me. "Damn right I'm eating it, I've gotta have my sustenance to keep these muscles lookin' sexy," I said, making a show of flexing my arm and kissing my bicep. It made her laugh. She loved it when I acted like an idiot.

8

We finished the rest of our meals in silence, enjoying the food.

It took me about five minutes to clear my plate. Suzie was always a little slower. I gave her a wink and stood up to make my way over to the jukebox to stick a few more songs on. I always brought a few quarters to feed the machine, knowing it'd try to rip me off at least once, no matter how much I fought it. I scrolled through the selection, looking for some good rock'n'roll.

"I swear, the amount of quarters you've put in that thing tonight, you may as well own it." It was the waitress again, the one who jiggled her ass. Her name tag read 'Kacey'.

"Hell, I think I've bought this thing five times over. Even if you had no other customers I'd keep the place in business through this damn thing. Any word from Benny on gettin' it fixed? It's still got a habit of eating the odd quarter or two."

"Not that I've heard, hun. The boss says he's been talking to the company but I doubt he'll get it fixed any time soon. He's not exactly gonna be complaining if he gets a few extra coins out of it."

"Suppose you're right, but it's a pain in that ass at times."

"That it is, sugar. Want me to get you guys anything else?"

"Nah we're good thanks, just the bill," I said, making my selections on the juke; Jerry Lee Lewis, Chuck Berry and Bill Haley, respectively.

Kacey gave me a smile and she set off to get the bill. "I'll get that for you then darlin'."

Suzie was right; she definitely wanted a piece. I sat my ass back down to the sound of Jerry Lee Lewis

9

going bat-shit crazy on a piano. In my nineteen years on this planet, I had yet to hear anyone go as nuts on a set of keys as that man.

"You get the bill?"

"Yup, it's on the way." I said.

Suzie chewed on the last of the food and swallowed. "We gonna split it?"

"Nah, I've got it."

"You sure?"

"Yeah, you can get the popcorn at the drive-in tomorrow," I said.

She thought for a second before grinning and saying, "Deal. You sure know how to spoil a gal."

"You know I'd go to Hell and back for you," I said, right as Kacey appeared with the bill.

"There you go guys, hope you've enjoyed your meals and hope to see you again soon." She gave us a wink then skipped off to serve the other customers.

"Yeah I'll bet she hopes we're back soon," Suzie said.

I laughed as I threw down the dollars to square up the bill and leave a little extra tip.

Suzie stood and flattened down her dress. I flipped the little bill book closed and stood up, putting an arm around her shoulders. She pulled me in a little closer as we walked out the door. It had gotten cold out but it only took about a minute to walk across the lot to my car. Well, I say my car; it was actually my old man's. He'd let me use it whenever he didn't need to.

I pulled out the keys and popped the passenger side door for Suzie before walking over to my side. It was a short drive back to Suzie's house and an even shorter one back to mine.

We pulled into the street not five minutes after getting out of Benny's and brought the car to a stop outside Suzie's house. I leaned over and gave her a kiss.

"So, I'll pick you up at eight tomorrow?" I said.

"Eight sounds good. Don't be late."

"I'll do my best but it's a pretty long drive ya know."

She laughed and rolled her eyes as she opened the door and stepped out. "You're such an idiot," she said, hanging on to the door, "but that's why I love you."

We shared a steamy kiss before she turned and skipped down the path. She spun around when she got to the door, gave me a wave goodnight and disappeared inside.

This had always been a little tradition of ours. Whenever I got to use the car, I'd pick her up and drop her off as if we lived miles apart when we actually lived right next-door to each other.

I pulled the car into the driveway, killed the engine, popped the car door and stepped out. Suzie and I had a week full of dates planned and I hoped I could get through another few nights without getting into some sort of trouble.

Something was nagging at me from the back of my mind down to the pit of my stomach. It was a sort of unconscious feeling I'd get whenever there was about to be trouble, a sickening, falling sensation in my stomach. I'd never taken any notice at first but over time, it had turned into a sixth sense, of sorts. The worse the feeling got the more trouble I was in for, and sweet Jesus, it felt like I had some serious shit coming my way. But then again, it could have been Benny's questionable hotdogs.

Little Punk

True to my word, I pulled up outside Suzie's place for exactly eight. I knew she was almost dressed and ready to go on the count of our bedroom windows facing each other, giving us a good view of one another whenever we wanted it.

I killed the car's engine but kept the radio playing as I sat and waited for her to leave the house. I could have waited at the front door or gone inside but her dad always weirded me out a little. Great guy, but he had these crazy eyes that made him look like he wanted to strangle everyone, even when he was happy. Her mom was nice, too, but she'd always want to feed me her home-made pies that she called 'man fuel'. Suzie's dad ate them like they were going out of fashion but I always thought they tasted like cat food that had been left out a little too long.

After a few minutes, Suzie appeared at the door with her dad close behind. She gave him a peck on the cheek and pranced down the path to the car. Her dad smiled and waved at me. I waved back. No use in being impolite, wouldn't want him to strangle me one day.

I reached over and opened the door for Suzie to get in.

"Dad says I've gotta be back by midnight," Suzie said as she threw herself down in the seat. On the previous night she wore a pretty dress, this time she'd thrown on an old pair of tight fitting jeans, ratty old

Converse All Stars and a white t-shirt with a big red love heart in the middle of it. And she looked damn fine.

"Midnight it is then," I said as I leaned over for a kiss.

She planted one on me and smiled. "Step on it, I don't wanna miss the start of the movie."

[Track 3]

As instructed, I put my foot down once Suzie's dad had gone back in the house and was out of sight. It was about a fifteen minute drive to the outskirts of town to get to the drive-in. I got there in ten. It had gotten nice and dark, the best time to see a movie. On this particular night, the movie of choice was the Tales from the Crypt movie. The drive-in entrance was lit up under a big neon sign. I pulled up to the ticket booth and handed some cash to the attendant. She counted it out, gave me some change and our tickets and waved us through. Suzie always liked to get near some speakers so we could hear nice and clear. I parked in a nice spot in the middle of the lot, not too far from the concession stand.

"I'm gonna go get the popcorn, I'll be back in a few minutes," Suzie said as she popped the door open.

"Hold up," I said, reaching into my pocket and pulling out a few dollars, "get us some drinks too, while you're there?"

"Sure thing," she said.

The trailers started up a second later. I flicked the air conditioning on to keep the car warm and got myself nice and comfy as the trailer for Deliverance started playing. I always loved watching the trailer before a movie. Missing them was like missing an extra scene

13

after a movie's credits, so I sat and enjoyed them. Suzie never really gave a damn about them, she was happy just as long as we caught the beginning, which is why she'd always be the one to get snacks from the concession stand while I sat on my ass.

A good few minutes had passed and Suzie hadn't got back yet, which was strange 'cos it usually didn't take long to get a few snacks. I decided to get up and go see if she needed a hand. She'd get excited sometimes and buy way too much and not be able to carry it all. I popped the door and hauled myself out the car, turning away from my precious trailers.

I could hear her voice as I got closer to the concession stand. She didn't sound happy. I found her standing outside, right in the middle of an argument with some sleaze-ball looking guy. Three of his friends stood behind him, smirking and nudging each other.

"Hey, what the fuck's going on?" I said as I approached, eyeballing the guy.

Suzie cut off yelling at the guy and turned to me.

"I was walkin' by to get our stuff and this asshole thinks it's fine to slap my ass," she jabbed a finger in Sleaze-ball's direction, "so I turn around, slap him on the chops, and the prick starts calling me a stuck up whore."

"This punk here?" I said as I eyed the kid she was pointing at. He looked to be about seventeen and was wearing a black leather greaser jacket. The assholes behind him were all dressed the same way, like a bunch of fifties rejects. They all seemed to think they were much bigger than they actually were. Even if he hadn't slapped Suzie's ass, just looking at the try-hard sleaze-ball kid was enough to piss me off.

14

The guy piped up. "Bitch, didn't your parents ever tell you it ain't attractive when a woman has a dirty mouth?"

His pals had a good laugh at that.

"How about you watch your mouth, asshole," I said, pointing a finger at him. "What's this about you smacking my girl's ass?"

"Man, with jeans that tight she was just asking for it," he said, checking out his reflection in the window of the concession stand.

"Well you're asking to lose your teeth, buddy."

This was always my weak spot; I was riled up far too easy, and disrespecting my woman was the easiest way to get me pissed.

"Whatever shithead, like I said, she wanted it."

Suzie cut in, "Fuck you."

I got a little closer to the guy. "How about you step back and beat it, you little punk."

The guy took a step forward and squared up to me, trying to look tough in front of his friends. "You wanna go? You wanna throw down right here? You wanna piece of this, huh?"

"Sit down before I knock you down," I warned.

He prodded a finger into my chest a couple of times then tried to push me over. It didn't work.

I planted both hands on his chest and gave him a hard shove. He stumbled backwards and almost fell on his ass.

One of his friends held him steady and decided to give some input on the situation. "Get 'em Sammy. Put a fist right on his god damn beak," he said.

I glanced over to the kid that was running his mouth and said, "You want some too? You're just a bunch of pussies."

Sleazy Sammy made a move to swing at me while I was distracted but I caught him getting ready to throw the punch. He took a second to step back so he could lunge forward and really put his weight into it. Just as he sprang forward and swung a fist, I stepped aside and stuck my foot out. He tripped on it, sailed past me and landed face first on the concrete. His nose made a loud cracking noise as it burst on contact with the ground and sprayed blood all across his face. He rolled onto his back and cupped his hands over his face while making a sort of moaning, crying noise.

I reached down and grabbed a hold of him by the shirt and pulled him in close. "You gonna get out of here or am I gonna have to make you bleed from more places?" I said to him.

"God damn creep," Suzie said and gave him a swift kick to the ribs.

I raised my free hand to give him a solid backhander when his friends decided to jump in to the rescue. Two of his cronies grabbed me and pulled me away from him while the other helped him up. Not a second later, Chris—the manager of the drive-in—came running out of the concession stand.

"Hey, hey, hey, now that's enough from you lot," he said, pointing at the little gang of greasers. "I thought I told you not to be causing any more trouble around here?"

The kids let go of me. I walked over to Suzie and put an arm around her.

"She started it," Sammy said, pointing at Suzie while trying to stem the flow of blood from his nose.

"That's always the case, isn't it?" Chris said, "You've been warned too many times now. Go on, get out of here and don't show your faces again."

"We've already paid for our tickets man," one of the friends said.

"Do I look like I give a shit? I run the show here and I say scram before I smack the lot of you myself."

"What a load of bullshit," Sammy mumbled as he turned to skulk off with his friends.

"Night, Suzie, you all good?"

We were pretty sweet with the staff here considering we came so often, and Chris was an old friend of Suzie's mom.

"Yeah thanks, Chris," Suzie said. "They were just being assholes."

"They always are. They show up every now and again and always end up hassling somebody. Everything okay though? They didn't hurt you did they?"

"Nah, one of them smacked my ass but I slapped him back and I think Night gave him a good scare," she said, squeezing my arm. I gave her a cheeky grin and kissed her on the forehead.

"Good to hear. I'll kick their asses myself if I catch them back here, I swear."

"I think they're gonna get their asses kicked sooner or later anyway," I said.

"Yeah but I wouldn't mind doing it myself," Chris said. "Anyway, what can I get you guys? Drinks? Popcorn? Whatever you fancy, it's on the house tonight."

"Sweet," Suzie grinned. "No queueing?"

17

"No queueing. I'll go get everything for you right now, you guys just head back to your car and I'll bring it over in a minute. So what'll it be?" he said, clapping his hands together enthusiastically.

"Large popcorn?" Suzie said, looking up at me.

"Sure, large popcorn, a lemonade for me and a...?"

"Another lemonade."

"Large popcorn, two lemonades and a hotdog," I said.

"Sure thing guys," Chris said, "go get comfortable, the movie's about to start."

"Thanks man, it's the ol' blue Cadillac over there." I stuck my thumb in the car's direction.

"Yeah, like I don't know what you drive by now."

With that, we smiled and made our way back to the car.

Suzie bumped her hip into mine. "You should get into fights more often if it means we'll get free stuff."

"Can't really call that a fight. I didn't even hit the kid; he practically broke his own nose."

"Yeah, real smartass he turned out to be, huh?"

"Real asshole is more like it."

She gave me another playful nudge with her ass as we got to the car. The opening credits of the movie were just starting as we sat down and pulled our doors closed. The car had warmed up nicely so I flicked the air-con off and shifted over in my seat a little to get an arm around Suzie. She inched closer and laid her head on my shoulder.

It was about five minutes into the movie when I heard a knock on the window. I sat up to see it was Chris and one of the girls from the concession stand with our snacks. I wound the window down.

18

"Here you go buddy, popcorn, two lemonades and a hotdog. I've supersized the lot and threw in some candy too. Sorry about all the trouble," Chris said, passing things to us through the open window.

Now that's some good service.

"Thanks man, you didn't have to but we really appreciate it," I said.

Suzie grabbed a hold of the popcorn and her lemonade while I took the other one and the hotdog. "Thanks Chris," she said as he gave us a wave goodbye and got back to his business.

We settled back down with all our snacks and kicked the seats back a little to watch the rest of the movie in peace.

"Now, try not to scream if you get scared," Suzie whispered with a big ol' grin across her face.

"I'll try my best," I whispered back, "but if it smells like someone's shat themselves, I swear it wasn't me."

Coconut Superstar

There was never much interesting around town aside from the drive-in and Benny's, but once a year, around July time, a carnival would come to town. It'd hang around for about a week before leaving and going somewhere else. We never missed it. The carnival was pretty much the highlight of the year for the town. We'd always hold off going 'till it started getting dark. It just seemed a lot more fun that way, kinda romantic. And considering it was the Fourth of July, there'd be lots of fireworks.

[Track 4]

It was about eight-thirty when I knocked on Suzie's door that night. My dad needed the car, so we were stuck with walking there and back. Suzie's mom answered the door, and that only meant one thing; I couldn't escape the pies. By the time Suzie made her way down stairs I had already been escorted to the dining table and had a suspicious smelling pie sitting in front of me, with Mrs. May sitting to my left doing a crossword puzzle. Being the perfect gentleman I've always been, I powered through it like a hero. I'd suffered through them since I was a little kid so I'd developed a damn good poker face while I was eating them. Suzie knew I hated them though, which is exactly why she told her mom I loved them.

20

Suzie came prancing down the stairs and into the dining room just in time to see me cramming the pie into my face as quick as I could, trying to get it out of the way fast, before my taste buds had a chance to know what hit them. "Enjoying that?" she said with a sadistic grin across her face as she walked over to her mom.

"Mhhphmm, phmmphhphh," I replied with my cheeks stuffed and crumbs all over my face.

Suzie's mom looked up from her crossword. "Oh Sooze, don't you look beautiful," She said, pinching Suzie's cheek. "Doesn't she look beautiful, Night?"

Suzie was wearing a pretty blue dress that I had bought her for her last birthday. I swallowed the mouthful of pie and smiled, saying, "Of course she does Mrs. May."

Suzie's dad walked into the room a second later. "She takes after her mother," he said, taking his wife's hand and pulling her from the chair into a twirl. "Now where's my pie? You ate them all, Night?"

I wiped the crumbs off my face. "No sir."

"Yeah you best not have, otherwise you'll get this." He shook his fist in front of his face.

And ya'know, I actually believed him. He was always nice and all, but his eyes said he'd murder anyone who dared come between him and a pie.

"Mom, you should really make more of them, Night says they're his favourite," Suzie said before smiling at me. She always knew how to torment me and make me enjoy it.

"I'm not opposed to you making more, darling," Suzie's dad said. "I might get morbidly obese in the end, but it'd be worth it."

I silently gagged at the thought of eating so many of those goddamn things.

"You ready to go?" Suzie asked.

"Sure," I said. I got up off the chair, thankful I wouldn't have to face another pie that day.

Suzie's dad said, "Remember, no later than midnight, Mr. Nightingale."

"Yes sir," I said, waving goodbye as Suzie dragged me towards the door.

"Love you darling," her mom shouted.

Suzie pushed me out the door before saying, "Love you too," and pulling the door shut behind her. She planted a kiss on me the second it was closed.

I took her hand and led her down the path. The sun was setting as we set off on our way to the carnival. It was shaping up to be a pretty nice night. The skies were clear, the air felt warm and the stars were just breaking through, trying to wink at us.

We got to the carnival for just after nine o'clock. Suzie got real excited when she spotted the lights on the big wheel in the distance. That was always her favourite ride, which was fine by me considering most carnival rides just made me sick on the count of all the spinning they do.

We made our way over to get a couple of drinks first. Suzie got herself a cola and I got lemonade, as always. With our drinks in hand, we made our way around the carnival, taking in the sights and seeing what we could spend our money on. Suzie had been eyeing the big circus tent in the middle of everything so we made our way over there first. They were just about to start a show that'd last an hour. We figured why not see it? The carnival was gonna be around for a few days so we could come back again to see everything we missed the first time around.

We handed over a few dollars to get in and bought a big puff of cotton candy, which Suzie practically buried her face in the moment the lady handed it over. We had just got to our seats when the show started. It was all pretty standard circus stuff; acrobats, clowns and the occasional person spitting fire or swallowing swords. I didn't think it was all that exciting, but Suzie seemed to love it. She barely took her eyes off the show the entire time and still had a look of amazement on her face when we left the tent.

"Did you see those guys swinging all over the top of the tent?" she said. "How the hell do they do that? There wasn't even a net to catch them. If they fell, they'd be dead."

"I'd say either they're insane or they've got some serious balls."

"Yeah they're definitely-OH MY GOD!" Suzie yelled, batting at my arm.

I was getting ready to throw a few punches, thinking someone had grabbed her ass again. "What?" I said, spinning my head to see what had her going crazy. I caught sight of her running off in the direction of a coconut shy and followed, wondering what was going on.

She started batting at me in excitement when I caught up with her. "Look at that," she giggled, pointing towards a giant fluffy cat toy sitting amongst the prizes at the stall. "I'm playing. I've gotta get it. Night, look at it."

She had caught the attention of the carny running the game. He came strolling over saying, "Hey there darlin', how'd you like to try your luck for a prize? Three balls for a dollar, all you gotta do is knock a coconut off a stand and you win yourself any prize. Whad'ya say?"

"Let me try," I said, handing over a dollar.

Suzie bounced with excitement. I would have watched her give it a shot, but I knew games like this were always fixed so there's not much chance of winning. I didn't wanna see her disappointed or swindled out of a load of money and I reckoned I had more of a chance considering I'd played baseball since I was old enough to walk.

The coconuts were each sat in a little bowl on the end of a stick that was stuck in the ground. I wouldn't have been surprised if they'd been glued into the bowl.

"There you go superstar, three balls. All you gotta do is knock one coconut off to win. Easy." The guy handed me three baseballs that were only half as heavy as they should have been.

I held back a little on my first throw to see what would happen. The ball hit the coconut and barely made it budge.

Suzie gave a grunt of disappointment. "Do it hard," she said, "go on. Whack the furry little bastard."

"I got a plan," I mumbled. I threw the second ball hard and whacked the top of the stick, just under the bowl. The stick leant back a little, making the coconut a bit more unstable. With the third throw I put all my strength in to it and threw the ball as hard as I could. It hit the coconut square in the middle and sent it flying out of the bowl and on to the floor. Suzie screamed as she threw her arms around me and planted a big kiss on my cheek.

"Hey well whad'ya know, we have a winner!" the carny announced in an underwhelmed tone. "Whad'ya fancy?"

Suzie pointed to the giant fuzzy cat toy. "That one, please."

"That one it is," he said before turning to get the prize, mumbling something to himself that sounded suspiciously like an insult.

He handed over the giant cat and gave me a shitty look. I couldn't blame him, in all honesty. I probably got lucky.

"Thanks," I said with a polite smile as we left with Suzie's new friend.

Within ten minutes we were eating ice cream at the top of the big wheel with the massive fluffy cat squeezed between us. The view from the top was quite amazing at night. The carnival lights glittered in all different colours, and then there were the lights in town, just over a mile away. We could see pretty much all of town when we were at the top of the wheel. It looked so small and peaceful at night. Quaint and cosy.

"So what's your new friend called?" I asked between licks of the ice cream.

"Hmm... Captain Flufftastic."

"I guess that's fitting. Do you even have space for this thing? It's almost bigger than you."

"I'll find space, or I'll just use it as a bed."

"It's definitely big enough."

Suzie nodded and took a few licks of ice cream. "Wanna come back tomorrow night and see the rest?"

"Sure, we haven't got around much of the place just yet. There's still a lot we can see and do."

"Yeah, I wanna get Flufftastic home early; it'd be a pain in the ass for us to carry him around all night."

"Should we start walking back after this then?"

"Sure thing," she said with a smile.

We sat and finished our ice creams in silence for the rest of the ride, taking in the sights and sounds of all the people having a good time. The carriage swayed back and forth a little. It was quite relaxing, especially when we reached the highest point and got the best view. After a few minutes the wheel slowed and came to a stop, moving now and again to let people off at the bottom. When it was our turn, I got out first and pulled Captain Flufftastic out with me before taking Suzie's hand and helping her step down from the carriage.

"Gimme," Suzie said with her arms outstretched, wanting to carry the giant cat.

"You're gonna carry that all the way home?"

"Nah, you can take him when we get halfway."

I handed her the toy. "Sounds fair enough."

I put an arm around Suzie's waist and pulled her in close. It was getting on to about eleven and the dark had crept in hard and heavy, so we left to get ourselves and Captain Flufftastic home.

Considering how dark it was getting, and how awkward the toy was to carry, we both agreed it would be better to take a shortcut through the woods to cut about ten minutes off our walk. We'd walked the trail hundreds of times in the past and never had any trouble so we set off into the woods, just the two of us and the giant cat taking a romantic moonlit stroll down an old dirt trail.

Within minutes we were completely surrounded by trees and darkness. The wind whispered through the branches as the moonlight marked out a lonely path.

It was beautiful, for a while.

Brick Shithouse

In all honesty, walking through the woods in total darkness was a little disorientating. The whole thing gave me that weird feeling in the pit of my stomach but it had been a great night; Suzie and I were practically high on our love for each other, so I just put it down to butterflies, and lots of them. (Yeah, after all the years we'd been together I'd still get them, shaddap about it.)

[Track 5]

Roughly halfway down our path through the trees we came into a little clearing where we'd always stop to try to spot some rabbits that usually hopped around. The moon shone through the trees. It made it all look nice, but kind of creepy at the same time. We stopped to admire the sight for a minute. There was no sign of any rabbits, just a nice display of fireworks flashing silently in front of the moon.

"Night," Suzie said, tugging my arm, "thanks for the past couple of days. It's been nice to get out a little more." She pushed herself up on to her tiptoes and kissed me on the lips. It was a one hell of a romantic kiss, too; bathed in moonlight with fireworks in the distance; something from a movie for teenagers to melt over.

"It's been a pleasure, Miss May." I put both arms around her waist and pulled her closer for another kiss.

Suzie would always have this little smile while we kissed. She was as cute as a box of kittens. We stood in the clearing for a while; just kissing and having a three-way hug with the giant cat while watching the fireworks. Well, Suzie watched the fireworks. I watched the reflections of them in her eyes. She turned and smiled when she caught me. I gave her a peck on the forehead and got the scent of her hair. It always had a delicate, flowery smell to it.

It was nice to stand for a while and watch the fireworks light up the sky. Things always seemed a little too hectic in my life so I appreciated taking a moment to just stand in the darkness, breathe some cool night air and watch some pretty lights in the distance. I was never really that fond of fireworks. They were too noisy for my liking, but from the little clearing we were at a perfect distance to see them and not have to deal with the noise they'd make. For a while, life was perfect.

When we had our fill of fireworks, I took Suzie by the hand and we got ourselves moving again. I didn't want Suzie to be late getting home. Her parents were always a little over-protective. We walked a couple of minutes down the trail, away from the clearing when I caught sight of two silhouettes walking in the opposite direction, heading straight towards us. It wasn't uncommon to pass the occasional person or two so I thought nothing of it but pulled Suzie a little closer to my side nonetheless. They seemed like nothing more than a couple of friends on their way to catch what was left of the carnival before it closed for the night.

Within a few seconds of seeing their silhouettes, they were standing right in front of us, blocking our path. The silhouettes belonged to two guys. They were pretty damn big too, I'll tell you that. One was short and beefy, with a good bit of muscle. The other was huge; built like a brick shithouse, reinforced with steel and clad in iron. A certified steroid head if I ever seen one; ain't no way to get so big without some help from the juice.

I didn't know what they were playing at and we didn't have time to deal with any bullshit so I put on my best gentleman voice and asked them if we could pass.

"Excuse us, fellas; just gotta squeeze by you there if you don't mind."

You know what they did? Jack shit. They stood there smiling like a couple of shit-brained goons. And one of the ugly bastards had his eyes all over Suzie.

So I asked to get by again. "Mind if we get through? It's getting pretty late, best we get home."

They stood there, grinning at us both. There was something strange about them that I couldn't quite put my finger on. Something just seemed off, like they weren't all there in the head. The smaller of the two had a real creepy look to him, like his greasy little face was sleaze personified. He had those small, beady eyes that'd leer at anyone with a set of titties. The brick shithouse just looked like a bull on two legs. His grinning face was equally as creepy but he had a glazed look about him that said the brain department was all out of stock.

Now, I was never known to be patient with anyone other than Suzie. I'd gotten myself into a fair few fights with guys who thought they could be assholes for the fun of it, or anyone who stared at Suzie's tits a little too long. In retrospect, I should have known better than to provoke these guys but I could be a mouthy little shit at times.

30

This wasn't the right time.

I'd tried being polite and I sharp lost my patience, so like a goddamn idiot I started running my mouth.

"Are you gonna stand there smiling like a pair of dick heads or are you gonna get out of the goddamn way?" I said to them with a hint of acid in my voice.

They glanced at each other and acted as if they were offended, then turned back to face us and carried on smiling. The smaller of the two dick heads—the one in front of Suzie—spoke first.

"Looks like we've got a tough little nut here," he said while glancing to his friend in front of me. "It'd be one hell of a shame if someone cracked you open."

The moment he heard those last three words, the goon in front of me swung a fist the size of a goddamn wrecking ball. It smashed into the side of my head, and it fucking hurt. I staggered sideways past Suzie but managed to keep myself upright long enough to hear her scream and see the sleazy looking guy seize Suzie's toy from her hands, tear it apart and stamp it into the dirt.

I dropped down on one knee to regain my senses but my head was a blur from the hit. "You fuckin'—" I slurred, "—you pair of asshats. You leave her..."

The smaller guy clicked his fingers and his big goon buddy walked around Suzie and came over to me.

"What was that?" he said. "Speak up boy, I can't hear you."

"I said..." I pushed myself back up on two feet and lifted my head. "I said leave her alone, you pair of fu—"

Click.

With a second click of the fingers, the big bastard swung another fist into the side of my head. This one

31

knocked me clean off my feet. I must have been airborne for a couple of seconds before the other side of my head came into contact with a tree and I hit the ground like a sack of shit. A mixture of pain and warmth spread over my head. It felt like my skull had been cracked open and my brain was trying to push its way out of my ears. The warmth trickled down the side of my face. I lifted a hand to my head to try and keep it from splitting in two. When I pulled it away I could see that it was covered in blood. My ears were filled with a ringing noise but somewhere in the distance there was the sound of screaming and a dull thud of another fist coming down on flesh. I didn't feel any pain from it, and the screaming quickly stopped.

It was Suzie that had taken that punch.

My eyes adjusted to focus on something a few feet away. Suzie was lying on the ground, crying and clutching her face. The ugly little shithead had punched her and bust her nose.

I staggered in an attempt to get back on my feet as I pulled myself up from the ground but didn't have a chance to speak before another 'roid fuelled fist came straight for my face. It smashed into my forehead and everything went black.

I must have only been out cold a few seconds. When I came around my vision was completely blurred and I felt like vomiting from the pain in my head. It took a few seconds to regain some of my senses and figure out I was lying face-down in the dirt, surrounded by a pool of blood. I made an attempt to push myself up from the ground and look for Suzie but couldn't see more than a few inches in front of me. Everything else was a blur of darkness. It took a moment for my mind to register that I could hear something other than the blood pulsing through my ears and out of my head. Suzie was screaming and there was a faint sound of fabric tearing.

I had just regained enough of my senses to understand simple English when I heard the words that'll ring through my head 'till the day I die…

"Hold this bitch down while I get my pants off, will you?"

Horrors, Part One

A couple of seconds after being beaten to the floor by the fucking Hulk on steroids, I regained my senses, only to see that the guy who'd ordered my beating was in the process of undoing his belt while his big buddy pinned Suzie to the dirt. I wouldn't really call myself an intelligent guy, but I'm not exactly dumb either. I knew what was about to happen. Fuck that shit, I thought. I had to save my girl.

[Track 6]

The little asshole caught sight of me trying to stand and nodded in my direction. His big buddy—let's call him Roids—gave Suzie a hard smack across the head that knocked her unconscious, then stood and came towards me. I flinched back as he neared, expecting another wrecking ball of a fist to crack my skull in half once and for all. The hit never came. Instead, I was whipped around and pulled into a vice-like bear hug. The son of a bitch put one arm around my body and one around my neck, forcing me to face the horror that was about to be unleashed upon my girl.

Pure dread raged through my body as I realised there was absolutely jack shit I could do to help. I tried, of course. Sweet Jesus, I tried but I couldn't so much as budge from the grip of the brick-shithouse that was hugging me like a kid with a teddy bear.

"Get away from her you piece of shit!" I yelled at the smaller goon—let's call him Rapey, 'cos he fit the bill—before his buddy tightened his grip, almost closing my windpipe.

He turned and smiled at me as he dropped his pants, giving me a quick wink before he threw himself on top of Suzie.

She slowly regained consciousness as she mumbled something and put a hand to her head where Roids had hit her, too dazed to understand what was happening.

Rapey took her arms and pinned them above her head with one hand while he pulled her dress up with the other.

Suzie's head cleared from the hit. She started to scream as she realised what was happening.

I kicked, yelled and tried to bite at Roids' arms in an attempt to escape, but it was futile. For all my struggling against Roids' embrace, I had nothing to show for it. I'd successfully accomplished sweet fuck all. Not a damn thing. I may as well have stood and watched with a tub of popcorn for all I'd accomplished.

But I wasn't the only fighter. As Rapey tried to arrange himself to make his assault, Suzie brought a knee up with the force of the gods and almost smashed his testicles up into his throat.

He howled in pain and rolled off of her. "You fucking bitch," he groaned, cupping his junk.

Suzie scrambled to her feet and wasted no time delivering a second kick, giving it all her might. Rapey's hands offered some protection this time, but still not enough. The howl turned into high pitched screeching as he tried to drag himself away.

"You're the bitch," Suzie spat, "you dirty fucking pervert."

Rapey backed up, dragging his bare ass across the dirt, still groaning.

Suzie turned to me and pointed at Roids. "Let him go you fucker." She marched over with the fires of Hell burning in her eyes, finger still outstretched, "I said, let him—"

"Behind you," I managed to groan, but not fast enough.

Suzie made to turn around as a rock crashed into the side of her head. She fell to the ground, hard. Rapey stood behind her, clutching the rock, pants still around his ankles. He dropped the rock and waddled over, eyes darting from me to Suzie.

She lay on the floor, out cold, with a concerning amount of blood leaking from her temple and running down her cheek.

"Enjoy that did you?" Rapey said, "I sure as hell did, bitch deserved that," he gestured towards Suzie.

"Fuck you," I wheezed.

"What?" he said, pretending to be insulted, "That's not very polite."

"Just you wait you sick bastard. I'll rip your damn dick off with my bare hands, I promise you."

He pointed at his still exposed crotch. "Oh, you mean this? How about I come over there and beat you senseless with it? I could do that, you know. Look at your girl, she's pretty senseless herself. What I've done to her with a rock, I'll do to you with my cock." He laughed as he bent down and pulled up his pants, making a jiggling motion with his hips, waving his junk about to torment me even more.

The goon holding me released his grip. I darted from his steroid pumped arms and ran straight for Suzie. I hadn't even covered a meter before Rapey kicked my legs out from under me, making me fall face first to the ground. I felt a sickening crunch go through my face as I gave the dirt a high-speed inspection. A coppery taste filled my mouth. I felt a few of my teeth shatter and my nose crack, spreading a warm sensation over my face as my nose burst into a fountain of blood.

One broken nose, a fractured jaw and four chipped teeth. Thank you very much.

Both assholes howled with laughter at the sight.

"Looks like you've hurt yourself there boy. Let us help you up!" Rapey yelled through his laughter.

I had almost managed to pull myself within reaching distance of Suzie before Roids grabbed me by the neck and dragged me away from her, back into his bulging, beef-like arms.

Rapey gave me a couple of slaps on the cheek. "You sit tight, sweet cheeks, show's not over yet."

That feeling of dread surged through my veins again.

Fuck, fuck, fuck!

Back in ol' Roids' bear hug, there was nothing I could do to fight, so I fought the only way I could and spat a mouthful of blood all over Rapey's face. "Go fuck yourself," I said.

On the list of traumatising events that night, witnessing the girl I love almost get raped, then bludgeoned with a rock was number one. Mouthing off to the assholes dropped down from the number two spot to be replaced by the decision to spit blood on Rapey's face.

Rapey stood there in front of me, taking long deep breaths as if he was savouring the smell of my blood on his face. With each breath his skin turned a paler and paler shade until the veins were visible underneath. What had previously happened was undeniably horrifying, but what was happening inched closer to a joint first place on the list of shit I just didn't want to see.

"What the fu—" I started to mutter, before trailing off

Rapey slowly stuck his tongue out of his mouth. Now, at first I just thought, 'This dickhead has a pretty long tongue' but the damn thing didn't stop. His tongue grew longer and longer as he stood there taking deep breaths, flicking it at me.

After it had grown almost a foot long—yes, a foot long—the damn thing split down the middle into two forks. The creepy bastard used both sides to slowly lick the blood from his face.

I was one hundred percent sure this was not normal.

When he next spoke his voice was close to being nothing more than a guttural growl, a noise straight from Hell. "Oh that's good," he said. His rancid breath hit my face almost as hard as his friend's fist. "Well, I don't know about you, kid, but I'm peckish."

My mind had pretty much broken from the shock of what I was seeing. I couldn't speak, nor think, so I swiftly replied by vomiting all over his shirt. And when I say vomit, I mean projectile vomit. It didn't even touch my tongue; it leapt from my stomach to his chest in one graceful arc.

He didn't even flinch.

As I stared at him in horror, his face continued to get even fucking weirder. The sides of his mouth split at the corners and his lips pulled back over his gums, showing tiny holes in them at the roots of the teeth. Within seconds, his jaw cracked and extended and his normal teeth began to fold back into his mouth as a new set of long, jagged fangs slowly pushed their way out of the holes.

I struggled against Roids' iron grip, not knowing whether I was trying to escape to attempt to save Suzie from this creature, or try and fight the Hell-freak that was standing in front of me. Whatever I was trying to do, it came second to trying not to shit myself.

I lashed out at him with my feet—the only limbs I could move—but he moved with inhuman speed. Before my mind could even register it, he was out of kicking range and standing above Suzie. He stood over her, grinning at me with his disgusting, freakish face while Suzie continued to bleed into the dirt below him. He bent down and began to stroke her hair. Suzie came to and recoiled at his touch. She pushed herself up to make a move towards me. Rapey let her wobble to her feet and stagger within reaching distance of me before he appeared behind her, pulling her away from me by her hair. Tears and blood ran down her face as she cried my name, reaching out for me. The bastards were taking every opportunity to torment us both, in every way possible.

Suzie began to kick and scream as Rapey pulled her into an embrace mirroring the one I was imprisoned in. My only solace was the fact that Suzie hadn't looked at Rapey's face since before he turned into whatever kind of monster he called himself.

Rapey stared straight into my eyes, just to make sure I was watching.

"Please," Suzie said through her tears, her voice faint and fragile, "please just let us go."

Something told me that pleading with these people, or things, would be useless. Her cries only seemed to entertain him more.

Rapey flicked his snake-like tongue at me as he ran his free hand over Suzie's chest and down between her breasts. His grotesque face contorted into a smile as his hand came to a stop on her stomach. His fingernails grew and turned a dark shade of yellow. He caressed the area under his hand for a moment before ripping a hole through the Suzie's dress and digging his fingers into her skin.

Suzie screamed out in pain as the skin on her stomach turned purple, the blood vessels braking under the pressure of his grip.

I struggled and yelled everything I could at him in hopes of making him stop, but as ever, it was pointless.

Suzie gasped for breath as he dug his fingernails into her flesh, cutting into her and drawing blood.

A low rumbling sound came from Rapey's throat. Laughter.

Suzie begged him to stop, and so did I, but he dug his fingernails in further, making Suzie cry out in pain. Blood trickled down her stomach, soaking into her dress and dripping from between her legs. The first few drops of blood spattered the ground and were absorbed by the soil.

I lifted my gaze to Suzie's face as Rapey sank his filthy fangs into her neck. Total devastation washed over me. Suzie's eyes were wide with terror. She knew what was happening and what it meant. She struggled against the ugly bastard's grip to try and reach out to me, to hold my hand one last time.

It never happened.

The parasite clenched his jaws and ripped the flesh from Suzie's neck. Flecks of warm blood hit my face as it gushed from the gaping hole. The creature threw back his head, gulped down what he'd torn from Suzie and let out a roar. Sinews of flesh hung between his fangs. Suzie might have screamed if she wasn't missing most of her throat. Her body had gone limp but she was still breathing, or trying to, at least. Blood bubbled and spluttered from the hole where her windpipe used to be.

After a few long, painful moments, the light left her eyes, and my own will to live died right alongside her.

Rapey sank his teeth into her again. From where I stood I could hear him gulping down the blood. My only consolation was that she probably couldn't feel what was happening anymore. At least that's what I hoped.

It's a terrible thing, I know, but I wanted it to be over fast so she didn't have to suffer.

A minute ticked by until the blood flow slowed to nothing but a trickle.

Her body fell to the floor as Rapey released his grip. The back of her head hit the dirt with a loud crack. Her eyes stared up at me, with no trace of the girl I loved behind them. And in that moment, I knew she was gone.

Rapey stepped over Suzie and strode over to me, looking all smug as his face twisted back to human. "I saw inside her head, you know," he said. "There's always a connection when I feed. I see my victim's thoughts,

41

know their feelings. She really loved you. She loved you more than anything, more than life itself."

What a touching sentiment.

He carried on, "But do you know what she was thinking as I sucked the life out of her? She thought you were a fucking coward. She despised you for doing nothing while she was torn apart right in front of you. She died thinking you're a worthless piece of shit. She wants you to remember that."

Both of them threw back their heads and roared with laughter as ol' Roids let me go. I fell to my knees. Too weak, too shocked, too sickened and too devastated to even try to fight. I just wanted them to kill me and get it over with.

Rapey crouched down in front of me and stared into my eyes again. Before I could even realise, he had a hold of my face. I could feel my skin bruising under his grip. The bones in my jaw felt as though they were about to snap.

"It's been fun, kid, it really has." He stroked my hair with his free hand while he spoke. "We should do it again sometime." After a few moments of savouring my sorrow, he stood and turned to leave. "Sorry about ripping the dress, by the way. It was real pretty, but your girl looks better in red, anyway."

As a final parting gift, he grabbed me by the back of the neck and threw me face first to the dirt right by Suzie's body. I tried to lift myself up to stop them from leaving, to tell them to come back and finish what they started and put me out of my misery, but it was pointless. I was far too weak, and they were already gone.

Broken

As you can probably imagine, when Suzie wasn't home by midnight her parents got a little concerned. By one in the morning they decided to head next door and pay my parents a visit to see if they knew what was going on. By two in the morning, they were going completely apeshit with panic and called the police. It took a short while, but the police eventually turned up, asked them a load of questions and then decided to start a search. They eventually found us just after dawn. I say 'us' but it was really just me clinging to Suzie's body with a thousand yard stare. Needless to say, it didn't look very good. I mean, it would have looked quite suspicious, don't you think? Suzie was dead, I was covered in blood—hers and my own—and my sanity had practically packed its bags and left.

Maybe just a little suspicious.

[Track 7]

I was the one and only suspect for the brutal murder of Suzie May. Salt in the wound, eh? Naturally, not a single person believed my story, aside from my parents of course, because they knew how much I loved her.

I can't really blame people for not believing. What could I say? "Hi there, how are you all doing today? Oh, this? Well, you see, we got attacked by a couple of monsters. I think they were vampires. And guess what?

43

One of them murdered Suzie whilst the other beat the shit out of me and made me watch. Then they both disappeared without a trace. Isn't that just crazy?"

Sure, totally believable.

I left out the whole monster bit and put more emphasis on how weird they were instead. Still, it didn't help in the slightest. In short, I was royally fucked and I knew it. My ass was going behind bars.

I didn't even get the time to grieve, nor attend Suzie's funeral.

From the moment I decided to be a smart-ass and run my mouth off to a couple of vampires, my life pretty much rolled downhill. It just kept rolling right on down to the bottom of the hill until I flew face first into shit creek.

And I didn't have a paddle.

I was considered too dangerous to be out on the streets, so I was kept locked up in jail all throughout the court proceedings.

Mom and Dad hired the best lawyer they could to defend me, but we weren't all that well off, and he just wasn't good enough. The evidence against me was too overwhelming. During the time I spent sitting in jail, waiting to be put in prison, I got regular visits from a nice, British psychiatrist lady. Of course, I'm being sarcastic by saying she was nice. She was a total bitch; one of those real uptight women, always wearing thick rimmed glasses and a pencil skirt that restricted her movement, with her hair tied back in a ponytail so tight it pulled her eyebrows up her forehead, giving her a constant look of surprise.

Did I mention she was a total bitch?

Harmony Maddison—the asshole in the pencil skirt—
scribbled some words in a notebook while I sat across
from her, chained to the desk of the interview room,
waiting impatiently for her next stupid question.

"Mr. Nightingale," she started.

"Just Night."

She looked up from her notebook and gave me a
big forced smile. "Yes, of course. Night. Have you ever
been diagnosed with any personality disorders in the
past?"

I chose not to mention that she had lipstick on
her teeth. "Such as…"

"I mean disorders such as schizophrenia,
paranoia or multiple personality disorder?"

"You calling me a schitzo? Look lady, I ain't crazy.
I know what I saw."

"I'm not calling you anything; I'm just doing my
job. Alright, how about drugs? Are you currently using
any, or have you used them in the past?"

"No, never touched them. I mean, sure, I ate a few
brownies at a party once and they made me feel like I
was made of time travelling marshmallows but I never
knew they were pot brownies. That was a couple of
years ago. And that's the only time."

"Hmm. Yes, alright," she mumbled after giving me
the same look people give their shoe when they step in
shit. "So, could you describe how the incident with Suzie
makes you feel?"

"Do I really have to answer that?" I asked. No
matter what I said, I was getting put away. Answering

her bullshit questions was a waste of time, and an annoying one at that.

She smiled that fake, toothy smile again, as if she thought it would make me want to confess my darkest secrets. "It'd certainly help."

"Do you have a husband?"

"Yes."

That was a surprise. Poor man. "Well, imagine watching him get murdered a few feet away from your face. How would you feel?" The corners of her mouth twitched, about to show another smile until I shot it down. "And stop giving me that god damn Cheshire-Cat-looking grin; it's not going to charm my pants off and I'm not going to go along with your head doctor bullshit."

Her face settled into how it really looked. Resting bitch face. Her true face. "Look, Mr. Nightingale, if you don't want to cooperate, I can't force you to, but I'm only trying to help."

"So stop asking pointless questions and do something that's actually helpful."

"If you'd let me ask my questions, I think you'd find that an honest answer would help me to help you."

I let out a heavy sigh. "Fine, give me some more."

"Good, now tell me, have you ever fantasised about harming a woman?"

"You mean aside from right now? No, I can't say I have."

"Mr. Nightingale," she snapped, giving me a stern look, "I am trying to help. One more remark like that and as far as I'm concerned you can go fu—erm, find someone else to help you."

"You told me to be honest."

"Right," she scribbled in the notebook. "Tell me, in more detail, about the men you say you saw."

"The men I *did* see. Did. They weren't normal."

"So you've said, but you haven't explained how they weren't normal. I need details."

"They were freaks. Both really strong. Stronger than any normal person ought to be."

My brain was doing its best to deny the existence of monsters and I didn't really want to tell anyone I thought a couple of vampires had murdered my girlfriend. My situation was bad enough; I didn't need to be spouting off about how one guy had a giant snake tongue and a spare set of shark teeth tucked under his normal ones. One word about what really happened and I'd be carted off to the looney bin and doped up to my eyeballs for the rest of my life. Telling the world the guy who murdered Suzie was 'just a bit odd' would have to do.

"Mmmhmm," Harmony mumbled. "And they just disappeared?"

"Yes. I took a pretty bad beating though, and it was dark, so it could have just been the darkness and my mind playing tricks."

"And you don't know what weapon the mystery person used, aside from fists?"

"It was dark, it was hard to tell."

"So you've told me," she said, peering over her glasses before pursing her lips and scribbling more notes.

I could tell she thought I was talking a load of balls and I was getting sick of the sight of her and her condescending looks, so I decided to cut to the chase

47

and get her professional opinion before politely telling her to stick said opinion up her ass and hit the road.

"Yeah, I've told you lots of things but you've been coming here and asking me the same obnoxious questions for weeks now and you haven't told me shit. And to be honest with you, I know I'm going away no matter what. I'm so sick of you bothering me that every time I see you and your pencil skirt shuffle in here, I just want to take a romantic bath with a toaster. So come on, sugar tits, spit it out. What's your professional diagnosis?"

She stiffened up at the sound of being called 'sugar tits' and slapped a perfectly manicured hand down on the desk before shooting up out of her seat. "I've had quite enough of your childish remarks Mr. Nightingale." I'd pissed her off big-time. "If you must know, I think you're completely defective. You've shown no signs of remorse for what you've done and you insist on pinning the murder of Miss May on two imaginary assailants. And frankly, I find you utterly abhorrent."

She sat back down and tried to compose herself.

"There, now that we're both being honest, things might be easier," I said.

"I'm sorry Mr. Nightingale but you're beyond my help."

"Good to see we finally agree on something."

"Yes, well, I don't think I'll be returning," she said as she gathered her things.

"You really think I murdered Suzie? You really think I don't feel like shit for what happened? I loved her. Still do. Why would I kill her when I'd die for her myself?" I asked.

"I'm not sure what to think. As there's so much evidence against you and no trace of anyone else being in the area at the time, I'm going to say yes, I do personally think you murdered her. Now I can't tell whether you're outright delusional and believe what you've said, or if you're just a damn good liar. But to put it bluntly, Mr. Nightingale, you're an insufferable asshole. Now, goodbye." She stood and pushed her chair back before twisting and hurrying for the door. Her skirt was so tight she could only take tiny steps. It killed her whole attempt at dramatically storming out of the room.

"Don't let the door hit you on the wa—" I said as she left the room. The door closed before I could finish my sentence. "—ah I hope it does hit you, bitch." I mumbled, finally alone.

I knew I'd been a total dick to her but she really did deserve it. She wasn't helping in the slightest and I'd gotten sick of her asking questions, looking for details on just how Suzie was murdered, as if she needed to know. It was pretty clear most of her questions were just to get some juicy details out of me. I knew she'd be selling my story to every newspaper in town, or writing a book about how she saw into the mind of 'The Blackwater Monster' or some shit like that, cashing in on my misery. Most of all, I had gotten sick of her constant dirty looks. She was one of those people that'd look at everyone—and I mean everyone—as if she was above them, as if they were a freshly curled turd on the sidewalk of her life.

I sat chained to the desk for about ten more minutes before one of the cops came in and un-cuffed me from the desk. He quickly slapped the cuffs back on a second later to escort me to my cell. I didn't mind being left alone in the holding cell, the enclosed space and solid door made me feel nice and safe. They'd keep the lights on all the time too, which was comforting, especially after what had happened. I've never been afraid of the dark but I'd get a little jumpy at times, seeing that demonic face every time I closed my eyes. It had spooked me so good I actually looked forward to being behind bars. I looked forward to being somewhere the two assholes from that night couldn't get to me.

Luckily for me, I didn't have to wait all that long. Within a couple of weeks, my court hearings came to a close with me being declared guilty for the crimes I didn't commit. Of course, I pleaded not guilty and that only added more time on to my sentence. I didn't care about the time. I didn't kill Suzie and I wasn't gonna say I did to get a couple of years knocked off my stretch. The girl who meant the world to me was gone.

I had nothing left to lose.

Iron Bar Hotel

It was early August when I was shipped off to prison. In the eyes of everyone but my parents, I was a maniac, an animal that deserved to be locked away. And so I was. Within a few weeks of Suzie's death I was nicely packaged and mailed to the nearest lock-up. This particular lock-up—Blackwater Maximum Security Prison—had a fantastic reputation. And by 'fantastic' I mean it was a fucking notorious shithole. Blackwater was the home of all the worst kinds of criminals. Rapists, murderers, child molesters, politicians, you name it. They were all sent to Blackwater. Considering I'd been judged to fit in to at least two of those categories, I was a prime candidate for the scum collection.

[Track 8]

I was picked up from the local jail soon after my trial and crammed into a prison bus that had the distinct aroma of stale piss. Roughly fifty other passengers eyed me as I shuffled through the security door that separated the driver and guard from the filth they were hauling. I stood and ran my eyes over all the sullen faces, trying to find somewhere to sit. One seat was left near the back so I wobbled down the aisle and sat my ass down next to a big skinhead guy that looked to be in his thirties. He was covered in tattoos of swastikas, switchblades, insults, and practically every other thing that would offend anyone but a heavily tattooed white supremacist. He turned to face me as I sat, showing the tattoo across his forehead that read "DEATH 2 NIGGERS". For a few seconds he simply stared straight into my soul as if trying to work out whether or not I had any black ancestors. He must have figured out that my ancestors were white, as far as I knew. He eventually stuck a hand out for me to shake. I took it and gave it a firm shake, or I at least shook it as best I could with cuffed wrists. I was never the kind to make friends with Neo-Nazis but this was one guy I didn't want to piss off, especially not while I was sitting next to him, chained up in an enclosed space. It would have been a shame to be strangled to death before I even got to prison.

"Wassup little cracker," he said as I shook his hand, "the names Big G."

"Night," I replied.

"This yo' first time going to the joint, Night?"

"Yeah. It's that obvious, huh?"

"You're all jumpy and shit, cracker. May as well have it tatted on yo' head," he pointed to his forehead. "But don't you worry. Us white boys, we stick together, you hear me?"

I wasn't sure where he was going with this, so I done what I always do in similar situations; smile and nod. "Sure," I said.

"You ever get any hassle from any of these NIGGERS,"—he yelled the word, probably hoping every black guy on the bus would be offended—"you come see Big G, you hear?"

"I hear," I nodded, hoping he'd stop talking.

"Good. Now I got some brothers on the inside, you hear? I can hook you up, little cracker. A fresh little vanilla face like you is gonna be eyed up by all the porch monkeys looking for a taste of white sugar. You come find Big G on the inside and I'll see you right. We'll shave that hair, get you some ink and make you a real brother."

Turns out I was being recruited. "Uhm, thanks, I'll see how things go."

"Think it over, brother. Think it over." Proud with his recruitment pitch, Big G nodded his head for a few seconds and smiled to himself before shutting up and turning to look out the window.

The rest of the ride was fairly uneventful, bar one small argument that broke out at the front of the bus because one guy thought his seat-mate's elbow was far too intrusive of his personal space.

When the bus finally came to a stop inside the gates of Blackwater Maximum, the guard swung the security door open and herded us out of the bus one by one to be attached to a long chain and led into the prison. We all shuffled in, chained at the wrists and ankles like a bunch of dogs on a leash. The guards led us inside, through grimy hallways and into a large hall-like room that led off to ten smaller rooms. The big room was empty except for about fifty guards lined against a wall—all carrying what looked like riot shotguns— ready to search us and escort us off to our new homes.

The guard in charge waited for everyone to arrive before speaking. "Line up against this wall, stand still and keep your mouths shut," he motioned to the wall opposite the one lined with guards. "As you can see, each guard is armed. If you make any sudden moves, you will be shot. If you raise your hands without permission, you will be shot. If you so much as breathe in a way I don't like, you will be shot. Yes, we are using non-lethal bullets but trust me when I say, they will take you down and you will regret it. Now, you will be unchained one by one, taken to a processing room, stripped, searched and given your new uniforms to change in to before exiting through the doors on the other side and escorted to your cell. Nod your heads to tell me I'm making myself clear."

We all nodded our heads in unison, standing with our backs against the wall. When he was pleased we seemed to understand, the guard that was with us on the bus took out a set of keys and unchained everyone's ankles. The guards against the other wall stepped forward two at a time, selected an inmate and led them away to a room. They took turns leading ten inmates at a time into the rooms.

Big G and I were in the fourth set to be selected. He looked over as he passed and whispered to me, "Remember what I told you, cracker."

I nodded and gave him a smile even though I had no intention of taking him up on his offer.

My guards picked me out a second later and gave me a push in the direction of one of the vacant rooms. I glanced at their chests and noticed name tags. Fontaine and Wilson. Fontaine, a big muscular black guy, pushed the door open while the other, Wilson, a small weedy looking white guy, shoved me inside and closed the door behind him. The processing room was much smaller than the previous. Much more cosy. A shelf was bolted to the left hand wall, holding my bright orange prison tuxedo and a box for my stuff. The guards stood in front of each door, Fontaine in front and Wilson behind me.

Fontaine spoke first. "I'm going to take the cuffs off you. When I step away, get undressed. Do it slowly now, no sudden movements."

I didn't feel like taking a shotgun blast to the chest so I followed his orders to the letter. I stood and let him take the cuffs off before stripping down to my underwear. Fontaine gave me a look and motioned towards my shorts with the gun, then pointed it towards the floor. I sighed, reluctantly dropped my shorts and stood there, bare-ass nude. The next five minutes consisted of me lifting my arms, opening my mouth, lifting my legs, wiggling my toes, squatting down and coughing, nut-sack swaying in the breeze. As unlikely as it is that anyone would have razor blades tucked up their ass, and even more unlikely anyone would be hiding a handgun up there, strange things can happen. You'd be surprised at what desperate people can smuggle into places by hiding it up their asshole. Not that I've ever tried, of course.

After a thorough searching, I was allowed to get dressed into my new uniform. Wilson came from behind me and collected the clothing I had been wearing then shoved it into the box to be taken away as Fontaine stepped forward. He took a hold of my wrists and slapped the cuffs back on then opened the door to lead the way to my cell. Wilson gave me a prod in the back to get me moving. I stepped out of the room and followed Fontaine like an obedient puppy. The walk to the cell led past a few rooms. One room was a large dinner hall. Some looked to be class rooms and one seemed to be a therapy room. The one that looked like a therapy room

55

was occupied. A man sat behind the desk facing the window. The patient's seat in front of it was occupied by someone that had a considerably large bald patch on the back of his head and a terrible comb-over on the rest. The man behind the desk glanced up for a second and caught me looking through the window. Seconds before I passed out of sight, the occupant of the patient's chair swung around to glare at me. He was one ugly son of a bitch. One ugly son of a bitch I instantly recognised. This man had his face plastered all over newspapers a couple of years prior to my imprisonment but the newspapers didn't do the ugly justice. The man in the chair was Harry 'The Balls' Garcia, a serial rapist with a penchant for young boys. Now, when I say ugly, I don't mean creepy vampire-face ugly; I mean the kind of ugly even a mother would struggle to love. This guy had a nose like a battered turnip, a pathetic, greasy comb-over, four teeth and three brain cells. He was a real big fucker too. Not the kind of guy you want to bump in to in a dark alleyway. Harry 'The Balls' Garcia gave me a quick smile before I was out of sight and in that moment I knew my ass was on the menu.

After a pleasant stroll through what looked like a good attempt to mimic Hell, Fontaine stopped in front of a door that I could only assume was my cell. My assumptions turned out to be correct. He fiddled with some keys before finding one with the cell number on it. He took a breath as he twisted the lock then cleared his throat to speak.

Wilson beat him to it, "Nightingale, welcome to your new home. We hope you have a pleasant stay with your roommate. If you have any problems at all, just remember nobody gives a shit." He burst into laughter as the door swung open.

His laughing rang through the cell even after the door slammed shut behind me. The lock clicked, and I stood to admire my new home. It was a dull affair, nothing but a small room with grey walls, a bunk bed, a sink and a shitter. My cellmate sat on the top bunk, looking over a book he had been reading. He put the book down and hopped off the top bunk to greet me.

He plopped down in front of me and stuck a hand out, "David Flowers," he said.

Yeah, Flowers. Not a good name to have in prison.

"Night," I said, shaking his hand while giving him a good eyeballin'. Of all the other inmates I'd seen, David was clearly the most out of place, aside from me. He looked to be in his late twenties and was a small guy in both height and build; he wore thick glasses and turned out to be a really friendly guy, which basically means he was the prison bitch. Poor David was the personification of the words 'prison bitch' in every sense. Friendly, naïve and a little too trusting, but I kept those thoughts to myself.

"Night? That's an odd name," David said.

"Short for Nightingale, Isaac Nightingale."

David stepped aside and got straight to the juicy bit, "Oh, I see, so what you in for?"

I passed him by and sat down on the bottom bunk. "A murder I didn't commit. How about you?"

"Robbery, and murder that I didn't mean to commit. I mean, I did. The robbery, that is, but I never meant to kill anyone. That was an accident."

I raised an inquisitive eyebrow, "Accident?"

57

"Yeah. I robbed a bank," David said, leaning against the wall opposite the bunk, fidgeting with his sleeves. "I needed the money and I needed a lot so I took a gun. It went off in my hands and killed a man."

"That tends to happen if you point it at somebody and pull the trigger."

He didn't realise I was joking. A slightly upset look crept into his eyes. "I didn't, it just... went off."

"I'm just joking, don't worry, just a bad joke. You don't seem like the type to kill anyone." I refrained from telling him he looked like a total dork.

"Oh, oh, I see," he said, beginning to smile. "I'm not. I never meant to hurt anyone but I did and now I'm here. I guess I deserve it. You don't seem like a murderer yourself, to tell you the truth."

"What makes you say that?"

"Well, you're having a polite conversation, you haven't been rude, you haven't tried to hurt me and you didn't try to take the bunk you seen me sitting on. You're quite young too. What are you, like eighteen?"

"Nineteen, actually, but age doesn't mean much. Anyway, you haven't been an asshole, so why would I be an asshole? If you jumped off that bunk and threw a punch, things would be different right now."

David stepped over and took his book off the bunk. He went back to the wall and slid down to lean against it, sitting on the floor. "I suppose that's a good point."

Memories of the night I lost Suzie flashed through my head. The image of that demonic face lingered before flashing to the memory of Harry Garcia spinning around in his chair and smiling at me. The old familiar twisting feeling in my stomach crept up at the thought. I hadn't felt it since the night Suzie was murdered.

As if he had been reading my mind, David piped up again, "I'll give you a warning since you seem a decent guy."

"Let's hear it then?" I mumbled, coming out of my thoughts.

"It seems a little too convenient that someone as young as you would be put in here with me."

"Why'd you say that?"

He took a breath, looking as if he was holding back tears. "Well, as shameful as it is to admit, I'm a coward, Night. I can't fight to save my life. People take advantage of this. They take advantage of me."

"By people, you mean..."

"Harry Garcia and his buddies."

I knew it. He was definitely the prison bitch, for lack of a better term. "They, uh, take advantage?"

He nodded. "This place is corrupt. Half the guards do whatever they please and a few of the worst inmates literally run the place, four of them actually. The warden lost control long before I ever got here. Garcia is one of the big guys at the top. He clicks his fingers and the guards practically have you served up ass-first on a silver platter. He must have gotten a look at the files for the new arrivals. He's most likely put in a personal request for you to be put in here with me, and if you're here with me, you're right where he wants you."

I knew from that split second smile that Garcia had taken a fancy to me, but I didn't even consider he had everything all planned out before I even got to the joint.

My ass was definitely on the menu.

The Balls

During the first few hours of my incarceration, David went on to explain the ways and workings of the prison. To break it down, the prison consisted of four neat little factions that would all cooperate with each other to practically run the place. The factions were: sex, violence, drugs and weapons. Each faction had a boss, a big bad at the top of the food chain. Garcia was the prison pimp, the sodomy specialist, the emperor of ass-fucking. He ran the prison's sex trade. If anyone was looking to get lucky, they'd go to Garcia and be supplied with someone unlucky. David was one of the unlucky ones. As one of Garcia's 'girls', he was frequently called upon to offer his services to whichever inmate was in the mood. His payment for the job was an extension on his life. As long as he did as he was told and dropped the soap whenever asked, he wouldn't be stabbed in the kidneys with a sharpened toothbrush.

David explained that this was the reason I happened to end up in his cell; I was being drafted in as one of Garcia's ladies. I was young, not bad looking—if I say so myself—and naïve to the ways of life behind bars; the perfect piece of ass flavoured candy. And Garcia wanted first taste, the dirty bastard. Now, don't get me wrong, I don't care if a man is into other men. Gay, straight, bisexual, it doesn't bother me. But rape is rape no matter what. I didn't want to see more, never mind be on the receiving end. So I found myself listening to

David talk about all the nasty stuff he had been forced to do at the hands of Garcia and his goon squad. And by nasty, I mean nasty. He was apparently into all sorts of weird shit. He even had his own set of tools—as David put it—that some cronies had smuggled into the prison for him. I didn't ask too many questions about the smuggling. I didn't really need an answer when it came to questions such as, "How did someone smuggle a bunch of dildos into the prison?" I'll leave you to figure that one out.

David talked my ears off all day long and right into the night. I didn't mind, he was only trying to help me out by telling me how things were on the inside. The talk was mainly about the horrors of life behind bars for people like him, but I was trying not to let it get to me. I wasn't like David. I'd happily fight and I wouldn't tolerate people's shit. Not that that's a good thing considering my intolerance got Suzie murdered.

The one comforting thing David said all night was that I'd get the night to settle in and rest before I was paid a visit from the guards that just so happened to be Garcia's pals. The knowledge eased my mind a little and I eventually drifted off into a restless sleep, pestered by dreams filled with Garcia's lecherous face.

The next morning we were all let out of our cells for breakfast. Everybody filed towards the food hall. I walked with David and found a seat in the hall the moment we walked in. I didn't have much of an appetite knowing I was due an appointment with Garcia later that evening. So I sat, trying to think of a million ways to avoid becoming the new fuck puppet. I had nothing. David sat down opposite me and gave me a smile. Or what could pass as a smile on a face that only had despair written across it. After hearing his stories, I was honestly surprised he hadn't tried to kill himself at some point. Most other people would have probably preferred to chew off their own hands and bleed to death but not Mr Flowers. He was a tough son of a bitch, I'll give him that. Physically he wasn't very tough but god damn his mind could take some strain. Even after all the shit he'd been through, he was still in a stable mental state, if a little scarred. He just wasn't the kind of person to fight back though, and that's why he was one of Garcia's bitches.

Breakfast went by in silence. It must have been quite clear that I wasn't in much of a mood to do anything but think of a way to escape Garcia's clammy grasp. It felt like my stomach was full of snakes. I wasn't prepared to be the new prison bitch but I didn't know what to do about it. David couldn't offer much in the way of help. He had been a victim for years and hadn't found a way to stop it. We sat for about thirty minutes before heading back to the cells. David told me we'd usually be allowed out into the yard but there had been a big fight outside the week before and as punishment there was no outdoor play-time for another couple of days. Instead, I lay in my cell and waited, waited for the inevitable, waited to be hustled out of my bunk to go for a friendly stroll with Garcia's chums. In truth, I probably only waited an hour or so but it felt like an eternity had passed before the cell door finally opened. Two prison guards stood at the threshold. One was a small and stocky middle-aged man with a big moustache that practically covered his mouth, the other was younger, in his twenties. The young one was tall, skinny and looked like the kind of guy that keeps children in his basement. You know the type.

"Nightingale," the older guard said through his 'stache as the tall one stepped into the cell and took out a set of cuffs, "off the bunk and behave. You too Flowers."

I hopped down from my bunk and stuck my hands out to be cuffed.

"Good boy," the tall guard, Andrew—as his nametag read—whispered while slapping the cuffs on. The guard with the 'stache's nametag read Jonah.

When we were both all nice and cuffed, Andrew and Jonah escorted us out of our cell to be delivered straight to Harry 'The Balls' Garcia. The guards didn't say a word during our stroll. They must have assumed that David had already told me what was about to go down, and that is exactly what he'd told me. You take it like a man—preferably an overly effeminate one, apparently—and you keep your mouth shut. That's about it. We came to a stop outside of cell number six hundred and sixteen. Unsurprisingly, it wasn't locked. 'The Balls' appeared to be free to leave his cell whenever he goddamn pleased.

The snakes in my stomach were at war with each other. *Fuck this*, I thought.

The door was opened by one of Garcia's henchmen, who also happened to be his cellmate. Apparently he always kept at least one of his most trusted henchmen near him, no matter what. You know, just in case someone tried to charge in and shiv him in the face while he was taking a shit. The henchman had a face like a dog's ass, just like Garcia. It must have been a job requirement considering Garcia was ugliest motherfucker in the entire state. I'm not even kidding.

[Track 9]

The guards left our cuffs on and prodded us into the cell with their nightsticks. They might have been the delivery boys but they were clearly too scared to even get near Garcia for fear he'd use their own nightsticks on their nether-regions. And that's if they were lucky.

The cell was a good size. At least three times the size of mine, with enough space for at least six inmates. Garcia lay on a comfy looking bed on the right hand side of the cell, reading what looked like an erotic novel. No bunks or scratchy sheets for this bastard. Garcia had luxury. I took a moment to glance around the room as the henchman closed the cell door and slid a deadbolt in place, locking it. My eyes scanned the room for anything I could use as a weapon. There was nothing in sight but a hefty glass ornament on a nightstand next to Garcia's bed. It was easily twenty inches long and suspiciously phallic looking. I'd never seriously hurt anyone before and I didn't really want to start by beating someone senseless with what was probably a giant glass dildo, but it'd do.

Garcia's goon passed us by and sat on his considerably smaller bed on the left hand side of the room as we stood there like a couple of scared sheep.

Garcia set the book down on the bed. "Nice to see my pretty little flower again," he cooed at David. Even his voice was sickening.

"Let's just get this over with," David said.

64

Garcia stood up from the bed and beckoned for us to come further into the cell. "Now is that anyway to talk to daddy?" he said, coming to meet us. "You be a good boy, Flowers, or I'll have to punish you." David stood his ground as Garcia reached out and stroked his face with a set of stubby little sausage fingers.

Garcia's goon piped up, getting up from the bed. "Boss? Whad'ya want me to do with that one there boss?" he asked, pointing at me with a vacant expression on his face.

Garcia looked over from David. His eyes twinkled a little. "Oh he's the main course." He nodded in the direction of the back wall, between the beds. "Take him over there and make sure he doesn't move while my little flower here gets things started. You can take Flowers soon, while I'm having a bit of that pretty little Nightingale. I'm gonna make that little bird sing."

Garcia didn't waste any time. He was already in the process of taking off his belt as his man-slave grabbed a hold of me by the arm and pulled me to the back of the cell. Garcia winked at me as we passed. My mind raced with thoughts of how to get out of the situation. I wanted to get out and I wanted to stop whatever Garcia was about to do to David but neither one of us had any way of freeing our hands. I watched as Garcia pulled David close to him and take a good sniff of his hair. He started to kiss David's neck while undoing the buttons on his pants. David had a mixed look of dread and pure disgust on his face, which was understandable. Garcia stood back and dropped his pants. It was like the night I lost Suzie all over again. I was being held back by one asshole while another took advantage of someone innocent and helpless. I closed my eyes as the memories of the night flashed into my head. I remembered the terror, the pain and the face of the monster that killed Suzie. The entire night surged through my head until I opened my eyes. The memories made me realise something, something that strangely hadn't occurred to me before. I had been afraid of the monsters coming back. Every day from the moment Suzie was murdered was spent in fear of reliving it, and here I was locked in a room with another set of monsters. They had the same intentions, but they weren't the monsters I'd faced. They were human.

A wave of relief washed over me. These guys clearly weren't vampires. I had seen vampires first hand and Garcia and his goon were completely different. My head flooded with ideas. I could hurt them. I could kill them. I could be the monster. I had been preparing to go against something I couldn't fight, something I couldn't hurt but this wasn't the case. Garcia and his goon may have been monsters but they were monsters I could beat the shit out of.

I snapped out of my thoughts as I heard Garcia speak. "Don't worry," he said to me, still facing David, "you'll get your turn in a minute."

Not if I could help it.

Garcia put one hand on David's shoulder and pushed him to his knees. I didn't have much time. Soon enough it'd be me on my knees. I had to come up with a plan and I wasn't gonna stand round and watch David get violated. My mind raced. What to do, what to do? Unfortunately for David, he was practically choking on 'The Balls' by the time I realised there wasn't much I could do, so without another moment's hesitation, I turned to Garcia's henchman and head-butted the bastard in the face as hard as I could. Blood sprayed in all directions as my forehead shattered his nose with a satisfying, squelchy crack. He stumbled back against the wall and fell on his ass. I took the opportunity to grab the glass ornament and take my best swing at his head. I swung that fucker hard, like a cock shaped baseball bat. The thing was heavier than it looked. By this point, I was definitely sure it was a dildo. I brought it down on the side of his head. It made a clear cracking noise as it connected with his skull. He didn't appear to be getting back up any time soon, if ever.

Garcia was completely caught in his moment of passion, making too many embarrassing noises to even realise I might have just beaten his friend into a coma with the big decorative shlong. When he finally realised what was going on, he was a little too late. Time seemed to slow, almost to a stop. In the moments between knocking out the henchman and Garcia slightly turning his head in realisation, I had already swung around and started my lunge towards him. Just a second too late, he tried to get his dick out of David's mouth. Within the space of a heartbeat, I was across the cell and directly behind him. I didn't even think. I had no other choice but to go on pure, primal, fight or flight instinct. I swung my foot with the devastating might of Zeus, right up between his legs, directly into his testicles. Harry 'The Balls' Garcia howled in pain as my foot came into contact with his smooth criminals, almost kicking them up into his throat. He hadn't even had the chance to move before I swung again, this time kicking harder.

I felt bad for a part of what happened next because it was honestly unintentional, but it was quite the twist of fate. For some reason, David was still, erm...

67

occupied. On the second kick I swung up under Garcia's legs a little too far and I ended up kicking David straight in the jaw, which hurt David, but hurt Garcia just a little bit more. Like I said, David was occupied, so while I was in the process of kicking Garcia's nuts straight to the gates of Hell, he hadn't had the chance to move away. That second kick sent David's jaw snapping shut hard, right on Garcia's goddamn pecker. David's teeth sliced straight through the damn thing. It sounded like a person biting through a carrot. Garcia squealed so loud it hurt my ears as he stumbled back and fell to the floor, grabbing the area of his crotch where his big ol' Johnson used to be. Blood pumped from his crotch and sprayed in all directions as he completely lost his shit and writhed around the floor.

David bent over and vomited profusely, sending the severed dingus slapping down on to the floor next to Garcia. 'The Balls' caught sight of his severed penis and howled even louder. It was a cry of pure despair for his lost manhood. As satisfying as I found his cries, I didn't feel like dragging things out. I took a few steps away from Garcia, bent down, then stood back up carrying a certain ornament. As far as I was concerned, Garcia was the kind of guy that deserved to suffer for his sins so I took my time in stepping over to him. The fear in his eyes was clear as I knelt down beside his head.

If things had gone the way he planned, he wouldn't have shown any mercy, so neither did I. With one quick movement I lifted the big glass dong high above my head then swiftly smashed it down into his skull, putting a sharp end to 'The Balls'.

Friends in Low Places

I had barely settled in and I'd already taken down one of the prison's most notorious criminals, one of the big bad bosses. Now that's how you do things. Harry 'The Balls' Garcia had lost his manhood, his reputation, and almost lost his life. He'd certainly never be called 'The Balls' again. My foreseeable future didn't seem so bad. For the second time I had escaped a monster and the terrible fate it had in store, but again, the other victim hadn't been quite so lucky. David was sent to the infirmary right alongside Garcia. He was a little traumatised and in shock but at least he was still alive. Garcia's fate, on the other hand, was dangling by a thread that deserved to be cut.

[Track 10]

Word spread quickly of how two cellmates had been taken to satisfy Garcia's perverse desires and ended up almost murdering him and his pet goon. Within twelve hours of the incident both David and I had become prison celebrities, especially among the unfortunate few inmates that Garcia had called to service.

The morning after, I strolled into the canteen to get what would come to be my daily dose of nourishing breakfast slop. Not one single motherfucker said a bad word to me. I was no longer the fresh meat to be tenderised by a hundred man-hammers. I guess once you castrate the rape-lord, all the lower level ass-fuckers understand that your ass isn't up for sale. They even stopped eyeing up David, which is understandable considering it was his mouth that really done the damage. He wasn't anybody's 'flower' any more. I didn't expect the respect to last all that long so I was going to take advantage of it while I could. Gotta milk the titties of life while you can, you know. She doesn't present them often.

After getting my shitty looking breakfast slopped all over my tray by the greasy guy behind the food counter, I took a seat on an empty bench in a corner. David quickly joined me, fresh out of the infirmary and looking fine. He gave me an uneasy look as he set his tray down but eventually grinned, slapped me on the back and sat down next to me. We sat in silence, both spooning through the gruel that passed as food. It tasted like wet cardboard. Wet cardboard that a hobo had spent two weeks sleeping on. We sat for about fifteen minutes, trying to quietly force the shit down our throats when another tray suddenly appeared on our table opposite us. It belonged to a tall, muscular Latino looking guy.

"Mind if I sit here, fellas?" he said.

I said nothing but eyed him cautiously and made a gesture that told him he could sit wherever he damn well pleased.

He nodded, "Gracias."

We sat in silence for a while until I noticed him eyeballin' us. He gave us both a good going over with them eyes of his, looking from David over to me and holding his gaze. He had a certain look on his face, the look of a man that meant business.

"Is there a problem, chief?" I asked him, beginning to get annoyed. I knew full well he could beat me to death with his bare hands if he felt like it but in wake of taking down Garcia, I was feeling pretty sure of myself.

He sat and stared while spooning his breakfast into his mouth. Eventually, he put the spoon down and spoke. "I hear you used this guy's face to kick Garcia's dick off?" he said with a heavy accent.

"You heard right," David answered, looking down at the remnants of his slop.

It felt as if everyone in the room had stopped eating to listen in on us.

The Latino studied me for a while longer. With a sudden roar of laughter he slammed one hand down on the table, reached over and gave me a smack across the shoulder with the other. "Well then, I owe a debt to both of you, mis hermanos."

"What?" David said.

"Garcia! That motherfucker, I've been trying to get to him for years. You've done me a favour and for that, I owe you."

I gave the guy a frown, "Oh yeah, how come?"

"I've been in here a long time. My brother came with me. What happened to your friend David here—and what almost happened to you—happened to my brother, Antonio. Garcia took a liking to him, screwed him daily. He was younger than me, quite a small kid. I couldn't protect him. We were put in separate cells, at opposite ends of the prison. Garcia seen to it that I couldn't get near him unless it was when we were having breakfast. I couldn't get to Garcia either; the guards kept a good eye on me and beat me within an inch of my life if I even tried to walk past him. We had breakfast together, Antonio and I, just like this. He'd never speak of what Garcia did to him but everybody else did, so I knew. I could see it in his eyes too." He took a deep sigh before continuing. "One time, this guy called Crispy sat his ass down next to us while we were having breakfast, started asking him shit, calling him things, shoving him, laughing at him—"

"Crispy?" I interrupted.

"Yeah, Crispy. Real asshole with a weird skin condition. One side of his face was all flaky, looked like half his face was covered in corn flakes, so people called him Crispy. Anyway, Anty was never much of a fighter, I did all that shit. This Crispy guy wouldn't stop being an asshole no matter how much Anty asked him to stop, so

I asked him to stop. He wouldn't. He just kept on being a dick so I threw myself across the table and beat the ugly bastard to death with my bare hands. He begged me to stop. I wouldn't. I almost beat him to death right here in front of everyone, just because I could get to him and not Garcia."

"Yeah, I remember that," David said, "locked you up in solitary, didn't they?"

"Yup, three fucking months. Garcia stopped targeting Anty for a while after that, I must have spooked him a little. It didn't last long though. Maybe a few weeks before I was out of solitary he started again, at least that's what I heard once I was out. There was still nothing I could do but talk to him during our breakfasts, I told him to fight so many times. I even gave him a shiv I'd made out of my toothbrush and a razor blade, just so he could give Garcia a fuckin' good cutting. He never did it though, and the raping just kept happening. One morning I was here sitting at this very table, waiting for Anty so we could have breakfast together. He didn't show up. The guards found him hanging in his cell. He'd made a noose out of his bed sheets and hung himself during the night. My brother is dead because of what Garcia did to him. You may not have killed Garcia, but you've both ruined his life. He'll never rape anyone ever again. That's why I owe you."

I exhaled the breath I had been holding, "Shit, if I'd known this beforehand I would have made sure to finish the job."

73

"Don't worry about that my friend; you've done more than I ever could."

"So," I said, "what do I call you?"

He stretched over, reaching out to shake my hand. "Alejandro," he said as I shook it, "Alejandro Santos."

"Nice to meet you, I'm Isaac. Everyone calls me Night, though."

"Night?"

"Isaac Nightingale, you know, Night for short."

"Makes sense," he shrugged, "and you're David Flowers, yes?"

"Yeah," David mumbled as they shook hands, "nice to meet you properly."

"So, Alejandro," I began. "What—"

"Nonono, just Ali, my friend."

"Ali? Fair enough. So, Ali, what are you in for?"

"A whole bunch of shit I'm not proud of. How about you?"

"A whole bunch of shit I didn't do."

"So what didn't you do?"

"Well, I didn't murder my own girlfriend."

"So who did?"

"Two huge motherfuckers. Well, one. The other watched. They were both bigger than you and stronger than you'd believe. Not that anyone's believed any of what happened. Apparently it's all a fantasy, something my mind made up instead of facing the truth. I didn't do shit. I know it was all real. I'm telling you, a normal man

74

isn't capable of what they did. They were something else."

Ali shrugged, "I believe you."

"What?"

"I said I believe you."

"Yeah, I heard that. But let me get this straight, you've just met me and nobody else will believe me but you do, without knowing the entire story?"

"I can tell these things, it's a family gift. Plus, it's all in the eyes," he leaned across the table and pointed his spoon at me, "and you my friend, you've got the eyes of a man whose seen The Devil."

"The Devil, huh?"

"Well, maybe not The Devil himself, but I'm betting you've seen something pretty damn close."

"I guess you could say that."

David nodded in agreement. "He's right. You do look like you've been through some bad shit."

"Seems like we all have," I said before getting back to my gruel.

After breakfast, there seemed to be a sudden change of heart about time in the yard. David had told me there'd be a few more days before people were allowed back into the yard but when breakfast time came to an end, the doors were opened and the inmates flowed free. I couldn't help but feel like my actions had pleased the gods of the prison and led to the decision to let people go out and play.

We all got up together, ditched our slop trays and wandered out into the yard to get some fresh air with our fellow criminals. It was a real warm day, too. The sun practically baked the dirt. Ali stuck around and followed us over to a bench in the shade. We all took a seat together. It appeared I had made another new friend. Life in prison certainly wasn't as bad as I expected it to be.

"You really wanna repay us for messing up Garcia?" I said to Ali.

He gave a nod. "The way I see it, I owe you both. If you need anything at all, you ask me. I don't care what it is, I'm not getting out of here any time soon and I don't know what I'd do if I did."

"Well, you said you almost beat a man to death with your bare hands, right?"

"That's right."

"How about you teach me how to do that?"

David cut in, "Me too? I think I need to learn to fight at some point. You clearly know how, so teach me too."

Ali let out a burst of laughter. "Mis hermanos, I don't think I need to teach you. You, Night, you beat two men with a glass cock. You almost killed them!" he roared between laughs.

"I don't carry a big glass dong everywhere I go, though," I said.

David shook his head and said, "Yeah, and I don't want to bite anymore things off of people, either."

76

Ali took a while to compose himself but he got there in the end. When he finally calmed down, he gave both David and I a good stern eyeballin' with a slight grin across his face. He opened his mouth to give his answer when a guard interrupted.

"Nightingale!" The guard barked. It was Fontaine.

"Damn it, what?" I snapped back.

He smiled as he slapped his nightstick down into his hand. "Follow me, boy. The warden wants a word with you."

Prison Favours

After rudely interrupting my conversation, Fontaine promptly cuffed me—which seemed a common occurrence—and led the way to the warden's office with a smug looking grin on his face that told me I could be in for an ass-whooping. While I understood that castration wasn't a very nice thing to do to somebody, Garcia somewhat deserved it on the count of him being a dirty rapist. I wasn't very fond of rapists, to say the least. They're not nice people. In my opinion, I didn't deserve to be cuffed and herded around like cattle.

The whole walk went by in an awkward silence. I figured Fontaine probably wouldn't want to have a conversation with me since he thought I was just another drop in the piss-bucket of criminal scum, and I didn't really care for striking up a conversation either, I just felt like slapping the smug look straight off his goddamn face.

After a short stroll, Fontaine knocked on the door to the warden's office and stood for a second before being given permission to enter. He threw a cautionary glance my way and shoved me into the office. The office was a large room, filled with all manner of nice, expensive looking things. The warden sat in a big leather chair behind a solid mahogany desk. The walls were lined with hundreds of antique leather bound books and the unmistakable smell of cigar smoke hung in the air. Such a room felt completely out of place. The warden himself was a thin, elderly looking fella with short grey hair, bushy eyebrows and an expensive suit that matched the colour of his hair. He didn't look intimidating in the slightest, but he had a sense of authority about him.

"Ah, Mister Nightingale," the warden beamed as I stepped through the door. He stood from his chair and made his way around the desk. "Fontaine my good man, take the bracelets off my guest, will you?" he said, pointing at my wrists as he perched on the edge of the desk.

Fontaine looked a little uneasy with the command. "You sure about that boss?"

"Of course I'm sure. Come on, off with the damn things."

He fiddled with the keys for a second before taking a hold of the cuffs and making a show of taking them off, as if it was a difficult thing for him to do. "There you go sir," he said.

"Thank you, thank you. You can go back to whatever you were doing now; I'd like to have a private chat with our friend here. I'll put a call out if I need anyone."

"Sir?" Fontaine said, unsure about whether or not he should really be leaving the warden alone in a room with a man who'd almost killed two other inmates.

"Sir?" the warden imitated. "I can take care of myself, now go on."

Fonts eventually gave in and obeyed. "Yes sir."

The warden waited for Fontaine to close the door behind him before stepping forward from the desk and extending his hand towards me. "Charles Spencer," he said.

[Track 11]

"Night," I said, as I took his hand and gave it a firm shake. For such an old looking guy he had one hell of a grip.

"You'd prefer to be called Night, rather than Isaac or Mister Nightingale?"

"Yeah, If you don't mind."

"Not at all, not at all. Give me a moment," he said, turning and walking back around the desk. "See the chair behind you, by the door?"

I turned and found the chair he was talking about. "Yeah," I replied.

"Could you bring it down here for me and take a seat?"

He was in the process of bringing his chair around to the front of the desk.

"Sure." I shrugged and made my way towards it. Seconds later, I sat comfortably as Warden Spencer poured two glasses of whiskey from a crystal decanter. The whole situation confused me. I didn't understand why he was being so pleasant.

The warden handed over a glass and turned to pick up a box from a shelf close by. He came back and lowered himself into the chair opposite me, glass in one hand, box in the other. I eyed the glass of whiskey in my hand, unsure on whether or not I should drink it. I had only ever snuck a few sips from bottles my dad left out. I wasn't sure I could handle a full glass just yet.

Spencer didn't seem to give any second thought to the whiskey, even though he knew I was under the legal age to drink. He set his box down on his lap, flipped the lid then lifted it in my direction, revealing a bunch of cigars. "Smoke?"

First whiskey and now cigars. I hadn't even smoked a cigarette, never mind a cigar but I thought why the hell not? When in Rome, you know. "Sure," I said, picking out a cigar. They were somewhat heavier than I expected them to be and I had no idea how to smoke one.

The warden caught me looking at it in confusion, like I'd just been handed a solid gold turd. "Never smoked one before now?"

"No sir."

"So watch and learn kid." Spencer set both the box and his glass of whiskey down on his desk, took a cigar and stuck it between his teeth. After a second of fumbling around in his pockets he pulled out a box of matches and an odd metal thing. He put the matches on the desk and took a hold of his smoke. "This here's a clipper," he said, holding up the metal thing. "If you get a cigar like one of these ones, you're gonna need to clip the end off so you can smoke it. Always use one of these if you can. Only bite the end off if it's life or death. A bitten cigar is better than no cigar at all." He used the clipper to snip the end off of the cigar then passed it over to me.

Good job he didn't just hand everything to me first or I would have made a total ass of myself, pretending I knew what I was doing. I copied his actions and snipped the tip off of my cigar then set the clipper on the desk. I watched Spencer strike a match then hold it under the cigar as he gently spun it around.

"You don't just light it up and take a few drags to get it lit?" I asked.

He shook his head in time with the spinning of the cigar. "Not at all, kid. You make sure it's lit evenly so it burns properly, like so."

Once the tip of the cigar was glowing bright orange he stuck the cigar back between his teeth and took a deep draw of the smoke before he handed the matches over, picked up his glass and reclined in his chair.

I struck a match and spun the cigar above the flame, imitating him as best I could.

Spencer took the cigar from his mouth to speak. "And before you go puffing on it, don't inhale the smoke. You'll goddamn shit yourself if you do, I'm telling you."

I flicked out the match and done as instructed by sticking the cigar in my mouth and taking a puff but not inhaling. The smoke filled my mouth with a flavour that was odd at first but not unpleasant. It was quite good, in fact. I blew the smoke, quite pleased I didn't make a fool of myself by coughing my lungs out all over the warden's nice shoes. The whisky was good too, if a little strong for an inexperienced drinker.

I took another drag on the cigar and exhaled before speaking up, "It's not that I don't appreciate it, but why such good hospitality for an inmate? Do all the new kids get this treatment?"

Spencer exhaled smoke. "Not at all, but then, not all new kids incapacitate the more undesirable inmates in their first forty-eight hours."

"So you heard about that, huh?"

"I'm the warden. I know everything that happens here. Controlling it is a different matter though, and that's where you come into the picture."

We both took a sip of whiskey. The burning sensation felt good on my throat.

"I don't get it. You're not mad about what I did to Garcia, or even put off because of what I'm in here for?"

Spencer's eyes searched my own through the haze of smoke before answering, "Where your past is concerned, I couldn't give a rat's ass. I've read your file and I don't see it in you. Sure, you've got some darkness in there but I've spent most of my life surrounded by the worst kinds of criminals. You're not like them."

"You think I'm innocent?"

"I'd like to think so. Aside from that, if I was mad at you, we wouldn't be having a chat over whiskey and cigars. No, I'm grateful. I'm happy about what you've done and that's why you're sitting here. You see, I haven't been warden here all too long. The place was out of control when I took over and it still is. Fuck all I can do about it myself. But maybe we can do something about it together. You're here because I want you on my side before the pig screwing, inbred hicks in this place get you on theirs. You follow?"

"Not entirely," I admitted.

"It's as simple as this son, you haven't even been here a week and you've quickly dispatched a major pain in my ass. Garcia has quite literally been a pain in a lot of asses, but he's been a gigantic pain in mine especially. Him and a few more of his criminal buddies think they own this place," he took a drag of his smoke then sighed, "you though? You've done something that commands their respect. I'm supposed to be in charge here so naturally they hate me, but you've got them in the palm of your hand right now, you know that? Most new kids think they'll take down the biggest, baddest guy in the joint and nobody will mess with them after that. Practically everyone that tries that goes for the wrong guy and leaves a day later in a body bag. Not you though. You fucked with the big guy and won. I'd like to propose an alliance."

I wasn't entirely sure about what he was getting at, but I was interested. If it meant I'd get special privileges, free whiskey, cigars and something to keep me occupied in the shithole called Blackwater Maximum Security, I was definitely interested.

"An alliance?" I asked, beginning to feel slightly lofty. "Go on..."

"What I mean by that is if you help me out by taking down the other main shitheads in this place, I can see to it that you get a few years off your sentence, plus some nice extras as an incentive."

"By take down, you mean..."

"To put it bluntly, I need you to kill the sons of bitches. Or maybe just seriously injure, I haven't decided yet. Just take them out of the picture as best you can, like you did with Garcia. Inmates have unfortunate accidents in prison all the time. What can I do if someone sustains a fatal injury from, say, falling down the stairs? The way I see it, I can't properly run this prison until a few roaches are squished. I just need you to be the boot that does the squishing. You've already squished one, so most of the others are aware of the boot, and they're scared. Now, you may or may not have it in you to kill a person, but I've been to the infirmary and I've seen first-hand what you can do if the situation calls for it. So, how about it? Want to earn a few extra years of freedom?"

"So you're saying you want me to murder a bunch of inmates to get out of here early, and I won't be blamed for it at all?"

"Like I said, accidents happen. It's already on file that Garcia had a freak accident with the zipper on his pants. Terrible things them zippers, if you're not careful."

It all seemed too good to be true but nonetheless, I had nothing to lose by agreeing to do the dirty work. I knew I couldn't do it alone, though. I'd need a friend or two. "I'd be pretty difficult to do alone," I said, "I couldn't have done Garcia in if it wasn't for David Flowers. How about I get him and another friend in on this? If that sounds good, you've got a deal."

Spencer took a moment to consider my counter-offer. "Fine, that sounds fair. There are three other people I need you to take out of the picture at the moment, but it could be more. If I need more taken care of we'll have another cigar, another whiskey and a nice chat about it. Out of curiosity, who do you want to ask for help?"

I nodded along as the warden spoke, then answered, "David and a guy called Alejandro; he says he owes me for Garcia. So who are the other three you want help with?"

"Ah, the Santos fella, yes he'll be good." He took a sip of whisky before continuing, "Anyway, the first job I want you to do could turn out to be more than one person, depending on when and where you find him. His name is Javier Rivera, the leader of a gang that call themselves Los Hijos De Puta. Now I don't speak border-hopper but I hear it means something along the lines of

'The Motherfuckers' or maybe 'Sons of Bitches' or something. Whatever it means, both are fitting names."

I finished off my whisky with a grimace from the punch it packed then set the glass down on the table. "The Motherfuckers?"

"Something like that, don't take my word for it. Anyway, it's Rivera and his cronies that are getting drugs smuggled into the prison. We take him down and we put a big dent in the drug supply. It's likely he'll always have a buddy nearby but I'm sure you can handle it if you take your friends along. After all, you did beat Garcia's crony up as well as the man himself."

"Doesn't sound too bad. We don't have to kill them though, right?"

"As long as they're out of the picture, I'm giving you and your friends free reign of their fates."

"David and Ali get the same deal too?"

"They do indeed," Spencer said as he pulled an ashtray to the edge of the desk and sat his cigar down in it. They were lasting longer than I ever expected. I set mine down, too.

"So who are the other two people you want rid of?"

Spencer shifted his weight onto his elbow and finished off his whiskey. "Let's just concentrate on Rivera and we'll come to the others later. For now, you and your friends take a couple of months to get yourselves ready for the work. No point rushing into it unprepared. I like your style but that Santos fella could probably show you a thing or two and I don't want you getting yourself killed, especially not straight off the bat. I need you, and you need me if you want to get out of here any time before you hit fifty. You just take a little time, make sure you can do the job and when you're ready to see to it that Rivera and his pals are no longer a pain in my ass, we'll have another chat. How's that sound?"

"Sounds good," I said, clapping my hands together.

Spencer leaned forward with a smile and put his hand out. "Do we have an agreement then, Night?"

I slapped my hand into his so we could exchange a good solid handshake.

"We have an agreement."

How to Knock Out a Motherfucker

Almost two months had passed since my talk with the warden. Ali was a good teacher but he was relentless. He refused to go easy on us, which was a good thing considering nobody else would. He drew up a schedule for us soon after hearing all about the offer. Mornings after breakfast were spent learning self-defence. Afternoons were spent working on offence and evenings were for working out.

[Track 12]

The first two weeks were the most difficult. We'd meet Ali in the canteen, have breakfast, then we'd go out into the yard and he'd beat the shit out of us. I always considered myself a half decent fighter but Ali was big, and he was damn strong. He'd beat me to the ground with ease. Turns out that being a smartass doesn't help when someone's got a lot more fighting experience than you. David got it worse, since he was never much of a fighter to begin with. Even though Ali would frequently hand our asses to us, we never had any hard feelings. It was all in the name of improvement, and that's exactly what we did. We improved. After the first two weeks, both David and I got the hang of all the self-defence techniques Ali taught us and we didn't get beaten up as much. Sure, Ali would still land a whole bunch of punches, but for the most part, we avoided them quite nicely.

When we weren't being human punching bags, we got to turn the tables and take turns trying to put Ali on his ass. It was three weeks before I managed to do it. We were having our afternoon offence lesson. Ali was defending himself while I was attacking. I threw a right hook, which he ducked, but he didn't see the left coming up from under him. I caught him under the jaw and put him on the ground. He looked shocked for a moment but eventually stood up with a grin. He slapped an arm over my shoulders and shook me with a celebratory cheer. David gave me a pat on the back then got himself ready to try his luck. Ali would always tower over David, and David just didn't have the strength to really land a solid punch. He'd land a few from time to time but he may as well have been trying to cut down a tree with a spoon for all the good it'd do.

The other inmates didn't pay us any attention at first. The general rule was that if a clean fight broke out in the yard, you'd not get involved and just let it finish, but if there were weapons involved, everyone got involved. With the rule standing, we were ignored for a while. Things changed when they realised that it was the same three guys fighting each other every day. By the end of the first week, other inmates had taken an interest and the warden had caught wind of it. Word had spread that the guys that fucked up Garcia were getting kicked all over the yard every day by some big Mexican dude for what seemed to be no reason at all. A few days later, Spencer had a storage room cleared out especially for us so we would be free to train, away from prying eyes.

During our training, Ali explained how the gangs worked in Blackwater. He told me that I had a certain degree of respect for accomplishing the feat of taking down Garcia. They respected me, but they weren't scared of me, not in the way the Warden thought. They were more cautious than scared, and also a bit pissed off because I'd fucked up one of their buddies. He told me the other inmates, and especially those in gangs, wouldn't respect me for long if they caught sight of me getting a beating every day. The gangs thrived on power, and took a liking to anyone that had even a whiff of it. According to Ali, one way or another, I couldn't avoid them. If I was weak, I'd be a target, a victim. If I was powerful, I'd be a different kind of target. One gang or another would want me to join them and that's not something I wanted. I had already turned down a neo-Nazi skinhead on the way to Blackwater. I didn't wanna do it again. Most people in Blackwater were fucking crazy. Not the fun kind of crazy, either. They were the kind of crazy that'd willingly stab someone with a shit covered shiv, just for a Sunday morning giggle.

It was a tough couple of months but after taking enough beatings, both David and I managed to give as much as we'd take. David had grown much more confident and a little surer of himself. Ali was proud, I was proud and the warden was proud when he got the news. I was due a meeting to tell him how much we had progressed. It was time to get things started. We were ready to put some hurt on Los Hijos De Puta, The Motherfuckers.

90

"Fucking do it, knock him out!" I yelled as David threw a punch that landed right between Ali's eyes.

David pulled back and threw another fist, sending Ali stumbling back against a wall. Ali hit the wall and put his weight on it, holding his hands up in surrender. David had won without so much as a bust lip, which was a big step forward. I threw a fist into the air and congratulated him.

Ali smiled and nodded, giving David a small round of applause. "Well done Flowers my friend, well done. That was good but I'm pooped. Let's rest," he said, sliding down the wall to sit on the floor.

David held his hand up for a high-five as I made my way over to them. I gave him five with a good hard slap. "That was some good fighting, man," I said.

David took a moment to catch his breath before dropping his ass down to the floor. "Thanks. I'm done too. A rest sounds good."

"You ladies best not fall asleep, it's my turn in a minute," I said as I sat down between the guys.

"How about we make it ten minutes?" Ali replied.

"Make it twenty for all I care. As long as you're ready to go all-out, I'm happy."

"You're eager to get your ass kicked, eh, brother?"

I gave Ali a backhanded slap on the chest. "Eager to kick yours."

He grinned back at me. "Really getting into this, aren't you?"

"I am now that you're not handing my ass to me every time."

Ali wiped his brow with his forearm. "Good. You both learn fast and can stand to take more of a beating now. That's something that'll always be useful, no matter what. Trust me, it pays to be able to take a punch and brush it off."

David chimed in, "I guess time will tell. After the shit with Garcia the only one that's done us any harm is you. I've had permanent bruises for weeks now."

Ali laughed and slapped a hand down on his thigh. "Right you are, my friend, but now you're the ones dealing damage. I couldn't be more proud."

I grinned at them both, looking forward to my own fight. "So whenever you're ready, I think it's time I deal some damage."

Ali had really helped us. I already knew how to fight and I could hold my own at times, but Ali was a much more seasoned fighter. He knew his shit and he taught us well. David was the one to really benefit from the lessons. In a short space of time he had gone from a quiet guy with no fight in him to someone brimming with confidence and a strong set of cojones.

We had taken a good share of beatings. The beating I was about to both give, and take, was our last fight before my meeting with the warden to tell him we were ready to go head to head with Los Hijos De Puta.

Ali stood a few feet in front of me, fists raised to his face, bouncing the way boxers do. I brought my fists up as he nodded to tell me he was ready. With one swift movement I sprang forward and ducked as Ali threw the first punch. His fist sailed over the top of my head, leaving him open. My right fist jabbed into his ribs hard. It was like punching a bull. Not that I've ever punched a bull, but you know. Ali took a step back and bent over slightly, rubbing at the area I'd hit. It was a good punch but he didn't seem too fazed by it. He came at me hard and fast. For his size he was damn quick. I didn't react fast enough and caught the first punch to my ribs and the second to my jaw. For a moment I thought the lower half of my face was going to tear off and shatter against the wall, leaving my tongue dangling from the bloody mess of a wrecked face. It's quite likely that it would have happened if I hadn't trained to take similar hits every day for two months straight. It took me a moment to recover from almost having my jaw snapped off but I pulled myself together and returned the favour, landing a hard right hook on Ali's chin. He staggered around for a second but brushed it off and came right back with a tackle that sent me crashing to the floor like a sack of shit. He stood over me as I lay on the floor. Anyone else could have kicked me while I was down at that point, but we had agreed to keep the fight clean, only using the upper body. No kicking and no hits below the belt. Definitely nothing below the belt. We may have been training to fight all-out but nobody enjoys a kick to the nuts no matter what the occasion. It's just not pleasant.

I took a few seconds to get to my feet. David switched from cheering for me to cheering for Ali. We'd do that whenever we had a fight, just root for both fighters and see who'd win. There were never any hard feelings when one of us inevitably received an ass kicking. Ali had won most fights and David the least. I sat nicely in the middle, not winning all that often but not taking too many defeats either, which I couldn't really complain about. I just wished I had been able to take a few more hits on the night Suzie was murdered. If things worked out that way then maybe Suzie would have still been alive. And if Suzie was alive then maybe I wouldn't have been in prison. The thought of such an outcome left a sour taste in my mouth because in reality, Suzie was dead and I was stuck doing time, accused of killing her. These were the thoughts that fuelled my fighting. All I needed to do was picture myself doing some serious harm to the assholes that murdered her and away I'd go, throwing punches, taking hits, having a damn good time.

David's cheer shifted back in my favour as I threw a strong left hook at the side of Ali's head and followed up with a quick right jab to the jaw as he staggered sideways and took a step back. He was looking tired and slightly dazed, which was understandable as he'd only just fought—and lost—against David. I shifted a little closer to make an attempt to put him on his ass. He saw me coming and threw a fist at my ribs to push me back a little. It would have hit but he was getting slow so I dodged it fairly easily. I took my chance, grabbed his arm to pull him in closer and threw all of my weight into a punch that landed square between his eyes. Ali stood for a second, seemingly trying to think about what had just happened before stumbling backwards and falling to the floor. I stood over him, giving him the same courtesy he'd given me; a chance to get up and keep fighting. He stayed down. David gave a count of three before Ali raised his hand in submission.

"A victory for The Nightingale," David said, imitating the voice of a boxing announcer, holding a fist in the air.

Ali kept his hand up until I took a hold of it to help him to his feet. "Mierda, hombre," he said, "I don't stand a chance against the two of you anymore. You win. You both win."

I gave him a slap on the back as I asked, "So how did I do, chief?"

"My friend, I couldn't have done any better myself." He pointed at the bruising swiftly appearing on his face. "That right there, that's how you knock out a motherfucker."

Sucker Punch

On the warden's suggestion, we took two weeks to rest and relax. Taking a beating every day doesn't give you much time to heal. If we were going to get into a potentially life threatening situation, we needed to be at full health. Ali made sure we stuck to his workout schedule, but at least we weren't getting kicked to shit for a while.

When the big day finally arrived, we were pumped. The warden had promised a whole host of rewards, the best being actual food at each of our meals, rather than wet cardboard flavoured slop. I hadn't been in prison long and I was already prepared to beat a man to death if it meant I'd get some chicken and fries or a nice cheeseburger. The thought alone was enough to spur me on. It must have been even more tantalizing to David and Ali considering they'd been locked up a lot longer and eaten a lot more of the prison's daily gruel. Our first taste of the high life came in the form of a good meal before our first big fight. By command of the warden, the guards that were loyal to him had set up a table in the room we had been using for training. That room was pretty much ours for all intents and purposes.

The three of us sat in anticipation, waiting for the food to come. The menu was roast chicken, potatoes, sausages, bacon and gravy. We even got a bottle of beer each. It was like Christmas. While the other inmates sat in the hall and spooned shit into their mouths, we dined on something with actual flavour. The smell alone gave me enough energy to fight for days.

By the end of the meal our bellies were full and we were ready to fight. In the few hours between dinner and bed-time-lock-up the inmates were free to roam the prison. We'd been given our instructions to head to a large communal room that was known to be the gathering place of Rivera and Los Hijos De Puta. Each little gang had their own turf, whereas Garcia's turf was his own cell and the shower rooms, the north-wing communal area was Rivera's. They all respected each other's turf but David, Ali and I had formed a new gang and we were about to do some serious disrespecting.

The northern communal area was a decent sized room, nicely tucked away at the back end of the prison. Like other communal rooms it had a range of things to provide entertainment. This room in particular was only ever visited by Javier Rivera, Los Hijos De Puta and their buddies so it was a fight free zone as long as any unwelcome inmates kept their distance. For this reason, their room had a few extra pieces of fun that the other communal rooms were lacking. While the others all had a television, radio, books and board games, Rivera's room also had a pool table, cues and everything. Such things were missing from the rooms that weren't faction turf. Fights were more likely to break out in those areas. This worked to our advantage. We'd have a better choice of objects to beat people with. It's quite difficult to beat a person with a selection of old novels and a Monopoly board. Trust me, I've tried.

* * *

We made our way to Rivera's turf in high spirits. David looked a little nervous but I told him that whatever happened couldn't be much worse than the near-constant ass kicking Ali had given us for the past two months. Ali was practically bouncing with excitement. He was a decent guy, but god damn, did he love a good fight.

I was about to shoot a question but David beat me to it. "How many do you think there'll be?" he asked, still nervous.

I replied with a shrug.

"Rivera will definitely be there," Ali said, "and probably a few others. Five or six, maybe ten. His gang is about twenty strong but I hear it's usually his favourite few buddies that hang in the room. We could take six. Easy."

"You think?"

"I don't think, my friend. I know."

This made David smile a little. Seeing Ali so confident seemed to ease his nerves a little, which was good. Turning into a nervous wreck wouldn't have worked out all too well for him.

A couple of minutes went by before we were within sight of Rivera's room. The door had a glass panel so we took a quick peek inside before we got down to business. As it turned out, there were seven people in the room. That meant we'd have to fight two each and have one to spare. Ali wanted the two biggest guys. David agreed to take on the two smallest and watch the door to make sure nobody got out of the room. Rivera was mine. Well, him and another asshole. Whoever put down two guys first got the bonus dude.

Ali gave me a sceptical look as we pulled away from the door. "We definitely get rewarded for doing this? Now that we're about to do this I can't help but wonder if we're being set up to take the fall."

"Spencer gave me his word. I don't see any reason not to trust him. Either way, if we pull this off, what's the worst that can happen? A few more years on our sentences?"

"Fair point, my friend. I just hope he keeps his word."

"Yeah," David cut in, "that meal we just had would make going back to slop a soul crushing experience."

"You got that right," I said.

Ali flexed his muscles and stretched out to limber himself up. "You both ready?"

"Yeah," I said.

David Nodded.

"Good. Remember, we're not fighting each other this time so we don't need to keep it clean. Grab whatever you can use as a weapon 'cos you can be damn sure they will. Pool cues would be good." He paused for a second. "Actually, let's all take a sock off."

"What?" David said.

"We each take off one sock. Whenever you get the chance, stick a couple of pool balls in it and swing the fucker at someone's face. Makes what I call a sweaty jawbreaker," Ali said, smiling.

Fair enough. We all kicked our shoes off, removed a sock and pocketed them for safe keeping before pulling our shoes back on.

"Ok," I said, "we gonna do this?"

They both nodded.

[Track 13]

"So let's crack some skulls."

Ali led the way, pushing the door open and strolling into the room like he owned it. I marched in after him and David followed close behind. Every eye hit us. Three guys watching TV, two playing checkers and two playing pool—one of them Rivera—stopped what they were doing to look at us. They simply stared for a while, seemingly in total disbelief that three strangers had the balls to stroll into their room.

Javier Rivera was, of course, the first to speak up. Warden Spencer had described him during our last meeting so I recognised him immediately. "What the fuck is this?" he asked, in an accent similar to Ali's. He set his cue down on the table and made his way around it. "I said what the fuck?"

David and I moved to Ali's sides, spreading out a little and keeping quiet.

"Maybe one of you would like to answer me?" Rivera said.

I moved over to the pool table, getting closer to him. Ali took a stroll around the room, having a good look around. David stood by the door.

"Javier Rivera?" I asked, knowing full well it was him.

Rivera was a mean looking bastard. He had his hair slicked back and was tatted up to the max. They covered his hands, arms, neck and face. It made him look like a Mexican version of my Nazi friend from the prison bus. He wasn't very big—just a little shorter than me and about the same build—but he was damn sure of himself. I could tell by his manner.

He looked me in the eyes and squared up. "Yeah, that's me," he said, "you gonna answer my question?"

"We're just paying a visit. I've gotta deliver a message." I said, staring back at him.

He tensed up. "And what's that?"

"Your business, I'd like it to stop. This place is bad enough without your guys running drugs through it."

Every member of Los Hijos De Puta had their eyes fixed on us. Most had stood up to watch and see how the confrontation unfolded.

"Excuse me? You think you can come in to my house and tell me what to do?"

"I'm not telling you, I'm politely asking."

He looked pissed. "Well I'm politely declining. Now I'm giving you ten seconds. I'm going to count down from ten and if you're not out that door when I reach one, you and your buddies are going to wish you never walked in here."

"Afraid I can't do that, chief."

"Ten," he began.

"I'm not leaving until you agree to quit the business."

He got all up in my personal space, his face almost touching mine.

Ali had made his way over to the pool table. Every member of Rivera's gang had their eyes fixed on me. Nobody was paying Ali any attention but I caught sight of him sneaking a couple of pool balls off the table before continuing his walk and circling back to the door to stand next to David.

"Nine."

Ali gave David a gentle nudge and flashed a pool ball at him before handing it over on the sly.

I stood my ground.

"Eight."

David cupped the pool ball and hid it behind his back as he slowly took the sock from his pocket and slid the ball inside.

"Seven."

The other guy at the pool table cut in, "Let's just fuck him up!"

"Shut up," Rivera said to him before turning back to me. "Six, asshole."

David and Ali had both armed themselves with their jawbreakers.

"FIVE!" Rivera yelled, getting riled up.

I shot a hand out for the pool cue on the table, shouted, "FOUR-THREE-TWO-ONE," then grabbed the cue and took a swing at his head.

He ducked it just in time, and all hell broke loose.

The other guy at the pool table made an attempt to hit me with his cue but Ali flew from the door and swung the jawbreaker at his face before he had the chance to get me. I heard the unmistakable sound of teeth shattering as the makeshift weapon smashed into his mouth. Good job the prison food was mush or he'd have a hard time eating for a while. He hit the floor, spitting out a whole bunch teeth.

One down.

One of the guys near the TV lunged at David and took a jawbreaker to the ribs for his efforts. He doubled over in pain but didn't go down so David swung again and again, right into the guy's spine. After three hits, he fell, howling in pain. He didn't bother getting back up.

Two down.

Rivera had darted to the other side of the room to look for a weapon. This left me open to the two guys that were playing checkers, but that was alright because I had a cue and they had nothing but their fists. The other two from the sofa took the opportunity to rush David. One guy managed to land a punch on David's face but the other didn't get so far. Ali had snatched up the other cue and within a heartbeat, snapped it over the head of one of the guys that were trying to jump David. He followed up with a jawbreaker to the side of the guy's head, possibly killing him.

Three down.

The checkers goons both came at me at the same time. The closest one took a sharp crack to the face with the thick end of my pool cue. Both of his lips split, splattering blood all over his chin but it wasn't enough to take him out of the action. He stumbled back, clutching his face. The next one threw himself at me and grabbed a hold of the cue. He made an attempt to head-butt me in the face but I dodged it just in time and returned the favour. My forehead came crashing down on his nose, completely fucking his shit up. He fell back and went down, still holding the cue. There was no way I'd just let him take my cue from me so I fell along with him and landed on top, pinning his arms under the cue.

I caught sight of the other guys. David was in the middle of a scrap with the asshole that punched him in the face; Ali had come over and straddled the split-lipped guy, using the thick end of his own snapped cue to beat him senseless. Rivera was scrambling around the room like a rat looking for a tasty morsel. So much for all that bravado when he was talking shit.

The asshole that pulled me down squirmed to get free. I shifted my weight and pushed the cue down on his neck. It made for the perfect opportunity to take him out of the picture.

"Going somewhere?" I said.

He bared his teeth and spat at my face before groaning the words, "Comer mierda," under the weight on his throat.

I've never been much good with Spanish but I'm pretty sure he told me to eat shit, which isn't very nice. Granted, telling me to eat shit wasn't polite but I didn't want to kill anybody if I didn't absolutely have to, so I searched for a weak spot to take advantage of. That weak spot just happened to be his nose, which was bent and broken, making it a prime target for a little more abuse. With one hand on the cue to keep the guy down, I raised a fist high above my head and swung it into his already busted up nose. My knuckles drove into it with ease on the count of it already being broken. It seemed to bubble and squish blood and gristle through my fingers as I beat it into pulp.

I expected him to react as most people in his situation would and scream out in pain before passing out, but he didn't. Instead of screaming he just gritted his teeth and made a loud noise that I can only describe as sounding like someone audibly straining to take an intensely bothersome shit. He continued to groan and strain until his face flushed to a bright shade of red. I eventually realised I was putting too much weight in the cue, practically crushing his throat. I lifted the cue, pulled it out of his grip and threw it in David's direction. The guy took a ragged gasp, filled his lungs with air and let it all out with the kind of scream I had been expecting. One more punch put an end to the noise.

I sat back on the now unconscious dude's chest and examined my fist as I pulled it away from his decimated nose. It was covered in blood, some of which was thick and falling from my knuckles in chunks. He was bleeding heavily from the nose-mush but he was still breathing.

Four down.

I hauled myself to my feet and stepped aside to assess the situation. The guy underneath Ali lay unconscious with a face like raw tenderised steak. He'd certainly never look the same way again, but he would live. Ali himself was still straddling him, leaning back with his eyes closed, and taking long slow breaths to calm his rage so he didn't commit murder.

Five down.

David's and his opponent seemed to be having a good clean fight. Neither had tried to take the cue that was lying near them. David was doing alright but the other guy looked tired and about ready to drop.

I came back to my own thoughts and realised I had lost sight of Rivera. Just seconds ago he was in front of me, scratting around the room. Now he was gone. I took a quick glance around but couldn't see him. Thinking he'd somehow scooted out the door, I stepped over my punch bag's unconscious body and tried to make for the door when something hard smashed into the back of my head.

"Ow, fuck," I yelled as I dropped to one knee and spun around.

Rivera stood behind me. He'd grabbed the eight ball from the pool table. The bitch had been hiding under the table while I was looking around and crawled out to sucker punch me the moment I let my guard down. He didn't have time to make himself a jawbreaker so he just straight up smacked me with the ball. Motherfucker.

Ali had opened his eyes and caught sight of my situation. He spun his broken cue around—the thick end now slick with blood—and lunged across the room with the pointy end towards Rivera.

Rivera panicked and threw the eight ball at Ali. It bounced off his chest and thudded to the floor. I heard a louder thud a second later. David had knocked out his opponent with a clean jab to the face.

Six down.

The eight ball had done jack shit to stop Ali. He didn't even blink; he just closed the distance and seized Rivera by the throat. David stepped over to my side and gave me a hand to get me to my feet and steady me. The whack from the ball had left me a little dizzy.

"Night," Ali said, "I think we've got this cabrón's attention."

I turned to see Ali holding Rivera by the throat, pressing the sharp end of his cue into his chest. Rivera had his hands held out in submission.

"Good," I said, stepping closer to him. Ali stepped aside but kept a hold of his throat. I got all up in his face and said, "I tried asking politely, now I'm going to tell you, not so politely."

Rivera nodded and made a noise to show he was listening.

"Stop running the damn drugs. If you don't, we'll pay you another visit. You hear? Garcia got off easy so we're giving you the same courtesy, for now."

106

He nodded, standing there like a deer in the headlights.

The message seemed clear enough but Rivera was the boss of Los Hijos De Puta. We couldn't just leave without making a point. So Ali threw him to the floor, and the three of us danced on his skull.

Shifty Bastard

I sat in the warden's office, puffing away on a high quality stogie with a glass of whiskey in hand, as I had done a couple of times before. Things were different this time. This time David and Ali sat there right alongside me. Whisky and cigars all round, the taste of success.

It had been just over a week since we put the hurt on Rivera and Los Hijos De Puta—The Motherfuckers—and since then, we'd been living like kings. Three solid meals a day, served with drinks of our choosing, and a whole host of other luxuries. It made our deal incredibly sweet.

Javier Rivera was alive but not all that well. He had been in the infirmary since we paid him a visit and done a number on him and his pals. Five of his friends were in there right along with him. Two were dead. It turned out Ali had killed two of them. One had died almost immediately after taking a madball to the side of the head. He had been dead before he hit the floor. The other had spent a couple of days clinging to life but eventually succumbed to the injuries Ali had inflicted. Those that survived would be out of the infirmary in another week or so; only time would tell if the message had been received with effect. It had certainly been effective for Harry Garcia—who was now out of the infirmary and spending his days hiding in his cell, pissing through a tube—so I didn't see why Rivera would continue his business.

Warden Spencer was in high spirits. According to him, the four of us were going to turn Blackwater Prison around. He told us that by the time we were finished the place would be held in high regard, a shining example of rehabilitation, the crown jewel of America's prison system. Warden Spencer would be hailed a hero, and he'd have the three of us to thank for it. In short, he was pleased with our work, but our work was far from over.

After a good round of patting each other on the back, stroking our own egos and dreaming of the future, it was time to get back to business. Two of the four big bad bosses had been taken out of the game and it was time to take out the next one.

Spencer took some time to explain how we had taken down the guys in charge of two of the big four crime factions—prostitution and drugs—before going on to tell us about the other two factions of the prison crime ring; weapons and violence.

The next target was a man named Bill Bingsley, leader of the Nazi skinheads, man in charge of supplying weapons, and a total weasel. We needed to take him down and sabotage the weapon supply in order to make it easier for ourselves when it came to facing the worst of the worst, the leader of a gang that ran a weekly fight club in the prison basement where only one contender ever left alive. The warden told us this guy only went by the name Uncle Jimmy, and he would have anybody that referred to him as anything else murdered. He was a real asshole. A real dangerous asshole, at that.

By taking down Bingsley, the warden explained, we would put a big dent in Uncle Jimmy's business. Without fresh weapons, the fight club and its organisers would be left with old merchandise at best. According to

Spencer, taking on Uncle Jimmy before Bingsley would inevitably end up in the three of us being butchered. That wasn't something any of us wanted, so we agreed to take care of the small fry before trying to hook the big fish.

Upon agreeing on the details and rewards of the next job, Spencer held up his glass in a toast to our partnership, and a bright future for all. We held our glasses in the air, clinked them together and drank. To us.

As we had done before our fight with Rivera and his chums, we took a couple more days after our meeting with the warden to rest, recuperate and prepare for our next job. Word on the street was that Bingsley was a bit of a loner during the evenings, and a lover of cooking who liked to spend his evenings alone in the kitchens. The other word was that he was a real shifty bastard, even around his fellow skinheads. People feared him because he was unpredictable. Spencer had told us a little about Bingsley but had recommended we do a bit of detective work before we paid him a visit, so that's exactly what I did. While David and Ali spent their resting evenings working out in our little club room, I was out questioning other inmates. Most weren't much help, but one gave me all the information I needed.

My fountain of knowledge on Bill Bingsley went by the name of Frankie Acara, a one-eyed Nazi skinhead and ex-follower of Bingsley, Acara had considered Bingsley a friend until he made a joke at his expense. As Acara told it, they were sitting at dinner with a bunch of other fellow skinheads when he made the joke. He laughed, Bingsley laughed, they all laughed right up until Bingsley suddenly stopped laughing, sprung across the table and gouged Acara's left eyeball out with a spoon. After that, Acara wasn't so fond of his friend Bill anymore, so he turned his back on Bill and the skinheads.

It was Acara that warned me not to trust anything Bingsley said or done. As he put it, Bingsley could be acting like a real friendly fella one second and have a knife to your throat the next. He was especially twitchy around anyone that wasn't Caucasian, which meant he'd be extra volatile in Ali's presence. He was also likely to have a multitude of weapons hidden where you'd least expect them to be.

We were in for a bit of fun.

* * *

I made my way our training room. It was time for dinner and after a long day of questioning inmates, I was famished.

It was a Wednesday, which meant it was spaghetti and meatballs night. We'd always have a nice meal but we made sure to have a damn good one before a fight. If we hadn't had a good meal before fighting Rivera and his chums, things might not have gone down as they did. Ali always told us to never fight on an empty stomach.

David and Ali were already sitting at the table awaiting food when I got to the room. I sat down at the end of the table with a sigh.

"Are we doing it tonight?" David asked.

"Yeah, he'll be in the kitchens 'till about ten," I replied.

The clock on the wall had just ticked over to seven thirty.

"Best make sure you clear your plates then, fellas," Ali said.

I smiled at Ali and said, "You especially. Word is he's likely to go bat shit crazy if he's near anyone that isn't an all-out white American."

He waved a hand is dismissal, "Ah fuck him, those Nazi assholes are all the same. They all talk big and act tough in front of their buddies but get them alone and they piss their pants."

"I hope you're right," I said, "but Bingsley is supposed to be a little unpredictable."

"Last time the three of us took down seven assholes, what's one lonely guy going to do?"

David chipped in, "Best to be cautious than reckless, right?"

I nodded in agreement. "He's the one that's getting weapons into the prison. It's usually things like knives but the three of us won't count for shit if he turns out to be packing a gun."

"This is true," Ali said, shrugging his shoulders.

I was about to dish out a little more information when the door opened.

The smell of our dinner filled the room as a guard called Carl Wilkins brought it in on a serving trolley. Carl was the usual guy to bring dinner and the sight of him always made us smile. He was one of the good ones, one of the guards loyal to the warden. Another guard I hadn't seen before followed behind him, carrying a small TV that we had been promised. He put it down on the opposite end of the table and plugged it into the nearest electrical outlet. Dinner and a show. We really were living the high life.

Carl set our meals down in front of us and presented a selection of drinks while the new guard tuned in the TV. We all chose a couple of beers each. It felt good to drink with the guys. Underage drinking somewhat inflated my ego. Plus, a little liquid confidence wouldn't do any harm.

After a minute of fiddling with the dials the new guy found a channel playing an interview with David Bowie. The picture was a little snowy but it was watchable. He turned around and made a face to ask if this channel would do. I was in the middle of taking a sip of beer so I stuck my thumb up to show my approval. The other guys nodded and thanked the guards before they left the room.

I put my beer down and watched the TV. Bowie was yammering away to a talk show host I didn't know the name of, explaining his alter-ego, Ziggy Stardust. The sight of him brought back memories of listening to his records in Suzie's bedroom; memories from only a few months back when I'd lie on her bed and watch her dance around the room in her underwear, singing along to 'Starman'.

"You alright?" Ali asked, pulling me away from my thoughts.

"Yeah," I lied. "Just thinking, you know? Suzie was a real big fan of this guy."

David swallowed a mouthful of spaghetti. "Want to change to something else?"

"Nah, it's alright. Good memories."

They both nodded and we continued our meals in silence. It was clear that they wanted to leave me to my thoughts and avoid any uncomfortable questions, which I appreciated. It'd be a long time before I could talk about Suzie without getting upset. The only good side of it was that the memories of her murder put me in the right mood to repeatedly hit somebody. That came in handy while in prison.

After the meal we left the room and made our way to the kitchens. It was almost eight thirty and the food hall was deserted. We could hear someone clinking around in the kitchen at the back. Bingsley.

"Just a moment," Ali whispered as we crossed the hall.

"What's up?" I asked as we stopped to listen.

Ali took a quick glance around the room then pulled something wrapped in cloth out of his pocket. He unwound the cloth to show a selection of three homemade shivs; a long iron nail duct taped to a wooden handle, a bunch of razor blades melted into the handle of a toothbrush and a sharpened screwdriver.

"Take one, mis hermanos. Just in case."

David looked somewhat reluctant but eventually shrugged and chose the duct taped nail. I picked up the sharpened screwdriver, impressed by Ali's craftsmanship.

Ali nodded, carefully pocketed his razor-brush and started towards the kitchen. With weapons in our pockets, I was fairly confident we would be able to take care of Bingsley quick and easy, preferably without killing him. I might have been accused of murder, surrounded by murderers and friends with a man that had recently killed two men and taught me how to beat the life out of someone, but I wasn't a killer. The thought of intentionally killing anyone other than Suzie's murderers made me shudder. I wasn't that kind of person. Not yet, anyway.

[Track 14]

I took the lead and strut into the kitchen like I owned the place. Bingsley was bent over a counter with his back to us. I took a moment to consider my options; I could do what most would consider the right thing and make my presence known, or I could sneak up behind him and jam the screwdriver into the side of his head and scramble his brains with it.

Like I said, I wasn't a killer so I done what I thought was right and made a show of clearing my throat with a loud AHEM.

Bingsley shot straight up into the air in fright and shouted, "SHITFUCKER!"

I bit my lip to contain some laughter.

He spun around to face us and pointed a knife in our direction. His apron was covered in suspicious red stains. "What the fuck are you doing sneaking up on me like that?"

I ignored his question. After taking a breath to calm myself I asked if he was Bill Bingsley.

"Yes, I'm Billy," he jabbed the knife through the air at us, "and who the fuck are you?"

I decided to play nice but keep cautious. "I'm Night, this is David," I gestured, "and this is Ali."

His eyes darted between us and settled on Ali for a while.

He looked like any other neo-Nazi; shaved head and a whole load of tattoos. Unlike Big G from the prison bus, Bingsley didn't have the words 'DEATH TO

115

NIGGERS' tattooed across his forehead. Instead, he had a neat little swastika right in the centre. His bare arms flashed a load of similar ink, most noticeable of which was a large tattoo on his bicep of a black man's severed head, complete with dripping blood and the words 'Jigaboo Butcher' written above it in a messy handwriting.

"What are you doing? Why're you here?" he asked, still holding the knife.

I raised my hands to show they were empty and edged closer with Ali and David close behind.

"We just want to talk."

He lowered the knife. "You're the ones working for the warden, aren't you?"

"Maybe..."

"Maybe shit. I know you're the ones going around offing inmates. It was only a matter of time, really."

"What are you doing in here? Is that blood?" I asked, nodding to his apron.

"Blood?" He said, shaking his head, seemingly calming down. "You've got me all wrong. It's food colouring. I'm baking a cake." He stepped aside to show what was on the counter; a large square cake made of red sponge with white frosting that he hadn't finished. "If you wouldn't mind, I'd like to get on with it so it's ready for tomorrow."

Bingsley didn't seem anywhere near as shifty as I'd heard but I still didn't trust him.

"What's happening tomorrow?"

"I'm giving the cake to Warden Spencer as peace offering."

"A peace offering?"

"Yes." He said, eyes twitching slightly. "Once I heard he'd roped a few inmates into doing his dirty work I knew it'd only be a matter of time before he sent you after me. But you see, I'm trying to get out of my old business. Time to retire, you know? I thought if I baked him a cake he wouldn't send you to kill me. Too little too late though, right?"

Ali said, "Not if you mean it."

I decided to take a stroll around the room to look for anything he could use as a weapon, other than the knife he was holding. "Yeah," I agreed, "if we can come to a peaceful resolution I'm sure that'd be fine. How do we know we can trust you though?"

"Come have a slice of cake? Call a truce?" He finished the frosting and moved over to a pile of clean plates. He grabbed a few and took them back to the counter. "I'm sure the warden won't mind if I give you all a slice, he'd probably offer it himself."

David took a careful step forward. Ali followed.

Bingsley turned to the cake and shaved the edge off one side with his knife, then cut the edge into four pieces and pushed them onto a plate each. He turned and held a plate out to David, who edged a little closer and took the plate.

Bingsley smiled and picked up another plate, extending it towards Ali.

Ali eyed him for a second then took the plate.

"Would you like some?" Bingsley said to me.

I stopped scouring the room and said, "Sure."

"Excellent," he smiled.

I made my way over and he handed me a plate before putting the knife down and taking the last one. I picked the cake up from the plate. It looked good. I gave

117

it a sniff. It smelled good, too. I was about to take a bite when I sensed some tension in the air.

Everyone was watching me. David, Ali and Bingsley all stood, staring at me as I gave the cake a good eyeballing. They hadn't touched theirs. I lowered mine to the plate. David and Ali looked back to Bingsley, who shifted his eyes between each of us.

He shook his head, smiled again and said, "Don't worry, it's not poisoned," before taking a bite.

The tension in the air dissipated slightly as we all took a bite of the cake now that we had confirmed there wasn't anything wrong with it. It tasted good. Not too sweet or sickly, just a nice sponge cake with vanilla frosting. Both David and Ali nodded in approval as they ate theirs.

"See? Nothing to worry about," Bingsley said.

We all nodded.

"Apparently so," I said.

Bingsley licked some crumbs from the side of his mouth. "Do you think Spencer will enjoy it? I'm not one to blow my own trumpet but I think it's to die for," he said as he stepped back and bumped his ass down to lean on the counter.

"Well, its damn fine," I said, "and he does seem fond of life's fin—,"

Something had caught my eye. When Bingley bumped his ass on the table, a bit of the cake crumbled away to show a glimpse of something inside of it.

Bingsley followed my line of sight and turned to see what I was seeing.

"Oh shite," he sighed to himself. "Looks like the jig's up, isn't it?"

"What the hell is that?" I asked, lowering my plate.

"It's a bomb you fucking shitnugget," Bingsley replied, completely deadpan.

Ali dropped his plate in an instant and tore his razor-brush from his pocket with total reckless abandon. David followed suit and whipped out his shiv. I kept mine pocketed for the time being.

"A bomb? What?" I asked, half in terror, half in amazement that he'd made a bomb from scratch and hidden it in a fucking cake.

"Yes, a fucking bomb. I fancied some fuckery so I made a motherfucking bomb." He paused for a second then added, "you fucker."

All of Bingsley's politeness had disappeared and gave way to what appeared to be some form of Tourette' syndrome paired with a fondness for the word 'fuck'. Don't get me wrong, everyone loves to say fuck, but this guy had crammed it into a sentence like nothing I'd ever heard.

"You fancy stepping away from that, chief?" I said.

"I say we just jump him," Ali suggested.

"I think I'll stay right where I fucking am, and you can keep your border hopping chilli-nigger on a leash if you don't fancy being turned to paste."

I edged aside and slowly put my plate down on the nearest counter, raising my hands to show I wasn't going to pull a fast one. "Nobody needs to get hurt. If you really want to change your ways, we can help."

"For fuck's sake kid, I was whistling Dixie. I don't want to change shit. I like what I do."

"Seems we have a problem then", Ali said.

"Seems we do," Bingsley sneered back, "and I can only see this ending one way."

"It doesn't need to," I said.

"I'm not a fucking retard. Spencer sent you here to kill me, and I'm not going down easy, I swear it. I know the only way out of this is in a box and I've made my peace with that. Now are we going to stand around kicking dick all day or are we going to shed some fucking blood?"

Ali seemed to have heard enough. He lashed out with his razor-brush and slashed across Bingsley's apron.

"Ow, you fucker," he yelled as the blades tore through the fabric and opened his skin.

"Watch out," I shouted, just a little too late as I saw a flash of steel in his hand. Bingsley had grabbed his knife as Ali lunged with the brush. He had let himself take a slashing just to get Ali within an easy stabbing distance. The flash lasted a split second before the knife was stuck between Ali's ribs.

"How's that feel, shithead?" Bingsley yelled.

Ali took a few steps back and dropped his weapon, looking down at the knife sticking out of his chest. Blood seeped through his shirt until he put his hand up to his chest and applied some pressure, leaving the knife where it was. He was clearly in a lot of pain but he had the calm composure of a man that had been stabbed more than once and knew how to handle the situation.

David backed away and lowered his shiv.

Bingsley threw his hands into the air and said, "Don't go yet, the party still needs to go out with a BANG!" In perfect timing with the end of his sentence, he turned and smashed a fist down into the centre of the cake.

Frosting and chunks of red sponge splattered all over the counter. I eyed David and Ali, wondering what had just happened before hearing a beeping noise coming from the cake.

Beep Beep Beep beepbeepbeepbeepbeepbeeeeeeeeeeee—

"HIT THE FUCKING DECK!" I yelled.

Ali had already turned to run but David was rooted to the spot in fear. I launched myself across the room, tackling him in an attempt to get him as far away from the cake and as close to the floor as possible.

The last I remember was the sound of laughter, right before an ear-splitting explosion.

Uncle Jimmy's Hot Sauce

When I awoke I found myself in a hospital bed, hooked up to an IV drip. I guess it was only fair that I ended up in the infirmary at some point since I was the reason a fair few others had paid a visit. It wasn't just me in there, either. David and Ali were in right along with me, on the opposite side of the room. They'd probably be alright. Bingsley, on the other hand, hadn't been fortunate enough to make it to the infirmary. I heard they had to mop most of him from the floor and scrape the rest from the walls. It was safe to say our little mission had gone completely tits up. We had heard he was unpredictable and dangerous but come on, who could have predicted a bomb in a cake? I guess we underestimated him a little.

David let out a small groan, stirring in his sleep. Ali lay still and silent. The knife in his chest had been removed and the wound patched up. From the look of him, he was going to be in the infirmary for a short while. David wasn't looking too bad. Some light burns and a few cuts and bruises but nothing worth complaining about. We had both dealt with worse from Ali's training and never really spoke of it. Me, though? I didn't even know why I was in there. Sure, the blast may have knocked me unconscious but otherwise I felt fine. From the look of things, David had taken the majority of the damage. If I hadn't tackled him and flung him to the ground, he would have been sharing a bucket with what was left of Bill Bingsley, so he could thank me for the cuts and bruises.

The door to the infirmary creaked open and a man in a white coat strolled in holding a clipboard. He looked tired. Not just physically tired, but mentally, too. Tired of life. Tired of everything. He caught a glimpse of me, looked away then done a double take. "Ah, good, you're awake," he said.

I nodded and asked how long I had been asleep for. The doc said I had slept for about fourteen hours. Bingsley had detonated the cake at around nine on a Wednesday. I was awake by around midday Thursday. Not bad.

"Any idea when I can leave?" I asked.

The doc glanced at his clipboard and said, "Today, if you're feeling alright. You didn't sustain many injuries if I'm honest. A couple of bruised ribs and a mild concussion, that's about it."

I raised my left arm to flash the IV tubes. "Is this really necessary then?"

"It appears not. We thought we'd hook you up as a precaution though, in case you were asleep longer, like your friends here."

"How are they?" I asked, nodding towards David and Ali.

He turned to look at them then turned back. "They'll be alright. Mr Flowers could be out of here not long after he wakes. Mr Santos could be in a while. I assume he was stabbed before the explosion. The explosion itself didn't do him much harm but it did knock him unconscious. He was unfortunately found lying face down, which drove the knife further into his chest."

I scrunched my face at the thought of the pain. "Doesn't sound too good."

"Well, no, it's best to avoid falling on a knife in the chest, if possible," he said with a hint of sarcasm. "As well as a stab wound, he also has a punctured lung, so it's not good at all." He paused, took a glance at the clipboard then gave me a judgmental look. "Although, he is in better condition than some people that have come through here recently. The people lucky enough to end up in here instead of the morgue, that is."

I shifted my weight awkwardly, avoiding eye contact.

He stuck with the judging look for a while before realising I didn't intend on taking the bait. "Anyway, the nurse will be around after her lunch break to unhook you from the drip and see if you're good to go."

"Can't you do it for me?"

He stood for a second before spinning on his heel and heading for the door. When he got there he opened it and turned to say, "I would, Mr Nightingale, but I have an important matter to take care of. An inmate recently had his penis bitten off, you see. He hasn't taken the best care of himself and what's left of his penis is severely infected. I now have the job of draining the pus out of it." He left with a forced smile, letting the door swing closed behind him.

That explained why he looked sick of his life.

I waited for about half an hour before an old, and equally tired looking nurse came and unhooked me from the drip and checked how I was feeling. All seemed fine so I was discharged and escorted to my cell by Carl, the dinner guard. He had been instructed to make sure I got there safe and sound, then to lock the cell door for a while to make sure nobody could take advantage of the opportunity to shiv someone that had recently survived a bomb attack.

"Gotta stay in here today, bud," Carl said when we got to my cell. "Dinner is at the normal time but it'll be brought here. Warden's orders, he wants you looked after."

I sat down on the bed, rubbing my bruised ribs. "That's alright; I could do with a day of doing jack shit."

"Good. You gonna need anything?"

"Nah I'm good. Got a few books here I've been meaning to read. I hear reading's good for the vocabulary and I need to work on my ways of insulting people," I said.

He shook his head. "Your mouth is gonna get your ass kicked one of these days, kid."

"It's happened before and it'll happen again. Shit happens. Getting your ass kicked isn't the most painful thing that can happen." I trailed off, thinking of how the pain of losing Suzie just wouldn't ease off. Not even for a second. A lifetime of receiving an ass kicking would be less painful than what I'd been through. What I'd seen. What I had to live with.

Carl nodded, looking at the floor. He clearly knew what I was thinking about. He didn't pry, either. He was decent like that. Instead, he handed me a brown paper bag he had been carrying before telling me he'd see me later and locking the door. The bag contained lunch.

Good ol' Carl.

Lunch was a chicken and bacon sandwich with red onions and barbeque sauce, my favourite sandwich. I pulled a book from the small shelf on the wall and sat to eat while reading. The book was called Naked Lunch.

125

The title seemed fitting for lunchtime reading but the book itself was a little bizarre, even for my standards.

I was a fair few pages through it when my cell door swung open sometime later, right on cue for dinner time. My stomach tightened in what I assumed was hunger. My lunch was nice but just didn't cut it.

Fontaine stood in the doorway, giving me the kind of disapproving and disgusted look people tend to give a dog that's just been caught eating another dog's freshly curled steamer.

"Where's Carl?" I asked, furrowing my brows at him.

"Had to go home sick. Said he had a real bad migraine."

After noticing the absence of Carl, I soon noticed the absence of food. "And dinner?"

"Your little club room, the usual place," Fontaine replied, totally deadpan.

"Carl said it'd be brought here today."

"Well Carl's gone and plans have changed. Now move."

I followed the command and pushed myself up from the bed. I put the book down on my pillow, pages spread and facing down to hold my place, something Suzie would have told me off for doing. She always liked to keep books in good condition and liked it when I did the same. I had eventually developed the habit of being careful with books but the copy I was reading was already well read and worn out. One more bend to the spine wouldn't do any harm.

Fontaine stepped forward and flashed a set of cuffs. "Arms out," he said.

"Really?" I sighed. "And here I thought you trusted me."

"Warden does. I don't. You're just another inmate as far as I see it." He slapped the cuffs on and put a hand on my shoulder to steer me out of the cell. He kept his hand there for the entire walk, not saying a word.

Fontaine took out his nightstick as we approached the room and prodded me in the back. I threw him a look over my shoulder to tell him it wasn't necessary but he took no notice, he just stared on ahead and nodded at something. I turned back to see two guards I didn't recognise leave the room and nod back at Fonts. They both took their places at either side of the door, nightsticks in hand.

Something didn't feel right. The strange feeling hadn't left my stomach, the feeling I had assumed was hunger, and that was never a good sign. I realised I wasn't hungry at all.

One guard stepped forward and pushed the door open. Fontaine gave me another prod to push me through the door and into the room. I stepped through the threshold and the knot in my stomach dropped right to my ass. Fontaine locked the door behind us.

It looked like shit was about to hit the fan.

[Track 15]

Instead of walking in and seeing the usual table set up with a fine selection of food and drink, I was met with the sight of other inmates sitting around it. I recognised a few faces, too. Big G, the Nazi from the bus was there, alongside Javier Rivera and Harry Garcia. Big G had two other tatted-up Nazi's at each side of his seat,

127

Rivera had two of his gang and Garcia had the goon I beat with the glass cock, plus one other. I didn't recognise the guy at the head of the table, but since all the other big bosses were there—aside from Bingsley, who had probably been poured down the shitter—I assumed the fucker at the end of the table was none other than Uncle Jimmy himself, the worst of the worst.

My suspicions were confirmed when the guy at the head of the table stood up to thank Fontaine for bringing me and Fontaine responded with, "My pleasure, Uncle Jimmy."

Uncle Jimmy was not what I was expecting. I thought he'd be a brick shithouse, covered in scars and tattoos, but here he was, a weedy little bastard with glasses that magnified his eyes and the worst hair-do I'd ever seen, except for Garcia's greasy comb-over. Uncle Jimmy had a bowl cut hair-do that made his head look like a mushroom, and it was sticking out in tufts at the top.

He didn't look threatening in the slightest. In fact, he looked totally ridiculous. The two goons flanking him looked more threatening and I could have probably taken them both in a fight. Both at the same time, even, considering they were both half the size of Ali and nowhere near as mean looking.

I was about to open my mouth to speak when I noticed blood splattered on the wall to my right. I followed the splatter down the wall until my eyes found the body of a guard lying in the corner of the room.

The guard lay on the floor in a pool of blood, his face smashed almost beyond recognition and his head split open from between the eyes. A mush of what I assumed was his brains circled his shattered head in a sickening halo. I almost retched at the sight. Seeing Carl lying there was the last thing I expected. Fontaine said he had gone home with a migraine. It seemed he most certainly did have a splitting headache after all.

I had witnessed some shit. I'd watched the girl I loved get murdered by monsters, a man's penis being bitten off and vomited out, people being beaten to a pulp and a man exploding in a shower of blood, but this was the first time I had seen a smashed head with brains leaking out, and it was straight up disgusting.

I turned back towards Uncle Jimmy—who had sat back down—and noticed a blood soaked hammer on the table to his left. His hands were laid out on the table in front of him, stained red.

"Got to set an example, haven't we?" Uncle Jimmy said. His voice was high pitched and smooth. He spoke gently; in the manner you'd speak to a child you're trying to teach.

"You son of a bitch," I said. "He didn't deserve that. Fucking hell, man, he was a nice guy."

Uncle Jimmy held up a hand. "Watch your language, please."

"Go fuck yourself," I spat.

Jimmy nodded to the goon sitting to his right. The goon nodded back then got out of the chair and made his way around the table, over to me. I prepared to take a punch but it never came. Instead, the goon took me by the cuffs and led me to his seat. He pushed me down into it so I was right next to Uncle Jimmy, who had turned to face me, his eyes huge through the glasses.

"I understand you're upset," he said, putting a hand on my thigh and giving it a gentle squeeze, "I really do. But I'm upset, too. You've hurt my friends. Darn,

129

some have even passed on, God bless their souls. And that upsets me, Night. May I call you Night?"

I said nothing but gave him a sideways look of disgust.

"Okay, Night. Here's the thing. I don't take too kindly to what you've done to my business associates. I like to run a smooth operation, and you're damaging that. You're damaging our reputation and—"

Big G cut in. "And you killed Billy, little cracker." He had a look of severe disappointment on his face.

"Actually, he killed himself with an exploding cake," I said.

Jimmy squeezed my thigh a little harder and said, "Please, Gregory, Night, let me finish."

Big G, or Gregory, glanced at Jimmy then and lowered his gaze in submission.

"As I was saying, I can't have you running around for Warden Spencer, harming my friends and my reputation. I hope you understand."

I was about to speak when the goon that gave me his chair put an arm around my neck. "What the fuck are you doing?" I grunted, trying to pull the arm away from my throat with my cuffed hands.

Jimmy put his free hand out and was handed a hypodermic needle filled with a luminous orange liquid. "You see this, Night?" he said, holding up the needle. "Of course you do. This is a concoction of my own design, an injectable enhancement for my fighters. Just one quarter of a syringe is enough to give one man the strength of ten. Just one quarter is enough to turn even the most timid gentleman into an absolute killing machine, filled with rage, and near unstoppable. This is why my fights are so popular, and why my fighters always win. It enhances the brain and body entirely. This is our little secret though. He paused for a second, holding up the drug, admiring it. "Yes, one quarter of a syringe is all it takes, and only one dose per week. No more than that. Any more and it'd have dire effects, you see. Any more than a quarter would cause unbearable pain before putting the user in a coma they'd likely never wake up from. Half a syringe would kill the person, easily."

I knew what was coming next, and I tried to tell Jimmy to go fuck himself, but his goon had practically closed my windpipe.

It looked like the end of the line and there was jack shit I could do about it.

At least I might get to see Suzie again, I thought.

Jimmy removed his hand from my thigh and took a hold of my chin, lifting my head. His grip was surprisingly strong. He jabbed the needle into my neck, started injecting the orange liquid and continued, "We call it Uncle Jimmy's Hot Sauce. I hope you understand, Night. We can't take any chances, so I'm giving you the full syringe. In about ten seconds, Mr Nightingale, you will be dead."

I looked him straight in his magnified eyes as he pulled the needle from my neck. Almost instantly, my hearing started to fade and my vision grew cloudy. My body filled with an intense, burning rage. It lasted about one second before being replaced by horrendous pain. Pain like I'd never imagined. It felt like my veins had been filled with gasoline and ignited. It burnt through every nerve, every cell. My heart thundered in my chest, hammering against my ribs until the hammering stopped and the pain fell away to nothing.

Uncle Jimmy was right. It took my body seven seconds to go through all the symptoms of his drug.

By the eighth second, my heart had stopped.

By the ninth, there was nothing.

By the tenth...

The Long Night

[Track 16]

I swam in infinite darkness. All of my senses had disappeared. There was nothing, nothing but the endless darkness of death. No pain, no pleasure, nothing.

It's a funny thing to feel your own heart stop, to feel the life slowly seep from your body, being pulled into oblivion. On the plus side, being dead really does put your life into perspective. When you're alive, everything has a time and a place; everything has a cause, an effect, a reaction, a consequence, a reason. Everything has meaning. And at the same time, none of it does. You get to reflect on how small and insignificant life is when you're dead, and then, you don't. All you have is time, but you don't have any time where there is none.

At least that's what happened to me when I died. I could have been dead an eternity, but in reality it was more like thirty seconds. Death is different for everyone. In the space of thirty seconds I had spent a hundred lifetimes floating in an endless void. After the hundredth lifetime, I saw the light. But the light wasn't Heaven; it was a doctor shining a penlight into my eyes.

A man spoke, but sounded like he was underwater. He said, "Yes, he's waking up."

It took a while but my hearing and vision finally came back to life, just as I was apparently doing.

133

"Can you hear me Isaac?" the voice asked.

"Yeah," I mumbled, struggling to get a handle on my vocal chords.

"How's your vison? Can you see clearly?"

"Sort of. Bit bluuury." I could see enough to notice he was perched on the right hand side of my bed.

"That should clear up in a second. Take your time, Isaac," he said.

I damn well intended to. My head felt like I had been smashed up by a jackhammer. It wasn't just my head, either. Everything felt fragile, like I was made of glass.

It took a moment but my hearing cleared up and my eyes adjusted to the light. It was then that I realised I wasn't in the prison infirmary. Everything was different; the beds, the room, the doctor, all of it. This doctor had a kind look about him. Not the kind of look a doctor would give a patient responsible for kicking off dicks and cracking people's jaws.

"Where am I?" I asked.

"Blackwater General Hospital," the doc replied.

I took a look around and saw that I was indeed in the hospital. There was a door facing the foot of my bed, a wall with a large window to my left and a curtain to my right, no doubt there to give another patient some privacy.

"What? Why?"

The doc gave me a reassuring look and put a hand on my shoulder, "You took quite a knock to the head. Don't worry about it. Confusion is common but you'll be alright."

Confusion was an understatement. "Knock to the head? What? I—"

134

"You've been unconscious for a couple of days, Isaac. You stopped breathing not long after being hit. Technically, you died for a short while." He paused to see if he was getting anywhere, but could probably tell he wasn't. "How about I let a friendlier face explain the details? She's been here the whole time. As luck would have it, she's left the room this one time to get some food and you wake up while she's gone." He stood up from the bed and made his way over to the door. "I'll head over to the cafeteria and let her know you're awake. I'm sure she'll be right over. I'll give you a bit of time to adjust, then I'll come back to explain everything properly and see how you're doing."

"Wait," I called before he left, "who's been here?"

The doc paused to look back. He gave me a smile before saying, "Suzie, of course."

Sweet Dreams

My head swam with a thousand questions. How was I still alive? How was Suzie still alive? Was prison just a dream? My mind had to be messing with me. Everything seemed so real. Had a couple of months really just been a couple of days? That's the thing. When you're totally out of it in a hospital bed, time doesn't count for shit. You could experience a minute that lasts for days, or go through years in a matter of minutes.

     I had been lost in my thoughts; there was a window on the left of the room and I had been staring out of it, even though I couldn't really see anything but the sky. I didn't believe Suzie would walk into the room until I heard the door swing open and I turned to see her standing in the doorway with a massive grin across her face.

[Track 17]

     She was really there. Denim jeans, black Rolling Stones t-shirt, scruffy converse and painted fingernails. The girl I fell in love with. The pretty blue dress she wore on the night of the carnival was probably safe in her wardrobe, not torn up, covered in blood and in some evidence locker.

     Her eyes looked wet and she was breathing heavy. She had a half-eaten sandwich in one hand. She must have hauled ass to the room the instant the doc told her I was awake.

"Jesus Christ," she said, still standing in the doorway.

"Nope, Isaac Nightingale," I replied.

She came over to the side of the bed and took my hand, smiling down at me. "Still a sarcastic shit, I see."

"Always," I said.

I could tell she was struggling to hold back tears. In truth, so was I. The sight of her was making me tear up and it was hard to keep from crying. I had so many questions but at that moment, none of them seemed to matter. Suzie was there, holding my hand, and that was all that mattered.

We spent a while just looking at each other, having a sort of Mexican standoff of emotions. Suzie broke first. A tear had escaped the corner of her eye and ran down her check. She rubbed her eyes with her free hand as she made a noise that was a mixture of crying and laughing. I pushed myself up from the bed and pulled her into a hug. My bones felt brittle and my head felt like a bullet had gone through it but I could at least manage a cuddle.

Everything was as it always was. Her hair felt soft against my face with that old familiar smell. Nothing had changed.

"What the hell happened?" I asked.

"I thought I wasn't going to get you back," Suzie murmured. "I almost lost you. I didn't think I'd ever get you back."

"What about the two guys from the trail?"

"Nobody's seen them. When the big one hit you, you fell and hit your head real hard. They panicked and

137

ran. They thought they'd killed you. I thought they'd killed you. They pretty much did, you weren't even breathing for a while."

I hugged her tighter, breathing through her hair. "I thought I'd lost you too."

"Huh?"

"Just a dream I guess."

"You've had plenty time to dream, don't you think?"

"Too much time. It felt like I was out for months."

"Better than years though, right?"

"That's true."

I loosened my grip and pulled back to get a look at her. She wiped the tears from her face and smiled.

"I missed you," I said, admiring everything about her face, right down to the freckles that ran under her eyes and over the bridge of her nose.

"Hey, at least you didn't have to watch me die," she said.

How wrong she was. I had watched her die, took the blame and faced the consequences. I decided not to tell her that though. It seemed to have all been a dream.

Best to let it fade away.

I smiled and held her face in my hands. "I don't know if I could live through that," I said. And it was true.

We sat and talked for a while. I asked about what the doctors had said, how long I'd be in hospital and if my mother had been to see me. Suzie told me I'd have to be in hospital a little while on the count of having a pretty bad head injury and that both my mom and Suzie's parents had rushed to hospital on the night I was injured. She said mom would be over to visit again soon.

The doctor would be giving her a call to say I'd woken up.

"Doctor Flowers is really nice. He's been taking good care of you," Suzie said.

"The doc's name is Flowers?" I asked.

Suzie nodded. "David Flowers."

Safe to say I was confused.

A familiar sounding voice from behind the curtain mumbled, "A damn good doctor, too."

I gave Suzie a questioning look. She looked towards the curtain then back to me and gave me a wink.

"Mr Santos," she said to the curtain, "I hope we didn't wake you."

Suzie stood and drew back the curtain as the voice replied, "Please, Ali, not Mr Santos. It makes me sound old."

The curtain fell back to reveal a middle aged Hispanic man lying in the bed. He set eyes on me and gave me a warm smile.

"This is Mr... erm... Ali," Suzie said.

He put a hand to his chest and said, "Alejandro Santos, my friend. It's good to see you're awake."

The voice belonged to the Ali I knew but the man looked completely different. My version of Ali was younger. He was beefed up and looked pretty intimidating. This Ali was older, smaller and gentle looking. It turned out he had been in the hospital for a while, a victim of a serious stabbing.

Suzie told me that Ali had been keeping an eye on me while she slept in a chair by the side of my bed. They had gotten to know each other and Suzie had told him all about me. He said they'd spoke so much he

139

considered me a friend even though I hadn't said so much as a word to him.

Ali joined our conversation for a while. All through the conversation, I was feeling odd. Happy, but almost too happy. Verging on euphoric. My head was fuzzy, too. Things didn't quite seem real. I could see certain things clearly but other things seemed distorted and unclear. Our conversation was difficult to focus on too, which was odd because I always loved talking with Suzie. The sound of her voice was soothing, making our conversations pleasant. But I just couldn't focus on it. A simple conversation was confusing me and I didn't know why. On top of that, having two different versions of both Ali and David had screwed my mind.

Suzie was in the middle of saying something when I cut in, "I'm feeling a bit funny."

"Oh?" she said.

"I'm not feeling very..."

She said something that I didn't quite hear. It sounded like, "You've got work to do."

"Huh?" I mumbled. My ears felt as though they were filled with water again.

A jolt of pain shot through my body. I hadn't noticed it for a while but I could feel my heart beating. It was suddenly pounding in my chest.

"Night?" I heard Suzie saying. "Night, come back." Her voice was different.

"Suzie..." I heard myself mumble, as if it was only in my head.

My vison faded. It was hard to focus on Suzie's face. I was losing her again. Or she was losing me. I heard her calling my name as I fell back into the darkness. The feeling of her hand resting in mine was gone. Oblivion had claimed me, again.

* * *

Pain burned through my entire body as a blinding light flashed through the darkness and I pulled air into my lungs. The darkness receded seconds after it had taken over. I looked around the room and down at the hospital bed. I recognised this one, though. I was strapped down in the room I knew as Blackwater Prison infirmary.

I tried to shout but I had no voice. I felt pain in my throat. I felt pain everywhere. The pain of reality. I lay in the bed, tugging at the straps and trying to scream. It was useless. I was in far too much pain to do anything. I felt like I was tugging at the straps but in truth I was struggling to lift my own arms.

I struggled for a while before the door opened and in walked a face I recognised as the doc from the exploding cake incident. I recognised him, but he was visibly older. He looked even more tired than I remembered and his hair was peppered with grey.

He made his way over to my bed and stood, looking down at me.

"Don't struggle Mr Nightingale. You've been in a coma for a very long time."

He picked up a glass of water with a straw from a table at the side of the bed and held the straw to my mouth. I moved to get it and took a few long draws before gasping and dropping my head back down to the pillow. "Thanks," I said. The water brought back some strength.

"You're welcome."

"I've been in a coma?"

"You have indeed. And you've had quite a miraculous revival. Actually, you've had a few of them."

I took a breath and tried to process the information, scared to ask what I knew I had to. I plucked up the nuts and asked, "How long?"

"The coma?" the doc replied, looking slightly uneasy.

"How long?" I repeated.

The doc inhaled, still looking down at me. He seemed to be holding his breath while pondering the answer.

"How. Long."

He finally exhaled. "Eight years."

Feelin' Saucy

When I came out of the coma it was Tuesday the 18th of March, 1980. I had been asleep for eight years. Eight goddamn years. Oversleeping for a few hours is bad enough, missing almost a decade of your life is something else entirely. I didn't know what to believe any more. I had woken up in a hospital bed in a world where Suzie was alive, and then I was back in the prison infirmary, in the world where Suzie is still dead. It was a bit of a kick in the nuts, to say the least.

I lay in bed listening to the doc prattle on about the coma and how I had died only for my heart to restart itself, multiple times. As he explained it, I had been given such a massive dose of Uncle Jimmy's Hot Sauce that—after killing me—it had kept on bringing me back. His best guess was that it was a freak reaction, like winning the overdose lottery. My heart had stopped multiple times but the sauce just kept on giving me a kick-start.

Thanks to the sauce, my body hadn't behaved as any other long term coma patient's usually would. My muscles hadn't atrophied as they should have. In fact, they kept as they were, as if I had stuck to my workout routine while in the coma (and judging from the straps on the bed, I might have been trying to). The only changes my body had gone through were the ones that every guy's body goes through. I had gone to sleep at nineteen as a baby faced smooth-chin and awoken from my slumber at twenty-seven as a bearded god. At least there were some positives in the whole shit situation. It was as if I had awoken from a nice nap, albeit with a slight hangover. For someone nearing thirty I still felt like I was about to turn twenty. I didn't feel any older at all aside from having the ability to grow a proper beard and maybe an extra inch or two added to my... shoulder circumference.

When the doc finished babbling on about how it was a miracle I was out of the coma, and that I was alive at all, he unfastened the straps around my wrists and ankles, then gave me a good checking over. To his total amazement, I swung my legs over the side of the bed and stood to stretch out and take a few steps. I felt weak, but my strength returned with each step.

"Astounding," he said, staring open-mouthed.

It was then that a nurse I hadn't seen before came into the infirmary. I caught her eye and she came over the doc's side to marvel at me. She was a short blonde lady with her hair tied back in a high ponytail. She was real easy on the eyes too.

I finished stretching and testing my legs, then turned and walked back to pick up the glass of water from the night stand. I sat down on the bed with the glass in my hand when I caught the nurse blushing. It took me a moment to realise I was wearing one of those open-backed hospital gowns and I'd just gave her a good eyeful of my ass. She seemed to have enjoyed the view.

The doc cleared his throat and said, "From the look of it, you're perfectly fine. I'd like to keep you here a while and run some tests, though."

"Can we make it quick? Seems I've got almost a decade to catch up on and I've been on my ass for too long. I'd kill for a cheeseburger."

A digital clock on the bedside table told me it was 1pm. The doc agreed not to keep me any longer than necessary. The necessary amount of time turned out to be a few hours. He seemed pleased and let me go on the one condition that if I ever felt anything unusual I'd go straight to him. As he told it, the hot sauce was still in my system, and always would be, so he wasn't sure how I'd react to a life permanently enhanced by a super-human creating ultra-drug.

By 5pm I was freshly shaved—after spending ten minutes admiring my new beard—back in my prison clothes and being escorted to my cell by a guard I didn't recognise. He told me that I'd get dinner brought to my cell and that the warden would be informed I was awake. Spencer would most likely want to see me as soon as possible, he told me. Hearing that Spencer was still in charge was a relief. I hoped what the guard said all turned out to be true. The last guard to tell me I'd have dinner in my cell had his head smashed in by Uncle Jimmy's hammer right before I was technically murdered, which reminded me, if Uncle Jimmy was still kicking about I'd have to pay him a surprise visit.

The prison hadn't changed much over the space of eight years. A fresh lick of paint was about the only difference. Even my cell was exactly as I remembered, except David's bunk was bare and there was no sign of his things. In place of his books on the table there was a large stack of newspapers. I picked one off the top as the guard locked my cell door. It was dated March 14th 1980, only a few days old. I figured David might have been moved to a different cell but brought some newspapers over now and again, in case I woke up.

Eight years is a long time. For all I knew, David could have been a free man.

I had flicked through the headlines of a bunch of newspapers when one dated August 17th 1977 finally caught my eye.

THE KING IS DEAD

ELVIS PRESLEY, THE KING OF ROCK 'N' ROLL FOUND DEAD IN HIS HOME.

I sat staring at the headline, reading it multiple times. It's a weird thing, you know? When certain people die you just struggle to believe it for a while. It could be a partner, a person you've spent years loving, or it could be a favourite musician, someone you've listened to but never met. You find out they're dead and for however long your mind just doesn't accept it. The King had been dead for almost three years. It was another kick to the nuts but the pain of it was nothing compared to the sudden heart-breaking realisation that while The King had been dead for almost three years, Suzie had been dead for almost nine. If this was reality—and I wasn't really lying passed out on a hospital bed with Suzie holding my hand—she would be nothing but dust.

I had read the entire article about four times when I heard my cell door being unlocked. It swung open to reveal the new (possibly old) guard. He shuffled into the room with a food cart, true to his word. It was stacked with exactly what I needed; a cheeseburger, fries and a cold beer. I was about to thank him when I caught sight of Ali standing in the doorway. He was smiling so hard it looked like he had a coat hanger stuck in his mouth sideways. He had really aged, too. A considerable amount of his hair had greyed and he had developed crow's feet around his eyes. He made his way on by my new dinner guard. I barely had time to stand up before he pulled me into a bear hug that lifted me off my feet.

"Mi hermano," he said, still crushing me, "it's so good to see you're awake. I'm glad you're not dead."

I sucked in some air. "Squeeze any harder and I might be."

He roared with laughter before dropping me and slapping a hand on my shoulder. Being closer to him I could see he had collected a few scars on his face. A somewhat fresh looking one sat just under his left eye, running down to the middle of his cheek. He noticed I was looking at it and traced a finger along it.

"Last year. Some new puta tried to jab my eye out in the yard. He left Blackwater not long after, though."

"Did he leave in a body bag?"

The guard let out a snort and shook his head before pulling the cap off the beer and handing it to me. I thanked him and he gave a nod in return, leaving us with the cart and swinging the cell door shut behind him.

Ali didn't even need to say anything about the scar. I knew from the look on his face that whoever gave it to him was stone cold and six feet under.

I dropped down to sit on my bed. Ali sat down beside me with a sigh. He picked a brown paper bag off the cart and dropped it in my lap.

"What's this?" I asked before I thought to just open the bag and take a look. It turned out to be my

147

favourite sandwich, chicken and bacon with barbeque sauce. I decided to eat it before the rest of the meal. I was starved so I knew I'd easily put everything away.

"You better enjoy that," Ali said, "I've brought you that thing and sat by your bed with it every day for eight years hoping you'd wake up and eat it."

I spoke through a mouthful of food, holding the sandwich up in front of me, "So you've kept this in a bag for eight years?"

He shook his head. "Still the same smartass, huh?"

"I might die a few times but at least nothing can kill my sense of humour."

"So it seems. But no, I've had that sandwich made every day for eight years. And when you haven't woken up, I've ate the damn thing. That's almost three thousand times I've eaten that sandwich. Now that you're eating it, it best be good."

I crammed the last of it into my mouth and swallowed. "Delicious." I licked my fingers to get the last of the crumbs. "What about David? Couldn't he have just eaten it if you didn't want to?"

Ali let out a sigh and shook his head. "He's gone, my friend. I'm sorry. It's been a long time now."

My stomach sank. "Gone? As in dead?"

He nodded.

"What? How? What the hell happened?"

He hesitated for a moment. "It was an organised thing, just like when they got you. Got him alone and took him out. Only, they made it more permanent."

I got straight to what I needed to know. "It was Jimmy, wasn't it?"

Ali gave me a pleading look, "Night, my friend."

"I need to know," I said.

"It was Jimmy."

My body temperature was rising, right alongside my heart rate. It should have been grief that I was feeling, but there was only a building rage. Rage like I'd never known, topped off by the old sixth sense in my stomach telling me that something was about to go down.

"How? The Sauce?"

Ali shook his head. "They went old school, made sure he'd never get up from it," he said as he drew a finger across his throat.

[Track 18]

The anger was building to the point where I was struggling to control it. "Where's Jimmy? Where's that little shit bag now?"

Ali could see the rage building up and tried to calm me. The doc must have told him there might be some adverse side effects if I ever woke up, considering the hot sauce would never leave my body. "Night," he said, turning his body to fully face me, "just sit a while?"

I pushed the food cart out of the way and stood up, about ready to murder someone with my bare hands. "He's in the basement, isn't he?"

Ali stood up and put a hand on my chest. "Don't, my friend. Let's just sit and have some food. It's been so long since we talked."

I pushed past him, barely hearing his words. The cell door hadn't been locked so I marched straight through and left Ali standing in the cell to debate whether or not he should follow me. I broke out into a jog, and then a run, heading for the basement to shatter Uncle Jimmy's skull against a fucking wall.

I passed a few guards on my way to the basement but they didn't pay any notice. That was Blackwater Prison for you. Even the decent guards were indifferent most of the time. Seeing an inmate running through the corridors was probably a regular occurrence and nothing to worry about as long as they didn't have a weapon or bunch of other inmates chasing them.

It didn't take long to reach the basement steps. I went down them three at a time and pushed through the door at the bottom. The basement was large and mostly empty—bar a few boxes filled with spare clothing and cleaning products—the perfect space for Jimmy to run his fight club. There were two other doors in the room; one on the opposite side to me, facing the door to the steps, and one on the left hand side. I stood and listened for a moment. My senses were going apeshit. I could have heard a mouse fart from half a mile away. Voices floated through the door to the left. Jimmy was busy speaking to one of his henchmen, organising the next fight and discussing which of his champions would get the Hot Sauce and be unleashed upon a fellow inmate. One other person was in the room. He wasn't weighing in on the conversation but his breathing was heavy enough to hear over the talking.

The rage felt like a mixture of anger and lust; the lust to beat the life out of somebody. Within a couple of seconds I had crossed the basement and was at the door, ready to kick it open and see who was going to take a thrashing right alongside Uncle Jimmy. I took a deep breath then practically exhaled fire as I lifted my foot and smashed it into the door. It flew clean off its hinges and clattered to the floor. I threw myself straight through the threshold towards the first goon I set eyes on.

Jimmy had himself a nice little set-up. He sat behind a desk in the centre of the room with a few comfortable looking leather chairs. He even had a few bottles of whiskey on a shelf behind him, and a refrigerator in the right-hand corner with a glass panel on the front that revealed a stack of needles filled with Jimmy's special drug.

Goon number one was sitting in one of the chairs facing Jimmy's desk. Number two was leaning against the wall to the left with his arms crossed. Number two was the first I set eyes on so he was first up for a beating, and I wasted no time in getting to it. I marched towards him as he pushed himself from the wall and put a hand out to tell me to stop walking. The hand had just finished rising when I wrapped my fingers around his palm and squeezed. It felt like crumpling paper. The guy let out a wail as his palm crunched, popped and folded in on itself. I kept squeezing until his fingers looked like a few breadsticks sticking out of a thin glass.

Like a fucking idiot, he used his free hand to try and pry my fingers away. He must have forgotten I had another free hand too. I grabbed his other hand and gave him a matching set of bread hooks. When they were about as smashed as they were gonna get, I loosened my grip and let him go. He stumbled back, screaming and holding his hands in front of his face, like a mentally challenged T-Rex.

He'd certainly not be jacking off any time soon.

Satisfied with my work, I turned to face Jimmy and goon number one. Number two wasn't a worry as he'd already had his ass handed to him. Number one was next and he looked reluctant to fight back after seeing his buddy's hands getting crushed.

"Darn it, will you stop standing there and get him!" Jimmy yelled to the goon.

"But boss, he's fucking jacked," he replied.

"Do your job and protect me!"

I watched the exchange in disgust, amazed to think that Jimmy had murdered David, and tried to murder me. He was nothing more than a snivelling coward that relied on other people to make him look tough. If it wasn't for the hired help, he'd have been kicked to death years ago.

Number one took a step towards me and put up his fists. He got close and threw the first punch. I let it bounce off my chin as I drove my fist into his stomach as hard as I could. The hit on the chin barely fazed me. The goon, on the other hand, doubled over and hurled up blood. It seemed like he wasn't in the mood to carry on fighting so I restrained myself for a second before he put one hand up and waved it in surrender, shuffling off towards the door.

"You damn coward!" Jimmy shouted after him. "I'll have you disposed of for this."

I made my way over to the front of his desk and sat myself down in one of the chairs. He stared at me with his magnified eyes, struggling to find his words.

"You—" he started.

"Sssssshhhhhhush," I said, bringing a finger to my lips.

He shushed.

"I bet you've got real beady little eyes behind those glasses, don't you? Pass them here, let me see."

I held my hand out over the desk. Jimmy stared for a moment then reached up, pulled off his glasses and handed them over. As I thought, his eyes were tiny.

"Can you see anything at all without these?"

"Not really, no."

I threw the glasses over my shoulder and held up my middle finger. "How many fingers am I holding up?"

"Two?"

"Good guess. Now, guess why I'm here?"

He opened his mouth then closed it again. "I, uhm... oh Lord."

"How's your memory Jimmy? Can I call you Jimmy? Of course I can. I don't know if you'll remember but a long time ago—not all that long to me—you said I had upset you because I'd hurt your friends. Since then, you've hurt my friends. That upsets me. It really does. You had a good guy killed, a guy that was only trying to do the right thing. You hurt my friends, and my reputation. I can't have you running around doing whatever you please, Jimmy. I hope you understand." I stood and made my way around the desk to put a hand on Jimmy's shoulder. I gave it a light squeeze. Jimmy gasped in pain. I stopped squeezing and held my hand in front of his face. Traces of luminous orange liquid shone through my veins. "You see this? You made this. Thanks to the Hot Sauce, I've just crushed your buddy's hands like a pair of paper cups. I doubt he'll be up to any mischief any time soon, but with you, I can't take any risks. I hope you understand."

"I understand. What I did to you was nothing personal, purely good business."

I nodded. "I'd say this is just good business too, but it's actually for pleasure."

Unleashed

By the time Ali found me in the basement I had officially committed my first murder. Sure, people had already died in my presence and I may have indirectly caused a death or two but Uncle Jimmy's life was the first one I personally ended. And by personally, I mean personally. Uncle Jimmy had murdered one friend, had goons try to murder another and technically did murder me. He needed to die and I was happy to do the deed.

His goons had abandoned him and lived to tell the tale. Jimmy, on the other hand, ended up having the life choked out of him so hard his eyeballs had almost entirely left his skull. He had it coming.

Ali found me sitting behind Uncle Jimmy's desk, feet up and enjoying his whiskey. Jimmy was lying stone cold dead at the foot of the desk. I had raided the refrigerator filled with Hot Sauce and emptied and the contents of the needles by injecting them into Uncle Jimmy's corpse. He'd certainly not be coming back to life, but he made himself useful as a trash can for his own product.

Ali crept cautiously into the room, "Night? You okay, my friend?"

I probably looked a little odd, sitting sipping from a glass and using Jimmy's dead body as a footrest, but I felt fine. The rage had disappeared. "Never better," I replied.

"You're not hurt?"

"I'm not, but he might need a Band-Aid," I said, motioning towards Jimmy's body.

Ali took a look at Jimmy and made a face that gave off a look of disgust. It was more of a disgust at Jimmy, and less of what I'd done to him. "How about we get out of here? Get you cleaned up, you've got blood on you." he said, paying no more mind to the stiff on the floor.

I nodded and threw the remaining whiskey down my neck. In truth, I hadn't even noticed the flecks of blood splattering me until Ali mentioned it, even though I could smell the iron in the air.

At my request, Ali helped me carry all of the whiskey back to my cell. There were six bottles in total. We split them three each before taking a walk towards the showers. On the way, we crossed paths with the guard that brought me my dinner, which was still sitting uneaten in my cell. The guard—Benson—looked shocked at the sight of the blood on me but Ali explained that there had been an accident in the basement and the warden would need to be informed. He seemed to understand what this meant and nodded before walking away as if he hadn't seen a thing.

By the time I had cleansed myself of all the blood and sweat, Benson was back and waiting outside the shower rooms, sitting next to Ali, who had come along to make sure nobody tried to jump me while I was all soaped up. I greeted him as I walked out of the showers and into the dressing room, bare ass nude.

"Erm…" he hesitated, "your dinner will be back in your cell. It's being reheated now. When you're finished I need to take you to see Warden Spencer. He'd like to have a word with you, both of you, in fact. I'm guessing it's probably about that uhm... accident in the basement."

"It'll be good to see him, it feels like it's been a while," I paused to laugh at my own joke. "How is he?"

Ali answered. "Tired, last I heard. Sick of this place I'll bet."

"Yeah, well, at least he gets to go home at night," I replied.

Benson shifted uncomfortably, clearly trying to put his eyes on anything but me and my dong.

Ali nodded and let out a deep sigh before saying, "Must be nice."

"Anyway," I said, pulling on some fresh prison rags, "How about that dinner?"

* * *

Dinner went down nicely and soon enough I found myself standing outside the familiar wooden doors of Spencer's office with Ali to my right and Benson to my left. Benson gave the doors a timid knock and waited for the warden to call us in.

We entered a second later. Warden Spencer was standing reading through a file. He set it down on his desk as we entered and beamed a smile at the sight of me. Out of all the people I remembered from before the coma, Spencer had aged the most. In the space of eight years he had managed to collect a fair few wrinkles, lose a good amount of hair and gain more than a few pounds. But he still looked as sharp as ever in a suit.

"Did someone kiss Sleeping Beauty?"

Ali slapped me on the back as he laughed at Spencer's wisecrack.

"Did someone raid the doughnut store?"

Spencer raised his eyebrows and put both hands on his stomach. "Is it that noticeable?"

"Looks like you've put on a pound for each hair you've lost."

"Oh that's a low blow."

We stood eyeing each other for a few seconds before breaking out into smiles and shaking hands.

Spencer broke off a moment later and made a beeline straight for the whiskey. He was going for the good stuff too, the kind that'd cost a regular working man about half a year's wage. Spencer dismissed Benson while handing a glass to Ali, then poured two more glasses. He handed one over to me while taking a sip of his own. I took it and thanked him before taking a nice long sniff. It even had the smell of money about it.

Spencer made his way around his desk and dropped down into his chair with a tired groan. Ali and I followed suit, sliding into the chairs in front of the desk.

Spencer took a sip of whiskey then said, "Barely a few hours out of a coma and you dispose of Uncle Jimmy, as well as seriously injuring two of his buddies. One of them has a ruptured stomach. He needs surgery. The other isn't going to be able to use his hands ever again. Care to explain that?"

I gave a shrug, "Hot Sauce kicking in for the first time, I guess. I couldn't control myself. Not that I wanted to, he had it coming. Ali told me what he did to David and I just had to go strangle him."

Ali nodded, just listening.

Spencer raised his glass. "Well good riddance to him. And I am sorry about David. He was a good man, he didn't deserve what happened to him and that's on me. I should have anticipated retaliation and I should have taken more precautions to protect my own," he waved his glass in our direction.

Ali said, "We knew there'd be risks."

"Yes but I should have looked after you better. A decent man died and that's on my conscience. I should have seen it coming."

I raised an eyebrow and gave both Spencer and Ali a questioning look. It seemed like I was missing some information. Spencer picked up on it and filled in the missing bits.

"Ah, of course," he said, "after Jimmy got to you I upped the security, had the guards tail the three of you night and day. Well, two of you. You were in your coma so you weren't exactly moving around much. I had just fired Fontaine for being a traitorous bastard and I thought I knew where my guard's loyalties were. Turns out I was wrong. My ignorance led to your friend's death. If it wasn't for my ignorance, David would have been sitting here with us, if not a free man."

"So after all we did, we didn't change anything?"

"You did, but not entirely. Jimmy was more powerful than ever. Garcia and Rivera were reluctant to resume their work at first but Jimmy coaxed them back out of hiding, mainly by reminding them of his little show of 'murdering' you."

"They're still around?" The thought of Garcia and Rivera still being alive got my heart beating faster, pumping me up for some more murder.

"Nope. Garcia eventually died a very slow and unpleasant death all because he couldn't leave his goddamn stumpy pecker alone. It never healed. Infection eventually killed him." Spencer nodded to Ali,

"And Mr Santos here made sure Javier Rivera went on his merry way, never to return."

"So they're all dead?"

Spencer took a look at his watch. "As of about an hour and thirty minutes ago, the mission you started all those years ago, has been complete."

I sat back and took a big gulp of my whiskey, absorbing the good news. I had lost a good friend but at least a whole bunch of cocksuckers had gone down with him. It wasn't all in vain, at least.

"So what now?" I said to nobody in particular.

Spencer sat up straight and put his whiskey down on the desk. "Now I honour my end of the deal, which is the main reason I wanted you both here." He turned to face Ali and said, "Mr Santos, I promised I would get a bunch of years knocked off of your sentence. I promised you both. Now, I had to grease a few palms but the best I could do is barter eight years per inmate. That'd mean eight years knocked off for your stretch and eight off Night's, upon completion of the agreed jobs. However, I've took the eight years owed to Night and had them added to your deal, meaning you've now got sixteen years off your sentence."

Ali looked as if he had just been told he had suddenly grown an asshole in the middle of his forehead. "Que?" he said.

"Yeah, what?"

Spencer turned his head and gave me a wink. "Congratulations Santos, with continued good behaviour you could be a free man in just a few more years." Spencer kicked back in his chair, opened one of the drawers by his side of the desk and pulled out a newspaper, a sheet of paper and an expensive looking fountain pen. "Night, you on the other hand," he threw the newspaper over the desk. It landed neatly in my lap. "You can read that."

[Track 19]

I gave him a disapproving look, hoping he wasn't playing some sort of shitty joke. I set my glass down on Spencer's desk. The newspaper was fairly recent, dated only a few weeks back. I picked it up and unfolded it to read the headline.

BLACKWATER BUTCHERS IDENTIFIED!
MAN ACCUSED OF MURDER DECLARED INNOCENT
AFTER ALMOST A DECADE!
BUTCHERS STILL AT LARGE AFTER ESCAPE FROM
LOCAL JAIL!

Underneath the headline were three pictures of people I could recognise in a heartbeat; the first was Rapey, the second was Roids and the third was my own teenage face staring back at me.

I looked up at Spencer with my mouth hanging open, completely speechless. He was sitting looking real fucking pleased with himself.

"You're innocent, Mr Nightingale."

"I fucking know that," I said looking back to the headline.

Ali stretched over to take a look at the headline before letting out a roar of incomprehensible Spanish. He necked his entire glass of whiskey in one go then sprang out of his chair. He bumped the chair back a little and done some sort of dance with his hands in the air.

160

There was no time to react before he stopped his jig and seized me from my chair to lock me in a bear hug.

He yelled in my ear, "Yes! I knew it my brother; I knew you were too good for a place like this!" He had squeezed all the air out of me before he dropped me and put a hand on my shoulder. From the looks of it, he was trying to hold back tears as he stood there nodding at me and shaking me by the shoulder. He eventually let out another burst of joyful Spanish as he let go of my shoulder, reached down for my glass and necked all of my whiskey. "Warden, another whiskey for my brother here!"

I had never seen him in such high spirits. I had seen so much of Ali, right down to witnessing him flat out murder people, but seeing him so happy was a first. It reassured me that even though the world is full of assholes and bad people, some people are genuinely selfless and love to see good things happen to others. Ali seemed to have forgotten he had sixteen years off his own sentence. He was just genuinely overjoyed at the news that he had a friend who would be getting out of Blackwater Prison without leaving in a wooden box.

The Warden cheerfully supplied more whiskey. Rather than pouring it, he just sat the entire bottle of the good stuff down on his desk so we could help ourselves. And that's just what we did. Quite gladly, too.

Over the space of a few hours we worked our way through a fair few cigars and a couple of bottles of the quality drink we had taken from Jimmy's place. Benson brought them from my cell at Spencer's request. Benson even had a glass himself before Spencer told him he could have an early finish and away he went. He seemed a decent guy.

During our little party Spencer explained that about a year into my coma another woman had met a fate identical to Suzie's. About a year after that, it happened again. And again the year after. And the year after. Bodies of women just kept on appearing. Raped and murdered around the same time each year, always in the same area. People had assumed there was a copycat at first, someone imitating the murder I supposedly committed, but someone eventually caught a glimpse of Rapey and Roids in action and lived to tell the tale. The witness's story and description of the two dickheads matched what I'd told the law. Whoever witnessed them doing their thing had also left out the bit about them being vampires, which was a wise decision.

Rapey and Roids were eventually spotted in town and arrested. They both confessed to the murders, including Suzie', and were promptly slammed up in the jail cells at the local police station, only to escape the night of their arrest. According to Spencer they hadn't been seen since.

The news was followed up by Spencer sliding a piece of paper across the desk for me to sign, declaring that I understood I would be released from prison immediately and generously compensated for my bindingly-fucking-obvious wrongful imprisonment. The compensation was already processed with help from my mother, considering I was proven innocent while still in a coma. This meant I would walk out of Blackwater Prison with a nice sum of a million dollars already sitting in my bank account, ready and waiting.

* * *

"What you gonna do? When you're out?" Ali asked.

We were sitting in my cell, finishing off another bottle. It was just after midnight and Spencer had gone home an hour later than usual thanks to the three of us getting shitfaced in his office. He'd be back in the morning to ensure I was released as quick as a fart. In the meantime, Ali and I had made our way back to my cell. He had decided to be my cellmate for the night once he heard I would be set free the next morning, and we were making the most of our last night as fellow inmates.

I downed the last of my latest glass and shrugged, "I dunno. Go home, see my mom. Buy a car, maybe."

Ali polished off his glass and held up the bottle to ask if I wanted the last of the drink. I shook my head and said he could have it. I was already plenty sauced and the room was starting to spin. One more glass and I'd have been spin-dancing with the porcelain princess. For someone that hadn't drunk in eight years, I'd held it together quite well.

"Yeah," Ali slurred, "get a car and go see my hometown, too. You do it."

I clearly wasn't the only one that was feeling the drink. I lay on my side on the top bunk. Ali was sitting opposite me on the floor, his back against the wall. I listened to him talk about how I should visit his hometown of San Filipe someday, about how much he loved the place, and about how much he'd like to meet again when we were both free. He went on for a while

163

before eventually drifting off to sleep halfway through a sentence.

Not wanting to leave him to sleep against the wall, I swung my legs over the bunk and dropped to the floor. Ali was heavy but I pulled him to his feet easily enough. With an arm around his waist to support him, I took him over and lay him down on the bottom bunk to get some decent sleep, sure that he'd want to wake up in the morning to say a proper goodbye before I left.

Morning came at eleven with a wakeup call courtesy of Benson wheeling breakfast into the room. The smell alone could have dragged me from the pits of Hell. Benson had wheeled in a trolley with a couple of plates full of bacon, eggs, sausages and beans. I poured myself down from the bed and dropped down to sit at the foot of Ali's bunk. Ali awoke from his slumber with a groan.

"Dios mio, my head." He mumbled, rubbing his eyes.

"I feel you," I said.

We exchanged nods with Benson before he left the cell. I handed a plate over to Ali, along with one of the glasses of orange juice we'd been given. Breakfast went by in silence as we focused of getting some food in our stomachs to soak up any residual alcohol from our night of heavy drinking.

Benson returned soon after we had finished eating. He gestured for us to follow. We both made our way past the food trolley and out of the cell. Ali was the last out so he pulled the cell door shut then done a quick jog to catch up. Benson escorted us to Spencer's office and pushed the doors open without knocking.

"Thank you Benny," Spencer said. He had his eyes closed and didn't bother opening them when he spoke. He was leaning back in his chair with his feet on the desk, clearly feeling the effects of the previous night.

Benson gave a nod and left the room, pulling the doors shut behind him.

"Warden," I nodded, even though he still had his eyes shut.

"Feeling the drink, huh?" Ali asked.

Spencer dropped his feet from the desk and rubbed his temples. "I've got the mother of all headaches today. The price of drinking so much hooch I suppose." He took a sigh and opened his eyes. They were bloodshot and watery. "Anyway, not to dwell, it's your big day Mr Nightingale. It's time to go home."

I looked from him to Ali. "So what happens now?"

Spencer pulled a box from underneath his desk, sat it on top then ducked back down for another smaller one. "These here are your personal affects," he said, pointing to the smaller of the two boxes, "It has the clothes you were wearing when you came here, anything from your pockets and anything else you had on you at the time. Although," he pushed the bigger box towards me. "I imagine your old clothes will be too small so I took the liberty of buying you some new ones, and a few other knick-knacks. You know, as a goodbye gift."

A shot of excitement flashed through my heart. I was getting some clothes, some real outside clothes rather than prison rags. "Shit, really?" I said, smiling, "You didn't have to do that." I reached over and took the box.

165

"I know, I know, but call it a good service reward. I've got the feeling it'll be smooth sailing without Jimmy around. I have you and Ali to thank for that. And David too, God rest his soul."

I pulled the box open and took a peek at the contents. There was a full—mostly black—outfit inside; brand new boots, jeans, a coat, a t-shirt, even socks and undies. On top of everything sat a box of cigars, a zippo lighter, a leather wallet and a bottle of bourbon.

"Very nice," Ali commented, nodding at the contents of the box.

"And you can expect a similar gift when you see the back of this place," Spencer told Ali. "So, let's take a walk. We'll take this back to your cell, you can box up whatever you want to take with you and then we'll see you off."

"This is great," I said, admiring my gifts, "thank you."

"Thank you, Night, for what you've done to help me. After all the shit you've been through, it's about time something good happened for you."

"You got that right."

Spencer pushed my box of old stuff across the desk and made his way around to walk back to my cell with me. Ali picked the box up, shaking his head at Spencer to tell him to leave it, he'd carry it. Spencer shrugged one shoulder and let Ali take it.

When we got back to the cell, the food trolley was gone. I set my box down on the table at the far side of the room, next to the newspapers. Ali followed into the room and put the other box at the foot of the bottom bunk. Spencer stood in the doorway, leaning against the frame.

"I'm guessing that was you?" I said to Ali, pointing to the stack of newspapers.

"It was David, at the start. He wanted to keep the best paper from each week for you. I kept it going when he died. Apparently I missed the most important one." He turned to Spencer and gave him a nod.

"Looks like I'm not gonna get to read them. Coulda done with catching up on things, too."

"Don't worry about it, not much interesting has happened in the world since you went to sleep."

I took a look around the room, scanning for anything I actually cared to take. My eyes eventually fell on an old copy of Steinbeck's Of Mice and Men. I remembered David telling me how much he loved that book so I picked it from what books we had left and stuffed it into my box of treasures. "Don't mind me taking that book, right?"

"Nah," Ali waved a hand, "I'm not as big on books as you are."

"Sweet," I nodded. "You can keep my share of Jimmy's whiskey."

"You sure?"

"Yeah, figure you could do with it more than me."

Ali snorted a small chuckle. "That's true, my friend."

"Maybe when you get out we can have another drink together?"

"Of course. But you're buying," Ali said.

"It'd be pretty shitty if I didn't, what with the all those dollars I'll be swimming in when I get out of here."

Ali shook his head. "Yeah, yeah, anyway. I have something for you."

"Is it my birthday? What's with all the gifts?"

"Shut up, here," he handed me a piece of paper.

I unfolded it, confused as to why he'd be giving me some paper until I read what he'd written.

San Felipe. Antiguo Torcida. Three feet under my rock.

Ali could see I was confused. "It's a tree," he said.

"You want me to have a tree that's under a rock?"

"No you dingus, Antiguo Torcida is a tree near my hometown. Find it and you'll see a rock with my name on it. I buried something there a long time ago. It was going to be a gift for my brother, but he's gone and you're the closest thing to a brother I have now."

I felt genuinely touched. "You sure about this?"

"Brothers?" he said, putting a hand out.

I took his hand. "Brothers."

He pulled me into a hug and slapped me on the back. A good manly embrace. "Then what's buried there is my gift to you."

Spencer piped up. "If you ladies are done having a cuddle, Benson should be waiting to open the gate. He's driving you home."

I took a step back and had one last look around the cell, not that I'd actually spent much time in it, but still.

Ali and Spencer stood outside to give me a little privacy while I changed into my new clothes. Everything was black, aside from the t-shirt, which was white, and it all fit perfectly. I thought I looked pretty fine, too. The coat was made of black leather and it came down to my knees. It added a bit of roguish charm to the outfit. The pockets were nice and deep too, perfect in case I ever needed to conceal a fair few weapons.

I swung the cell door open and nodded my approval of the clothes. Spencer and Ali nodded right back, agreeing that the outfit suited me even though it was odd to see me in anything other than prison clothes. I gave my thanks for the gifts again and made my way back into the cell to pick up my boxes.

Ali took one again and followed me out of the cell. Spencer closed the cell door for us before telling us to follow him. We made our way to the prison gates and true to Spencer's word, Benson was there, sitting at the wheel of a car parked on the prison's side of the gate. Spencer walked up to the driver's side and took the keys to pop the trunk. Ali and I placed the boxes in the trunk and pulled it shut with a loud clack.

"Well, this is it son," Spencer said, thrusting his hand towards me, "you're a free man."

I slapped my hand into his and gave him a strong handshake. "Thanks for everything. I'll hopefully see you on the outside."

Spencer nodded and gave me a wink as I turned to Ali.

"And you," I said, "Don't have too much fun without me."

He grinned and gave my chest a backhanded slap, "You too, you lucky motherfucker. Don't forget about me."

"I'll see you in the future." I put a hand out. Ali shook it and held on.

"When we're older," he said, "until then. Take care, my friend."

"You too, man, you too."

He let go of my hand and took a step back to stand beside Spencer. I gave them both a smile and

169

turned to walk to the passenger's side door. I popped the handle and pulled the door open.

"Night," Ali said, "when you find the assholes that murdered your girl; you give them hell, brother."

I paused to take one last look at the people I considered to be my only friends.

"When I find them, Hell will be like paradise compared to what I'm going to do to them."

Welcome Home, Son

After a good half hour of thinking about what to do, I had Benson drive me to my parents' house, even though I was a little apprehensive about the thought of going back. To me it felt like it hadn't been all that long since I'd seen them, but to them it had been years, and I didn't think they'd recognise me, but they were my parents. I couldn't live with myself if I left them waiting for a knock on the door.

[Track 20]

It was about a forty-five minute drive from the prison to town. It had ticked over to two in the afternoon when Benson brought the car to a stop outside home. Way back before I was locked up, around this time of day my dad would either be out working or out mowing the lawn. From the lack of car in the driveway, I assumed he was working.

I caught sight of a curtain moving a little, no doubt my mom peeking to see why a car had pulled up outside. I sat for a moment and got my thoughts together before pushing the car door open and stepping out on to the sidewalk. Benson had already got out and opened the trunk. He told me he'd take care of my stuff while I got the door, so with a deep breath I took the plunge and made a slow walk up the path. I had gotten about halfway up when the door creaked open to reveal my mother standing at the threshold, holding her hand over her mouth. I guess she actually recognised the man that used to be her boy.

"Isaac?" I heard her ask from behind her hand.

"Mom," I said with a nod.

With the confirmation that the stranger in front of her was her son, she hurried through the door and rushed towards me with her arms outstretched. Her eyes sparkled as she pulled me into a long hug, the kind of hug that only mothers can give.

Benson had the decency to wait 'till we'd hugged it out before asking what he should do with my stuff. Mom led him into the house and told him to drop the boxes anywhere, and that's exactly what he did.

"Thanks for the lift," I said, walking him back to the car, "and I mean this in the best kind of way, but I hope I never have to see you again."

Benson gave a wink and said, "Stay out of trouble then, kid." We exchanged a firm handshake and said a quick goodbye before he stepped into the car. I watched as he drove off and waved so long to my last tie to Blackwater Prison.

Mom stood at the door and put a hand on my shoulder as I got close. She closed the door and followed me to take a seat on the nearest sofa. The house was pretty much as I remembered it. The only thing that had changed was the photos that used to hang above the fireplace. They were gone. Where there used to be a collection of family photos, there was just the one photo of Suzie and I. Before I could ask where the rest had gone, I turned to see Mom with tears streaking her cheeks.

"Hey, what's wrong?" I asked.

She wiped her eyes on the sleeve of her cardigan and took a moment to compose herself, "I just can't believe I've got you back. I always knew you didn't do it," she said, putting a hand on my cheek. "I told everyone. I did, I told them my boy loved Suzie May like nothing else. And now you're home. The warden called me when you came out of that coma and called yesterday and told me you were being let out today. I could barely believe it, any of it. Even when you were proven innocent I thought I wouldn't get you back. "

I could see her tearing up again so I kept my trap shut and just gave her another hug. She probably had more questions for me than I did for her but ten minutes after being reunited wasn't the time for questions, it was the time to hug one of the only people I had in the world outside of prison walls. We hugged the bad feelings away for a few minutes before mom offered me a cup of tea and something to eat, and I thought she would never ask. There's nothing quite like being fed by your parents, especially after being in a coma. I followed her into the kitchen and sat at the dining table while she made two cups of tea. I offered to help but she insisted I sit. Mom was always like that. She loved to do things for people. So I sat and watched as she made the tea and pulled a sandwich out of the fridge. She put it on a plate and set the plate down in front of me then shuffled to the counter to pick up the tea.

"I thought I'd make you your old favourite, for when you got here," she said. Chicken with barbeque sauce. Mothers always know. "It is still your favourite, right?"

"Of course," I said, offering her half.

She put up a hand and shook her head, "Oh no, I couldn't eat right now."

I tucked in to the sandwich and watched mom as she took a sip of tea. She had aged considerably. Her hair was greying and she'd lost a good bit of weight, which made her look a little gaunt. Something about her eyes had changed too. They seemed to have faded.

She fiddled with her cup and searched my face with her tired eyes, which always meant she wanted to say something but didn't quite know how to say it.

"Is everything okay?" I asked.

"It's just... something."

"Something?"

"Your father."

The sixth sense in my stomach kicked in, telling me the conversation wasn't going to be all sunshine and roses. "Dad? When's he getting home?"

She laid her hand over mine, "Look, there's no good time or way to say it and I know it might be a lot considering you've just got home, but he's not coming home... he passed away."

I was about to take a bite of my sandwich but sat there open mouthed instead. "Dad's dead?"

Mom nodded.

"How did he... when?"

"Just about three and a half years ago now."

"What happened?"

"Well... after, you know what happened," she squeezed my hand, "and they put you in prison, he fell ill. We thought it was from the stress at first but doctors eventually found cancer, all over his body. There was nothing they could do, just chemo, but even then it wouldn't cure him, just keep him here longer. He didn't want it, so he went out on his own terms."

"Own terms?"

"That's probably not the best way to put it. He didn't commit suicide; he just waited it out until the cancer got the better of him."

I nodded, "Figures. I woke up from the coma to find out one of my friends had died, and now I get home to find out Dad is gone."

Mom gave me a sympathetic smile. "You're taking the news quite well."

"I guess it needs time to sink in, a lot of stuff has happened in such a short space of time. It'll hit me all at once, sooner or later."

"Well you know I'll always listen."

"I know, you and Dad always did. So how have you been? You haven't been alone all this time have you? What about Suzie's parents, how did they deal with things?"

"I've been alright. I just worried about you mainly, especially when you fell into the coma. They wouldn't even let me visit to see you. It's been a tough eight years, not knowing how you were doing. Suzie's parents moved away almost immediately. I guess they just couldn't stay here anymore, too many bad memories. I did meet somebody though. About a year ago I took up dance classes to get myself out of the house. I got partnered with a man called Edward. He comes over a few times a week. He's a nice man."

I finished off the sandwich. "Well I'm glad you haven't been alone the whole time. How come he doesn't come over more often? Not thought of moving in together, or is it not like that?"

"We've spoke about it but his mother is housebound and sick, so he stays with her to look after her. I like it like this, though. It's nice to have the place to myself, I've gotten used to the quiet. It'll be nice to have you back though." She squeezed my hand again. "You are staying, aren't you? You'll stay for a while, at least?"

"I've just got back, of course I'm staying. At least until I find a place of my own, you know, considering I'm getting on in years now."

She let go of my hand and took a sip of her tea before saying, "Good, your room is how you left it, only a little tidier."

I smiled and shook my head; glad that she could still crack a joke after all she'd dealt with. Mom watched as I drained the tea from the cup, a little bit of light creeping back into her eyes. A good cup of tea always made things better but something was niggling at me. I had to ask something, get an answer to something I'd needed to know for a long time. I hesitated for a moment before firing away.

"You know after everything happened?"

She nodded, knowing what the question would be before I could ask.

"What, uh, where…"

"They buried her, under the old willow tree in East Street Cemetery. Your dad's in East Street too."

"Can we go see her? And Dad, too?"

"Of course, we can go today if you like?"

It was nice to have a bit of freedom, but the first day out of prison felt a little too soon to go visiting graves. The day after would do though.

"How about tomorrow, if you're free?"

"Tomorrow's good, I had nothing planned. We could take some flowers for Suzie?"

"Yeah, yeah she'd like that."

"We'll do that tomorrow then. Get yourself settled in today. It's so good to finally have you home."

I nodded in agreement, both looking forward to visiting Suzie's grave and dreading it at the same time. It would be the final nail in the coffin, so to speak; the completion of my loss. After eight long years I'd finally get to lay some flowers on my girlfriend's grave.

East Street Blues

After the best breakfast I'd had for longer than I could remember, I rode the bus into town with Mom sat next to me. It gave me a somewhat nostalgic feeling of when I was a kid and we'd get the bus into town so she could buy me a new record. The thought of seeing town almost a decade after I'd last visited gave me a tang of excitement, mainly out of interest to see if there was anything new. New stores, new things, you know? For all I knew there could have been some bitchin' new technology released while I was visiting the iron bar hotel.

After a ten minute ride we stepped off the bus and on to Barker Avenue in the centre of town. The first thing I noticed was the amount of cars. There was a hell of a lot more than I remembered, and most of them looked real different to what I was used to. A few storefronts were familiar but the majority of them had changed. One in particular caught my eye; a store on the right side of the street with a big neon sign reading 'Vidstar Video'.

I nodded in its direction. "What's that place?"

"That's the VHS store, it opened about a year back," Mom replied.

"What's a VHS?"

She paused and gave me a puzzled look before catching on that a lot of things would be new to me. "Oh, they're video tapes. Like music cassettes that play movies. You hook a video player up to the TV set and put the tape in just like a cassette player. I've thought about getting one but they're expensive. You can rent the movies from the store to watch at home. Want to go have a look?"

In truth, I very much did want to have a look. My brain had almost frazzled at the thought of such an amazing invention, but it wasn't the right time. I had come to town to get flowers and visit the graveyard, not go crazy for new technology, so I just said, "Nah, maybe another day."

The florist's was only a five minute walk from the bus stop, passing the video store, and in the same direction as the graveyard. Mom linked an arm around mine and led the way down the street. I took a quick glance into the window of Vidstar Video and saw a whole store filled with customers browsing through shelves loaded with video tapes. A visit was definitely on the cards at some point. I made a mental note to visit the bank at some point too, considering I was practically sitting on more money than I knew what to do with.

After a couple of minutes we neared the florist's. You could always smell the place before you could see it, especially if you were downwind of the place. The storefront came into view soon after, looking exactly the same as I remembered. I stepped forward and held the door open. Mom said, "Thanks sweetie," and walked in, taking a deep sniff of the floral air as she entered.

We spent a few minutes browsing the selection of flowers. Mom pointed out a few she thought Suzie would have liked. She knew Suzie well back when we were together, so she completely avoided roses. Suzie was never a fan of them. In the end we left with two bouquets. I picked out a bunch of lilies for Suzie and mom picked tulips for Dad, even though he never cared for flowers when he was alive.

East Street Cemetery wasn't much farther. We walked and arrived after about ten minutes. The cemetery gates faced Barker Avenue—the street we were on—with the East Street road running adjacent. The cemetery itself was a pretty large place for being in such a small town, and it was real nice as far as such places go. The entire place was circled by trees, and it had a fair amount of them dotted around inside. We took a slow walk down the main path through the centre. When we were around the middle, Mom led me off to the right with a slight tug on the arm she had linked. We walked a few meters and stopped by a bunch of graves that were clear of any trees. I ran my eyes over the headstones until I found the one with my dad's name written on it.

[Track 21]

"There he is," Mom said, taking her arm from around mine and stepping towards Dad's grave. The headstone was fairly simple. It didn't bear any meaningful inscriptions or heartfelt messages; just a name, age and a date, which was exactly what Dad would have wanted if he had any say on the matter. Any time we'd pass the cemetery he'd always say, "All this fancy shit for a dead person is a waste. When I'm gone, toss me in a cardboard box, drop me in the ground and mark my grave with a couple of sticks in the dirt. Done and dusted."

I kept quiet as Mom placed the flowers on his grave. The sight brought home the fact that he was gone, but as with everything else that had happened since I came out of the coma, it didn't hit me as hard as I expected. I knew in time it'd all hit me at once but for the time being, I just felt numb.

After standing for a minute, Mom gave me a little smile, said, "Come on then," and linked my arm again to direct me towards Suzie's grave.

We made our way to the left hand corner of the cemetery, towards a large willow tree. I'd seen the tree plenty of times during my life, and actually spoke to Suzie about how nice it would be to be buried under it someday, and she agreed. She'd always said that once we'd grown old and our time had come, we could be buried there together. I'd never thought she'd be there so soon, or without me beside her.

Suzie's headstone lay exactly where she would have wanted it to be, resting directly beneath the willow. The stone was an elegant white with black script-like engraving reading:

Suzie Lorelai May
Dearly beloved, deeply missed.
April 5th 1953 — July 4th 1972

The sight brought a dull ache to my chest. Another wound in my broken heart. I stepped forward and bent down to one knee, taking a moment before placing the flowers at the base of the headstone. As I lifted my hand from the bouquet it was brushed by something delicate. A satin moth fluttered around for a second and landed on my hand; an unexpected surprise considering it was the middle of the day. It sat for a few moments before taking flight again, fluttering over to the flowers. Mom placed a hand on my shoulder and gave me a reassuring smile as I stood and took a step back, rereading the inscription on the headstone. Dearly beloved, deeply missed. We stood in silence for a while and watched as the moth fluttered from the flowers then over to us, eventually going back to the flowers, and finally settling on top of the headstone. I was probably just being overly sentimental at the time but I felt the moth was trying to send a message, to tell me that Suzie was with me in some way, and I hoped she was. In my head the moth's movements said, "Suzie see's you. She sees the flowers. She's right here. She's with you." I hoped she could see that I still loved her. But most of all, wherever she was, I hoped she could see what I would do to her killers if I ever got my hands on them.

The weight of everything lay heavy. I needed to get home before it came crashing down.

* * *

I tried to keep myself busy over the next few weeks as I adjusted to almost a decade's worth of changes to life outside of prison. About a week after getting home, I got acquainted with Edward, my mom's new boyfriend. He was a nice guy and he made her smile. I was happy for them. I was also happy he had a car. During the days he came over and spent time with my mom, he'd let me use his car to go for a drive and just do whatever I needed to do, which mainly consisted of paying multiple visits to the cemetery.

I had only known Edward for a couple of days when he offered to let me use his car for the first time. I jumped on the chance to go for a drive, and I'm pretty sure he was happy about it considering it'd get him some alone time with my mom. So with my ass behind the wheel of a 72' Ford Pinto, I took a drive into town and made straight for the bank. The clerk behind the desk recognised me almost immediately as I walked up to the desk, most likely from being in the newspapers more than a few times over the years. Over the course of an hour I filled in a number of forms, signed a bunch of papers and had a few chats. By the end of it I walked away with a shiny new card which I took to the nearest cash machine.

After a few moments of pressing buttons the machine spat back my card and a slip of paper. I took a look at the paper and ran my eyes over the number one, followed by a whole bunch of zeros and a fifty. I was the proud owner of one million and fifty dollars. With a grin that almost touched my ears I walked straight back into the bank and withdrew a cool two thousand dollars right then and there. The clerk brought the dough and I quickly gathered it and filled the wallet I'd gotten as a parting gift from Spencer. It left a fair bulge in my back pocket and I had to take it out and set in on the Pinto's dashboard so I could sit comfortably while I drove around town to find a nice spot to leave the car while I done a bit of shopping.

I eventually pulled up and parked outside exactly where I wanted to be; Vidstar Video. I killed the engine and pushed the car door open, picking the fat wallet up from the dash as I stepped out. The weight of the wallet was impressive. It felt good to carry so much cash. I had more cash than I'd ever known in my hand and more than I knew what to do with in the bank, but I knew exactly what to do with the cash I had on me. I strode into the video store feeling like a king. The place was one big neon nightmare, but the owners had clearly put their hearts and souls into it.

After the longest time I'd ever spent browsing a store, I waltzed up to the counter and had the guy behind the cash register ring up a bunch of VHS tapes—which were damn expensive to actually buy at the time—and a fresh VCR.

I spent a few more hours splashing cash around town before I eventually set off for home with the trunk of the car filled with various treasures. Mom and Edward were on the sofa enjoying some wine when I nudged the front door open. Edward jumped up and gave me a hand when he saw all the bags I was carrying. We carried them up to my room and dumped them all on my bed. I thanked him and handed him his car keys once his hands were free.

"Any time, buddy," he said with a smile.

After unpacking my purchases—which were mostly new clothes since I'd grown out of my old ones—I piled the VHS tapes on top of the VCR and carried them downstairs to present to Mom. I cleared my throat to catch their attention as I set her gifts down on the coffee table and announced, "I'm sure someone said she wanted one of these, so ya'know..." I finished with a shrug.

The look of surprise on her face was priceless. She sprang up and pulled me into a hug. "Honey, you shouldn't have," she said, almost speechless, "that's a lot of money."

"Hey, I can afford things now that I have a lot of money. You looked after me when I was a kid, so I'll be damned if I can't look after you now."

Mom spent the next hour or so reading through the VCR manual as Ed and I tried to figure out how to get it hooked up and working the way men always do, by reading jack shit on how to do it and just giving it a shot. We got there in the end and tested out one of the tapes. It worked nicely so we all sat and had our first viewing of a movie on VHS. The movie of choice was Jaws, and it still remains one of my favourites.

Once the movie finished I was feeling a tad peckish so I made my way into the kitchen for something to eat. I had just about finished fixing myself a sandwich when I caught sight of Rapey and Roids' faces. A newspaper sat on the dining table showing their mugshots underneath the headline:

BLACKWATER BUTCHERS SIGHTED IN LOS ANGELES! MURDERERS STILL ON THE RUN AFTER ESCAPING LOCAL JAIL!

The hot sauce kicked in and immediately set my heart on fire. It was quickly doused as my mom walked into the room and found me staring at the paper, trembling with rage.

She put a hand on my arm to calm me. "I was going to show you when you got in but it slipped my mind when you brought the VCR down."

"Don't worry about it," I replied, "I'd have seen it sooner or later."

She gave me a pat on the shoulder and a peck on the cheek. "Let's just hope they're caught soon so they get what they deserve."

I gave a silent nod in reply as I finished reading the article before flipping to the back of the newspaper. They were certainly going to get what they deserved, and I was gonna serve it to them. I scanned through the classified ads with the sudden urge to find a nice fast car.

I felt like taking a road trip to Los Angeles.

Highway to Hell

After finding out Suzie's killers had been spotted in Los Angeles. I browsed the ads every day for a couple of weeks before I found the ideal car; a black 1969 Pontiac Firebird. I needed it and I needed it bad. Sure, I had the money to buy a brand new one right away but I figured I'd rather have my money in the hands of a fellow Blackwater resident that needed the cash than in the hands of some rich moneygrubbing CEO. That evening, I gave the owner a call and arranged to have a look at it as soon as possible, which happened to be the morning after.

The next morning, I said bye to Mom with a quick peck on the cheek and left to catch the bus and buy my first car. After about a twenty minute wait at the stop, it finally appeared. The wait itself would have made me glad I'd never have to use a bus again, but the ride was worse. This bus in particular seemed to be the one smelly bus that every service has, and that was just peachy. It had the faint smell of piss and vomit floating from the back. Needless to say, I sat at the front.

When the peasant wagon eventually pulled up at the stop on Barker Avenue about a half hour later I stepped off and sucked up some good odourless air, then got stepping towards the meeting point we had agreed upon, right outside Vidstar Video. There was no sign of the car when I got to the store but I was somewhat early. We agreed to meet at eleven. I had another ten minutes to waste so I decided to have a quick browse and see if I could find any decent movies. By the time my watch hit the hour, I was waltzing out of the shop with copies of Alien, Death Race 2000 and Psycho. I stepped out on to the sidewalk just in time to see the Firebird pull up. The driver killed the engine and got out, looking around to see if his buyer had arrived.

"Hey," I said, giving a wave as I walked up to the car.

He spotted me and walked over to the sidewalk, sticking out a hand. "Hi there, uhm... Isaac, yeah?"

"That's me," I said, shaking his hand.

"Nice to meet you Isaac, the name's Will," he flashed a smile and gestured to the car, "well, here she is."

And she was a beauty. Everything was immaculate; no rust, no scratches, nothing, just a perfect jet-black sheen on the outside, complete with a spotless black leather interior. I made my way around, inspecting every inch of it.

"Wanna take a closer look?"

"Sure," I said, eager to get in the driver's seat.

Will made his way over and held the door open for me. I stepped in and got myself comfortable behind the wheel. The entire car had a satisfying smell of clean leather.

Will shut the door on me, walked around to the passenger side then dropped down in the seat a few seconds later. He was a young looking guy, maybe in his mid-thirties. He was pretty eye-catching too, on the count of all the piercings in his ears. I assumed he worked at the local tattoo and body piercing studio but I didn't care enough to ask. The car was all I cared about.

188

"How does she run?" I asked as I took a hold of the steering wheel.

"Like a dream," Will replied, "I've had her a few years now and took good care of her. Best I could, anyway."

It all seemed too good to be true. I didn't understand why anyone would sell such a good car. "How come you're selling her?"

"I've just got a lot on my plate at the moment. She takes a bit of upkeep and I just don't have the time right now. I'd rather she went to someone that can look after her and enjoy it. Got all the papers sorted, so if you want her she's yours, right here right now."

I nodded, "How does cash sound?"

"He sounds great on this stereo," Will said before chuckling to himself.

I gave him a wide grin, appreciating both the wisecrack and the fact that he was a fan of ol' Johnny.

"Jokes aside though, cash sounds great."

"Excellent," I said, popping the door open. "I'll be back in a minute."

I actually took a few minutes, but I soon returned with a neat stack of dollar. I popped the door and dropped back down in the driver's seat, flashing the stack.

His eyes widened when he saw the cash. "Shit, you got that together quick. I thought you'd maybe want a few days to think it over and get the cash together."

"Got the dough ready to go, so why wait, ya'know?"

"I'm not complaining," he said.

"In that case, I'll take her. Right here, right now." I handed him the cash along with a receipt from the bank confirming the amount.

He thumbed through the cash, nodding to himself before pulling open the glove compartment and taking a bunch of papers and a pen out. "All the papers are here," he scribbled on the paper, "here's my name, address and phone number. Gimme a call if there's any problems, or anything you need to know." He finished scribbling and stuck the papers back into the glove box.

"Groovy, thanks. So, we square?"

"We're square," he said, handing over the keys.

"Thanks very much, I'll take good care of her." I patted the dash.

"Glad to hear it," he said as he pulled the handle to open the door. He paused before pushing it open. "One more thing though…"

"What's that?"

"Any chance I can get a ride home? I hate buses."

* * *

[Track 22]

After getting home and showing Mom the flashy set of wheels, we sat and had a good long heart to heart so I could break the news that I'd be leaving home. My reason—as far as she needed to know—was that I had promised a friend I would visit his home town and collect something for him, and that after being cooped up in prison I wanted to be out on the road for a while, stretch my wings and fly a little. I needed to find a place of my own, too. Mom seemed a little troubled by the decision at first but she knew how much I loved driving and eventually agreed that it would probably be the best thing for me to do. I wasn't her little boy anymore. I was a grown man and couldn't live at home all my life. Her one condition was that I stayed at home for one more week before flying the nest, and to make sure I called regularly while I was away, no matter how long I'd be away for. In her eyes I had been away for eight long years. She wanted a little more time with me. I happily agreed to all the terms and conditions.

On the day I left home I sat and had a big breakfast with Mom. Edward even came over to say goodbye, and to keep Mom company for the day so she didn't feel too sad about me leaving. We spoke a little more over one last cup of tea before I hit the road. I told her I would keep in touch and that I'd be home for Thanksgiving and Christmas at the very least. She seemed content with that. It meant I wouldn't be gone for too long.

After drawing out the tea for as long as we could, Ed gave me a hand with getting a few things into my car. I didn't need all that much so I packed light. One rucksack filled with clothes and another filled with essential travel items was all I needed. Ed stuck the rucksack filled with clothes into the trunk of the car as I came out with the other slung over my shoulder. Mom watched with a bittersweet expression as I threw it into the trunk alongside the rest of my stuff and pulled the trunk shut.

"You'll be back soon right? And you'll call at least twice a week?" she said, coming over to my side.

"Sure thing," I said, giving her a reassuring smile.

"And don't go looking for trouble."

"I never do, it always comes looking for me."

191

"You just keep safe and enjoy yourself."

"I will, don't worry," I said. "Oh, and you might wanna check your bank account next time you're in town."

She gave me a concerned look. "What's wrong with it?"

"Nothing, I just had a bit of money moved into it during the week. Thought I'd leave it to be a surprise but ya'know, best to tell you just in case."

When I said a bit of money, I actually meant half of all the money I was given as reparations for my imprisonment. Half a million for me and half a million for Mom. It only seemed fair considering she probably suffered more from it than I did.

"Isaac, that money is yours. You deserve it."

"I don't need all of it, and we both deserve it. Besides, I only gave you a couple of hundred dollars. You can buy yourself something nice," I joked.

"I'll miss you," she said, patting my arm, "even though you are a smartass. Seriously though, promise me you'll take care of yourself and don't go getting into fights like you used to."

"I promise," I said, and I meant it. I wouldn't be getting into fights like I used to. I damn well knew I'd be getting into fights, but with the hot sauce jacking up my entire body and mind I'd be fighting like never before, so it wasn't entirely a lie.

With one last handshake from Ed and a good long hug from Mom, I said my goodbyes. Mom handed me my car keys and watched as I popped the door and got behind the wheel. The engine roared to life with a turn of the key. I caught sight of Mom waving goodbye in the rear view mirror. I stuck an arm out of the window to wave back as I stomped the gas and tore down the road.

I waved goodbye to Mom, I waved goodbye to Ed, I waved goodbye to the sleepy little town of Blackwater. Most of all, I waved goodbye to my last chance at having a normal life.

Rest in Peace, Isaac Nightingale

I had been on the road for about sixteen hours with only a couple of stops here and there. Safe to say, I was pretty tired. Not long after setting off, I decided to make my way down to Mexico for a day or two before heading over to Los Angeles. I didn't know when I'd be bothered to take another long ass drive and I was curious to see what Ali had buried under the old tree in his hometown. With my destination set, I made my way down Minnesota, through South Dakota and Nebraska before finally stopping for the night in Colorado.

It was almost two in the morning when I pulled up to the Rest in Peace Motel in the middle of Fuck-Knows-Where, Colorado. The surrounding area was a thing of beauty, and the night sky took my breath away. Unfortunately, the motel was a run-down looking shit-hole, but it was somewhere to sleep. When you're tired and in the middle of nowhere you've got to choose from a shitty motel or the back seat of your car. Considering I had the cash, I felt like taking a bed. The place made my stomach churn but I was tired so I chose to ignore it.

[Track 23]

I killed the car's engine and stepped out into the cool night air, stretching out and looking around as I did so. Not another soul in sight, aside from the motel's night attendant. The reception was illuminated by a few dull, flickering lightbulbs. It looked like something straight out of a bad horror movie. The guy behind the desk could have easily been the next Norman Bates. He had a long skinny face with thin lips, beady eyes that looked completely black in the dingy light, and a pristinely combed hair-do with a middle parting. Even his skin looked wrong, as if it was moist.

After taking a few moments to admire the state of the place, I pushed through the door and made my way up to the reception. I was completely unsurprised to see that Norman Bates was reading a porno magazine. No shame at all, just flicking through it like a goddamn catalogue. His choice of reading material didn't bother me; I only hoped he had pants on.

He completely ignored me as I strolled up to the desk, fully engrossed in his titty mag. I made a show of clearing my throat before speaking up. "Got any rooms free?"

He sat and stared at the porno for a few more seconds before setting it down on top of the desk and looking at me. "We've got a few. Would you like one? Fifty bucks a night," he said through pursed lips, barely opening his mouth. "They're real nice beds. Soft. Very soft." He stopped abruptly, looked straight back down at his magazine and ran a long thin finger over one of the tit-pics.

"Erm, yeah I'll take one," I said, pulling a fifty from my wallet.

"Name?" he asked, grabbing a guest book from under his desk.

"What?"

"I need your name."

"Isaac Nightingale."

He scribbled my name, time of arrival and a room number in the book. "Cash?" he mumbled, damn well seeing I had the cash in my hand.

I held it out. "Yeah."

He stretched a skinny hand and plucked the bill away with his spindly fingers before slowly getting up and disappearing into the office behind the desk. Thankfully, he had pants on. A few seconds later he crept back to the desk with my room key. "Room number sixty two." I took the key and thanked him before turning for the door. As I pushed the door open I heard him say, "Rest in peace, Isaac Nightingale."

"Yeah, thanks," I said as I backed out and let the door swing shut, thoroughly creeped the fuck out.

I got back into my car and drove around the blocks of rooms until I found mine. A minute later, with my bags out of the trunk and slung over my shoulders, I was jimmying the key around in the lock on the door. It took a few tries but it eventually gave and clicked. The door creaked as I slowly pushed it open and took a peek inside. I had been expecting a total shit-hole but the room itself wasn't all that bad. There were a few spots of mould in the corners of the ceiling and everything had a musty smell to it, but other than that it was alright.

I threw my bags down on a well-used sofa then threw myself down on the bed. It wasn't as soft as Norman Bates had made it out to be, but it'd do. The only thing about the room that stood out was some strange gurgling noises coming from an air vent near the floor. I got up to inspect. The vent itself was loose so I lifted it off and took a look inside. There was nothing to see, but an odd smell wafted through with the noise and the vent had something sticky on it that I didn't even want to question. I put the cover back down and shuffled to the bathroom to wash my hands. Screw it, I thought. I'd slept through worse noise.

The drive had left me exhausted. I went out like a light. By two thirty I was sleeping soundly, stretched out on the bed wearing nothing but my shorts. It was a warm night so I was on top of the covers. For a while, everything was fine, but a couple of hours into my snooze I was awoken by the noise I had heard in the vent. It was louder than before. I opened my eyes to a dim view of the ceiling. A quick turn of the head and I saw the bedside clock flashing five in the morning. It wasn't until I tried to turn to lie on my side that I noticed I couldn't feel my legs. The only sensation I could feel was something cold, wet, and sticky. It was slowly spreading. Icy fingers crept up past my waist. I took a look down and almost shat myself. Instead of getting a look at my bare legs, I caught an eyeful of a pale humanoid looking creature with a long tongue, licking at my legs, spreading foul smelling saliva all over them.

"WHAT THE FUCK!" I roared, trying to pull myself up to get whatever it was off me. My legs didn't move at all, I could only push myself up with my arms.

It apparently hadn't realised I was awake until I yelled at it. The long tongue quickly flicked back into its mouth as it raised its head to look at me in fright. The thing was straight out of a nightmare. Its entire skeletal body was covered in smooth, pale, translucent skin with what looked like a thin coating of slime all over it. The hands and feet were webbed, and if all that wasn't fucking weird enough, it had gigantic jet-black eyes and two large tarantula-like fangs tucked into the hole that passed for a mouth.

"Get off me you alien looking motherfucker," I yelled. It had surprised me, to say the least. I already knew there was some weird shit in the world, and I expected to find it eventually, but I didn't expect to find it so quick. Just my luck, eh? I get out and about one damn time and I end up being served for dinner. I should have really payed attention to my gut feeling about the place.

The creature made a loud gurgling noise and slid off my legs as I pushed myself up and took a swing at its head. I couldn't get close enough to hit it but I must have scared it. After seeing me lash out, it slowly crawled off the bed and dragged itself towards the open air vent. I grabbed a handful of the bed sheets and used them to scrub the slime off my legs as I watched it crawl into the vent and slide out of view. The gurgling noise stopped as a splashing sound floated through.

After about a minute of scrubbing, I'd wiped the slime off my legs and I was starting to regain feeling. Once I was confident enough to walk, I swung my legs over the side of the bed and shuffled over to my bags to throw some clothes on. Within moments I was freshly clothed and nope-ing the fuck out of the room with all my stuff.

I had just abandoned the room, thrown everything into the passenger seat of the car and was about to pull the driver's side door closed to drive off when I heard a holler coming from a room a few doors down. I glanced at the steering wheel, then to the room, then back to the wheel before giving it a slap and darting out of the car to help whoever was yelling. As I closed in on the room I prepared to kick the door down, hoping someone actually needed help, rather than it just being a frisky couple getting noisy during the no pants dance.

I raised my foot and heard the gurgling noise, putting the doubts to rest. I slammed my heel into the door and sent it snapping open. I flicked the light on to reveal a guy lying on the bed screaming his balls off, with one of the creatures squatting over him and licking at his face, fangs out and all. By the looks of it, he had been asleep with his girl. She was lying closest to the door but all that was left of her was slimy pile of blood soaked skin shaped like a person with two large puncture holes in the chest. She looked like a deflated blow-up doll, literally nothing but skin; no eyes, no teeth. Nothing.

The creature let out a gurgle and tucked the fangs away as I rushed towards it. It made an attempt to get off the guy and slide onto the floor but it was far too slow. I was by the bed before it could get anywhere. With the hot sauce sending my body into super-human overdrive, I flung a fist straight at the creature, connecting with its head. The force of the punch sent the creature flying from the bed and crashing into a heap on the floor, one hundred percent dead from a hit that had caved in half of its skull.

I stood looking down at the creature for a second, surprised at how weak it was. I expected to knock it unconscious but I wasn't expecting it to have such a brittle skull. Even the fall to the floor looked like it had broken a few bones.

"Help!" The guy cried, snapping me back to my senses.

"Shit, are you okay?" I said as I pulled up some bedsheets and wiped a coating of slime off my knuckles.

"I can't feel anything! I can't move!"

I bundled some sheets together—taking care not to move his dead partner's remains—and used what sheets I could gather to wipe as much slime off his as I could. "One of them tried to get me," I said, "their saliva must numb you. You should get feeling back once it's off. That's what happened with me at least."

"Oh fuck, thank you. It was gonna kill me. Look what it did to Jenny! It fucking ate her!"

I took a look at Jenny lying there like a rubber diving suit and thanked myself for waking up on time and not becoming a human Happy Meal. I'd even saved someone else in the process, and killed my first monster.

I took another look at the creature on the floor and pulled together the pieces of information I'd been given. Whatever they were, they were so weak they could die from one punch. Their eyes were large and black, and they were horridly thin and slow. Norman Bates back at reception had to be in on this. I used my brilliant detective skills and deduced that he was probably one of the creatures wearing a previous victim's skin, ushering unsuspecting guests to their death at the slimy hands of his buddies.

When the guy on the bed was clear of slime I stepped out of the room to give him a moment to pull some pants on.

"You dressed?" I asked, leaning towards the doorway.

200

"Yeah," he said.

I took his word for it and walked back into the room to find him sitting on the bed, staring at Jenny with a stricken look across his face. He was most likely in shock, too much shock to cry or do anything other than follow a few simple orders. "Let's get you out of here," I said, offering a hand to pull him to his feet.

"What about Jenny?"

"We can't do anything to help her now. Come on, you've had a pretty shitty night. I'm taking you to a hospital."

"Pretty shitty night," he repeated before taking my hand.

I led him out of the room, over to my car and sat him down on the back seat, leaving the door open as I went to collect his things. I bagged everything that seemed important and gave the room a quick going over. Happy that I'd found all his—and Jenny's—stuff, I hauled it out of the room and tucked everything on to the back seat beside the dude. He didn't even move, just sat staring ahead at nothing in particular. I got into the car to drive around to reception to pay Norman a visit.

He was still sitting behind the desk when I pulled up, and he still ignored me as I walked up to the door. And yes, he was still staring at a porno mag, although if my suspicions were correct it was probably more like a menu to him. I didn't bother announcing my arrival this time. Instead, I just marched right up to the desk and snatched the magazine right out of his hands. He jumped with fright and looked up at me, his black eyes searching my face with fear.

"How many more people are in the rooms?" I asked.

"What?"

"I said how many? How many people are on the menu tonight?"

He began to scoot his chair in the direction of the office. "I don't know what you mean."

I pointed to the office, watching him slowly pull the door closed, blocking my view of the inside. "What's back there then?"

"There's nothing there."

"Fuck it, I'll see for myself," I said as I hoped over the desk and pushed past him.

The office was small and dingy. All it contained was a wall of hooks with keys hanging from them and a large stack of TV's, showing surveillance footage. Each TV was hooked up to a hidden camera in each of the rooms. I checked the hooks to see which keys were missing, looking for the rooms that should have been occupied. Five other rooms had been taken. I found the screens that matched the missing keys, all of which showed footage of the other guests in various stages of being eaten. Three of the rooms showed the guests looking the same as Jenny, just blood, skin and slime with no creatures in sight. The other two showed the remaining guests in the process of being turned to soup. All of them were dead, their bodies collapsing in on themselves with mush oozing out of their face holes.

A sudden clanking noise tore me away from the screens. I turned just in time to see Norman's skinny feet disappearing into an air vent close to the floor. I hadn't noticed it until then and the sneaky bastard had crept straight past me and crept inside without making any noise.

202

"Oh no you fucking don't," I said to his feet as I threw myself down to follow him. A splashing noise followed by a bunch of gurgles came through the vent a moment later. It was dark inside the vent so I pulled my head out and rummaged a pocket for my zippo. A quick flick open gave me a decent flame. I stuck my arm into the vent, followed by my face. The flame lit the vent enough for me to see, and I quickly pulled my arm back. Norman had turned himself around to face me and my hand had ended up inches away from his face. He had his mouth wide open and his spider-fangs were out, confirming my suspicions about him.

Whatever he was, they may have been weak but I didn't want the fangs anywhere near me. I made a move to push myself back out of the vent. In my haste to stand up and back away, I dropped my zippo into the slime trail that Norman had left. It ignited like gasoline.

"Fuck!" I yelled as I jumped away and watched the flames dart into the vent.

The flames spread fast. Moments after dropping the lighter, the inside of the vent was ablaze and Norman was screeching as his skin suit melted. I took a look back to the screens and saw flames spilling out of each vent in every room. The flames shot across the trails of slime and up to the creatures that were still in the middle of dinner, immediately setting them alight. I didn't mean to torch the place, but hey-ho. Some accidents are just lucky.

I snatched my lighter from the fire and backed out of the office as the flames spread up the walls and across the ceiling. It seemed about time to hit the road again, and I was happy to do so. I may have only had a couple of hours sleep, but almost being eaten is one hell of a wake-up call. With the Rest in Peace Motel turning into an inferno, I hurried back to the car, threw myself in and gunned the ignition to get the fuck outta there.

Rest in peace, my ass.

The Sisters

I glanced at my new companion in the rear view mirror. He looked totally out of it. I couldn't blame him, he'd seen some shit. "What's your name buddy?" I said.

"Billy," he replied.

"Listen Billy, I know what you're feeling right now. I lost my girl in pretty similar circumstances a few years back. You're not insane, but it's best not to mention what you saw. Easiest story is that you stepped out for some fresh air and we saw each other at the vending machines getting snacks when the motel went up in flames. We got lucky and survived; I helped you to a hospital. That's it, I'll swear to it if you need me to."

Billy nodded.

"I ain't gonna lie; you're in for a tough time bud, just stay strong. You'll get through it."

Billy nodded, again.

I knew a conversation wasn't on the cards so I shut my trap and drove in silence. It took a while, but I finally found a town on route to Arizona. I dropped Billy off at the local hospital, took a few hours to nap in the waiting room then got back on the road. There was nothing more I could do for the guy. I'd made sure he was seen to and gave him my Mom's phone number in case he ever needed to get in touch with me. That's about all I could do to help.

It was another long drive down through Arizona, just cutting off California as I drove into Mexico and down to San Felipe. I spent about a solid eighteen hours driving, with about four two hour stops for a snooze—in the car this time—so I didn't get too tired and fall asleep at the wheel. Everyone fantasises about road trips but they're pretty hard work; especially when you're alone.

I woke up from my last scheduled nap with the sunrise and drove into San Felipe at about midday, and let me tell you, it was hot. Damn hot. I had never been anywhere near Mexico so I didn't know how warm it'd be, even with the air con on I was sweating my nips off. After a damn long drive, and in such heat, I needed a drink.

Once I was sure I had arrived in San Felipe I drove until I found a bar. Any bar would do as long as they served cold drinks. The first one I came across was a small place called El Tirador; a traditional looking, dusty old saloon with flaking white walls. It would do just fine. I parked up a second later and grabbed my wallet off the dash as I pushed the door open. The heat hit me hard and made me sweat even more, giving me the good idea to hurry inside.

I pushed the door open and strolled inside, catching the looks of everyone in the bar. By the looks of it, it had been a while since a stranger had dared to walk in. I sat myself down on a stool at the bar, pulled a fifty from my wallet and said, "I'll take a cold lemonade, your best whiskey and some good information. Keep the change."

The bartender eyed me for a moment before taking the money, saying, "Si mi amigo." He was a tall, wiry looking guy with a head of thick black hair, dark green eyes and a weathered looking face. He clicked his fingers at a young, curvy, dark haired girl sitting at one of the tables and said something I didn't understand while pointing to the back room. The girl rolled her eyes as she got up, walking to the back like a stroppy teenager. She appeared a second later with an ice cold bottle of lemonade, popping the cap off as she walked. I took the bottle and thanked her. She gave me a wink in return, making a show of wiggling her ass as she walked away.

"So what can I help you with?" the bartender asked as he set a glass down and poured a measure of the good stuff.

"I need to know where I can find something; a tree. I can't quite remember the name though. Antique Torpedo or something, hold on," I said, making to reach for my wallet so I could get the note Ali gave me.

"Antiguo Torcida?"

"Yeah that's the one."

"Outskirts of the city is where you want to look."

"Know anybody willing to show me exactly where it is?"

He shook his head. "Won't find anybody to take you there."

"Why not?" I asked before draining half the bottle of lemonade.

"It's cursed."

I raised an eyebrow. "Cursed?"

"Cursed. Used to be an old hanging tree. They say the spirits still haunt it and bring harm to anyone that goes near."

"Yeah, well, there's only one spirit I believe in and it's been good to me so far."

The barkeep looked at my whiskey, then back to me and rolled his eyes.

"So there's not one single person that'd take me? I'm not planning on staying long so I'd like to find it as soon as possible."

"For price, Miss Isabella might do it."

I finished off the lemonade and pulled the whiskey closer. "Three more questions then. Who's Miss Isabella, how much we talkin' and how do I find her?"

"She's an old fortune teller. Most stay clear of her; they call her a misfortune teller. She might take you for a hundred dollars. Here," he pulled a napkin from under the counter, a pen from his back pocket and drew a rough map, "this is where you'll find her." He pointed to a dot that symbolised the bar, then tapped a cross for the fortune teller.

"Thanks, I appreciate it," I said, taking the napkin.

"You didn't hear this from me. You were never here."

I drained the whiskey and clacked the glass down on the bar and said, "Never here," before standing up and smacking another twenty down as a tip. "For the map."

Following the directions on the napkin, I drove through the streets of San Felipe. After a couple of wrong turns I finally pulled up to a shabby old house with 'Isabella the Fortune Teller' stuck above the doorway, hand painted on a sign in big mystic blue letters. The sight of it didn't inspire much confidence but I parked up and knocked on the door anyway. There were a few bumping and scraping noises but after a few seconds a croaky old voice called through the door, "You may enter."

I rolled my eyes and walked inside to the sight of the fortune teller sitting with her eyes closed, waving her hands over a crystal ball. The room was filled with shelves, each one covered in all manner of strange trinkets, curios and knick-knacks, hiding her choice of terrible pink wallpaper. Isabella herself looked like one of the curiosities, just another part of the collection. She was a tiny old woman, all wrinkled and leathery looking. She wore a dark purple dress and shawl, with an unnecessary amount of cheap looking costume jewellery.

"I'm guessing you're Isabella the Fortune Teller?"

She waved her hands around, putting on a show. "I am indeed, my child. I have been expecting you."

"You must know why I'm here then?"

She opened one eye and gave me a good long eyeballin' before closing it and stretching out a hand. "Cross my palm with silver and all shall be revealed."

"I don't have any silver but I'll give you a hundred dollars if you help me find the cursed tree. Another fifty if you cut the shit," I said, reaching for my wallet.

She opened her eyes and dropped her hands. "Fine, hand it over. I'm getting too old for this shit anyway."

I handed over the dollars and took a seat at the table on the other side of her crystal ball. "So are you really a fortune teller, or is it all just a show?"

"I have my gifts. Now, tell me, why do you want to find the tree?"

"A friend buried something there, said I can have whatever it is if I can find it. I've heard you're the only person that'll take me there."

"Is that what you've heard? It'll cost you."

"What? I've already paid you."

"To help you find it, yes. And I can do so by telling you how to find it, or by drawing another shitty map like the one on that napkin in your pocket. But to take you there myself? That'll be a few dollars more."

I frowned at her then looked down at my pocket. The last time I took the napkin out, I was in my car. There was no way she could have known I had it. "How the fu—"

"Gifts," she said, cutting me off.

I stared at her for a few more seconds, trying to get a good measure of her. "Fine," I sighed, "how much do you want to take me to the tree?"

"Another hundred and fifty should do it," she smiled, showing some loose fitting dentures.

I muttered under my breath, pulling my wallet out again to fork over more cash. She snatched it up before it could even hit the table and made it all disappear up her sleeve.

"Well," she clapped her leathery old hands together, "shall we embark? I'd rather get this over with quickly, my time is valuable."

"If you're so eager, sure, let's go. You don't happen to have a shovel I could borrow, though, do you? I'm gonna need to do some digging."

She gave me another crooked smile. "I've got a shovel you can buy. Fifty dollars."

I shot her a look of disbelief. "Damn it, I only need to use it once, and then you can have it back."

"Fine, I've got a shovel you can rent. Fifty dollars."

"God damn old goat," I muttered, pulling my wallet out. Again.

"I heard that," she said.

"Yeah, well, good, I'm surprised you can still hear anything at all."

She put a palm out and clicked her fingers for the cash. I handed it over, giving her a disapproving look. Sure, I could afford it all but she was clearly taking me for a ride. The cash disappeared a moment after hitting her palm. She nodded her head in thanks and pointed at something behind me. I turned to see a shovel propped up against the wall by the door. "Oh, and you're going to have to drive me there and back," she said, "I don't have a car."

* * *

[Track 24]

After a tense ten minutes of driving that mainly consisted of me getting eyeballed by Isabella the Fortune Teller, she eventually jabbed a finger at a barely visible dirt road that led up a hill on the very outskirts of town. I pulled the car around and followed the trail up the hill. Once over it, a large ancient looking tree came into sight that I assumed to be Antiguo Torcida.

"Stop here," Isabella said once we were about a hundred meters away from it.

"What? Why? It's right there."

"This is as far as I go."

I eased on the brakes. "No further?"

"No."

"Not even for another fifty dollars?" I said with a hint of sarcasm.

She gave me a sideways look. "No."

"Fine," I said, pulling to a stop and pushing the door open, "I don't know how long I'll be so you'll have to wait here 'till I've found what I came for. Just don't go rummaging through my shit, okay?"

She nodded, staring out at the tree.

I left the door open and grabbed the shovel from the back seat, swinging it over my shoulder, making sure I had my car keys in my pocket just in case Isabella fancied a joyride. Happy that she wasn't going anywhere with my car, I made my way down the trail to the tree on foot. It was an old, creepy looking thing; sun-bleached white and long dead by the look of it. Its gnarled branches spun out in all directions. Even the trunk was all twisted and crooked. I searched around for a few minutes, running my eyes over every rock until I eventually found a rock with the initials 'A.S.' scratched into it.

"Found you," I said to myself, or the rock, or whatever tree-haunting spirits may have been listening.

Ali had told me that my gift would be under the rock so I bent down and hauled it aside before sinking the shovel into the soft dirt underneath. After a good hour of digging, the shovel struck something hard about an inch deeper into the soil. I tossed the shovel aside and used my hands to scoop out and brush away the remaining soil, hoping I hadn't just found another rock. Luckily, I hadn't. I brushed the last of the soil away to reveal something silver with the inscription 'Las Hermanas' across the top. One good tug pulled the entire thing out from the dirt. It was a box. An ornate box, made from what looked like solid silver. I put it on top of Ali's rock so I could free my hands to get out of the hole and shovel the dirt back where it belonged.

After refilling the hole, I tucked the box under one arm as I strolled back to the car under the watchful eyes of Isabella. I popped the trunk and threw the shovel inside before taking out an old rag to give the box a clean before opening it. A good scrub got it nice and fresh. I admired it gleaming in the sun for a second before throwing the rag into the trunk and pulling it closed.

Isabella eyed the box the moment I dropped myself down on the driver's seat. "Dios mío," she said, crossing herself.

I looked down at it sitting in my lap, about to open it. "What's wrong?"

She shook her head in response, keeping quiet.

I gave her a shrug and pulled the lid. It scraped open and tipped back on dirt creaking hinges, revealing the most beautiful pair of guns I'd ever laid eyes on.

"Las Hermanas," Isabella whispered with reverence. "The Sisters."

The guns were a set of two large, ornate revolvers, similar to the .44 Magnum. Eight inch barrels, each with carvings of two beautiful naked women set on silver grips. They looked used, but especially well cared for. The box was fitted with a soft lining so they fit snugly and displayed nicely.

"You've seen these before?" I asked.

"No. And until now, I thought they were only a legend."

The guns were damn impressive, but talk of them being legendary made them even more so. I raised an eyebrow, "A legend?"

"These guns are old, said to be passed down through generations of a family of infamous bandits.

They say that the original owners were a pair of sisters, the very women you see adorning the weapons; Maria and Sofia Santos, twin sisters that would never part. Like a couple of Robin Hoods, they'd rob the wealthy and give every coin to the poor. They robbed together, they murdered together, and once they were finally caught by the law, they hanged together," she pointed her wrinkly finger, "from that very tree."

"Is it all true?"

She shrugged. "Dunno, I'm not that old."

"You sure?"

"Yes I'm sure you little shit. But I guess it must be true. Anyway, shut up, there's more." She cleared her throat and waved a hand. "They say that the Santos Sisters had a younger brother whom they provided for; always sickly and weak. He watched his sisters hang from that tree and he cursed it. The guns—their most valuable possessions—fell into his care, and as the legend goes, he was awoken from his bed on the night of the hanging by the sound of his sisters, whispering to each other through the darkness. It is said—"

"Seems a lot is 'said' in this story," I remarked.

She threw me a dirty look before continuing, "It is said that the souls of Maria and Sophia Santos reside in those guns, that the souls of the sisters themselves guide each bullet, and that whomsoever may own them... shall never miss a shot."

She finished by waving both hands around. I nodded, impressed at the tale as I took a hold of one of the guns, getting a feel of the weight in my hand. It felt good. Heavy but well balanced, even comfortable to hold.

"Anywhere in town I can buy some bullets?"

"Give me the napkin."

I pulled the napkin from my pocket and handed it over. She snatched it away and began scribbling away with a pen that seemed to have appeared from nowhere.

"Here," she said as she handed it back, "go here and ask for Benito. He owns a… aah… a legitimate vehicle maintenance business. He'll have whatever you need, as well as any other items you may want to buy." She eyed the guns as she spoke.

"Why'd you think I'd want to buy more guns?" I asked, frowning.

"I've met people like you before, Isaac Nightingale. You're one of the cursed. You're the kind of man that attracts evil everywhere he goes. No matter what you do, it will find you or you will find it. Mark my words, boy. Before your life is through, you will come face to face with The Devil himself. And people like you, you always need more guns."

I had to admit, the old goat was right. I did seem to have a knack for attracting trouble, and it wouldn't hurt to stock up on a bit of firepower. A set of nice black leather shoulder holsters would complement the Sisters nicely, too. With that in mind I slammed the door and stomped on the pedal, sending the Firebird soaring across the dirt and back towards town. It was time to do a little shopping.

I needed to see if the Sisters lived up to their legend.

Let's Dance

After spending a few days in San Felipe picking up a few treats from Benito—San Felipe's resident chop-shop kingpin—I took a drive up to somewhere I'd been dying to visit; Good ol' Los Angeles. The first thing on my list was to test the Sisters on some poor asshole, see what damage they could do. LA seemed like the ideal place to find a few back-alley bloodsuckers. If what Isabella the Fortune Teller said was true, it'd be a matter of minutes before I'd end up face to face with a sight that'd make me want to pull out the hand cannons.

It was getting on about seven in the evening and I was working up a thirst for blood and whiskey when I pulled the Firebird into a parking lot right by the Santa Monica Pier. I killed the engine and popped the door. The cool sea air caressed my face as I stepped out of the car and propped myself against the roof with an elbow. Santa Monica was a pretty sight, but it wasn't pretty sights I was looking for. I wanted the ugly sights; the dirty, nasty sights.

I pulled a cigar out of my pocket and put it between my teeth before locking the car door and strolling around to the trunk, lighting the cigar as I walked. I was looking for some trouble and I needed my gear. With a dull click I unlocked my trunk of treasures and threw it open. Benito had kitted the car out exactly as I'd requested. The box containing the Sisters sat on top of my leather coat, with a set of shoulder holsters at the side. I strapped on the holsters and flipped the lid to

216

reveal Maria and Sofia. They were a pretty sight. After fitting them snugly into their new holsters, I set the box aside and pulled out my coat, revealing even more treasures underneath. I stood admiring the contents for a moment before pulling the coat on and nudging the trunk shut, making sure nobody had caught a glimpse of what lay inside.

With the pier at my back, I took a hard drag of my cigar and set off in the direction of Colorado Avenue. In line with what Isabella had told me, it didn't take long to wander into the trouble. I figured following the sound of police sirens would get me to where I needed to be and I wasn't wrong. Within the space of half an hour I had wandered over towards Santa Monica College and into what seemed to be gang territory. I was ripe for a mugging, or worse, and I was absolutely looking forward to it.

My watch had just ticked over to eight when I heard a woman scream from an alleyway about two blocks away. Bingo, motherfucker. My heart rate jumped a little as I went from a leisurely stroll to an all-out sprint towards the alley. It looked to be a really shitty one too; the stereotypical alley filled with dirt, dumpsters and the token murderer lurking in the shadows, which is exactly what I found.

I crept down the alley and found an overweight, sleazy looking guy bearing down on a woman who looked like she'd had a fair few drinks. She was on the floor, whimpering and struggling to crawl away. By the look of her broken stilettos and scraped legs, she'd tried to run, broke a heel and hit the ground hard. Her wannabe Romeo was making his way towards her, tugging a large knife out from the inside leg of his pants as he walked.

[Track 25]

I stubbed my cigar out on the wall before catching his attention. "Hey, sugarnuts," I called out.

The creep swung around to face me, bringing the knife up in front of him. He looked like a kid caught with his hand in the cookie jar. I don't know what his deal was but he was sweating profusely and breathing real heavy. Something about his face was unnerving, too. Unnerving in a way I hadn't seen for a long time. His eyes were small and beady but far too dark, his mouth too wide, his teeth too odd. It looked like I'd hit the jackpot. This asshole was a certified bloodsucker and I knew it. I'd caught him just as he was beginning to change his face to scare the poor lady.

I took a look at the knife. It was a real big one with a nice sharp edge and an impressive length. "I think you're overcompensating for something there, buddy," I said, nodding at it.

"Get outta here before I gut ya," he said in what sounded like a bad attempt at an Australian accent. His face seemed to shift to look a little more human as he spoke.

I slid a hand into my coat and pulled out Sofia, making sure he got a good eyeful. "Now that is a nice knife, but mine's bigger," I said.

"That's a fuckin' gun," he replied.

"Ten points for that great observation."

"Fucking shoot him!" The woman on the floor wailed.

Romeo spun and hissed, "You shut up, whore!"

I edged closer, pointing the gun at his head. "That's not very nice. What kind of a man talks to a lady like that?"

"If you come one ste—"

"You're not entirely a man though, are you?" I interrupted.

He looked offended. "Well I ain't no eunuch if that's what yer asking."

"You know what I mean," I said, growing impatient, "and I know what you are, so you've got five seconds to show me or I'm gonna paint the alley red, sucker."

"Don't you fuckin' call me a sucker. I'll cut yer goddamn throat, ya hear me?"

"Well, let's dance," I said, "Five."

"You ain't gonna pull that trigger. Ain't got the balls."

"Four."

Silence.

"Three."

"Fuck you!" He yelled, beginning to turn from a sleazy looking pervert to a nightmarish hell-spawn. His eyes quickly faded to an inky black and sunk back into the sockets, pulling his nose up into a permanent snarl. His mouth split at the sides and a set of shark-like teeth pushed out from above the human ones, folding them back in on themselves.

I called it.

Not a second after showing me his true face, he was running at me with the knife outstretched. It was time to see what my toys could do. I cocked the hammer on the revolver and took aim, waiting for him to get a

219

little closer to make sure I didn't miss my first ever shot and totally ruin the moment by getting stabbed in the neck.

When he was close enough to smell, I pulled the trigger. An ear splitting bang thundered from the gun and shook the alleyway. The sucker's head exploded like a watermelon loaded with dynamite, raining blood, brains and bits of bone all over the alley. I stood in awe of the awesome power of the gun. The sucker was still standing upright. I stared at the ragged stump of his neck as it squirted blood for a couple of seconds before the body realised the head was gone and fell into a heap on the floor.

I stood in awe, looking from the corpse to the gun. It was more powerful than it had any right to be.

The woman on the floor seemed to be in shock. I stepped towards her and offered a hand to help her up. She took my hand, shaking and stumbling while trying to get to her feet. I put an arm around her and led her past the headless corpse, giving the sucker a hard kick just for good measure.

He was already smelling foul and appeared to be swiftly decomposing. The body let out a rattling fart as I drove the toe of my boot into its gut. We hurried out of the alley before the smell got even worse.

* * *

I walked the woman—Lucy was her name—back to her apartment. Luckily, it was pretty close by. When we got there I made sure she got in safely and told her to call the police if she wanted to, but asked her not to mention me. She said she'd call them but say she didn't see who blew her attacker's head off.

When I was fully satisfied that she was safe, I said my goodbyes and made for the door. She threw herself forward before I could leave and hugged me tightly, thanking me for saving her life. I told her to think nothing of it, literally. Like, actually try to forget the whole thing ever happened and pretend it was a bad dream. She nodded and wiped away a few tears, smudging her makeup. I said another goodbye as she closed the door behind me. I waited to make sure she locked it. She did. Happy that I'd managed to test out one of the Sisters, take down my first vampire and save a life all at once, I strode out of the apartment building feeling pretty smug about myself.

I arrived back at the pier about forty minutes later. The Firebird sat looking as fine as ever. I unlocked the door and pulled it open, dropping myself down on to the seat. My thirst for blood was quenched. I only had my thirst for whiskey left to tackle. With the thought of a good drink floating in my mind I gunned the ignition and pulled the door shut as I stepped on the gas and took off to the nearest dive bar.

It wasn't all that long 'till I found one. I drove back in the direction of the shady alleyway to see if any cop cars were flying around the area. A five minute drive down the road from there led me to a place called The Black Cat. I pulled into the nearby parking lot and found a space. The place seemed pretty popular judging from the amount of cars in the lot. I killed the engine and pushed the door open, making sure to pick my wallet up from the dash before getting out. The air practically carried the smell of alcohol and cigarettes from the bar to my nose; a welcome aroma. With my coat on, Sisters by my side and a hefty amount of dollars in my pocket, I made my way over the entrance only to be greeted by three assholes standing outside. They were mouthing off to a fourth guy in a wheelchair, who seemed a bit mentally unstable. The poor guy had bright ginger hair sticking out in all directions and had a broad Scottish accent that was easily heard on the count of how loud he spoke.

I caught wind of their argument as I approached.

One guy with a slicked back hair-do and a black t-shirt that looked two sizes too small said, "Why not piss off back to where you came from, huh, hot wheels?"

The guy in the wheelchair replied completely deadpan, "I've been in this country since before you were sucking on your momma's titties. And I should know 'cos I got to suck 'em first!"

The two guys at Hair-Do's flanks made a wooing noise and nudged him to egg him on and continue arguing.

Hair-Do looked Hot Wheels up and down. "You ain't been near any titties with a face like that."

"At least I don't look like you," Hot Wheels yelled in response. "You've got a face like a beaten up scrotum! Not even ya ma' could love that face." He sat back in his chair and widdled his thumbs. "Although, she was beating my scrotum last night and she quite enjoyed it."

I couldn't handle it. I burst into a howl of laughter that caught everyone's attention.

"Something funny?" one of Hair-Do's buddies asked me. He had his shirt collars propped up like some Walmart value-bin Dracula. An unlit cigarette hung from the corner of his mouth. He looked like a total douche.

"Yeah something's funny," I said, waving a finger at the guy in the wheelchair, "this guy right here. He's handing your asses to you."

Hot Wheels gave me an insane looking grin, seemingly pleased that he had an admirer. "Aye, now run along ladies, I don't want to embarrass you in front of this gentleman any further," he said.

"Go fuck yourself, cripple," Hair-Do spat.

"Hey, the man said run along, so beat it," I said.

Hair-Do eyeballed me, no doubt getting the measure of me to see if he could take me in a fight. "The only thing beating anything will be me beating your face in, punk. Only reason hot wheels ain't shitting teeth is 'cos it'd be way too easy."

The guy seemed to have gotten into a fair few fights and took a few too many hits to the head from the sound of how he put a sentence together.

I was getting tired. "Look," I said, brushing my coat aside to flash the guns, "I've had a long day and you're getting in the way of my drink."

The looks on their faces told me they'd caught sight of the merchandise.

"Pffft, fuck these homos," Hair-Do said, clicking his fingers at his buddies, "let's get outta here, they ain't worth the time."

They took turns giving me the stink-eye as they stepped aside and passed to skulk off down the parking lot.

"Appreciate the backup there pal. Didn't need it, but appreciate it anyway," the guy in the wheelchair said. He was about to say something else when he paused and gave me a funny look, leaning forward to

223

sniff the air. He eventually sat back and put a hand in my direction. "Rusty's the name, Rusty Shacklejacker."

I forced back a chuckle as I shook his hand and introduced myself as Night.

"Night, eh? You'll join me for a drink. What's your poison?"

"I appreciate it but it's alright, I'm just having a quick one," I lied.

"That wasn't a request."

I took a look at him for a second before figuring why not. "Alright then, I'll have a whiskey. Any kind, it's all good to me."

"Good choice."

I turned to enter the bar when I noticed there were a couple of steps up to the door and not a ramp in sight.

"You, uh, need a hand getting in?" I asked.

"Just get in there and hold the door open for me," Rusty replied.

I did as instructed and pushed the door open. I stood and held it open as Rusty wheeled his chair back from the entrance and turned to face it. Without a single doubt or moment of hesitation, he set his wheels spinning and raced towards the entrance. It looked like he was about to crash into the steps and fall out of his chair, but a few inches from the first step he grabbed the frame of the chair and bunny-hopped up the steps, soaring right over them and through the open doorway like a majestic eagle on wheels.

I took a glance around the bar as I let the door shut. Not a single person batted an eyelid at Rusty's feat. I later found out that the entire bar had seen him do it on a daily basis. Still, I was impressed.

"Over in the corner, this way," I heard him say as he steered himself down the room.

He led me down through tables filled with a whole assortment of people, some odd looking, some normal looking, but all emanating a strange energy. The table he led me to had the strangest feel about it. It was in the far left hand corner of the bar and was occupied by four other people; three guys and a woman; a particularly eye-catching brunette. I took a look at the group as Rusty introduced them one by one. He introduced the pretty brunette as Harriot. She wore a deep red lipstick that complimented her chocolate coloured curls. She gave me a wink as way of a greeting. The guy to her left was a tattooed, muscular fella with jet-black hair and a beard so strong he could probably curl a dumbbell and impregnate a virgin with it all at once. Rusty introduced him as Khearo. Khearo gave me 'the nod', a universal greeting between all men. To Khearo's left was Morgan, a slender guy in a suit so sharp I had to take a step back so I didn't cut myself. This guy had the kind of look that told me he'd charm the pants off of your wife, then you.

"Evenin'," Morgan said with a tip of the hat.

I replied with the nod and looked to the last person. The last to be introduced was the guy sitting to Morgan's left, and the person closest to me. His name was Michelangelo. He was wearing sunglasses. Indoors. At Night. And he appeared to be completely asleep.

"Don't mind him," Rusty said, "we call him Mystic Mickey."

"Why Mystic Mickey?"

"He has visions of the future. That's what's happening now, he's not sleeping, just having a vision."

225

"Visons of the future, eh? Bet that comes in useful."

"It might, but every vision he has is wrong."

I took the empty seat next to Mystic Mickey. "Wrong? How'd you mean?"

Khearo answered, "It means if he has a vision of me getting stabbed, I know I'm not gonna get stabbed, because his visions never come true."

"Seems like a useless talent then," I said.

"It is," Morgan replied, "Unless you care to know whether or not you'll be getting shat on by a heard of flying cows sometime in the next four days."

The group let out a chuckle, and Mystic Mickey continued sleeping, because I swear he was actually asleep.

"Drinks then," Rusty announced, "whiskey all around?"

"Rum for us," Morgan said, gesturing to Khearo and himself.

I got myself nice and comfy in my seat as Rusty wheeled himself away to get a round of drinks. Morgan and Khearo gave each other a look, and then looked over to me. Harriot was giving me the same look. They all seemed to be sniffing at something and looking at me. It made me feel a little self-conscious, just in case I stank and hadn't even realised it. Like how most smelly don't know how bad they smell. I was about to ask why they were staring when a hand clapped down on my shoulder. Rusty was back with a tray on his lap, carrying our drinks.

"Be a good lad and pass these over," he said, handing me the glasses of rum.

I took them and set them down on the table near Morgan and Khearo as Rusty handed a glass to Harriot and set one on the table in front of Mickey. He handed a glass to me and took his own before pulling his wheelchair around to sit at my side, completing a circle around the table.

We all took a sip of our drinks. Rusty let out a gasp of relief and reclined in his wheelchair. "I've got a confession, Night," he said.

"Go on," I replied, somewhat interested.

"You see, believe it or not, Khearo, Harriot and I, we're all what you'd call werewolves. Morgan there is a vampire, and you don't even want to know what Mickey is. The vampire you recently murdered was a man named Keith Gooseman. You've got his scent and death stink all around you. Care to tell us how a human like you managed to do that?"

I took another sip of my drink, thinking I was completely screwed.

Letting the Darkness In

After asking how I'd killed a vampire and giving me an intense stare-down, Rusty finally cracked and told me not to worry about it. Apparently, they could tell I had murdered the sucker from the smell of his rotten blood on me. I couldn't see or smell any myself, but an insane sense of smell came as standard for supernatural folk.

I had been sipping my whiskey and getting ready for a fight, but my tension soon eased off after a bit of conversation. As Rusty put it, "Not all supernaturals are evil. They're born naturally evil but can turn out good, just as humans are born naturally good but can turn out evil." He explained that they may be different, but they tried to be good people. And that's how I ended up befriending a group of monsters. They called themselves The Monster Squad; a bunch of monsters that tried to be more human. As they put it, it was rare for them to welcome a human into their circle but thanks to my set of abilities, I qualified for membership.

After sharing our stories and having a few drinks we agreed to meet the next day so they could show me a thing or two about their kind. I pulled out the napkin I had picked up in San Felipe and had Rusty write down the directions to the meeting place. Once he finished, I stuffed it back into my pocket and shook hands with everyone except—still sleeping—Mickey and bid them goodnight.

As I'd found out over time, it takes an unnatural amount of alcohol to get me drunk; a side effect of the hot sauce. I could drink an entire bottle of hooch and be stone cold sober, but I had drank a fair bit more than that, so I left the Firebird in the bar's parking lot and stumbled off to the nearest decent looking hotel. No more cheap shit-holes for me. One experience of almost being eaten in my sleep was plenty.

When morning came, I awoke lying face down on the bed, still wearing the previous night's sweaty clothes. Luckily, I had the good sense to grab my bag of clothes from the car before making my way to the hotel. A quick shower and set of fresh clothes later, and I was ready to go. I dropped a twenty on the bed as a tip for the housekeepers. With the Sisters at my sides and bag on my back I left the hotel room and made my way back to my car.

The Firebird was right where I left her, gleaming black in the LA sunshine. I threw my bag down on the back seat and got behind the wheel. The heat inside the car was intense. I flicked the stereo on, turned the volume up and wound the window down. Creedence Clearwater Revival's 'Bad Moon Rising' rang out from the sound system. With my directions in hand, I gunned the engine and took off down the road.

The meeting location turned out to be a large abandoned looking warehouse, tucked away down a side street somewhere around Oakwood. Not suspicious at all, right? I cast a wary eye over it as I pulled up out front. The entire thing seemed to be made of grey, rusting steel with a bunch of smashed windows scattered here and there. I stepped out of the car and made sure all my valuables were out of sight. The Sisters gently tapped at my sides as I walked around the car, double checking the locks. Happy that none of my shit would be stolen, I took a stroll towards the warehouse entrance. The doors groaned on rusted hinges as they opened; unleashing the smell of stale, damp air. The place was almost empty, save a few old wooden pallets and a bunch of mouldy cardboard boxes.

"Glad you decided to come," Rusty called out from the back of the warehouse. The Monster Squad were gathered at the far end, shrouded in darkness. They were all sat on old wooden chairs around a makeshift table, having a game of cards.

"I never cancel a date," I said.

Rusty's wheels squeaked as he pushed himself towards me. "Join us back here," he said before spinning his wheelchair and heading back into the shadows.

"What's this all about then?" I asked.

"We're going to murder and eat you," Morgan said, completely deadpan.

Rusty came to a stop beside his buddies and threw Morgan a 'shut up' look. "We don't know how long you're gonna be in LA, but be it a week, or a few years, we want you to join us properly. And to do that, we need to get to know each other a little... better."

"How do you propose we do that?"

"Well," Rusty adjusted himself in his chair, "have ya heard of a jumping in?"

I thought for a second. "You mean where a new kid joins a gang and his initiation is getting the shit kicked out of him by the rest of the members?"

"Exactly!" He yelled. "But not quite like that. We want a fight. Or more like, we want you to fight us. Well, no, I want you to fight Khearo and Morgan. Yeah, that's it. It'll just be a bit of friendly sparring. No harm."

"What's the point in that?"

Khearo answered, "To see what you can do."

"Exactly that, pal," Rusty said, "we want to see what you can do, and to show you what we can do. After our chat last night, we think we may be of help. You want to find the vampires that killed your girl, and put them down in return. We can teach you how to fight. Fight like a monster, instead of just a man. As you know, Khearo here is a werewolf, and he's the strongest out of Harriot, himself and I."

"And Morgan is a vampire," I finished, nodding in his direction. "What about Mickey?" I asked, turning to him.

He kept quiet.

Morgan answered for him, "He'll not be fighting."

"Why not?"

"Because he'll fucking kill you."

I raised an eyebrow. "Thought you said a bit of friendly sparring?"

"I did," Rusty said, "but Mickey's kind have an uncontrollable reflex. Most creatures in this world have the fight or flight reflex when faced with danger. His reflex is to immediately suck your soul out. Even if it's in a friendly manner, you startle him; you're fucked."

I looked over at Mickey, who seemed completely uninterested as he raised his sunglasses, revealing his eyes. Instead of a normal set of eyes, he had a pair of florescent yellow orbs with no pupils. He gave me a quick wink and flicked the shades back down. Cool as a cucumber.

"I see why you wear them all the time," I said.

He nodded in reply.

Harriot piped up, her voice smooth as honey. "He doesn't speak, in case you're wondering."

"No?"

"His species don't have mouths, or throats... or vocal cords."

"But he has a mou—"

"That's not his mouth. That's not even Mickey. He's a Murnock, and they look nothing like humans. They just take over the bodies of freshly dead humans. What you can see is basically a suit for him."

"This just keeps getting weirder. So how does he talk?"

"You need to be around him long enough. Eventually you'll build up a telepathic link and be able to speak to each other. It's like radio for the brain; you just need to tune in."

I stood and eyed the entire group. The others were nodding along to confirm what Harriot was saying. "Okay, so you, Khearo and Rusty are werewolves," I looked to each person as I spoke, "Morgan is a vampire, and Mickey is a corpse-inhabiting, clairvoyant, telepathic soul eater?"

Rusty clapped his hands together. "Precisely!"

"Just think of him as Mickey the Murnock." Harriot added. "That might make it easier to remember."

"Mickey the Murnock. Got'cha. Cool." I nodded along, deciding on what to make of the situation. When it came to humans, I knew I could handle them, and vampires I knew I could shoot. Hand to hand fighting wasn't something I had planned on when it came to fighting supernatural creatures, but learning wouldn't hurt.

232

I pulled off my jacket, unhooked the Sisters and set everything down on the table. "We gonna do this, then? I do like a good fight."

"Nice guns," Harriot said.

"Thanks. I picked them up in Mexico a few days ago."

She looked me up and down. "Those aren't the guns I was talking about."

Khearo shook his head. "Calm your tits, Hair Riot, we're here to see how he fights, not how he fucks."

"Fuck you," Harriot spat.

"Hair Riot?" I asked.

"It's what my old 'friends' used to call me," she said.

I kept quiet, waiting for an explanation to follow.

Harriot sighed. "Werewolves always have fur when they turn, yeah? When I turn, I'm a little furrier than most."

Morgan let out a chuckle. "A little more? You out-fur Khearo by a mile. You look like a walking rug."

She gave them both the middle finger, hard.

"Alright lads, that'll do before she goes apeshit and slaps the lot of us," Rusty cut in. "let's get cracking then we can all have another drink, whad'ya say?"

"Sounds a plan," Khearo and Morgan said in unison.

"Who's up first then?" I asked, getting myself pumped.

Morgan stepped up and removed suit jacket. "Me."

[Track 26]

233

He wasted no time in getting to it. By the time the jacket hit the table, he was in full vampire mode. His fingernails had turned to thick, dark claws. His eyes had sunk into the sockets and turned black. His mouth split at the sides, and the shark teeth had pushed through. He was ready to go.

The hot sauce had already kicked in and my senses were in overdrive. Morgan made the first move, swinging a fist at my ribs. He was fast. Damn fast. I deflected the punch with a smack to the side of his fist and followed up with a left hook aimed at his throat. He dodged it and jumped back a few meters, putting some distance between us. The atmosphere in the warehouse was electric, fizzling with a supernatural energy. Morgan crouched and pounced, sailing through the air, claws outstretched and fangs bared. We may have agreed on a friendly bit of competition, but I was convinced Morgan was actually trying to kill me. I stepped to the side and watched him pass, still airborne.

"Shit," I heard Rusty say, "for a human, he's fucking fast."

Morgan landed with a spin and lashed out with his claws. He caught my forearm and raked his fingers down it, effortlessly tearing through the skin. It wasn't a deep scratch but it cut deep enough to draw a fair amount of blood.

"Shit, what happened to 'no harm'." I said.

He licked my blood from his claws and shrugged. "Accidents happen."

"Hold up," I said, doing the time-out gesture.

"Quitting already?" he said.

I shook my head and turned to the rest of the group, feeling pretty damn confident with myself. "How about we make it a little more interesting? I'll fight Morgan and Khearo at the same time."

"Are you having a fuckin' chuckle?" Rusty said.

I gave a shrug.

He slapped his hands together and gave them a good rub. "Fantastic, you've got balls kid. This should be a show!"

"Don't mind, do you?" I said to Morgan.

He replied with a look that told me he wasn't trying to kill me before, but he'd damn well try now.

Khearo stood, immediately whipped his t-shirt off and began undoing his jeans.

"Hey now, that's not the kind of three-way I'm asking for," I said.

He grinned and shook his head. "I get bigger when I turn, smartass. Don't wanna tear through my clothes."

"That's okay then," I said, with mock relief.

Khearo stripped down to a set of over-sized boxer shorts and kicked off his shoes.

"Wait, when you say 'turn', don't you need a full moon? I thought you'd just be fighting as you are."

He gave me a mischievous grin. "The full moon thing's bullshit, we can turn whenever we feel like it. You're getting the full package." His sentence had barely ended before he was sprouting hair and getting taller.

While he had said he'd get bigger, with this being my first experience seeing an actual werewolf, I didn't know exactly what he meant by "bigger". As it turned out, "bigger" meant an eight foot tall, snarling hybrid of human, wolf and tank in red silk undies.

"Shit," I muttered under my breath.

I readied myself, waiting for everything to kick off. A second later: chaos. My world exploded into a blur of fists, claws and teeth; a furry tornado of pain. For his size, I expected Khearo to be slow. I was wrong. He had one hell of a reach, too, making his fists—and claws—difficult to dodge. Fighting both Morgan and Khearo turned out to be one hell of a challenge. I landed a few good punches here and there, but they were mostly wasted on Khearo. His fur cushioned the blows, and he was huge. Morgan took the most damage from the hits, when I could actually hit him. He dodged my attacks as much as I dodged his.

It felt like the fight went on forever. The hot sauce slowed my perception of time, making what was probably a five minute tussle feel like a five hour battle, and the faster my heart raced, the slower everything seemed. It came in handy for avoiding attacks, at least, especially Morgan's.

When Rusty eventually called for a time out, I was well and truly pooped. I hadn't had such a tough fight in my entire life. My entire body ached, all bruised and partially bloody. No harm, my ass. I dragged myself over to the table and dropped down into the seat next to Harriot. She gave me a pat on the back then bent down and picked up a bag from under the table. Morgan and Khearo pulled out the two remaining seats and sat down, both looking human again. I felt a hand on my shoulder and looked down to see Harriot wrapping a bandage around the forearm that had gotten acquainted with Morgan's claws. The bleeding had stopped, but it was still sore even with the hot sauce numbing the pain. Luckily, I wasn't the only one with a few bruises. Now that they were both looking human again, Khearo and

Morgan looked like they'd taken some damage. Morgan had a seriously bust lip. One side of Khearo's face was bruising badly, and they both had black eyes developing.

"That was fun," I said, still trying to catch my breath.

"Best fight I've had in a long time," Khearo agreed.

Morgan nodded. "I'd be chewing your bones right now if you'd given me the chance but I could barely get a hit in."

"You got enough in, I reckon."

"Have yourselves a little rest then we'll hit the bar. Sound good?" Rusty said.

We all nodded.

Once we'd all tended to our wounds and found the energy to stand up again, we agreed to meet back at The Black Cat. Harriot had parked down the road. She gave Mickey and Rusty a lift. I took Khearo and Morgan. We met in the parking lot shortly after and walked up to the bar together. Mickey held the door open as Rusty done his trick of getting up the stairs. I gestured for everyone to go ahead and followed in last, letting the door swing shut behind me.

Within seconds a loud screeching noise burst out, filling the entire bar and bringing it to a deathly silence as something, or someone, shot toward me with arms outstretched. It was Lucy, the woman I had saved the other night. She charged towards me, full of glee. She slung a drunken arm over my shoulder and waved the other around to make sure she had the bar's full attention.

"This is him!" she yelled to the entire bar. "This is the guy that killed the vampire!"

Heavy Reputation

Life got pretty damn hectic in the month following that night in the bar; the night Lucy outed me as a vampire killer to everyone that'd listen. People didn't really react to Lucy's claims at first. It seemed to me that people just brushed her statement off as nothing but some drunken chick's ramblings. As I soon found out, LA happened to be full of vampires. It was—and still is—the vampire capital of the world. Vampires turned out to be so much more common than I could have ever imagined. Walk down a street in LA and you'll pass by about four of them. It turned out that people damn well knew of their existence, too, but they chose to ignore it and keep talk of such things down to nothing more than hushed whispers in dark corners of dive bars. Maybe they were hoping the vampires would go away if people didn't believe in them, but the vampires stayed. And so did every other weird-ass creature that came in to town.

I didn't have to wait long until people approached, asking me to take care of problems they'd been having. Problems like seeing someone with lots of sharp teeth hanging around their house at night. Within a week, I had turned into LA's most sought-after exterminator, and boy, did I have some fun. I didn't need money, but as the saying goes, "If you're good at something, never do it for free," so for a price, an unlucky sucker got to spend some quality time with the Sisters. All profits from my business went to The

Monster Squad, because they were the original exterminators, and I couldn't have done it without them.

[Track 27]

In the space of a month I'd hunted down a whole bunch of suckers thanks to The Monster Squad's guidance. Mickey and Harriot gave moral support, Rusty provided the wisdom. Khearo and Morgan handed out lessons in being a total fucking beast. Thanks to Khearo, I soon knew the best ways to take down a hostile werewolf, and that the full moon thing was bullshit, just like as the need for silver bullets. Morgan taught me how to avoid getting turned into a sucker's bitch, by showing me exactly how most suckers fought. And just as Khearo had done, Morgan taught me that certain myths about vampires were also a crock of shit. For one, sunlight and garlic wouldn't do a damn thing to harm them; the only way to take out a sucker is to destroy the head or heart.

And finally, Rusty taught me how to control my rage, and in turn, control the hot sauce. After spending a few weeks with them, I had learnt to truly hone my senses and make use of their enhancements. Thanks to The Monster Squad, it seemed like life as a full time badass would be a piece of cake.

* * *

"You'll never be free of it, you know," Rusty said one night over drinks at The Black Cat. He had a few things to tell me, and I was all ears.

"Free of what?"

"What you are. You're the hunter and the hunted. Our kind," he gestured to the group, "we can feel what's inside of you. Your soul is too clean. It's like a target, a neon sign above your head, or dog piss on a lamp post. And that's why our kind won't stop hunting you. You're a marked man, Night."

"Well at least I'm not gonna lead a dull life," I said, raising my glass to take a drink.

"Just be careful," Harriot said, "or it could be a short life."

Khearo spoke up. "He doesn't need to be careful; we'll always have his back."

Morgan nodded in agreement and raised a glass. "He's one of us, a true monster."

We all clicked glasses.

"I never really asked, but why do this? Why make me a part of the group?"

Rusty answered, "It was someone like you that started this whole thing way back when. He was human, but he found us and brought us together. You remind me of him."

Khearo added, "Plus you're like us. We see the world for how it really is. We're not slaves to our instincts, or slaves to a system. We do what's right, for ourselves and others. Sure, our ways might be different but we get things done."

"Simply put," Morgan said, "sometimes you just need to kill a motherfucker."

Mickey gave Morgan a punch on the arm as way of agreement as his telepathic laughter rang through my head. We all took a moment to drink. The bar was full and the smell of cigarette smoke hung in the air. It made me want a cigar. It had been a while and a good smoke felt well deserved for all my progress in the field of ass kicking. It just so happened that The Black Cat kept a stash of damn fine smokes behind the bar, ready to light and available for purchase for those in the know. I quickly excused myself from the table and made my way over to the bar, admiring the range of bottles on display along the back wall as I approached.

Even with a full bar, I managed to get some snappy service. Davy—the short, pudgy and heavily moustachioed bartender—came right over to serve me. "What'll it be, Night?"

"Five of your best smokes please, Davy, oh and a Gin for Harriot."

Davy disappeared to the far side of the bar and came back a second later with five fat cigars and a glass of booze. He handed everything over as I palmed him a Benjamin. He unfolded it and made to hand it back to me. "They're on the house, for the favours you've done me."

I gave him a wink. "Consider it a tip, in that case."

He nodded and said, "You're a saint, Isaac Nightingale."

I stuck a cigar between my teeth and spoke through it. "I know, but I'm also a dirty, dirty sinner."

Raised glasses welcomed me back to the table. The alcohol seemed to be doing its work. I handed out the goods and sat down, pulling out my lighter. The smokes and drink were gladly received. Everyone gave a nod of thanks as the lighter made its way around.

"So, what's this important thing you needed to tell me?" I said to Rusty.

"Oh yeah," he said, taking a puff, "you'll fuckin' love this. You know those fuckers that killed Suzie?"

"Of course."

Rusty paused for dramatic effect. "Mickey's found them."

I looked over to Mickey. "What?"

"Yup," I heard him say in my mind.

"Where?" I thought back to him. To anyone but the group, it would have looked like we were having a staring competition.

"They were in LA 'till last night. Word is they're heading back to your home town for the Fourth of July."

"Shit, seriously?" I said to the group.

They nodded in reply.

Morgan said, "We've asked around for you. While you were out hunting, Mickey managed to track down a friend of theirs, and Khearo beat the information out of him. According to their buddy, they move around constantly but always visit the same places at the same times every year. They're going on a road trip, should be in Blackwater in a few days."

I took in the information. In a matter of days it would be nine years since Rapey and Roids murdered Suzie. If my suspicions were right, they'd be paying Blackwater a visit to relive that night and recreate their Fourth of July celebrations.

Rusty took a long draw on his cigar and exhaled smoke. "You might wanna hit the road, kid."

Don't Flip

The afternoon sun beat down heavy. I had the car windows rolled down so I could soak up the cool rush of air as I cruised down the long stretch of Arizona road. Los Angeles sat about eleven hours behind me, and Minnesota, about eighteen hours ahead. The plan was to get back to Blackwater with a few days to spare before the Fourth of July, the ninth anniversary of Suzie's murder. Things to do, people to see, suckers to kill. You know the drill.

I had put down some serious mileage before hunger set in. I was making good time so I kept an eye out for a roadside diner, because a man needs a break from time to time. Sure, driving is great but so is a nice greasy hamburger, and I had worked up an appetite so big I needed a heart attack in a bun. For about another half hour of driving, the only things the road brought were sand and dirt. Not a scrap of food. Eventually, though, the road led me to my Zion. Under a great big neon sign sat Tumbleweed Joe's, "Home of the Sweet Jesus burger," according to the sign. I needed no more convincing. Tumbleweed Joe's would do just fine.

With a rumbling in my stomach, I swung the car into a dusty parking lot out front and promptly stepped out into the dry desert heat. I took a look around. Three cars sat out front, and that was about all there was to see. Tumbleweed Joe's stood like a monument to life in a barren land, buzzing with bright paintwork and glowing neon signs. I pushed the door open and felt a rush of cool air flow from inside. The breeze of the air-con was welcoming enough, but on top of that, the welcome came with a smile as I stepped through the threshold. The smile belonged to a young blonde waitress—maybe in her early twenties—with a powder pink uniform composed of a mini-skirt and a tight, half unbuttoned shirt. She had a fair bit of cleavage showing. I generally tend to avert my eyes, but when a girl is putting forward so much titty, you can't help but cop an eyeful. I pried my eyes away and read her nametag; Mindy.

Mindy smiled even wider, knowing damn well I had been staring at the merchandise. "Hey there," she said in a bright tone as she handed me a menu and gestured for me to follow. "I'll be your waitress for today. Let's get you comfy."

"Thanks," I said as I followed. I sat down in the booth she had taken me to. "What's the Sweet Jesus?" I asked, without as much as a glance at the menu.

"Sweet Jesus is our special. Two big, juicy chicken breasts, with soft, fresh buns filled with bacon, hot chili sauce, onions, tomato, and lettuce. The chicken breast is especially fantastic."

I examined her face as she spoke. She was incredibly pretty but was wearing a lot of makeup, probably trying to hide some fading bruises under her left eye. "Well, I do like some fantastic breasts," I said.

Mindy giggled and gave my shoulder a playful nudge. "We have a special offer on, if you're interested? For an extra five dollars, you get a large drink and a choice of dessert."

"Sure, I'll take that."

"So, one Sweet Jesus. With Fries?"

"Of course," I nodded.

"And to drink?"

"I'll take a lemonade, please."

She wrote down my order. "Aaaand, what can I get you for dessert, sweetness?"

I scanned the menu for ice cream and pointed to my choice. "This one right here, Tutti Frutti."

"Tutti Fuckin' Frutti," she said. "Coming right up, honey."

Mindy touched my arm before sauntering away to pass along my order. Tumbleweed Joe's was my kinda place; colourful décor and colourful language.

I took in my surroundings as I sat and waited for my order. Three other customers sat dotted about the place, all looking like worn leather that had been left in the sun. As for the place itself, the walls were a light blue, recently painted by the look of it. I followed the walls to a large service window that gave a good view of what was going on in the kitchen. A couple of fry cooks went about their business. To the right of the service window, a jukebox sat spinning out some gentle music. Mindy bent over the service window, almost showing her ass, clearly doing so on purpose. A good way to get a tip, I guess.

Mindy stayed bent over the counter for about thirty seconds; more than enough time to turn every head in the joint; all three of them. She eventually pushed herself off the counter and stood up straight once she was handed a glass, much to the disappointment of the customers that had been enjoying the view. She strolled over a second later and placed the glass down in front of me, touching my arm and bending over unnecessarily as she set it down. Her cleavage ended up inches away from my face.

"For fuck's sake, Mindy," a voice called from the kitchen, "get your goddamn tits outta that man's face." The voice belonged to a gruff looking, slightly overweight, balding man that looked to be in his late fifties.

"Sorry," she said, swiftly moving away from me with her eyes on the floor.

I watched as she quietly tended to the other customers as I waited for my order. It seemed like the scolding had upset her, and she wasn't being flirty anymore as a result.

I had downed most of my lemonade by the time my food was ready. A new voice yelled, "Order up!" and the food appeared at the window. Mindy quickly brought it over and said, "One Sweet Jesus," as she set it down, eyes cast to her shoes.

"Thanks," I said with a smile. She was about to get on with her work when I spoke up, saying, "Hey, is everything alright?"

"Huh?" she said, turning to face me.

"The guy in the kitchen, is he giving you bother?"

"Oh, no," she fiddled with her fingers, still avoiding my eyes, "that's just my dad. He owns the place. He doesn't like me being too friendly, you know?"

I took a bite of the burger as she spoke and quickly swallowed to reply, "It's not my place, but don't let anyone tell you what to do. Sure, it may be his joint, but I'm betting a lot of people come here because of the good service. Burger is great, but the service is better." I gave her an encouraging wink.

"Thanks, that's real sweet. You let me know if I can get you anything else. Wanna top up on that lemonade there?"

"Mmmhmm," I mumbled through a mouthful of food before sticking up a thumb and nodding. Mindy giggled and gave me a smile as she took my glass and made her way to the kitchen.

The Sweet Jesus burger had a good name, 'cos sweet fuckin' Jesus, it was damn fine. I practically inhaled the entire thing, including the crumbs. I just needed that glass of lemonade to wash it down nicely but Mindy was taking a while. After licking the last of the sauce off my fingers I turned my attention towards the kitchen. I could hear Mindy's voice floating through the service window. She sounded upset. The sound of her dad's voice followed a second later, and it had an unpleasant tone to it. I slid out of the booth with a sigh and made my way over to the window. It gave a good view into the kitchen so I propped my elbow on the counter. Just in time, I caught sight of Mindy's dad raising his right hand, threatening to back-hand her across the face. Mindy squeezed her eyes shut and flinched back. Judging from Mindy's bruised eye, this wasn't the first time he'd raised his hand.

[Track 28]

"Hey!" I called into the kitchen. Mindy's dad caught sight of me and dropped his hand. "I'm still waiting on that lemonade." They exchanged a look and Mindy sulked away out of sight. Pops disappeared for a moment then reappeared with the lemonade. I gave him a hard stare as he made his way to the counter. He put the glass down harder than necessary and was about to turn away when I caught his attention. "Pssstt, asshole," I hissed under my breath.

He froze for a moment. "The fuck did you just say?" he said, looking me in the eye and leaning over the counter a little.

I leant over a little more, too, and whispered, "You like that right hand of yours? Raise it again and you'll have to learn how to jack off with your left."

His eyed widened and his face reddened. "Who the fuck d'ya think you're talkin' to, punk?" he hissed.

"I'm talking to you, dick face. When I leave, I'm leaving your daughter one hell of a tip that you're not seeing a cent of, as well as a number she can call if you ever touch her again. And if I hear that you do, I'll be back here for another Sweet Jesus, only it won't be the burger, it's what you'll be screaming when I break your damn legs."

My little speech had Tumbleweed Joe shaking with rage. His face had turned a shade of purple. "You get the fuck outta my joint," he groaned through gritted teeth.

"Are you having a stroke?"

The remark set him off.

From where I was standing I couldn't see behind the counter so he probably thought I'd get a fright when he pulled a meat cleaver out from under it. Unfortunately for him, the sauce had kicked in long ago. While it took him a second to make a move, it felt like fifty to me. He rose it above his head and brought it swinging towards the hand I had resting on the counter. I batted the side of the cleaver as it came down, knocking it out of his hand. It went clattering across the kitchen floor. He watched it spin away from him then looked back at me as if to verify I had just done what he thought I had. His face dropped when he realised I had indeed done it.

"Now go get Mindy," I said, raising my right hand as if to slap him.

He flinched and took a step back before taking another step, then scurrying away. I reached for the glass of lemonade and took a long gulp. Mindy appeared a few seconds later. She looked like she'd been crying.

"Hey," she said with a meek smile.

"Hey. Walk me to my car would you?"

"Sure," she said.

I grabbed a few napkins from the counter as she made her way around. We walked to the door together. I held it open and motioned for her to go ahead. She gave a little nod and walked out into the parking lot. I followed her over and propped myself against the hood of my car.

"Got a pen?" I asked.

She nodded and pulled a pen from her back pocket. I scrawled my mom's phone number on one of the napkins and handed it to her.

"What's this?" she asked.

"My mom's number. I'll be back there soon, for a short while. If your dad ever even thinks about hitting you, you call that number and say you're Night's friend. I'll hear about it. I don't know what he'll be like right now, probably feeling like a bit of a dick for being shown up in his own place, but if he ever hits you, I'll make sure he never does it again."

Mindy smiled and wiped at the corner of her bruised eye. I handed her a napkin. "Thanks," she said. "You really mean it? You'd do that?"

"In a heartbeat."

"I wouldn't want him hurt, but that's real sweet," she said. She hesitated for a moment then stepped forward and gave me a peck on the cheek.

"Don't mention it," I said. My back pocket was feeling heavy so I nudged myself off the hood and pulled out my wallet. There was about a hundred dollars in cash left. I whipped it out, took Mindy's hand and folded the cash into it.

She stared at her hand. "What's this?"

"Your tip; and I mean yours, nobody else's."

"Shit," she breathed, "I don't know what to say."

"Don't say anything, to anyone. Just treat yourself."

She threw her arms around me and gave me a squeeze. "You're a hero, erm, is it Night?"

"It is indeed."

She let go of me and took a step back towards the diner, "Well, Night, I'll hope to see you back here sometime. It's rare to serve someone who isn't an asshole."

I popped the car door and said, "Oh I'm the biggest asshole there is, I just don't get along with other assholes."

She gave another giggle as she stepped backwards. "Well you're the best asshole that's been by. See you again?"

"Sure thing," I said.

Mindy made her way to the door of the diner and turned to wave goodbye. I waved back as I dumped

250

myself down behind the wheel and pulled the door shut. She stood and watched, still waving as I put the car into reverse and swung around to face the road. The wheels spun and kicked up dust as I stomped the accelerator. The engine roared, the tires gripped and the car took off down the highway.

I watched Mindy and Tumbleweed Joes disappear in the rear view window. A few miles were already down by the time a sudden, horrifying realisation hit me.

I forgot my Tutti Fuckin' Frutti.

Shit

The engine of my Firebird roared as I tore down the dusty desert road. It was one hell of a hot day. You know those days when it's so hot your pants cling to your ass so tight they may as well be tattooed on to you? Yeah, well this day was hotter, and I needed a drink.

[Track29]

The next town was about 20 miles ahead of me and I planned to drink it dry. So, armed to the nuts and ready to get into a good ol' drunken brawl, I put my foot down on the pedal and hauled ass to the nearest bar I could find. Within a matter of minutes I was greeted by the sight of a run-down ghost town, the ideal place to pick a fight. I passed by a bullet-hole riddled welcome sign that read; "Welcome to Saltstone! Population: 112 and a half." Somebody had spray-painted the 'and a half' bit on to it, along with a badly drawn picture of a dick next to it, 'cos you know, if someone has a can of spray-paint it's only a matter of time before something has a huge dong drawn on it.

The town was pretty much just one street, all wooden buildings like something straight from an old western movie. I brought the car to a stop outside of what looked to be Saltstone's only drinking

252

establishment, 'The Salty Dog'. I later discovered that the town was home to an old salt mine, hence the apparent fixation on salt.

From outside of town I expected the place to be a shit-hole. I was wrong. Calling this town a shit-hole would've been a compliment. On my short drive from the welcome sign to the bar I passed by at least four piles of garbage, two mounds of manure and the carcass of one rotting cow; all by the roadside.

I hesitated as I opened the car door in an attempt to brace myself to be slapped in the face with an abominable stench. It hit me hard. Shit, decay and heat all combined to make the smell of death. It'd certainly put you off your lunch. Luckily, this wasn't the first time my nostrils had taken such an assault so I adjusted to it pretty quickly. I didn't mind the state of the place so much to be honest with you. You see, it usually works out that the shittiest places sell the strongest drink. By those standards, I expected this place to sell pure, straight alcohol.

I pushed though the heavy wooden doors. Every single fuckin' eye in the place hit me. It looked like a true saloon, complete with cowboy hats and at least five different groups of people playing poker and smoking pipes. The only one that wasn't eyeballin' me was a guy sitting in the corner, on what seemed to pass as a stage. While everyone else watched every step I took towards the bar, he sat strummin' away on a guitar, singing a song about devils in the desert. The song seemed pretty damn appropriate considering the bar was crawling with suckers. I spotted them all immediately; at least fifty of them, likely half of Saltstone's entire population. One big vampire nest.

I tried to get a good look at the singer but he was wearing an old worn out cowboy hat covering most of his face. He was clearly human, though, and only one of the dozen or so dotted around the bar.

Fuck it, I thought. Drink time.

Not a second after my ass cheeks hit the bar stool, there was a bartender in front of me. Now that's service. He was a sucker but I decided I might not murder him if he could pour a good drink. It was a pretty big 'if' though.

"What'll it be, son?" he said with a heavy southern drawl.

This place had clearly been here a while, at least since the eighteen-hundreds would be my guess. The barman had probably been here just as long, from the look of him.

"Bourbon, over ice. Fill the glass," I said.

His hands trembled slightly as he placed a glass down and poured. "That'll be four dollars for the bourbon, kid."

"Start a tab," I replied, taking the glass. "And don't call me that."

He hesitated for a moment, before realising I wasn't handing my money over any time soon.

Of course, I didn't actually intend on paying him. Come sundown I'd be blowing his entire bar to the darkest pits of Hell. His payment would be a few more minutes on earth.

Maybe.

The heat was so intense I could actually see the ice melting, watering down my drink. I took the glass, downed the contents in one go and slammed it back down on the bar. The drink was strong, but it tasted like piss.

"Keep 'em coming," I said, still looking at the glass.

There was the sound of a bar stool scraping across the floor to my left. I took a glance to see that someone had sat themselves down next to me, which didn't please me one bit. My personal space was being invaded by a short, fat man with a handlebar moustache and dark purple lines under his eyes. Another sucker. Hungry too, judging from those eyes.

"Ain't seen you around town, friend," the creep said.

I swiftly downed another glass of the strong piss before replying. "That's 'cos I ain't from around town, friend." I put a good bit of emphasis on 'friend', hoping he'd realise that I was the exact opposite. It seemed to go straight over his head.

"How about you and me have a few drinks to give you a real Saltstone welcome? I'm buying, whad'ya say?"

Now this here, this is how the suckers in places like this get you; it's one of the first things Morgan taught me. Every non-sucker in the bar would have got the same welcome. They act all friendly, real nice. They'll get your drinks so they can make sure you stick around 'till you're good and sauced then BAM! Darkness falls, fangs appear and the dismemberment begins. An easy meal when the victims are all so shit-faced that running isn't an option for them. In fact, with hooch this strong they'd struggle to walk, never mind run.

Putting all of that aside, I came to the place for a drink and I was gonna stick to that, so naturally I accepted the kind gentlemen's offer. As they say, a fool and his money are easily parted. This particular fool was competing for the gold medal.

I sat and listened to my chubby little companion prattle on about the history of his crappy town, occasionally offering a grunt of acknowledgement or a nod of the head. The man was paying for my drinks, after all. His name was John, by the way. John Salter. Now there's a surprise. Salt. He told me about his family, his job, even his god damn cat. All lies, of course. Fuckin' suckers. Always lying through their dirty rotten teeth, most are quite the silver tongued bastards too.

After maybe an hour of sitting listening to stories from the jabbering ball of fudge, the drink started doing the Tango with my intestines. It was due time for the second coming of Sweet Jesus. I excused myself, jabbing a thumb towards the toilets. Salter nodded and raised his glass in acknowledgment. As I turned, I caught a glimpse of the sky through a grime covered window. Almost sunset. Shit would be hitting the fan in about ten minutes.

I strode past the croonin' cowboy on my way to the toilets and caught the chorus of the song he was singing:

> When the blood moon raises high.
> Staining red the midnight sky.
> Hell will tear this world apart.
> So son, grab your gun.
> And let the shooting start.

He sang with a voice filled with gravel.

My trigger finger twitched as he repeated the words. There was something about this guy that I couldn't explain. If I can't explain it, I don't like it, and if I don't like I usually try shooting it. I decided to ponder the matter whilst in the sanctuary of the gent's.

Now, this town was a shit-hole, this bar was the filthy heart of the shit-hole town, but this room, this was something else. This one single room transcended all filth. The stink alone burnt my nostrils and stung my eyes. A weaker man could have died from the stench. No word of a lie, this room was the earthly equivalent of The Devil's shitter. The walls themselves were covered in all manner of stains, and the floor was even worse. Not far from the first cubicle there was a guy lying passed out, face down in a puddle of his own vomit. Well, I say 'passed out in his vomit' but that was just a guess. He could have been dead in somebody else's vomit. Either way, I wasn't gonna bother to check. I had my own business to take care of. Cubicle one was caked in shit, literal turd all over the floor. I passed.

Stepping over the possibly dead guy and the large amount of vomit, I made my way to the second cubicle. My stomach started to rumble, anticipating the embrace of a toilet seat. I took a breath of the foul air as I pushed the door of cubicle, my hands trembling, expecting the worst. A tidal wave of dread and grief washed over me as I glanced past the door. My worst fear had been realised, they were out of toilet paper.

I was never the kind to turn to prayer, but in this moment of need, I had no other choice, so I prayed. I prayed with all the might I could muster as I moved on to the next cubicle. The blood drained from my face as I slowly pushed the door, afraid to look inside. A bead of cold sweat ran down my cheek as I prepared to face oblivion. I took a swift peek inside and almost shat myself in joy at the sight of toilet paper. Not a lot, but just enough to do the job, with a little extra to wipe the piss off the seat first.

Jackpot.

After the world's fastest seat cleaning job, I swiftly hung up my coat, dropped my pants and mounted the throne, pulling out a tattered old comic I had stashed in one of the pockets of my coat. No, it wasn't a porno, you dirty bastards. I've just always been partial to reading comic books on the shitter. This particular comic was an old issue of Iron Man, a personal favourite of mine.

Roughly ten minutes had past when I heard the door to the gent's open and close again. I could hear two voices, whispering, sounding like they were plotting something. I had a bad feeling in my stomach that certainly wasn't the second coming of my pal Sweet Jesus. Judging by how long I had been on the throne, sunset would be right about now. The voices sounded panicked, rushed. I tried to listen in on what was going on. The voices quietly shushed each other.

As my ears adjusted to the quiet, I heard one of voices whisper to the other. "Ten," it breathed. "Nine."

A sudden realisation hit me.

"Eight."

This isn't happening, I thought.

"Seven."

Nope nope nope nope nope!

"Six."

I stashed the comic back into my coat pocket.

"Five."

I was right to have a bad feeling.

"Four."

I pulled my coat off the hook, reached in and pulled a sawn-off shotgun from one of the many inside pockets filled with weapons.

"Three."

I took two shells from another pocket and loaded the gun.

"Two."

I took a split second to judge my shot.

"One."

A moment after the voice whispered 'one', a guttural roar tore through the shit-house. I snapped the gun up just in time and aimed low, right for the nuts. One of the suckers from outside the shitter burst through the door of my cubicle as I sat back, pulled the trigger and blew the fucker's head clean off.

This guy must have been the 'and a half' that the welcome sign mentioned. His face was right where I expected his balls to be so what should have been a shot to the nuts tore straight through his mouth, instead. The shot blasted the sucker's fangs right through the back of his head before taking the rest of his face with it. Blood, brain and bone sprayed out of the cubicle and splattered all over the other sucker that was standing staring at me, open mouthed and covered in bits of his friend. One of his buddy's fangs had embedded itself in his chest.

"You gone and shot Salty Sal!"

"I did, yeah," I shrugged.

"You blew his fucking head off maaan!" he squealed.

"Well I'm trying to take a goddamn deuce, what the hell did you think I was gonna do? Ask him if I could wipe my ass before he chewed my face off?"

"But you blew his HEAD clean off!"

260

"Well I wasn't meaning to was I? I was gonna blast his nuts off as a warning to you both; I didn't exactly expect a midget to burst through the door."

"You motherfucker, don't you call him a midget. He's just short!"

"Yeah, well, he's about a head shorter now, isn't he?"

"Fuck you!"

"No, fuck you and fuck that little asshole! Suckers or not, what kind of person tries to kill a man while he's taking a shit? There's low, there's rock bottom and then there's trying to eat a man while he's dropping a deuce. I should have aimed my ass at that door and pinched one off right on his forehead."

He opened his mouth to talk but quickly shut it again as I aimed the gun at his head.

"Don't test my patience, asshole," I growled. "Now, here's what's gonna happen; you're gonna stand right there while I finish my business and if you move as much as an inch, I'll blow your fucking head all over that wall. We crystal?"

Silence.

"That's what I thought." I kept the gun steady with one hand while I finished up my business with the other. "Now, come here," I said, still sat on the throne, "I'm gonna stand and you're gonna pull my pants up and buckle 'em up for me."

"Fuck y—"

"You've got three seconds to get my pants up before I redecorate the walls with bits of your face." I stood up, pants around my ankles, gun still pointed at the sucker's face.

He stood looking at the gun, then down to my pants, then to my exposed crotch.

"They ain't gonna pull themselves up," I said, grinning at him. "Three."

He hesitated.

"Two."

He started to panic. "Fine, fine, I'll do it!"

"That's a good boy," I said, "and don't be getting any ideas. Your friend tried to bite me with my pants down and that didn't work out so well for him did it?"

He made a grunting noise as I motioned for him to come closer. He crouched down, grabbed my pants and pulled them up. The look of humiliation on his face was priceless.

"Buckle 'em up good and proper for me now, I wouldn't want them falling down in front of everyone in the bar."

"There," he said as he fastened my belt. He sounded like a scorned child.

"Much obliged," I said to him as I stuck the barrel of the gun in his face and pulled the trigger. His head erupted in a fountain of blood and gristle, splattering all over me. The headless body jerked around for a second before falling to the floor.

I stepped out of the cubicle and looked down at the rotting suckers. "Pair of dickheads," I said as I gave both corpses a good kicking.

The sound of gunfire floated through the shit-house doors. The party had started.
I put the shotgun back in its hiding place and took out the Sisters, fully loaded and ready to dance. I stepped over the vomit guy and with one last breath of the foul stench I smashed the heel of my boot into the door. It came straight off the hinges and went flying across the bar.

There was one hell of a fight kicking off and I was itching to get in on the action.

Gunslinger

[Track 30]

I tightened my grip on the Sisters as I ran through the doorway and threw myself into the fight. The entire bar had descended into one almighty slaughter-fest.

     The doors and windows had been blocked off or chained up to stop anyone from escaping. I watched as the limbs of a few innocent civilians flew through the air. Now, I know what you're thinking, you're probably asking yourself; 'Why didn't he just kill all the suckers right away and save all the people in the bar?' Well, smartass, if I started shooting the place up as soon as I waltzed in, every sucker in the joint would've pounced on me. You know how difficult it is to kill over fifty suckers in one go? No? Well, it's fucking hard. I'd probably just get myself killed, and if I was dead I couldn't kill any more suckers, could I? No, I couldn't. I'd be dead and anyone that got up and tried to do a runner out of the bar before shit turned ugly, well they wouldn't get very far. It's a small town and most likely entirely populated by suckers. Better to live and save a few than get killed and save nobody, right? Anyway...

The cowboy was still on the stage but he wasn't playing his guitar anymore, he was using it to smash in the skull of a sucker he had on the floor in front of him.

That's one damn well built guitar, I thought.

A sucker at the other side of the bar set eyes on me and came charging forward, his mouth wide open with fangs on show. He was the first sucker of the night to earn a kiss from the Sisters. I stood and waited for him to get a little closer as I caressed the handles of both guns with my thumbs. It only took a second 'till I could see the whites of his eyes. In a heartbeat I whipped the Sisters up to greet him. He was fast, but I was faster. I put a bullet through each eye. The back of his head blew out and sprayed brains all over the floor. The body fell to the floor and rapidly decomposed, making the entire bar smell even worse than it already did. The smell caught the attention of a few other suckers. Within seconds I had four of the bastards surrounding me; one on each side, one behind and one in front of me.

The one to my right moved first, so naturally, I looked him dead in the eyes, took a shot and blew the teeth right out of the face of the sucker on my left. This is another thing they'll do. They'll get you surrounded then one of the fuckers will jump at you to get your attention. While you're looking the other way, the one on the opposite side will get you. Lucky for me they're not as fucking clever as they think they are. I easily played them at their own game. My time with the Monster Squad had really payed off.

While the suckers in front and behind me were watching their friend's teeth vacate his face, I was busy taking out the one that tried to distract me. He had quickly gotten all up in my personal space. I didn't like that. I held my shot and plunged the barrel of one of the guns straight into his right eye socket. He let out a deafening screech as the barrel pierced his eyeball and pushed through with a squishing noise.

I holstered my free gun, grabbed him by the neck and gave the gun in his eye a tug to pull him in front of me.

He howled in pain as I manoeuvred his head like a grotesque puppet. "No, no, no," he screamed, "stop pulling at it! Shit!"

The sucker in front of me had a confused look on his face. He looked at his friend on the end of my gun, then to his friend behind me. He stood glancing over my shoulder for a few seconds. The look in his eyes told me he was trying to get his buddy to jump me from behind. I didn't even need to turn around, I knew he wasn't gonna pounce any time soon. The gun in his friend's head served as a good warning.

Most of the other suckers were occupied with their own fights for blood but a couple of them had started to take notice of my little Mexican standoff. I could feel the tension in the air. We stood in silence for at least thirty seconds, eyeballin' each other as the carnage raged on around us. I could even feel the sucker behind me staring at the back of my head.

I broke eye contact first, for a damn good reason. One of the suckers at other end of the bar was crawling up the wall on his hands and knees. I watched as he went up the wall and scurried across the ceiling, heading in my direction. He stopped directly above me.

In the space of two seconds, a whole bunch of shit happened.

The sucker on the ceiling spun his head around to face me; his neck twisting a full one-eighty degrees. His face was a grotesque mess of fangs and twisted flesh with deep black pits that housed beady little eyes. I still recognised the bastard though. John fucking Salter.

While I was distracted by Salter, the other two suckers decided to make a move. I didn't have time to grab my other gun so I gave the gun in the sucker's eye a good twist to get him moving. I aimed the back of his head at the sucker in front of me and pulled the trigger. The face on the end of the gun exploded with a wet bursting sound. Two corpses fell to the floor. I had shot the other sucker right between the eyes.

I quickly spun around on my heel while grabbing my other gun. The sucker that was now in front of me was a little too close for comfort. I threw up both guns to blast him back a few meters but before I could take a shot, his head made a jolting motion and a spray of blood spat out of the right side. I was about to make an attempt to see who shot him but I was flattened by what felt like a ton of bricks. That cocksucker, Salter, had dropped from the ceiling and landed right on top of me.

The back of my head smashed off the wooden floor boards. It hurt, but that wasn't the worst of it. Salter's ass had landed square on my face. I could practically feel his goddamn nuts on my chin. A moment later I felt him lean forward, no doubt to tear my stomach open and feast on my guts.

My arms were pinned so all I could do was kick at anything and everything, which seemed to pay off. My right knee made a connection with something, something that cracked. Salter let out a yelp and sprang to his feet. I quickly sat up, thankful to have Salter's fat ass off my face. From the looks of it, I had broken his nose, or whatever the fuck passed for a nose on that mess he called a face. He looked pretty pissed.

I quickly assessed the situation. I had nine shots left in both Sisters combined and most likely no time to fumble around in my pockets for more ammo if I needed it. Salter flew at me. I put a bullet between his beady little eyes. He didn't go down.

The first bullet clearly didn't bother him so I put another two in his head. He didn't even flinch. I tried two shots to the heart. Nothing. Fuck it, I thought as I stuffed the guns in to the side pockets of my coat, I was gonna have to do it the hard way.

I braced myself for impact and caught movement to my right. A split second before Salter could slam in to me, the cowboy sprang from the side and tackled him to the ground. They began to roll around on the floor in a struggle, both trying to kill each other. Salter managed to get on top of the cowboy and pin him to the floor.

Big mistake.

Without a moment's hesitation I was at Salter's back. I took my chance and wrapped one arm around his neck and the other up and under his jaw, then hauled him to his feet. I looked the cowboy in the eye. He knew the plan. He sprang to his feet, grabbed Salter's arms, pinned them to his sides and wrapped his own arms around Salter's body. I nodded to him, he nodded back. A moment later he was pulling Salter's body in one direction while I was pulling his head in the other. If his mouth wasn't pinned shut, Salter would have been screaming.

I put all of my strength into it as I watched the skin of his neck turn bright red. I gave another good pull. The skin started to tear. The cowboy pulled harder, too. Blood squirted in all directions as Salter's neck began to split apart.

"Awh shit, man," I heard the cowboy shout. Salter had pissed himself and the cowboy was soaked. He gave me a look that said 'fuck this guy'. It was time to end our tug of war.

We both gave one last heave. I heard a grisly breaking sound as the muscles in Salter's neck completely snapped in half and his spine cracked apart. There was blood pouring everywhere. I stumbled backwards and fell on my ass while cradling Salter's severed head. There was a good seven inches of spine hanging out of the ragged stump of his neck. I stood up, threw the head into the air and booted the thing right in the face to send it flying at a bunch of suckers at the other end of the bar.

The cowboy had already disappeared.

I spied a couple of people cowering under a table; they looked like husband and wife. The guy was clinging to a broken bar-stool leg, as if it would save either of them from being butchered. I guess I could sympathise with him considering I'd once been in a similar situation.

A sucker had set her sights on them. Yes, this one was a woman. I wouldn't have expected to see some she-devils in a place like this—you don't tend to see the females all that often, they're sneakier and more intelligent. I guess this one was an exception—but a sucker is a sucker and even female pigs will roll in shit. With one good slap, she sent the table-shaped sanctuary flying through the air, leaving the couple out in the open slaughter. She flicked her tongue across her fangs like a snake with tits.

The guy stood up, swung his makeshift bat and took it straight to the she-devil's head. He had some balls, I'll give him that. Unfortunately, the bat didn't do shit.

I wasn't gonna give the bitch a chance to pounce. She was far too fixated on the couple, probably thinking about all the ways she could slaughter the guy while she made his wife watch. She didn't notice me in the slightest. All I had to do was stroll up behind her, whip out one of the Sisters, point it at the back of her head and pull the trigger. An easy kill.

Her corpse fell to the floor and began to decompose.

"Stay close," I said to the couple.

They both nodded frantically.

I spun around and made my way through the obstacle course of severed limbs, broken tables and decomposing vampire bodies, some of which I hadn't killed myself. The cowboy certainly seemed to have an appetite for slaughtering vampires. Well, I assumed he was responsible for the non-human corpses, considering he was the only other person that seemed capable of killing them on his own.

I felt a slight tug on the back of my coat, I glanced back to see the woman holding on to me and the guy following close behind her with his makeshift bat at the ready. I snapped a leg off the nearest table. A good angled kick will snap a table leg and leave quite a sharp end, a good steak. Good enough to kill most suckers, anyway. I handed the woman the steak. Yeah, I had plenty of guns that I could have handed out but most people tend to shoot blindly when they're panicked and I didn't feel like getting shot with my own toys.

"Grab another bit of wood. If any of those things get close to you, make a crucifix and they'll back off. If they get too close too quick, stab them in the heart with the pointy end of your sticks and don't be a bitch about it. You'll be alright," I shouted to the couple. I didn't have time to do much else; I had guns to load and suckers to kill.

A quick search through one of my special pockets yielded fresh bullets for the Sisters. I loaded them up as quickly as I could and prepared to give out more kisses.

The people that had survived the first few minutes of the slaughter had formed into groups to fight the suckers. There were four groups of survivors, five if you included my own. The cowboy didn't count as a group, he was alone. I caught brief glimpses of him darting around the bar, picking off unsuspecting suckers. It seemed like they barely even noticed him. He'd clearly been doing this a lot longer than I had.

I led my little herd to the most vulnerable looking group of people. From the look of them they seemed like a bunch of tourists on a road trip. They were a group of four, two girls, two guys, all in their early twenties. There had been three more people in their group, but they were face down on the floor, each equally as mutilated as the next. Two suckers were dancing around them, tormenting them. One of them was another she-devil. It seemed like the group had gotten an idea of what they were up against after seeing their friends die. The two guys were holding makeshift crucifixes, one girl had a can of pepper spray and the other had a pocket knife that looked recently used.

"Hey, assholes!" I roared at the suckers. It caught their attention. They both eyed me suspiciously before turning their backs on the group. "Come take a piece of me, you dirty fucks."

The offer seemed to entice them. The male sprung towards me, he looked weak and sickly. Not worth wasting a bullet on. With perfect timing I launched myself into the air, just high enough to deliver a punishing kick to the sucker's jaw. The force of the kick made him drop to the floor like a sack of shit. The back of his head hit the wood. My boot hit his face a moment later. I heard a sickening crunch as I drove my heel down on his nose. He groaned then spat a load of his own blood, and a couple of teeth, out on to the floor.

"Nnnooooo," the she-devil screeched.

I looked up to see her staring at the sucker on the floor. I lifted my foot from his face. He made no attempt to get up.

The she-devil's eyes widened in horror.

"Oh, I'm sorry; does this ass-hat mean something to you?" I said.

The group at her back edged closer, all four of them about to pounce on her.

"You let him go before I feed you your own intestines," she hissed.

I looked her dead in the eyes as I stomped on the sucker's head again. I felt bone cracking under my boot. The sucker made a gurgling noise and coughed out more blood.

"You son of a bitch!" she screamed.

The group moved closer. One of the guys pressed his makeshift crucifix against the back of her head. She squealed in pain and spun around to an eye-full of pepper spray.

She howled as she reeled back, shielding her eyes. Both guys came at her with their crucifixes, one at each side. The girl with the pepper spray kept spaying as the girl with the pocket knife darted behind the she-devil. All at once, they pounced on her. While both guys pressed crucifixes on either side of the she-devil's head, the girl with the knife furiously stabbed away at her kidneys.

The sucker squealed as the skin on her face began to burn as if it was covered in acid. She fell to the floor a few seconds later and burst into flames.

"Finish her!" I shouted to the group. "Stab her through the heart or smash her head in, she's not dead yet, just stunned!"

One of the guys quickly obeyed and stuck one of his broken chair legs through her chest. The flames turned green and engulfed her corpse.

"Good teamwork," I said to them. "Let's get the rest of these assholes together."

Their group quickly joined with mine.

The weak sucker on the floor made a groaning noise and rolled over on to his stomach, blood dripped on to the floor from the mess of his face.

"Going somewhere?" I said to him.

With what seemed to be the last of his strength he turned his head, looked me in the eyes and flipped the finger at me.

Even though he was weak as shit, I admired his balls. Not literally, of course.

I rolled my eyes and smashed my boot into his head. He twitched around on the floor for a moment before laying still. He seemed to be dead but I wasn't taking any chances so I put all of my power in to one devastating stomp that completely shattered his skull. I ground my boot into the remains of his head as bits of brain oozed out on to the floor, you know, just to make sure he wasn't getting back up.

Most of the suckers had been taken care of. A quick look around the bar and I got a count of seven still alive. Each of the three groups had two suckers to deal with. I caught a glimpse of the cowboy flip a seventh sucker over his shoulder and throw her down on to the leg of an upturned table. The moment she was impaled on it he darted away to help the people closest to him. That meant one group was covered, so they'd be alright.

The group closest to me looked like they could take care of themselves. They were five strong and all clad in leather. They looked like what was left of a biker gang, holding their own pretty damn well. I passed by them and moved towards the group that looked most vulnerable.

Two women and a man were stuck in a corner, each holding a crucifix to keep their two suckers at bay.

Seemed like the ol' broken-wood-crucifix trick caught on pretty quickly. The suckers caught sight of my group approaching. They panicked. One of them sprang straight upwards and latched on to the ceiling. He tried to scuttle away but was far too slow. I followed his movement with both of the Sisters glaring right at him. He stopped to look back for a moment to see if he was escaping. He wasn't. I pulled both triggers and sent one bullet through his head and other straight through his ass. He decomposed in mid-air, faster than any sucker I'd seen before. The remains of his corpse made a sloppy splattering noise as it hit the floor.

I turned back to see that my group had teamed up with the trio. They were all beating the shit out of the remaining sucker. I took a look around; each group was finishing off their own suckers. The biker gang had chained their two together and were having a great time pummelling them to death.

I was about to holster the Sisters in victory when I got that strange feeling in my gut. I spun around and whipped up both guns, only to be greeted by the business end of a Colt .45, right in my face.

The cowboy held his gun steady, unflinching, regardless of the fact I had two guns on him. We stood in silence, staring each other in the eye. It seemed to me like he was making a judgement, getting a measure of my soul. One twitch of his trigger finger and both of mine would be twitching back. We both knew it. For the first time since I walked in, I got a decent look at his face. His eyes were a bright, piercing blue, the kind of eyes that can see right into your heart and soul. It was unsettling. Despite the bright eyes, the rest of his face was a little more worn and weathered, half hidden under a salt and pepper beard. He narrowed his eyes for a second then lowered his gun with a grunt.

I lowered mine.

He stood for a second and looked around the bar. "Ah," he grumbled as he made a move towards something. He kicked a dead sucker aside and picked up his guitar. There wasn't as much as a scratch on it.

I practically had to dance around the corpses on the floor as I made my way to the exit. With one swift movement I put away the Sisters, pulled out a sawn-off shotgun and blew the lock and chains clean off the doors.

A heavy hand slapped me on the back; it belonged to one of the members of the biker gang. Most of the survivors stood in shock at what had happened but the bikers didn't seem too phased by it. They each gave me a nod of gratitude as they passed by on their way out. The cowboy was nowhere to be seen.

After a few seconds, everybody else wandered out of the door with stunned looks still on their faces.

"Hey, um, thanks for what you did in there," one of the guys said. It was the guy from the first couple I helped out. "We'd all be dead if it wasn't for you."

"Not a problem," I said to him.

"Name's Robert, this is my wife, Michelle. Don't forget that. You saved us. Seriously, thank you," he said while extending his hand. I reached out and shook it. "Were those things... those people, were they—"

"Things," I said. "You were right the first time. Those things weren't people. Yeah, they were vampires."

The colour drained from his face. Well, what colour was left, that is. "Fuck," he sighed.

"Yeah, I thought the same thing the first time I seen them too. Now it'd be a good idea for you to get in your car and get the hell out of here just like I'm about to do. The town's probably crawling with suckers and I've had my fill of brawling for the night. Get yourselves to the nearest city and find somewhere safe, you'll be alright."

They both nodded and took turns to shake my hand and thank me before hurrying off to their car. Everyone else had already taken off, which was damn smart of them. The moment any other sucker noticed that the bar was torn to shit, the whole town would most likely explode into chaos. With that in mind, I made my way to my car while fishing my keys out of a pocket full of bullets.

The sweet smell of leather greeted me as I opened the door. It was a welcomed scent, like the smell of the girl you love after you ain't seen her for a while. Or maybe the smell of a guy, whatever you prefer.

I threw myself down on to the seat with a sigh and stuck the keys in the ignition.

"Evenin'," a voice growled.

"JESUS TITTY FUCKING CHRIST," I roared as I practically jumped out of my skin, "who the fuck? How'd you get in here?"

It was the cowboy, sitting in the back seat. Fuck knows how I didn't notice him before and fuck knows how he got in my car. "Old trick of mine," he said, grinning at me.

"I almost shat my goddamn pants, you son of a bitch."

"I have that effect on most." He chuckled as he shimmied through the gap and plopped down on the passenger seat before kicking off his boots and making himself at home with his feet on the dash. "You were good in there kid, real good, was like you had chainsaws for arms. You sure know how to dance but if you wanna be as good as me I'm gonna have to show you some new grooves."

"What you gettin' at?"

"What I'm getting at is you could be one of the best damn creep killers in the world and I can show you how."

"That right?"

"You're goddamn right it is," he said as he pulled a couple of fat, ready to smoke cigars from a pocket inside his jacket. He handed one over to me. I took it gratefully. I needed a good smoke.

He struck a match, lit his cigar and flicked the still-flaming match at me. I caught it and lit my own cigar before waving out the flame and throwing it out of the door. The sweet smell of smoke comforted me. It was a real nice cigar, too.

I pulled my door shut and turned the key. The Firebird rumbled to life. "This all sounds like a nice little idea, but I've got a question or two," I said to the cowboy.

"Shoot 'em."

"Who the hell are you, and what are you doing in my car?"

The cowboy took a long draw on his smoke. "Texas Dickson's the name. Most call me The Gunslinger; ladies call me Big Dickson," he said with a grin, "you though? You can call me Tex. And you're driving me home."

A Terrible Mistake

The road ahead was streak of ink across a parchment desert. It was a clear night and the temperature had plummeted so the asphalt was sleek and glistening, illuminated by the light of the moon. The sun had set pretty damn quickly so it's no surprise that Saltstone was a hotspot for suckers. With that in mind, I put my foot down hard in an attempt to get the shit stain of a town far behind us. I didn't doubt that the entire town would have caught wind of the events that had recently gone down in the Salty Dog. Putting a few miles between us seemed a pretty fine idea, so I drove the way driving is meant to be done, hard and fast. There wasn't a single car in sight, which was nice considering I was hauling ass down the highway at full speed. The sight of the empty highway and the feel of the smooth leather on the steering wheel made all my tension melt away into the night.

The cowboy puffed on his cigar, taking long drags and savouring each one. I had decided to let him stick around and see what his idea of mentoring was. From what I'd seen in the bar, he clearly knew his shit. Plus he seemed alright and I somewhat appreciated the company. He took a drag and exhaled the smoke with a relaxed sigh. "Where you from, son?"

"Blackwater Lake, up in Minnesota," I said, tapping some ash out the open window.

"Uff da, I'm from Minnesota dontcha know," the cowboy replied in a terrible attempt at an accent.

I gave him some side eye and returned the sass in his own style, "Well darn-howdy ya done guessed it partner, yeehaw."

He eyeballed me for a moment then huffed, "I wouldn't have guessed if I'm honest, you don't have much of an accent. Is mine that strong?"

"My mom's originally from northern England, my dad's from Cali. She taught me to speak the Queen's growing up. I ended up with a bit of a blend between them both and not much of anything from Minnesota. And yes, yours is rootin' 'n' tootin'."

"Fair enough," he said, "So how much experience you got then, kid?"

"Enough, I reckon," I said through the cigar in my mouth.

"Enough, eh? Well come on kid, spill the guts, how long you been dancing?"

"Dancing?" I asked, even though I knew fine well what he meant.

"Dancing with the devils, taking out the trash? Killing the fuckin' monsters, kid."

"Oh, right, a couple of months now. I had my first encounter with suckers a long while back. I spent the last eight years in the big house, got out in March. I've spent most of my time killing suckers for people in LA since then."

"Shit son, you call that experience? You ain't even got hair on your balls." He laughed, loud and strong.

"My balls are plenty hairy," I grumbled at him.

"So give me a selection of your finest, kid. What have you sent back to Hell? I need to know whether you're worth my time or just some punk that hasn't gotten himself killed yet."

"Well, I've killed my fair share of suckers, if that's what you're asking? Saw it yourself back there in the bar."

"Yeah, I saw it. I also saved your ass a time or two."

He had me there, I'll give him that. I got a little cocky and I ain't gonna deny it. My balls would have been sitting on John Salter's mantle by now if Tex hadn't been killing suckers right along with me. "Appreciate it," I said, giving him a nod to show I meant it.

"Yeah, I know you do," he grinned. "Come on then, what else?"

"Okay, just vampires mostly, but I took out a bunch of these weird blue things a while back. Also fought a werewolf."

"Blue things? There's lots of blue things, son. Gimme specifics."

"I dunno what they were; just skinny, creepy things. Pretty sure they wear their victim's skin. I stayed at a motel that had at least three or four of them. I woke up in the middle of the night and one was about to eat me, spreading a kind of numbing saliva all over me."

"Hmmph," he snorted. "We call them Tentaclari. They're real bastards, I'll give you that. They're weak as shit, but damn sneaky. You say you killed a bunch?"

"Yeah, punched one in the head and killed it then set the motel alight and fried the rest."

"Not bad, kid. Not bad. The motel wasn't the Rest in Peace in Colorado by any chance was it?"

"Yeah, how'd you know?"

"Read a story in the papers, said the place burnt down with only one survivor. Something seemed a little fishy about his story."

"Yeah, they ate his girlfriend. That'll screw any one up, trust me."

" Well, I guess that's a couple of achievements. Tentaclari can be tricky but vampires are like rats, pretty standard amateur stuff, 'sept Iscarions. They're bastards to kill, as you discovered when you put a few useless bullets in your fat little friend."

"The fuck is an Iscarion?"

"They're descendants of the first vampire himself, the one and only Judas Iscariot."

"You expect me to believe that shit?" I laughed.

"Believe it or not, I don't care. I got the proof though, a bunch of ancient texts, old as the Bible, 'sept this is the true, unaltered stuff. Most of the modern Bible is a load of bull, stuck in by God knows who."

I gave Tex the sideways look of doubt, "Got them texts on you? I'll believe it when I see it."

"Don't be stupid. They're worth about as much as a small country. I ain't gonna carry something so valuable in my pocket, am I?"

"I 'spose," I muttered.

"I 'spose," he imitated. "They're under lock and key, son, and it's a pretty big lock we're talking about. Play your cards right and you might just get to read them yourself someday."

"I guess I've got no reason to not believe you," I said, exhaling some of that sweet cigar smoke.

"Exactly, son. You stick with me and you'll see things that'll tear your mind a new one. Now give me a nudge if you want me to drive. I'm gonna get some shut-eye in."

With that, Tex stubbed out his cigar, pulled his hat down over his eyes and made himself even more comfortable as I tore down the highway and enjoyed my cigar in peace.

After maybe ten minutes or so, I decided a bit of driving music would be nice so I flicked the switch and turned the dial to find a station. The radio crackled to life and let out a low hum of white noise. I didn't seem to be getting many stations so I kept turning, hoping to find something decent to listen to. It was all shit.

[Track 31]

The noise seemed to have disturbed my new companion. He made a grunting noise and flicked the hat back up on to his head then without saying a word, reached over on to the back seat of the car and pulled his guitar case over to the front. I hadn't even noticed it was there, even though it was bigger than most normal guitar cases.

"You gonna provide the music?" I asked, half expecting him to actually start playing something.

"Nope," he said, flicking open the locks on the case. He hesitated for a moment, leaving the case closed. "Got many scars, kid?" he asked with a hint of concern in his voice.

"Good few, yeah," I replied, still puffing on my cigar. Shit, I didn't get a Cuban every day. I had to savour it good and proper.

"See this here?" he said, pulling his left arm out of his jacket and pointing to his shoulder. It was covered in some pretty brutal looking scars all circling his entire shoulder and the upper half of his bicep. "Got this one ten years ago in Venezuela, courtesy of a Ventripede."

"The hell's a Ventripede?"

"Nasty, ugly fuckers is what they are," he said, pulling his jacket back on once he'd made sure I'd had a good look at the scar. "From the waist up you'd think they're normal women. Well, you would if they didn't have four pairs of tits. Bottom half though? Giant fuckin' centipede."

286

"Any point in this conversation or are we just comparing the size of our dicks now?"

"Shut up a minute and stub out that cigar will you?" he said, flicking the radio off and killing the white noise. "Know why Ventripi are so nasty? Course you don't, so I'll tell you, son. A Ventripede will lure you in, hide behind something like a bush and only show their head and maybe the first set of titties. They'll act like they need help, or they'll try to seduce you from behind their chosen shrub. Once you're close enough, they'll grab you and take off to their burrow. They're lightning fast and they're strong, trust me."

"Uh-huh, yeah, and then what?" I said, stubbing out my cigar on the ash tray.

"And then they'll open their mouths wide enough to show their teeth and let out these weird pincer things they have inside their cheeks. The teeth can tear straight through skin. I learned that the hard way. Bastards will try to bite off your arms and legs so you can't escape."

"And the pincers? Whadda they do?"

"They'll use them just before taking your arms and legs from you. What they do is inject a sort of venom into you. It doesn't kill you though. Nope, what it does is stop the blood from flowing to your arms and legs and directs most of it straight to your penis. You'll be lying there with no arms or legs, but have a raging hard-on. Jack shit you can do about it. That's how they mate. You listening?"

"I'm listening," I nodded.

"Good. As I say, that's how they mate. There's no male Ventripi, so they use humans. A big beast of a bug-woman tried to dismember and screw me. I'm not even gonna get into how the fuckin' works. And that's the story of how I got my worst scar."

"So why you telling this story?"

"You listening?"

"Yes, I'm listening," I snapped.

"Good. I'm telling you this because I think I'm about to get a few more scars and I'm hoping you're not gonna be a bitch about getting a few more yourself." He opened the guitar case. His guitar was sat snugly inside, not a single scratch or speck of blood on it.

I didn't know what he was talking about or what he was doing but I certainly hoped he wasn't about to beat the shit out of me with the guitar like I had seen him do to a sucker or two. "Wha'cha doing?" I asked, eyeing him suspiciously.

He pulled the guitar and lining out of the case in one swift movement, revealing a stash of guns and ammunition hidden inside. "You've been driving slower and slower since I started taking a nap, must have drifted off into your own world. If you'd really been listening you'd know that we currently have a mix of about thirty cars and trucks on our asses and I'm guessing they're all loaded with the residents of the town we recently vacated. And guess what?"

"What?"

"One of them is playing the fucking banjo."

288

True to his word, someone was playing the banjo. Tex was right about me drifting off into my own world. I should have heard the banjo a long while ago, but the drive had practically sedated me, making the hot sauce die off for a while. For the first time since I got in the car, I checked the rear-view mirror. True enough, I saw the headlights of about thirty vehicles creeping up on us and it was at that moment I realized why he was prattling on about getting new scars. We were *fucked*.

"Shit!" I roared, "Why'd you not say something sooner?"

"Just testin'," he smiled.

"Testing? Testing my patience is what you're doing, mister."

"Call me Tex, kid."

"Fine, Tex. You see all those vehicles back there?"

"I see em."

"So why the *fuck* are you smiling?"

"This'll be fun."

"Well I hope you can drive 'cos in about five minutes you're gonna be taking the fucking wheel."

Tex was about to say something when a loud cracking sound went off in the car. Cracks quickly spread through the windscreen. Some fucker had took a shot and sent a bullet straight through the middle of the car. A couple of inches to the right and it would have gone straight through Tex's head. A couple to the left and it would have been mine.

"Get them guns ready," I said, "we're gonna need them."

"Best get some of yours out too, this is gonna take the both of us."

"Friend, I've got all I'm gonna need. It's time to go wake up Betsy."

"Betsy?"

"Betsy."

"But, Betsy?"

"Yes, Betsy."

He looked at me with a puzzled expression. I wasn't gonna ruin the surprise though. After staring at me for about five long seconds he realised I was keeping quiet so he started rummaging through the case, picking out guns and making sure they were fully loaded. Another cracking sound went through the car. They'd taken out my right wing-mirror.

"Take this," I said as I took my hands off the wheel to take off my coat. "It's got a load of pockets sewn inside it. They're either filled with weapons or ammo. Load what you can, use what you like. I'm keeping these two beauties on me though," I nodded down at the shoulder holsters that contained the Sisters. I handed the coat over. He was clearly surprised by the weight of it. "You're gonna have to load 'em fast, those bitches are catching up and I'm gonna need a couple of minutes to wake up Betsy."

"Sure thing," he grunted, beginning to rummage the pockets.

I gave him a couple of minutes to load and check the guns, both his and mine. He'd need them all. Another bullet whizzed and pinged off the roof of the car. The suckers were getting close.

"Here," I yelled over the roar of the engine as I put my foot to the floor, "take the wheel!"

"The fuck you doing?" he roared back.

"You'll see!" I quickly budged over and hauled myself out of the seat as Tex took the wheel. A few more bullets pinged off the car. That fucking banjo was getting louder too. I threw myself over into the back of the car. I aimed for the seats but I fell straight down the gap and landed with a thud.

"Ain't no time to be taking a nap, son," Tex yelled over to me.

"You're one to talk," I called back as I dragged my ass up from the floor.

I got on to the back seats and took a look out the window. The suckers were getting real close and they were firing off more bullets by the second. Luckily, not many had hit the car just yet. I put my ass into gear and got going in an attempt to stop more damage from being unleashed upon it. You see, this car was special. This was my car. *Mine*. And I'd rigged her with up some good shit. I didn't want my money going to waste. I smiled to myself in anticipation of using Betsy for the first time. We were seriously screwed, but I had faith that she'd pull us through.

Within a couple of seconds of running my hand along the back of the seats, I had found the button that flipped the middle of the seats down, leaving an opening just big enough for me to fit through and get me in the trunk of the car. I threw myself through the hole and dragged my legs through, pulling the seat back up behind me and locking it in place. It was dark in the trunk and I couldn't see shit, but that didn't matter, I knew what I was doing and some things are just more fun in the dark.

The banjo was getting louder and louder as the hail of bullets grew stronger. I heard a few shots go off from the front of the car. Tex was kicking off the action. I wanted in on it. I ran my hands over Betsy, feeling every bit of her. She was all prepared and ready to go. I had been waiting for an opportunity like this since I paid a visit to Benito down in San Felipe.

I felt the back of the car getting rammed by another behind us.

"They're here!" I heard Tex roar over the sound of his gunfire.

I waited a second longer until I was sure the suckers in the car directly behind us weren't packing much heat. The Firebird would have taken a lot more bullets if they had lots of guns, so I guessed I was safe for a few seconds. Regardless, my car was taking damage. I was pissed. And the motherfucking suckers had just woke up Betsy. It was time to dance.

I slammed my shoulder in to the hood of the trunk. It went flying open. A moment later I was on my knees, hauling up Betsy, locking her in place and praying I didn't get shot.

The gunfire paused the moment I burst out of the trunk. I was faced with a mix of thirty vehicles and maybe sixty suckers all crammed into them.

They were faced with Betsy; a fully loaded Gatling gun.

Fury

[Track 32]

The two suckers in the car closest to me were grinning, showing their blackened fangs, eager to be the first of the mob to tear into some sweet flesh. The smiles didn't last very long. It took them a moment to register that they were no more than a few meters away from the business end of a machine of pure destruction. They had made a terrible mistake. I watched as their ugly faces went from sickening grins to looks of terror, both seemingly mouthing the word 'shit' at the same time.

I gave every single sucker a couple of seconds to drink in the sight of the Gatling gun. It had certainly stunned them. I glanced back to see Tex hanging halfway out the window with his mouth hanging open and eyes all over Betsy.

"Yes!" He roared. "Now that right there is what I'm talking about, son." He pounded a fist on the car door and threw his gun over on to the passenger seat. His face looked like a child's on Christmas morning.

The sound of the banjo filled my head. I glanced around the crowd of vehicles to see where it was coming from, and I couldn't quite believe it. Right at the back of the convoy, one sucker was sitting on the god

294

damn roof of a pickup truck, playing the hell out of his shitty little instrument. It looked like it was hooked up to some amplifiers in the back of the truck, which would explain why it was so loud. We were all cruising at one hundred, easy, and this asshole was sitting on the fucking roof. Jesus Christ, I hate banjos but I hated this prick even more for having the balls to sit and play one during a car chase. Even the sight of Betsy didn't stop him. On the plus side, I had found my main target. With the sound of the hillbilly music ringing through my head, I began to crank Betsy's handle around, unleashing a storm of bullets on the nearest suckers.

The chambers spun, spitting out round after round straight into the car in front of me. The bullets flew through the windscreen with unrelenting fury, completely tearing through the suckers in the car. The noise was deafening, but damn, it was a beautiful sight. The suckers in front didn't stand a chance; the heavy rounds tore through their heads, chests, arms, legs, pretty much every bit of them. They were both dead in seconds. The driver immediately decomposed, practically melting in an instant. His car swung out of control, swerved, flipped and began rolling down the highway as flames engulfed it. The other vehicles swerved to avoid it, but it was a prime target so I slammed a few more rounds into it. Not a second had passed before the flames took over and the car exploded, sending debris flying in all directions.

The force sent two other cars—one on either side—spinning through the air before crashing back down on the desert sand, a good few meters clear of the road.

Three down.

The rest kept coming, driving past the wreckage of three cars Betsy had already wiped out. I could feel her getting hot. A few more minutes and she'd need a while to cool down.

I caught sight of the fucker playing the banjo. It was his turn to feel Betsy's fury. I swung the gun to face the bastard and cranked the handle. The bullets hammered from the chambers. I hit the banjo sucker dead on and practically tore him a hundred new assholes. A loud din of Christ knows how many noises rang through the air as the banjo exploded into a thousand pieces, each bit mixing into the cloud of blood that was spraying from its owner. The idiot didn't even try to move when I swung the gun at him, he damn well deserved to be filled with holes just for being so cocky. His body jerked around violently as the bullets kept tearing through him until I was fully satisfied that he, and his banjo, were totally obliterated.

I began to turn my attention on some fresh meat. A bullet flew past my ear and another caught me on the left leg. It was just a graze but it was enough to remind me that while I was clearly handling the largest weapon, the suckers were still playing with theirs.

The cars up in front took priority now. They were a little too close for comfort. I swung the gun to stare them down but she let out a hiss of disapproval. She was getting a little too hot, and a tad hungry for more bullets.

Shit.

With Betsy needing a rest, I kicked the stand, spun her sideways and tucked her back into the trunk then threw myself down for cover. The chambers of the gun were a spider's ass hair away from my face and they were damn hot.

The gunfire picked up again the moment Betsy was out of sight. Tex put his foot down hard, sending the car jolting forward. I felt a tingling in my side that told me the Sisters wanted to come out to play. They were speaking to me. They told me they wanted to redecorate the upholstery of the cars that were trying to ram the trunk. I couldn't deny them their fun.

"Are you a man of God, Tex?" I roared.

"In my own way, yes, why'd you ask?" he bellowed back.

"I want you to pray I don't get shot," I said, then sprang up from cover, straight into sight of too many guns.

I didn't waste any time. I had barely cleared the rim of the trunk before I eyed the two suckers in the closest car and put a bullet through each of their skulls. Their car swerved left, then right, and then left again before rolling off the road and settling on the sand to rot. I had cleared a bit of space and gave myself some safe time while the others swerved in all directions to avoid the car and get back on our asses. While I had a moment, I quickly holstered my left gun and reached into a small bag that was tucked into the side of the trunk. I rummaged for a moment until I felt a small round object. Oh yes, I'd found the sweet stuff. I pulled out a grenade, swiftly bit down on the pin, gave it a tug and held for a moment then threw the sweet little piece of anarchy straight at a car right in the middle of the convoy. The target had a few bullet holes in the windscreen. The grenade sailed through the air as if in slow motion before crashing down on the glass, shattering through it and coming to rest on the drivers lap. Nice and snug.

I couldn't actually see the exact landing spot but the sucker gave his crotch a horrified look so I assumed it had landed in his lap, which was probably soaked with piss in less than a heartbeat. He took a hand from the wheel to grab at what I'm sure was the grenade, considering it wasn't the time or place to be scratchin' his nuts. It was too little, too late. I ducked into cover as the grenade went off and the driver exploded dick first. Both his passenger and his car followed suit. Bits of the car went flying in every direction.

The gunfire stopped in wake of the light show. I took a peek over the rim of the trunk to assess the damage, and damage there was. The car on the left of the grenade victim had done a flip and was upside-down, screeching to a halt on the highway. The car to the right was swerving wildly. This one only had one occupant, a sucker with a giant shard of metal sticking through one side of her head and coming out of the other. Her eyes were rolled back, blood was pouring from her nostrils and her tongue was hanging out. Quite impressively, she was still trying to steer the car as she jerked around like a fish out of water, clinging on to life with her last few breaths. She eventually slumped forward and hit her face on the steering wheel, setting off a Dukes of Hazzard style Dixie horn. Everything seemed to be going well.

A moment later, the cars got back into whatever formation they were trying to keep and the hail of bullets started again.

"I've got a plan," Tex roared before immediately putting it into action without bothering to explain. He slammed down on the brakes and swung the steering wheel. It threw me back down on to the floor of the trunk. Before I knew what was happening, I was facing empty road. Tex had swung the car in a one-eighty to face the shit-storm head on. The wheels screeched as he put his foot down on the gas and sent the car flying forward.

I took a glance at the front of the car to see that the windscreen was completely gone. Tex was steering with his knees; he had a gun in each hand. Either this was the dumbest idea in the history of dumb ideas or he had one hundred percent pure steel testicles. Maybe a bit of both.

The car went head on into the swarm of vehicles. They all swerved to avoid a collision. It was like Moses parting the red sea. Within a second I had Betsy hauled up and ready to dance. We went flying past cars that had swerved out of the way. I could hear Tex roaring with laughter through the noise of his guns. He was firing off rounds in all directions, no fucks given. As the first cars passed by, I cranked Betsy's handle and hammered bullets into the ass end of every car I could. They were helpless.

It took a matter of seconds to get clear through the convoy. We both got out with little more than a few scratches; the suckers on the other hand had lost a total of ten cars thanks to Tex's stroke of madness and Betsy's appetite for destruction. I swung her back down to rest again. All was silent for a while as we flew down the highway back in the direction of Saltstone.

"You mind taking the wheel?" Tex said.

"Not at all," I grunted as I squeezed through the space in the back seats and clambered over into the passenger seat. I grinned as we switched places and I took the wheel. "How'd you like Betsy?"

"She's mighty fine. Mighty fine indeed," Tex said while pulling a handful of bullets out of one of my coat pockets. He thumbed the bullets into the chambers of a heavy revolver. "Told you this'd be fun, didn't I? We're doing alright."

"I 'spose. You could have warned me a little sooner though, don't ya think? My damn car's fucked now."

"Your car was fucked the moment we left that bar. One way or another, this was gonna happen."

"How come you're so sure?"

"Seen them rallying up behind the bar before they locked down the doors and windows, while you were in the bathroom. They'll have been doing this for decades; of course they'd be prepared to chase down anyone that managed to escape. Clearly, they ignored everyone else and sent the whole gang after us."

"Guess I missed a few things while I was on the shitter."

"Guess you did. Anyway, you might want to check them hand cannons of yours. We've got about thirteen cars full of biters left and they'll be on our asses again in a minute," he said as he pulled out a couple more cigars and handed one to me without asking if I wanted one. I tucked mine into the little compartment on the side of the car door, for safe keeping. Tex struck a match with his thumb and lit his cigar in one smooth motion. He flicked the match out of the hole where the windscreen used to be and sat back to take a long drag.

The peace was short-lived. A bullet cracked off the trunk, letting us know that the second part of the show was about to commence. Tex took off his hat and set it down on the back seat. He looked older without the hat. His hair was thinning and completely grey. The hat hid his age quite well.

"Keep an eye on that for me," he said. "An' slow down a little."

I didn't know what he was thinking, but everything had worked out alright so far. I let up on the gas a little, letting the car roll with its own momentum for a while. The suckers were catching up fast but I assumed that was all part of Tex's plan. The bullets started pinging off the car a little more frequently, but it seemed like the suckers had lost their balls after witnessing Betsy's fury. They were cautious.

"What's the plan, chief?" I asked, glancing at the all too relaxed old man sitting in the passenger seat.

"Let 'em catch up and don't fire back 'till you can smell the shit on their breath."

I came to the conclusion that Tex didn't give a single fuck. Not one. I mean, he could have a whole bag full of fucks and he physically couldn't part with one.

We cruised along and waited for the suckers to catch up while Tex calmly puffed away on his cigar. It wasn't long before they caught up, considering we let them. One sucker had decided to grow a pair and take charge of the remaining crew. He had put his foot down and cruised up alongside me, keeping the pace, keeping parallel. I kept my cool as I turned to face him. I was greeted by the business end of a rifle. He was aiming with his right hand while his left was on the wheel. I knew he wasn't going to fire, if he did the rifle would kick back and probably take his teeth out. I knew it. He knew it. It was an empty threat but his face sure was a mask of rage. I could hear him shouting all sorts of abuse at me, all of which I replied to with a smile and a nod.

I took a moment to see what Tex was up to, only to catch him halfway out of the hole where the windscreen used to be, climbing onto the hood. I watched as he hauled himself onto the hood and stood, surfing the car. He pointed in the direction of the angry sucker with the rifle. I nudged the wheel and got a little closer to his car. The sucker's attention was still on me, still shouting his abuse. I didn't like that. It just wasn't polite.

He quickly shut his mouth as Tex jumped over on to the hood of his car and put a foot through the windscreen, shattering it. The sucker practically shat his breeches. He swung the rifle up in front of his face to take aim at Tex but he didn't pull the trigger fast enough. Tex kicked the barrel of the rifle with the heel of his boot, sending the stock crashing into the sucker's nose. His beak cracked and bent sideways before blood began to stream from it. He let go of both the rifle and the wheel at the same time to nurse his face. Tex wasted no time in snapping up the rifle, pointing it at the sucker and pulling the trigger. The sucker's head exploded all over the back window.

A moment later, Tex was in the driver's seat, kicking the corpse out of the door. "Throw the guitar over!" He bellowed.

"What?" I yelled back.

"I said throw the damn guitar. It's time to end this," he yelled as he kicked his passenger door open.

He gestured for me to hurry so I snapped the case open and pulled the guitar out. I dangled it out of the window and threw it over into the other car. It landed nicely on the passenger seat.

I put a little pressure on the gas. Tex did the same, keeping parallel with me as he let go of the wheel, picked up the guitar and started strumming away.

"What in the holy fuck are you doing?" I shouted.

He didn't respond, just kept on strumming out a frantic tune. I stared over at him a while, hoping for a reply. I didn't get one but I kept on staring nonetheless.

After about thirty seconds of vigorous guitar playing, he shimmied over into the passenger seat and stuck the guitar down between the wheel and the gas pedal. His car jolted forward. I put my foot down, trying to keep level with him. About a second before I was parallel again, Tex flung himself from the hood of his car and on to the hood of mine. "Drive!" He roared, "Drive son, fuckin' drive!"

I didn't bother asking any questions. I floored the pedal and took off down the highway as Tex clung to the hood. He dragged himself in and plopped down in the passenger seat. It was only then that I noticed he was still smoking his cigar. Cool as a cucumber.

He reached over for his hat, set it down on his head and leaned back in his seat, kicking his feet up on the dash again as if he hadn't just been hopping between two speeding cars with bullets pinging all over the place.

I took a look in the mirror to see the rest of the suckers closing in around the car that Tex had abandoned.

"Hold tight," he said.

I was about to ask him what the hell he was smiling about when the loudest damn noise I've ever heard went off behind us. I jerked the steering wheel in shock and sent the car spinning in circles. As we spun I caught glimpses of an almighty inferno where the last of the suckers used to be. I slammed down on the brakes. The car eventually came to rest facing the right direction, away from Saltstone and back towards what had turned into one big burning pile carnage where the suckers used to be.

I sat and stared at the sight open-mouthed. "Was that the guitar?"

"Yep," Tex grunted before nodding to his handiwork, "and that there, that's the kind of fun you can expect if you stick with me, son."

In the moment, I realised it was all over, I also realised I'd never been that scared since the night I first set eyes on a vampire, and I realised something else, too. I hadn't felt so alive in a long time.

"Yeah." I said, my heart still trying to break out of my chest.

"Yeah?" Tex repeated.

"Yeah." I nodded, and that was all that really needed to be said.

I put my foot down and took off down the highway once again. We were hauling ass away from Saltstone for good this time. The explosion had almost cleared the road. There was a burnt out car or two to avoid but the rest had been thrown off the road and out to the desert. We passed by the carnage. It was quite the sight, but one god damn thing just had to ruin it. One car, just one, had managed to escape the explosion. Luckily, it didn't escape completely unscathed. It was lying upside down on the road, crumpled and broken with a trail of blood leading down the road. A few meters ahead, my headlights caught the source of the blood. One last sucker was dragging himself away from all the wreckage. He was bleeding heavily and both of his legs were clearly shattered. I brought the car to a crawl behind him. He screamed. I looked at Tex, he looked at me, we both nodded. Tex burst into a shrill scream, doing his best impression of a frightened little girl. It sounded just like the sucker on the road. I inched the car forward nice and slow, closer and closer. His screams grew louder as I inched ahead until I felt a bump under the car and his screams turned into something else entirely. Through the noise he was making, I could hear the strangely satisfying crunch of bones being crushed under the wheel of the car.

The screaming stopped the moment I heard a hollow crunch and squelch. Sort of like the sound you get when you drop an egg and it breaks on the ground. I hung my head out of the window to check I'd finished the job. Sure enough, the asshole's head was shattered and smeared all over the road like a burst watermelon.

They were done. Dead. Neatly wrapped and tied with a bow to be delivered first class straight to the steps of Hell.

I breathed a sigh of relief and put the car into reverse to run over the son of a bitch a couple more times, just for good measure.

Voice of an Angel

We drove in shifts. I drove a while, Tex drove a while and I drove a while again. You get the idea. It took about sixteen hours of straight driving to get where we were going. We made a few stops along the way, of course, 'cos you know, a man's gotta take a piss now and again. And no matter how wrecked my car was, there was no way I'd let any fucker risk taking a slash in a bottle or out the window while still in my car. Bullet holes, smashed windows and scratched paint? I can deal with all that. Piss on my upholstery? No. Not a chance. Not a god damn chance. Benito and his crew could have the car looking brand new but once someone takes a slash in your car, that memory lasts forever.

After an ass-numbingly long drive, we finally rolled up to a real pretty little town in the middle of nowhere. Sonora, Texas, Tex's hometown. Yeah, a man named Texas living in Texas. His parents must have been real imaginative. It was a nice little place though, all peaceful and the like. Seemed the kind of place where the whole town knew each other. Truth be told, it wasn't my cup of tea. Never been a fan of everybody knowing my business.

We pulled up to a pretty sizeable house with a good bit of land surrounding it. Tex guided the car into the driveway in front of a garage and brought it to a stop outside. The engine rattled as it died out. It sounded damn tired and in need of some good ol' TLC.

We hadn't spoken much over the course of our little road trip. It had mostly been spent driving, sleeping or pissing. Tex had asked me to drive him home, and considering he saved my ass a time or two back in Saltstone, I figured it was the least I could do. I needed a place to stay for a while too, and Tex seemed to be lookin' to pass his knowledge on to a man of similar mettle. I just so happened to be that man.

Tex grabbed his empty guitar case and threw the car keys to me before stepping out of the car and stretching. He took a nice deep breath and let out a long sigh. It was about midday and the sun was shining bright. "Welcome to my humble domicile," he said, pulling his house keys out of his back pocket, "come meet Gabriel."

"Who's Gabriel?" I asked, getting out of the car and having a stretch too. My ass had fallen asleep long ago.

"You'll see."

In all honesty, I found Tex's penchant for not explaining anything a little annoying at first. I mean, it could have gotten me killed and it pretty much did get me shot within an hour of meeting him, so I had a good right to be slightly pissed about it.

The thought brought back the stinging of the graze I took from the bullet during our balls-out car chase. Both the hot sauce and adrenaline had worn off hours ago, so the wound stung like a bitch. I sucked it up and dealt with it as I limped alongside Tex, up the path to his front door. I could feel blood trickling down my leg. The hole had been healing pretty fast during the drive but standing seemed tear it right back open.

Tex stuck his keys in the lock, gave a quick twist and kicked the door open. I heaved myself over the threshold and into the house. The living room was nicely decorated, neat and tidy with two doors to my right and a corridor in front. It didn't even look like anyone lived here; it looked more like a show house. Tex gestured for me to take a seat on the sofa. I made my way over, checking I wasn't trailing blood along the nicely carpeted floor behind me. All was clean, so I took a seat. Tex gave a whistle to announce his arrival and I was immediately greeted by Gabriel.

"CUNT!" A high pitched voice screamed at me as I was battered in the face by an unknown assailant.

No word of a lie, I almost shat myself. Whatever it was, it was big, black and all over my face, screaming the word 'cunt' over and over again. My arms flailed wildly as I tried to get it away from me.

"Gabriel!" Tex roared.

My attacker immediately stopped screeching before flying back a few feet and perching itself on a lamp. Gabriel turned out to be a gigantic raven.

"Sorry about that," Tex said, nodding towards the bird, "it's been a while since I've had any visitors, and he's an asshole."

"You could have warned me you have a fucking flying guard dog."

"I didn't think he'd get so excited, to be honest with you."

"And did it actually call me a cunt, or..."

"Yeah, like I said, he's an asshole. Don't let him sit on your shoulder or head, he'll shit on you. I guarantee it."

"I'll keep that in mind," I said, eyeing the bird, "but if it ever drops a fresh one on me mid-flight it'll be plucked, roasted and served for dinner before it has the chance to call me a cunt again."

Tex shrugged. "That's fair. I've thought about putting the bastard in the oven myself a few times, but unfortunately, I need him."

"He has a use other than making people turn their blue jeans brown?" I asked, giving both Tex and the bird a quizzing look. As expected, I didn't get the reply I hoped for.

"Yeah, I'll explain later. Come on, I'll show you where you'll be staying, then you can get that leg seen to."

[Track 33]

With that, I hauled myself up off the sofa and hobbled after Tex as he disappeared down a corridor. I shuffled across the room, following Tex. I stopped at the edge of the corridor and turned back to stick my middle finger up at the overgrown pigeon.

Tex waited outside a door on the right of the corridor. He pushed it open as I approached and let me shuffle past and into the room before following behind. Keeping with the theme, the room was real nice. The bed was immaculately clean with a nice little nightstand beside it. There was also a chest of drawers, a bookcase filled with books and a walk in closet.

"Make yourself at home," Tex said, "move whatever you want into the room and stay as long as you like. All I ask is that you keep the place clean, help me out with the jobs I'm given and don't kill the bird no matter how annoying it gets."

I sat myself down on the foot of the bed and let out a groan of pain over the hole in my leg. "We just met, how come you're offering me a place to stay so easy?"

"I'm gettin' old, son. People like you and me are a dying breed and I've been doing what I do since before you were suckin' on your momma's titties. There's a lot I could show you. Plus, somebody needs to carry on the work when it's my turn to inspect the dirt. You're the first I've met in a good few decades that seems capable, and I'd like to think I'm a good judge of character."

"You really don't mind me staying? I can't stay long but I've got money. I can pay my way as long as I'm here."

"Keep your money, son. You'll earn your keep by helping out and learning what I teach. Consider it an apprenticeship, pain in lodgings. Everything crystal?"

"Sure, yeah, I appreciate it."

"Good," Tex smiled, "now hold on a second, I'll get you something for that." He nodded towards my leg before disappearing down the corridor again.

I took a moment to survey the room. Aside from a few bits of furniture, everything else was bare and empty. Pretty much all of the house was the same way.

Tex popped back around the door. "Here," he threw a roll of toilet paper, a bottle of bourbon and a bandage on to the bed, "get yourself cleaned up and rest a little, I'll give you some privacy. If you need me I'll be in my workshop, back into the living room, first door on your left."

"Sure, thanks," I said while unbuckling my belt to get my pants off and tend to my wound.

Tex gave a nod and a grunt before closing the door.

I somehow managed to get my pants off without getting a drop of blood anywhere. The bullet had caught me good. The graze was deep. I gave my leg a quick wipe and pressed some toilet paper against the wound to stop the blood. The wound itself had been covered with dried blood, but it hadn't bled that much, all things considered. It seemed to stop bleeding not long after the gun fight and only started again whenever I set foot out of the car.

I bit down on the cork in the bottle of bourbon, gave a pull and spat it on to the bed. The bourbon smelled good. I took a good swig from the bottle before splashing a dash on to the wound and covering it immediately so I didn't waste a drop. It's a sin to waste good alcohol.

The wound stung like a motherfucker. I took another swig to kill the pain before putting the bottle down on the nightstand. I wrapped the bandage around my leg nice and tight, pulled my pants back on and got up off the bed. If I was gonna stay, I'd need to grab some stuff from the car. I had worn the same pants for over two days. It was time for a change.

I made my way to the door of Tex's workshop and gave it light a knock. I didn't wanna barge right in just in case he was striding around with his balls swinging free. He seemed to live alone, and if a man lives alone, at least eighty-five percent of his time in the house will be spent naked.

"Yeah? Come in," Tex called through the door. It gave a little creak as I opened it. Tex was sat in the corner of the room, tapping away on a typewriter. A work bench sat against a wall covered in wood chippings and various tools and other bits of equipment. The walls were practically lined with guitars.

"Shit, you sure like guitars don't you? You build them all yourself?"

"I do, yeah. Nobody makes them like I do. When was the last time you saw a person use a guitar as a bomb? Can't buy them in a store, son."

"Fair point," I said. "Wha'cha working on there?"

"Could call it a novel, or a memoir of sorts. Think I might be just about finished. No peeking now, I don't want anyone else's eyes on it yet."

"No peeking, you have my word. I'm gonna get a few things from the car, any chance I could get a hand?"

"Sure," Tex sighed as he stood and set a blank sheet of paper over the top of the stack by the typewriter. We made our way out to the car. She was pretty damn messed up. The windscreen was gone, the upholstery was fucked and the body was riddled with more bullet holes than I could count. Tires were good, at least.

"Wanna swap places?" Tex said. "We can put yours in the garage and I'll keep mine out on the drive if you like?"

"It's alright, I'm gonna have to make a call to get her picked up, it'll be easier to just keep her on the drive."

I popped the trunk and reached over to the bags behind Betsy, one bag filled with various weapons and ammunition, one filled with clothes, cash and a nice bottle of bourbon. Almost everything I owned that wasn't on my back. Tex grabbed the bag full of weapons and ammo as I shut the trunk and made my way to the driver's side door.

"You're getting the car picked up?"

"Yeah, gotta get her repaired after last night's shit storm. I've got a friend that works magic for cars like you do with guitars. He's got a shop in every state. I give him a call; the car will be gone by morning, and wherever I need it to be within a couple of days, good as new" I explained before a question popped into my head. "Anyway, you said you've got a car?"

"Yeah, so?" Tex shrugged.

"So how the fuck did you get to that shithole town without one?" I asked as I pulled the door open and sat myself down in the passenger seat, pulling my bag on to my lap.

"Hitched a ride."

I unzipped the bag and opened up the glove compartment. "Pffft," I snorted. "Hitched a ride. Mighty convenient that is. I'll wager your car is all nice and safe in that garage, not a scratch on it, and look at mine..." After emptying the glove box of bullets, jerky, a pack of cards and a Twinkie, I stashed a nice stack of cash inside and threw my car keys in, too.

"Yeah, sorry about the car. You got a place to stay, at least."

"Yeah, can't argue with that," I said as I shut the glove box and punched a seven digit code into a little keypad on the side. I knew the cash would be safe. With the code punched in, it'd need the correct code to safely open the glove box again. If somebody tried to break it open –BOOM– they're dead. Yeah, the cash would go up in flames, along with the car but so would the fucker trying to steal my shit.

Tex started back to the house. I hauled myself out of the seat and used my ass to close the car door. Still limping, I dragged myself up the path and stopped at the door to take one last look at my car before she'd be gone a while.

"Hey, Tex, you mind if I use the telephone a little la—"

Something odd was happening. I had backed into the house and turned to see Tex standing rooted to the spot, staring at the bird. He was mumbling something fast and incomprehensible. The bird was a few feet away, perched on the back of the sofa, staring back at him and making weird noises just as quickly as he was. I moved a bit closer. "Hey. You alright?"

No response.

"Tex? Hey!" I waved my free hand in front of his face then in front of the bird. Neither reacted. Not so much as a blink. It went on for about two minutes before both stopped their ramblings at the exact same time. The bird flapped off to sit on top of the TV in the corner of the room. "What the fuck was that?" I asked, staring at the bird.

"Just talking to Gabriel," Tex replied.

"I could see that. You two have an interesting conversation?"

"Did indeed. We've got a job to do, gonna have to perform an exorcism in a town called Ozona, about half an hour's drive from here. There's a family. Man, woman, two kids. The man's possessed."

"What?"

"Good ol' case of possession, we gotta fix it."

"And who told you this?"

"Gabriel. You just saw us talking."

"I just saw you mumbling gibberish to a bird. You weren't even speaking anything close to English."

"It was Enochian."

"It was whatnow?"

"Enochian, language of the angels."

"Oh, I see, you were talking to the bird in an angel language. It all makes sense now," I said with as much sarcasm as I could cram into the sentence.

"I wasn't talking to the bird; I was talking through the bird, son. He's a vessel to Gabriel himself. He's the one who tells me where I need to be and what I need to do. This is how I knew I'd find you in that bar yesterday. I was told exactly where to go and when to be there, and here you are now, questioning the very thing that sent me to save your ass in the first place." Tex seemed a little annoyed at my scepticism.

"By Gabriel, you mean the angel?"

"Archangel Gabriel, the very man."

"So you're telling me that the archangel Gabriel himself speaks to you in a weird angelic language, and he chooses to use this bird as a feathered walkie-talkie, a bird that likes to scream 'cunt' at people over and over again? Is that all correct?"

Tex shrugged. "Pretty much, yeah."

Fuck my life. I didn't know whether or not to believe him, but all the other crazy shit he said turned out true so far, so I decided to go with it. After all, there was a time when I'd have called somebody crazy if they believed in vampires, and look at me now.

"So, are we going now?"

"Fuck nah, son, it can wait 'till tomorrow. Halloween's on TV tonight and I can't be missing that.

317

Pray

We spent the night drinking beers and watching horror movies on TV, occasionally being interrupted by Gabriel squawking offence at me. It amused Tex to no end. Through all his mystery and over-spontaneity in the face of death, Tex seemed a pretty decent guy. He told me a little about himself while we sat and drank into the night. He lived alone, with only the bird for company. He made and sold guitars from his home for a living—aside from being a hitman for the angels—and he used to travel a lot when he was younger, which is how he got most of his scars and experience in killing things.

I asked him if he was married on the count of him wearing a ring on his left ring finger. He didn't really respond to the question, other than grunting and saying "I just like the ring is all."

I had a suspicion that it wasn't all a case of just liking the ring but I left the matter at that. I gave Benito a call during some commercials. He said my car would be picked up during the night and left wherever I wanted it in no time. I told him the code to the glove box so his man didn't obliterate himself and what was left of the car. Tex apologised about the car again but in truth, I didn't mind the damage all that much. As far as I see it, I owed him for helping me out in The Salty Dog as much as he owed me for getting my car torn to pieces, even though it wasn't entirely his fault. Gotta blame somebody though.

We sipped on cold ones 'till about midnight when Tex dozed off in front of the TV with a half-empty bottle still in his hand. He looked old without his hat on and even older when he was sleeping. I gave him a careful shake to wake him up, making sure I didn't make him spill his beer. He made a few tired grunting noises before opening his eyes and realising he had dosed off.

"Shit," he mumbled, handing me his bottle. "Finish that off, would you? I'm gonna get some proper shuteye. Gonna be a long day tomorrow, son."

"Yeah," I sighed, sipping the last of what was left in my own bottle. "Reckon I'll catch some Z's soon myself."

"Get rested good and proper now. Fighting vampires is one thing; going against a demon is something else entirely, even if it only possesses somebody."

"Sure thing, chief." I yawned as he shuffled off down the corridor and into his room.

I sat and watched the TV for a while longer, sipping at the remains of the beer until it was gone. The house was quiet when I came to turn the TV off. Tex seemed to be sleeping and even Gabriel had gone all still and silent, which was nice considering he was quite the mouthy little fucker.

I dragged myself through the house, stopping off at my room to grab my toothbrush and a towel out of my bag before heading to the bathroom for a quick shower before bed. I needed to cleanse myself of two days' worth of blood and sweat. The shower felt beautiful. I cranked up the heat until it almost burnt my skin. I took the bandage off my leg and gave the wound a good wash. It was healing fast. The hot water stung but

319

by god it made me feel clean. After about ten minutes of washing myself and fifteen of contemplating all manner of things that people contemplate while taking a shower, I was satisfied. It was time to dry off and hit the pillow.

True to Benito's word, by the time morning came around, my car was gone. I stood in a borrowed bathrobe, admiring the lawn and the morning sun. The smell of bacon caressed my senses. I found Tex in the kitchen sharing the bacon out on to two plates that had already been filled with sausages, mushrooms, eggs and beans. The man had taste.

"How'd you sleep?" he said without even seeing me enter the kitchen.

"Like a tranquilized rock."

"Good." He brought both plates over to the table that sat in the middle of the kitchen and set them down on opposite ends. "Enjoy. You'll need a full stomach today."

"Where'd you say we're going again?" I asked as we both sat down to eat.

"Ozona, it's about a thirty minute drive from here."

"And we're gonna be there all day?"

"Depends on how badly the poor bastard's possessed, but we could be. I've already packed us some lunch for later."

"You plan on having a lunch break in the middle of an exorcism?"

"Of course. It's tiring work, son."

"Are you even a certified exorcist? I thought you needed permission from the Vatican before you could do that kinda stuff?"

320

"I am indeed," Tex said through a mouthful of bacon, "and I don't need shit when I'm being sent by one of the messengers of God. I've got more authority than the pope when it comes to these matters. I'm sent by the angels. I tend to be the last resort, though. The church usually send their own exorcists first and if they can't get the job done, I finish up."

"How'd you get permission? You don't look like a man of the cloth."

"I'm not, not really, but he personally certified me anyway."

"Who?"

"The Pope."

"Piss off," I snorted through a mouthful of beans.

"Seriously. It was a while back now, Gabriel sent me to see him. I needed to collect a few things for my work."

"You needed to meet the pope to help you make guitars?" I said with a sarcastic grin.

"No fuck-wit, the other job. I needed a few items to make the job a little easier."

"So you're telling me you met the pope, and he personally gave you things to help you kill supernatural creatures?"

"Yeah, basically."

"Mmmhmm," I grunted while shoving a load of eggs and bacon into my mouth.

"The church ain't all about screwing the choirboys and getting hammered on communion wine, you know. Yeah, they'll cover that up but they also need to cover up the existence of beings that aren't exactly human. The pope knew all about me before I even knew I would be meeting him."

"An' how's that?"

"Keep up, son. He's got his own vessel. If I've got one then the pope's damn well gonna have one too. His is a dove though. Funny, ain't it? I do all the hard work and the pope gets nice fancy dove and I get stuck with a scraggy fucker that calls everyone a cunt."

"So what'd he give you? Anything interesting?"

"He gave me a whole bunch of stuff. I'll show you sometime," he said before stuffing the last of his breakfast into his mouth and excusing himself. He took his plate over to the sink and gave it a quick wash. "Meet me out front in ten minutes, time to earn your keep, son."

I was busy shovelling beans into my mouth so I responded with a thumb up and quick nod before he left the kitchen. The food was amazing. It had been a while since I had a proper breakfast, so this one was damn well appreciated. It made a nice change from eating a Twinkie and a candy bar whilst lying on the back seat of my car or a hotel bed. I spent another few minutes appreciating the food as I practically inhaled it.

The bag full of clean clothes sat tucked under the foot of my bed, the dirty ones were strewn all over the rest of the room. I picked my leather coat up off the floor and emptied all of the contents into the bag of weapons. I didn't imagine I'd need to take any weapons to an exorcism.

I gave the place a quick tidy and bundled the dirty clothes, as well as the coat, in a corner to see about getting them washed later on. A casual varsity jacket sat at the top of the bag of clothes. I pulled it out along with some jeans, a plain white tee-shirt and my favourite underpants. Within seconds I was feeling all nice and crisp in my clean clothes. I'd slept in a nice bed, I'd had a proper breakfast and I was wearing silk underwear. I was ready to take on anything.

[Track 34]

Tex was out in front of the house, already sitting in his car and puffing away on a cigar with his hat pulled down, shading his eyes. He really was a man after my own heart. His ass comfortably sat in a '67 Chevy Impala, one damn nice set of wheels. I popped the door and sampled the comforts myself. Tex handed me a cigar, which reminded me I'd left my last one in the car before I sent it off to be repaired. I knew it'd be safe though. This cigar was shorter and thinner than most; a quick smoker. A swift rummage in my jacket pockets yielded a box of matches. The match lit with one strike. The smell of the struck match made my nostrils tingle as I lit the cigar and puffed the sweet smoke.

Tex gave the keys a twist, making the engine purr to life. "You set?" he asked.

I gave a quick nod and Tex stomped the accelerator to tear off down the road.

It was a nice day, a good day for a drive. The sun beat down through the windscreen making me damn warm in my jacket. I decided to bear it, I was far too happy to just sit back, relax and enjoy the ride while having a smoke without the risk of any suckers popping out of nowhere to try and bite me on the ass.

After about ten minutes of silent smoking, Tex perked up. "Ever encountered a demon, kid?"

"Nah, can't say I have."

323

"Well, lemme clear up a few things before we even attempt to take this asshole. First, they're fuckers. Real fuckers. They won't just try to hurt you physically; they'll do it mentally too. They know things you don't want anybody to know and they'll use it against you. Don't let them get to you that way. Second, they lie. They all lie and they're good at it. Don't believe a thing they say and I mean it, not a thing. Third, if you know its name, you've got power over it. They're bound by their names, if you can get it out of them, you're winning. Like I said though, they lie, so if they tell you without putting up a damn good fight, they're lying."

"Seems pretty straight forward."

"It is, you'll see. And one more thing, don't forget that the demon is possessing a person. This is probably just an innocent guy. Shit will happen and we could get hurt, just don't hurt the person. It's him you'd be hurting, not the demon. That means no punching the poor bastard in the mouth, no getting too rough and definitely no shooting."

"Good job I left my guns in the house then," I said.

"Good, 'cos I'm telling you now you'll be damn tempted to shoot the fucker."

I took a while to ponder the situation. I already knew some of the stuff Tex told me from my talks with the Monster Squad, but I'd only ever seen demons in movies. This wasn't a movie. I was about to be face to face with something worse than a sucker, something entirely new. The thought creeped me out a little. I already knew vampires were some kind of demonic devil offspring, but an actual demon was some next level shit. The only comfort I had was that it was only a possessing demon. By demonic standards, any demon that chooses to possess a human is weak. They don't have their own physical body so they try to take over a human instead. They're considered filth; the degenerates of the demon world. If we'd been sent to face off against a true demon with its own physical body, things would be totally different. I'd have packed my shit and legged it in the opposite direction. Regardless of all that, any demon can still totally ruin your day.

I snapped out of my daydreams as I felt the car pull to a stop. I had been in my own world for a while. We had pulled up to the kerb in front of an old but nicely maintained looking house. The walls were covered in ivy, giving the place a slightly sinister look.

"Make sure you've got your balls fastened on tight, son. This should be interesting," Tex said, stubbing his cigar out in the ash tray and taking off his hat, setting it down on the back seat. He popped the glove box and took out a small bag.

"Wha'cha packin'?" I asked, eyeing the bag as I stubbed my cigar.

"Only the essentials, a Bible, crucifix and holy water.

"Got any toys for me?"

"You can have some holy water if you play nice. Least that way it's not something you can use to beat the poor bastard with if the demon pisses you off."

"Deal," I smiled as I clicked the handle and swung the car door open.

The heat was pretty intense, it was about midday and the sun was high. I decided to leave the jacket in the car. Tex seemed to have the same idea. He shrugged off his heavy leather trench-coat and threw it to the back seat to keep his hat company before clicking the locks down on the doors and heading off down the path to the front door of the house. I followed close behind him. He turned and gave me a look that said 'here we go' before knocking on the door. A second later the door creaked open and a small, tired looking woman peeked through the gap. She seemed to be in her forties, but somehow looked about sixty from stress.

"Can I help you?" she squeaked with a distinct British accent.

"I believe you should be expecting me," Tex said with a friendly smile, trying his best to sound a little less Texan and a little more British.

"Are you the man the priest told me about?"

Tex held up the Bible. "I am indeed. May we come in?"

"Yes, yes," the woman murmured, opening the door to let us in.

Tex strode in like he owned the place, which didn't seem to bother the woman, though she gave me a suspicious look as she closed the door behind us.

"Mrs. Williams, is it?" Tex smiled, holding out his hand.

"Yes," she sighed as she gave his hand a weak shake. The poor woman looked half dead from exhaustion and fright. "Would you like a drink, mister...?"

"Dickson. Texas Dickson. Please, just Tex though. This here's my, uh, apprentice, Isaac Nightingale. And a drink would be marvellous, thank you."

"I hope you both like gin. I'd offer you tea but you're going to need something stronger before you see my husband. Please, take a seat," she mumbled, forcing a smile.

We both sat down on the nearest couch. It was nice and soft.

"Gin's perfect, thanks."

I nodded in agreement, letting Tex do all the talking. He was a lot smoother with the ladies, especially married ladies.

"How long has your husband been like this?" he asked as the lady poured three glasses of gin.

"About two months now. I've had priest after priest come see him and they've all said there's nothing they could do. The last one said they'd send for someone else—a special kind of exorcist—to help, and here you are."

"Two months? Damn," Tex mumbled under his breath, giving me a look that made it clear we were soon to be knee deep in a whole load of shit.

"Forgive me for saying, but neither of you look like priests," she said as she handed us each a glass and perched herself on the edge of a footrest that sat in front of the sofa.

"We're not priests, but we specialize in matters like this. More so than any priest they could have sent, in any case," he smiled reassuringly.

The woman downed the glass of gin in one go. "Fair enough. They could have sent Chuck Norris for all I care, as long as my husband gets the help he needs. I just pray you're the ones to finally do the job."

"Lady, Chuck Norris ain't got shit on us." Tex downed his glass. "Shall we begin?"

Torment

Mrs. Williams led us up the stairs to the door of the master bedroom. Seven different locks and four deadbolts were keeping the door shut. She clearly didn't want her husband getting out.

"He's tied to the bed, but I thought the locks would be a good idea," she said as she twisted the keys and pulled each lock off the door before standing back, giving us both a weak smile. The smile said 'good luck', but her eyes said 'God help you'. "I'll leave you to it. I can't go in there."

"That's understandable. Are your children at home?" Tex asked.

"No, they're staying with their grandparents until this is over."

"Good. I'd suggest you put on a nice record and turn up the volume, you might not want to hear this."

She nodded as her eyes teared up a little, then she was off, away down the stairs to escape the oncoming tidal wave of shit. Tex nodded at me and gave the door a nudge. It opened slowly with a loud creak, just like they do in old haunted house movies.

"Let me do the talking. Try not to draw his attention and don't engage him if he speaks to you directly," Tex whispered.

I nodded to show I was listening.

Tex went in first, holding the bible out in front. I followed a second later, pulling the door shut behind me. The room was cold and bare. The only thing in the entire room was a king sized bed with Mr. Williams strapped to it, and he looked pretty vacant himself. He lay there and stared at us with dull yellow eyes that had sunk back into bruised and blackened sockets. He snarled with lips pulled back tight over his teeth, in fact, all of his skin was tight across his bones, a pale canvas of yellow and purple bruises with veins bulging through. Basically, he looked about as good as a corpse that had been left out in the sun a little too long. The leather straps around his wrists and ankles had cut in to him and left painful looking red marks.

We stopped at the foot of the bed. Tex set his bag down and looked at the demon. Its mouth curled into a smile as a low, guttural growl came from his chest.

"Hello gentleman," the demon breathed. "It's such a beautiful day, isn't it?

"Hello Mr. Williams," Tex responded, "it is indeed a lovely day out, how are you feeling?"

"Never better," Williams grinned.

"Are you sure? You don't look so well."

"I'm sure."

"Do you know who I am?"

"Yes. I know him too," the demon said, nodding towards me.

"You do?"

"I do."

"So can you tell me why you're here? Why you're strapped to the bed?"

"My wife is a kinky bitch."

"Do you usually call your wife a bitch? It's not very nice."

"She loves it. She's a filthy whore," he croaked with a twisted grin.

329

"I don't believe that. I'm sure she's a very nice lady."

"Drop your pants and whip your cock out. She'll be up here the moment she hears your belt hit the floor."

Tex glanced sideways at me, giving me a disapproving look. I was having a hard time containing a fit of laughter and it was making me shake.

"I'm not going to do that, Mr. Williams. Your name is John, right? Can I call you John?"

"You can call me whatever you please, sweet cheeks." He winked and blew a kiss.

"Is that your name? My memory isn't what it used to be."

"Yes."

"Are you sure?"

"Yes."

"Could you just confirm for me by telling me?"

"No."

"Why not?"

"Because I know what you're playing at you shit-fucking son of a whore," the demon spat.

"So you know why I'm here?" Tex said, his tone growing more serious.

"I know everything."

"In that case you know that I'm aware you're not really Mr. Williams, and that I'm going to have to ask you to leave this man's body and go back to where you came from?"

"It's my body now, pig fucker."

"It's not your body and you need to get out, now, demon."

"Fuck you," the demon growled.

330

"No thanks," Tex said with a sarcastic grin.

"What?"

"You offered to fuck me, but I'm politely declining."

"I never offered to fuck you," the demon said with a confused look plastered across his face.

"You did, you said 'fuck you,' so you clearly wanna fuck me."

"I didn't say that!" he roared, tugging at the straps.

"Didn't say what?"

"I wanna fuck you!"

"Oh, so you're admitting it now?" Tex smiled.

"What? No! Aaaarrg, I'll fucking—"

"You'll fucking what, fuck me?"

The demon thrashed around, growling illegible words in annoyance. The whole thing seemed a little ridiculous.

"Tex," I cut in, "a moment?"

"Yeah?" he glanced.

I took a few steps back and lowered my voice. Tex followed. "What is this? What are we doing here?"

"He's being a cheeky bastard; I'm just giving him a taste of his own medicine, getting him riled up a little. Gotta get them to react if you wanna get them out."

"This all smells like bullshit to me. He's probably just crazy, look at him, he doesn't know shit from chocolate," I whispered.

"That's exactly what it wants you to think. Trust me, it's the real deal."

"It looks like someone's watched The Exorcist one too many times."

"Remember who sent us here? You think Gabriel would get this wrong? He's never been wrong once. Trust me on this."

I gave him a sceptical look. "Fine, I guess. But if it turns out to be bullshit, you're buying drinks when we're finished."

"Deal," Tex smiled, turning back to the bed and its ugly inhabitant.

The sickening smile was still plastered across the creature's face. I hadn't noticed at first but I didn't see him blink a single time. Those freaky yellow eyes just seemed to stay fixed, constantly staring into our souls. I stood at the foot of the bed and looked at him. His eyes flicked up to meet mine, staring straight into me. I stared back. It felt like I couldn't take my eyes away. We could have been staring at each other for seconds or hours, I don't know. It felt like time had stopped. There was a scratching feeling inside my head, like bugs crawling over the inside of my skull. A weak sound whispered into my ear, repeating itself, growing louder each time. I recognized the voice and what it was saying but if felt like it was miles away, like it couldn't reach me. There was something choking me, icy hands around my neck, with more hands holding me still. More hands than I could count, all over my body, grabbing me in a vice-like embrace. The creature's eyes grew brighter as the hands around my neck got tighter and tighter until I couldn't breathe. A sharp pain spread across my face, then again, and again.

"NIGHT!" Tex roared as he gave me a hard slap across the face.

I snapped out of whatever trance I had been in and gave my face a rub. It felt like he had been slapping the shit out of me while I was away with the fairies. "What happened?" I asked. My head was a blur. It took me a second to realise we weren't in the room anymore.

"You let it inside your head. Don't look directly in its eyes. It'll fuck your mind in ways you don't even want to imagine."

"Yeah, I think we've established that."

"So, you think this is all bullshit now?"

"I think I believe you. It was like it was strangling me. It felt all too real."

"Good. Are you alright to keep going? Play time is over now. It's time to kick this asshole back to the deepest pits of Hell."

"Yeah, let's do it," I nodded.

Tex lead the way back into the room, keeping an eye on me as he opened the door and stepped in. "Alright sugar tits," he said, addressing the demon, "it's time to—oh shit!"

A second after he said it, I realised what was wrong. Mr. Williams was gone. The fucking bed was empty. Oh shit indeed.

"Where'd he go—ooh," I trailed off as I bumped into Tex. He had stopped dead in his tracks in the middle of the room and was standing, staring upwards. I followed his eyes. Yep. It was just as I suspected, send Sherlock home, the case was solved. Mr. Williams was on the goddamn ceiling. The straps lay on the floor in shreds and there he was, twisted around in some weird crab-like position, practically moonwalking his way across the ceiling like a spooky Michael Jackson.

"Would you mind coming down from the ceiling?" Tex asked, nice and polite as the demon lined himself up above his head.

333

The demon's response was a little less polite. Instead of responding vocally, he decided to open his mouth and vomit out a foul smelling, sticky black liquid, all over Tex's upturned face. It gushed out of his mouth for a solid twenty seconds. Tex made an attempt to move out of the stream but the demon scuttled across the ceiling and kept in line to get maximum coverage.

This was some real B-Movie shit.

Tex stood and wiped the puke from his face as the downpour came to an end. The demon chuckled and shuffled off to the top right hand corner of the room, above the bed.

"God damn sonuvabitch," Tex muttered to himself, "had hoped to make it all nice and easy, but no, this asshole goes and ruins my day. Damn good job I left my coat in the car." He handed me a bottle of holy water as he took out a crucifix. "When he's off the ceiling, toss that on the fucker."

"Gladly."

Tex turned to face the demon. "Now I'm giving you one more chance. Get down and don't pull any shit like that again."

"Fuck your mother," the demon growled.

"Don't say I didn't ask nicely," Tex shrugged before throwing the crucifix at the corner of the room with all his might.

The demon yelped and dropped from the ceiling in an attempt to avoid being hit by mini Jesus, but he wasn't quick enough, it smacked him on the head as he fell to the floor. I decided to make my move and pulled the cork out of the bottle of holy water.

The demon eyed the bottle. "Don't even try it, cocksucker," he hissed before flying towards me.

I braced for impact but the hit surprised me. For being trapped in such a frail, weak looking body, he slammed into me like a damn freight train. My feet came off the ground as he kept on moving, slamming me into the wall. My head snapped back with the force. I felt the skin on the back of my head split open, followed by the warm sensation of blood trickling down the back of my neck. He had me pinned. Luckily, I didn't spill any holy water until I upended the entire bottle over the creature's head. It made a loud hissing noise on contact with his skin. He screeched in pain, reeled back and spun around to retreat, only to be greeted with a face full of crucifix, courtesy of Tex.

The demon howled in pain and dropped to its knees as Tex pressed the crucifix into its forehead. The black vomit oozed from the sides of the creature's mouth and his eyes rolled back 'till they were all white, then Tex unleashed the fury.

"Feeeeel the power of Jeeeesus Christ, you vile piece of filth!" He roared with conviction so powerful the room almost shook. The demon fell to the floor and shook like an epileptic at a rave. Tex pointed to the bag to tell me to bring it as he knelt down beside the demon. I shuffled over to the bag and kicked it over to him. He rustled through it and handed me more holy water. "Don't use it all at once this time," he said before turning back to the demon and shouting, "Give me your name."

I sprinkled some of the Jesus Juice on the ugly bastard for good measure. The demon growled and writhed around in pain.

"I have many," he groaned through the pain.

"Give me your name, demon," Tex hissed as he held the creature's head with one hand and pressed down on the crucifix with the other.

[Track 35]

"My name... my name... So... is Sonn... my name..." his eyes flashed open, "my name is Jenny," he sighed as his voice softened. "My name is Jenny."

"You son of a bitch," Tex mumbled, staring at the demon, still holding the crucifix in place.

"It's me, Tex. I'm here. Billy too." The voice was completely different. Even the yellow in the eyes had faded to white.

Tex released his grip on the demon's head and pulled the crucifix away slightly. "It's not you."

"Dad?" the voice had changed again, this time it was filled with sadness, like a child on the verge of tears. "It's Billy, let us go, you're hurting us. We don't want to hurt anymore."

"It's not you."

"It's us. Please don't hurt us anymore. Don't hurt Mr. Sonny, he's a nice man, he found us brought us here to keep us safe from the cold. Don't make us go back. I'm scared of the cold."

Tex's hands trembled slightly. "Who's Mr. Sonny?" he said.

"The man you're hurting, he's helping us. He says he's sorry he was nasty to you; he just wanted to keep us safe and warm. He says he's like Uncle Luke, people think he's a bad person but he's not really, he's good."

336

"Billy?" Tex muttered, dropping the crucifix. He was clearly caught off guard by what was happening and seemed genuinely upset. It was difficult to watch.

"Tex," I cut in, pulling him to his feet and taking the crucifix to point it at the demon myself. "You said yourself that thing would lie and fuck with your head. That isn't who you think it is."

"It's just—"

"It ain't shit. It's a demon and it's fucking you over."

The demon got to its feet and took a step back from the crucifix. The eyes were slowly turning back to that pissy shade of yellow.

Tex looked at it, then back to me, then back to the demon and took a long breath. "It's not you," he said, pointing a finger at the creature. "You're not my wife. You're not my son."

The demon's eyes widened as it spoke. "Your precious little boy is being sodomized by the legions of Hell." he growled in his spooky voice, "Every day he dies a torturous death, Shall I tell you how he cries? How he screams for his father to save him? How his tears taste when daddy never shows up?"

"You shut your damn mouth," Tex snarled through gritted teeth.

"Tell that to your wife," the demon grinned. "Not a day goes by when she doesn't use that mouth of hers to clean assholes of the Hordes of Hell. So many... so many."

Tex took a step forward and took the crucifix out of my hand. "How about I personally jam you back up The Devil's asshole, you lying piece of shit? I know they're not in Hell," he said.

337

The demon took a step back and came into contact with the wall. Tex edged closer. The demon planted his hands on the wall and done a backwards crab walk up to the ceiling.

"I've got you, Mr. Sonny, you son of a bitch. From the moment I walked in I could feel it, I could feel the hatred. That's what you are, the pathetic demon of hatred. Your name is Sonneillon, isn't it?"

The demon's face contorted into a sickening scowl as he bared his teeth and scurried across the ceiling, looking panicked. Tex had figured out his true name. He was fucked. It was time to pack up and go home. I flicked some holy water to try and get him off the ceiling but he was having none of it.

"Fuck you both," he spat. A fat black glob landed next to my boot with a large splat. He was still moving across the ceiling. I made sure he didn't scurry in my direction. I didn't fancy getting covered in whatever he had spewed all over Tex.

Tex perked up again. "You've got one last chance to leave peacefully. You know you're fucked no matter what you do. Leave this man's body, Sonneillon."

"It's mine," the demon cried, scuttling to the corner and planting his feet on the walls, keeping his back to the corner of the ceiling.

"Sonneillon, I command you to leave!"

"No," he screeched, his resolve weakening.

"Sonneillon, I command you to vacate the body of John Williams," Tex roared.

The room fell silent; unnaturally silent.

We stood and waited for someone to make a noise, or a move. Anything. After a few seconds the demon spoke gently. "Fine," he seemed to sigh, looking me in the eyes, "I will leave. But if I can't have this body, no one can. I'll see you in Hell." Mr. Williams took his hands off the wall, reached up, took his own face in his hands and before Tex could shout 'no', gave a sharp, powerful twist.

His body fell to the floor with a heavy thud. He lay flat on his front but his eyes faced the ceiling. The yellow had washed out of them. For the first and last time, I saw Mr. Williams' true face and not the face of a man possessed by a demon.

"Shit," Tex muttered. We both stood and stared at Mr. Williams' body for a while, in a sort of stunned disbelief that the demon had decided to kill him so quickly. Tex bent down and picked up his bag of tricks, stuffing the crucifix inside. "Take a swig of them waters," he pointed at the bottle in my hand.

"You want me to drink the holy water?"

"You can do it and not be the demon's next home, or you can leave it and take your chances. Drinking holy water stops them from getting inside you once they've been exorcised from the last person."

I shrugged and took a sip then handed over the bottle so he could have some too. He gave it a quick pull before sticking the cork back in the top and dropping it in the bag.

Tex motioned for me to grab Mr. Williams' legs. As respectfully possible, we hoisted his body up on to the bed. Tex took a moment to adjust his head so it was facing the right way again.

"What do we do now?" I asked.

"Now we go home and drink," Tex sighed, fumbling in his pocket and pulling out the car keys. "Go wait in the car; I'll sort everything from here." He threw the keys over.

I didn't want to make things harder than they already were so I did as he asked. He followed out the room and down the stairs to have a word with Mrs. Williams. She turned her record off and sat as Tex sat opposite her. I was just closing the front door when I heard her ask how her husband was doing. I popped the car door and dumped myself down in the passenger seat where I sat in silence.

About twenty minutes passed before Tex appeared, walking down the path from Mrs. Williams' house. He pulled his door open, threw the bag on to the back seat and sat down at the wheel to join the silence. The entire journey home went by without either of us speaking a single word. Tex had taken the scenic route, too, so it was a good while.

It was about four in the afternoon when Tex pulled the car into the drive and killed the engine. He sat for a second and let out a heavy sigh. We both left our things in the car and made our way to the house. Tex headed straight for the whiskey and poured two glasses, almost to the brim. He handed me one and took a damn big sip of his.

"There's a few things I need to sort out in my room, it's gonna take a while so I'll catch up with you tomorrow if I'm not done by tonight."

"Sure thing," I said, knowing he probably just wanted some time alone.

I spent the rest of the day sitting drinking in front of the TV, pondering what had happened and why. My head was full of questions. How was it all over so fast? Why did the demon kill Mr. Williams like that? Who the hell is Uncle Luke? Every now and again I heard the dull sounds of things being moved around in Tex's room but he didn't appear at any point. By the time night came I was good and numb from the drink. I decided it was time for bed. My glass had a little whiskey left so I drained it and shuffled to the kitchen to wash the glass but ended up just leaving it in the sink.

Tex's room had gone silent a while ago but I had the feeling he was still awake. I staggered up to the door and was about to knock to say goodnight but I changed my mind a second before my knuckles hit the wood. I pulled my hand away and dropped it to my side as I shuffled away to the unmistakable sound of a man quietly sobbing.

Haunted

When morning came around I was the first to wake. Tex's room was silent so I decided to return the favour and cook breakfast, hoping Tex wouldn't mind. I gathered up all the ingredients and got cooking. It was about halfway done when the door to Tex's room creaked open and he came shuffling out. He looked a little rough around the edges.

[Track 36]

"Hope you don't mind," I said, nodding to the stove. "I thought I'd cook today since you made me a breakfast yesterday."

"Don't mind at all. Appreciate it, in fact." He made his was over to the table and sat down with his head in his hands. He seemed a little uneasy so I kept quiet while I prepared the food.

We sat and ate breakfast in silence, but the whole time, I could tell Tex had something he wanted to say. After clearing his plate and taking mine to wash them, he finally spoke up. "Look, I haven't been entirely honest about a few things."

"I don't mind," I said, leaning back in my chair, watching as he gave the plates a quick clean.

"I do though. I should have told you about my family. Now I know it might not seem like you need to know, but hear me out, alright?"

342

"Sure."

He finished giving the plates a scrub then stuck them on the rack to dry before sitting back down opposite me. "Good. Okay. Truth is I was at that bar in Saltstone for a reason. Gabriel sent me to find you, and I already know why you were there."

I raised an eyebrow, "That so?"

"Yup. You were on your way home to find a couple of vampires. I know all about it. I know about them and I know about Suzie."

It felt weird to hear someone say her name.

"Now, I know you want revenge for what they done and that's entirely your choice, but I want you to know I was in a similar situation myself once. My family is gone thanks to a vampire, and just like you I wanted the fucker dead. Thing is though, I eventually found him and I killed him. I got my vengeance. And it didn't bring me any peace. It didn't bring my family back. I wanted revenge and I got it but it didn't change shit. So sure, find them, kill them and enjoy it while it lasts, but don't expect the pain to go away."

"I can't honestly say I want it to go away. It's my fault Suzie's gone."

"Well, it's not but you feel like you should live with the pain, right?"

"Pretty much," I sighed.

"I can't lie, Night. It's gonna haunt you. Shit, what happened to my family has haunted me every day since. What happened yesterday made it even harder. It wasn't supposed to go down like that. I let myself get compromised. A man is dead and another family is broken. That's on me."

"You can't blame yourself for that. You said yourself demons are unpredictable."

"They are, but I could have saved him. The point is; don't let anything use your past against you. Not even your own emotions."

I nodded along. "Noted. Mind if I get some juice?"

Tex waved his hand, "Help yourself, and pour me a glass."

I poured two glasses and sat back down to let Tex finish what he needed to say. "You were saying?"

He took a sip before continuing, "Night, I've already told you I'm gonna need someone to carry on my work when I take a dirt nap, so what I'm saying is I want to help you find the assholes that murdered your girl, but I also need your help."

"You need my help?" This came as a surprise. Tex seemed capable of just about anything.

"I do. It's the reason Gabriel sent me to you. As far as he sees it, you could be the best there is at what we do. And there's not many like us left. From what I seen on the drive back from Saltstone, I've gotta agree with the bird."

"There are others?"

"There's a few. They're dotted here and there, but not many."

I sipped my juice. "So what's the deal?"

"Well, the deal is I help you finish what started when you were a kid then I teach you everything I know, and eventually, someday, you help me take out the meanest son of a bitch you'll ever have the misfortune of setting eyes on."

"Sounds interesting," I nodded. "Sounds like it could also get me killed."

"There's a decent chance, I ain't gonna lie. But I'd rather we avoided that. See, the thing is, I've been doing what I do for a long time. I'm getting on in years and I need someone to take over when I'm gone. The plan was to show my son the tricks of the trade, but he was taken from me. I want to teach you what I know, for when I'm gone. I know it's a lot to think about, especially considering we just met, but you're the only hope of carrying on the work."

I took a moment to ponder the offer, trying to weigh up the pros and cons. "So who's this mean asshole you mentioned?"

Tex sighed and fiddled with his fingers. "They call him Dominus Atrocitas, the self-proclaimed king of vampires."

"Dominus Atrocitas? What the hell kind of name is that? Sounds like an angst ridden teenager that's read a few too many shitty horror novels."

"It might sound ridiculous by today's standards but he's ancient, one of the original descendants of Judas. He's also extremely powerful. Like nothing you can imagine. He's the endgame for me, but going up against him alone would be suicide."

"Shit, that bad?"

"That bad. In fact, that vampire we killed in the bar—"

"We killed a fair few between us."

"You know the one. He didn't die when you shot him so I grabbed him and you pulled his head off."

"John Salter?"

"Yeah, him. Dunno if you'll remember much from the drive here, but like I told you in the car, he was a descendant, albeit a weaker one. You saw how a bullet wouldn't kill him."

"Fuck, yeah."

"Well imagine a vampire immensely more powerful and you've got Dominus Atrocitas. There's a kind of hierarchy. At the top of the pyramid there's the first ever vampire, Judas. He's long gone now, though. Second from the top are the likes of Atrocitas. They're the direct descendants, the pure bloods. There's only a couple left. Below that are those like John Salter, they call themselves Iscarions, after Judas. Then at the bottom you've got the regular old vamps. As far as I know Atrocitas practically has an army protecting him, with a fair few of Salter's kin thrown in there. So you can see why going after him alone would be suicide."

"So you want me to help you fight an army of ultra-vamps, to try and kill their dorky king."

"It's a lot to ask, but that sums it up. Just have a think. We'll go get the guys you're after and then see how you fe—"

"I'll help," I cut in.

Tex looked a little dumbstruck at my reply. "What?"

"Fourth of July is two days away. If we leave in an hour and drive fast we can be in Blackwater sometime after midnight. We leave soon and find them, then I'm in."

"You're sure? I didn't think you be entirely up for it."

"I said sign me up. Once the two assholes I'm after are dead, it's not like I'll have anything better to do."

Green Meanie

After my talk with Tex, we got straight on the road to Blackwater. Tex promised to honour his word and help me find Rapey and Roids, and I would honour mine by helping him take down Dominus Atrocitas, because why not?

[Track 37]

Before leaving I gave Mom a call to see if she was happy to have Tex as a guest for a couple of days. She sounded overjoyed at the thought of me returning with a friend. After Mom, I called Benito and gave him my mother's address so he could have my car dropped off there instead of back at Tex's place. I had no doubts that it'd be there within the next couple of days, looking good as new.

With a hunger for vengeance building inside me, I threw on some clothes, grabbed my stuff and hit the road. Tex sat behind the wheel of his Chevy Impala while I kicked back and enjoyed the cruise with one arm out the window. It was gonna be a long drive back to Blackwater, and one we'd have to do in shifts, so I intended on relaxing hard until it was my turn to take the wheel.

"Don't you have any questions?" Tex asked, keeping his eyes on the road.

347

"Plenty," I said, "Just depends on whether or not you'll answer them."

"Don't see why not."

I eyed him for a moment, considering what to ask. "Well, back when the demon was talking to you, he mentioned someone you haven't mentioned yourself."

Tex already knew who I meant. "Uncle Luke."

"That's the guy. What's the deal with that?"

"He's not really any relation," Tex said, taking his eyes off the road for a moment, "you know how kids will call a friend of the family their aunt or uncle? Just that really, he's an old friend. You'll meet him someday."

"It said people think he's a bad person, what's the deal with that?"

"Not exactly, he's aah... got a bad reputation, but he's a decent guy, he's um... look, it'll be easier to explain when you meet him. He helps with my work; let's just leave it at that for now."

"Fair enough," I sighed, unsurprised at him being cryptic again.

"Anything else? Not gonna ask the big question, get it out the way?"

"What's the big question?"

"Well considering I talk to an angel through a bird and you recently met a demon, I was expecting you to ask if it's all true, you know... Heaven and Hell."

In truth I hadn't really put much thought into it, just assumed it was all true without really thinking about it. Sure, the idea of Heaven sounded nice and I liked to think that Suzie would be waiting for me there, if I ever got there. But chances are, if it all turned out true, I'd probably be going down instead of up.

"Is it all true then?"

348

Tex glanced sideways, giving me a crooked smile. "It's all true," he said. "Heaven, Hell, all of it."

"So God exists?"

That one seemed to catch him. For painfully long second, he didn't answer. "Yes and no." He eventually said.

I kept quiet, but gave him a look that told him to continue.

"The being we call God exists, but isn't around anymore."

I raised an eyebrow. "So what does that mean? Does God take vacations?"

"Apparently so. God created our universe, but according to Gabriel, God's been missing for a while now, probably off watching what happens in another universe, or playing cosmic poker with some other gods. Either way, all any of the angels know is that he abandoned them and us a long time ago."

"When did God leave? Who runs Heaven?"

"Apparently he, or she, disappeared not long after Christ's crucifixion. It's all down to the angels now. They run Heaven, they make the decisions."

"It seems to me like the world's getting by just fine without God."

"It is, thanks to people like us keeping the supernatural under control."

I gazed out the window, pondering the possibilities of Heaven and Hell. "If Heaven is real, is Suzie there?"

Tex gave me a sympathetic look. "I don't know. Souls are funny things, apparently. Some go to Heaven, some go to Hell. Others go somewhere else entirely. They go wherever they're called. That's why the demon,

Sonneillon, got to me. I don't believe my family are in Hell, I'm ninety-nine percent sure they're not. But there's always the possibility. You know, what if? And one percent of doubt is enough for a demon to take advantage of you."

"Can't you just ask Gabriel if they're up there? See if Suzie's up there?"

"I've tried," he sighed, "they don't know. Angels don't know everything. No omnipotence for them, only the big man. They can do a lot and know a lot but not everything. Heaven is an entirely different plane of existence, son, and supposedly endless. Earth is a speck in comparison. An angel trying to find one specific person up there would be like a human trying to find one specific grain of sand down here. Sure, angels are immortal so they could search but I'd be long dead before they could find them. God would know but it seems we just aren't worth watching over anymore."

It was a lot to take in. It's not every day you learn the secrets of the universe while cruising down the highway. I had an endless amount of questions but thought I'd best cut it short and only ask a couple more.

"So, is the whole idea of seeing your loved ones again bullshit?"

Tex grumbled. "According to Gabriel if two souls are linked in this world, they'll find each other in the next. Are you remembering all this? I don't wanna have to answer so many questions again if you forget."

"I think stuff like this would be pretty difficult to forget," I said, staring straight ahead. "One more question?"

"Shoot."

"You said some souls go somewhere else. Where's this other place?"

Tex shrugged his shoulders. "Fuck do I know, son. Gabriel himself hasn't got a damn clue. Theory is that the soul can go to a different universe entirely. There's supposedly an infinite amount; just different planes all with different laws and gods, but they're all linked somehow. Don't ask how, 'cos I don't know. But what I do know is souls can travel. If they're needed somewhere else they can go there, and when they're done they can return. Apparently they'll disappear from what we consider existence and reappear just as suddenly. They reckon it's got something to do with the other gods, possibly borrowing them for some unknown reason. Like I said, they're funny things."

"And here I thought I was just gonna have a few drinks in the Salty Dog the other day. I'd get moderately sauced, sleep it off in the back seat and be on my way by morning. One minute I'm there and the next I'm getting lessons about the meaning of life from a guy who talks to angels."

"It's a lot, I know. I went through it all myself. You'll be fine though. If you weren't gonna be fine your sanity would have taken a hike long before now."

"Sometimes I think it wandered off nearly a decade ago. Sometimes I wonder if I'm still in a coma and just dreaming all of this. Hold up, pull over," I pointed at the side of the road about fifty meters away, "over there, by those cactuses."

"You mean cacti?"

"Whatever, just pull over, I've just thought of something."

Tex gave me a confused look but eased the car on to the side of the road and came to a stop. "Gotta take a leak or something? There's a gas station a few miles ahead."

I pushed the car door open and slid out of the seat while saying, "Nope. I just want a cactus, they make good gifts," before closing the door and strolling out into a patch of land littered with them.

It didn't take long for Tex to get out of the car and wander over to my side. I told him I was looking for the perfect cactus. I gave him a brief description of the kind of cactus I had in mind. He shrugged his shoulders and wandered off in another direction to help me search.

Five minutes passed before Tex called from about thirty feet away. "What about this one?" He said, pointing downwards.

I made my way over to him and took a look at what he'd found. There it was, standing proud, a big green meanie. Twelve inches long and three inches thick; the perfect cactus.

A cactus to die for.

The Hunt

Luckily, Tex had a shovel in his trunk, so I uprooted the cactus with ease. His explanation for having a shovel in his car was: "In my line of work, you never know when you're gonna need to dig a grave." I couldn't argue with that.

Given how accepting I'd been of Tex's stories and general oddness, he decided not to ask about the cactus, which was fine with me. I even asked him to pick the spikes off the lower quarter while I took my turn driving, and he did it without so much as a questioning look.

The drive back home to Blackwater took a fair few hours. Even with driving in shifts and the pedal on the floor, it was long after midnight by time I drove over the hills that surrounded town and saw the familiar lights glittering down below. With it being so late, I decided to pull up outside one of the little hotels on the outskirts of town. I didn't want to wake Mom and have her fuss over things at such an hour.

Tex was asleep, leaning against the car door with the brim of his hat covering his face. I gave him a slap on the chest and told him we were here. He flicked his hat up and took a look around. "Where's here?" he said.

"Home," I said. "Think it'd be best to spend the rest of the night in a hotel. We can head into town in the morning."

"Good idea. I could do with a bed," Tex grumbled.

Within minutes we had grabbed our stuff, booked a couple of rooms and agreed to meet back at the car for ten in the morning. Getting a room each felt necessary, mainly so we wouldn't have to take turns showering, shitting, you know. We weren't that well acquainted just yet.

Sleep came and went. It felt like I'd had my head on the pillow for no more than thirty minutes before I was getting back up to face the day. When morning came around, I shuffled my way downstairs with my bag slung over one shoulder. The long drive had taken its toll. I felt like shit. Tex wasn't looking much better either. He stood propped up against the car, looking like he'd be on the floor if it wasn't there. As I got closer I noticed the dark circles under his eyes. He looked worse than I felt.

"Sleep well?" I asked.

"Like a log, just didn't get enough. What's the plan then?"

I pulled a few newspaper clippings from my pocket and handed one to Tex. The clippings had pictures of Suzie's killers, Rapey and Roids (or Wane Wachesky and Brad Jones, as they were officially known). "Reckon we take a tour around town; ask a few people if they've seen this pair of assholes. First stop is my mom's though. We can drop off a few things, get you both acquainted."

Tex nodded and pulled the car keys out of his back pocket, "Sounds good."

354

"No sweet-talking my mother, though." I said.

"I can't make any promises," he joked, throwing the keys to me. "You're driving by the way."

I caught the keys in one hand and begrudgingly got in the car. It made sense for me to drive considering I knew the town, but I'd had enough of it for a few days. Luckily, it only took about ten minutes to drive from one side of Blackwater to the other. I was pulling up outside Mom's place within five. From the look of the place, nobody was home. I didn't exactly give my Mom a time for when we'd be arriving so I wasn't all that surprised. "Looks like you're gonna have to save that sweet-talking for later," I said. "But we may as well drop our stuff off, since we're here."

"She won't mind?"

"Nah, I'll just put it all aside somewhere and leave a note."

Tex hauled his ass out of the car and made his way to the trunk to collect our stuff while I set about opening the door. I didn't bother taking a spare key with me when I left, but Mom always kept one hidden in case of emergency. I found the key hidden under a plant pot filled with Lavender, just where she always left it. Tex brought our stuff inside. Just the travel gear though, the essentials such as guns and ammo were left in the trunk, alongside my cactus.

I scribbled a short note telling Mom that I was home, and that we'd be back later, then set off to the centre of town to start the hunt. After throwing out a few ideas, we agreed to split up to try and cover more ground. I parked the car in a small parking lot right in the centre of town, just by the Barker Street bus stop. Tex said he'd just wander around for a while and meet me back at the car in a few hours. First stop for me was Vidstar Video. I reckoned the shining jewel of the town would probably attract anyone that visited, so it seemed a good place to start. The clerk turned out to be a dopey-eyed teenage guy that couldn't even fake an interest in my questions. He glanced at the newspaper clipping and shrugged.

"They're pretty memorable. You've never seen them?" I said.

"I dunno man," he droned, "I don't really take notice of who comes in here."

"Really?"

He gave another shrug, without even bothering to grunt a half decent response.

I turned away shaking my head then set about the store to ask any customers if they'd seen the two assholes. Not a single person had. Maybe my love of movies was making me biased, but I couldn't understand why anyone wouldn't at least take a look in the only video store in town. I thought they would have at least called in to check out the porno section, but no.

After visiting Vidstar I spent a couple more hours calling in to every store I could find, even stopping random people on the streets. The day turned out to be one big 'fuck you'. Not a single person had set eyes on Rapey and Roids. A fair few recognised them from news stories, but nobody had actually seen them in the flesh. Feeling completely beaten, I called into the florists for the second time that day. I didn't have any questions; I just wanted a bunch of flowers. It was time to go apologise to Suzie for being so useless. I had travelled all the way to Los Angeles and back looking for her killers and I'd found a grand total of jack shit. Everything I'd been through seemed to be leading up to one big, shitty anti-climax.

I sulked my way to the East Street graveyard with my hands in my pockets and a big bunch of flowers tucked under my arm. I knew Suzie wouldn't have been mad, but I was mad at myself. The Fourth of July was a day away and I hadn't so much as had a peek of anyone suspicious.

Suzie's grave was exactly as it had been the last time I visited; beautiful yet sombre. In what had been almost nine years since she died, I was visiting for the second time. I crouched down to place the flowers at the base of the headstone and rocked backwards to fall to my ass. I sat with a dull thud that kicked up a bit of disturbance in the grass. I stared at the headstone, wishing Suzie was still with me, and for the second time, a moth fluttered out from the grass and danced around in the air. I watched as it fluttered about, getting closer to me. It was the same kind of moth I'd seen when I last visited, a nice looking one, a kind that Suzie would have liked. It flew around me a few times then eventually fluttered up to my face and landed on my nose.

A voice behind me said, "Night?"

I turned and found Tex looking down at me, giving me a concerned look as I sat on the ground, looking like a lunatic with a bug on my face.

"Take a look at this," I said.

"Yeah, you've got a moth on your face there buddy."

"It was here last time I visited."

"Wasn't that a while ago?"

"Yeah. Obviously it's not the same one but still, it's the same type. There must be a bunch of them living around here."

Tex looked a little awkward. "I guess... I, uh... didn't mean to disturb you, I was on the way back to the car and spotted you. Thought I'd come see if you'd found anything."

I sighed then said, "I ain't found shit. Let's just call it a day."

The moth twitched its wings and took flight.

Tex held out a hand to help me up. "Maybe tomorrow then," he said.

I took another look at Suzie's headstone and nodded, "Maybe tomorrow."

Same Time, Same Place

After a disappointing day looking for Rapey and Roids, we made our way back to my mom's place. Mom was home when we got there and I was greeted with a strong hug that no woman her age should have been capable of giving. Tex was a perfect gentleman around my mother and she took an immediate liking to him as they got to know each other. True to his word, he held off on the sweet-talking, which was just as well because Edward—Mom's boyfriend—was also there.

Another good thing was that Tex had the damn good sense not to mention anything we'd been up to together. I don't know how my Mom would have reacted if he had casually mentioned he'd met me at a bar-slaughter, shot up a load of vampires, and then talked me into joining what was essentially a war against them. "By the way Mrs. Nightingale, your son is a talented murderer, and we've spent the past couple of days kicking ass and talking to a bird." It wouldn't have made the best dinner conversation.

No, everything went perfectly. It felt great to be home and see Mom so happy, too. We spent the evening having a good catch up and just talking about anything and everything. When the time came to hit the sack, I fell into the bed in my old room and had the best sleep in a while. Tex got the spare room after being talked into taking it rather than sleeping downstairs on the sofa.

When morning came around I was feeling refreshed and optimistic about questioning more people. A quick glance out of the front window gave me the pleasant surprise of finding my car sitting by the sidewalk, looking as good as new. I made my way into the kitchen to join everyone, already sat around the breakfast table. We ate, we laughed and we enjoyed each other's company. The day got off to a great start, and considering it was the Fourth of July—a day I'd come to dread—even I was in high spirits.

Unfortunately, the fun didn't last long. Just like the day before, my best attempts at finding Rapey and Roids offered sweet fuck all.

By the end of the day, I gave up looking.

* * *

[Track 39]

Tex and I sat in Benny's diner, the place I'd often visit with Suzie, during happier days. We had looked all over town before I eventually gave up and decided to call it a day. We'd even brought both cars out—Tex's and my own—to cover as much ground as possible. Neither of us had any luck, so we decided to grab something to eat. Time was getting on and the sun was going down by the time we got our food. Just like all those years ago, I'd ordered lemonade and an extra-large hot dog. Only this time, it was Tex sat across from me and the food was served by some scrawny guy rather than the feisty waitress I remembered.

Tex sat sipping a light beer, washing down some of the steak he'd ordered. The place had a completely different atmosphere to what I remembered. The staff members weren't as fun and the food just wasn't as good. Or maybe it was all exactly the same, but the lack of Suzie made everything a little dull. Tex seemed to be enjoying himself, at least. I watched as he sunk a fork into the steak and cut off another piece. He noticed me watching, sitting with my half-eaten hotdog in front of me.

"Too much on your mind, huh?" he said.

I nodded, looking down at the hotdog. It was going cold.

"Don't worry. We'll get the guys. It's what we're here for."

"I ain't so sure," I said.

Tex chewed on a piece of steak, "Look, the way I see it is things tend to fall in to place one way or another. Look how Saltstone turned out."

"Yeah but you had an angel to tell you where to go. You were sent there, you weren't sent here. I wasn't sent here. I'm going on Chinese whispers and newspaper clippings."

"Have a little more faith. Not in them," he pointed his knife upwards, "no, have faith in you, in us. Besides, they don't tell me everything. For all we know, the plan could have been to send me to Saltstone so I'd end up here to help you. Maybe you don't spot the guys, but I do? Maybe the fact that I'm sitting here taking too long to eat this steak is what makes us find them? Or perhaps your decision to quit looking could be what makes you find them? Things play out, son, sometimes you've just gotta let them."

"Guess I'll take your word," I said, picking up the hotdog.

I had completely lost my appetite but I finished my meal anyway. Tex finished his steak and drained his beer soon after. Even though place just didn't have the spirit I remembered, I still left the waiter a damn good tip before we left. We agreed to meet back at my mom's place as we walked out to our cars. I figured spending the rest of the evening there might cheer me up a little. Tex stood by me as I leaned against my car and pulled out a smoke. The sun had set fast and the parking lot was bathed in the soft glow of the diner's neon lights.

"Got a light?" I said, patting my pockets for my lighter before remembering I'd left it in the trunk with the Sisters.

Tex grunted and pulled a pack of matches from his pocket.

I struck the match and was about to spark up when a cry rang out from the darkness. My heart missed a beat and I quickly handed the matches back to Tex. He looked at me. I looked at him, and we were both off in the direction of the noise. The streets were lit by dull street lights. Shadows flickered everywhere. As we got closer to where the noise came from we heard what sounded like a scuffle going on down a nearby alleyway. I broke out into a run. Tex followed close behind. We were about to turn the corner into the alleyway when a man stumbled out of the darkness and fell at my feet. He landed face down on the sidewalk. I crouched down as he rolled on to his side. His face was all beaten and bloody.

"Please," he said, "please help. They've took my wallet."

I put a hand on his shoulder and turned to look down the alleyway. My blood froze. There he was, the man himself. Wane Wachesky stood staring me right in the eye. Rapey. And Roids was behind him. He held eye contact for a second then spun on his heel and ran in the opposite direction. Tex recognised them a second after I did. As I helped the man from the floor to his feet, Tex whipped out a Model 29 revolver and pinched off a round. It hit Roids in the thigh. He steadied the gun to take another shot.

"Wait," I said. "Take care of this guy. I'll take care of them."

He didn't question the matter. In the blink of an eye the gun was gone and Tex was reaching to put an arm around the guy. He nodded in the direction of the alleyway and said, "Things play out."

I gave him a nod and took off running down the alleyway. I had found them, seen them in the flesh and looked into the eyes of the man that murdered Suzie and left me to rot. I had just about been to Hell and back because of these two fuckers, and after nine years, they were almost close enough to touch.

In the time it took to hand the injured guy to Tex and actually start chasing them, they had disappeared. As with all suckers, they were fucking fast. Lucky for me, I had Uncle Jimmy's Hot Sauce burning through my veins. And it was burning like never before; my heart was on fire. Unlucky for them, Roids had been shot in the leg and had left a trail of rancid blood. I could find them with my eyes closed. All I needed to do was follow the stench.

The sound of tires screeched in the distance behind me. Tex was on the road. The unmistakable sound of his engine roared as he passed the alley, the roar spoke to me. And I knew just what it was saying.

I ran out the other side of the alley to find Rapey and Roids running down the road, way off in the distance. They were heading for trees; to the cover of darkness. I put the sauce to work and catapulted myself towards them. From the look of it, Tex had hit Roids in the femoral artery. He was bleeding heavily and beginning to limp and lag behind. Rapey took a hold of his arm to encourage him to hurry up. They were making a damn good escape attempt but I was having absolutely none of it. I pushed myself forward, closing the distance. They were nearing the end of the road. Their options were to turn right or left and run up another road, or stay straight and run into the trees. I knew what they'd be choosing. Fifteen seconds and they'd be in the trees. That's not what I wanted. Sure, I could still catch them but it'd likely be more difficult with trees in the way.

Ten seconds. I sucked in a lungful of air and channelled my rage to my legs. I needed this. I needed to catch them. I needed to kill them. I needed them to suffer.

Five seconds. I was close, but they were still getting away. I let out a roar, a battle cry, yelling nothing in particular. I wanted to startle them, make them stumble. One moment's hesitation was all I needed.

Two seconds. For a moment, I thought it had worked. Rapey's face dropped in fright as he glanced back to see where I was. It lit up in a look of horror. And by 'lit up' I mean the headlights of a fast approaching car had flashed on from the darkness, literally illuminating his face as he undoubtedly sprayed shit all down the legs of his pants. They had less than a moment before they reached the treeline.

Tex's car shot towards them from the right hand road. It smashed right into them both at a devastating speed. Rapey and Roids went barrelling over the car like a pair of ragdolls. I watched with grim satisfaction as their unconscious bodies fell to the hard ground, their skulls bouncing with a pleasing crack. If they were human they'd have been dead before they even hit the ground. No doubt about it. But they weren't human. They were suckers.

Tires squealed as the car skidded to a sudden stop. Tex burst out of the car, yelling, "YEAH! I GOT YA GOOOOD DIDN'T I?"

I closed the distance and slowed my run as I made my way over to him. "Shit," I said. "For a second I thought I was gonna lose them."

He slapped me on the back. "What did I say? Huh? Things play out."

I smiled and nodded. "Things play out."

The injured guy from the alley was sitting buckled up in the back seat of Tex's car. He looked horrified and happy all at once. Tex followed me over to Rapey and Roids' unconscious bodies.

"What now?" he said.

"Help me get them in the trunk then get me back to my car. I'm gonna take these cocksuckers for one hell of a ride."

Horrors, Part Two

With Tex's help I got Rapey and Roids back to my car, tied them up and piled them into the back seat. I took a minute to check the contents of my trunk. Betsy the Gatling gun sat snugly folded away at the front. My box of explosives was tucked nicely into the top left corner. The box for the Sisters—which were now strapped to me, where they belong—sat up in the right corner. My cactus sat in the bottom left corner, resting on a bed of old newspapers. To the bottom right sat my miscellaneous items (chains, a hammer, crowbar, a sack, duct tape). The sides had a nice assortment of guns and ammo, with a clear spot in the middle for a space to sit when putting Betsy to work. The thought of putting my toys to use made the hot sauce burn in my heart. It was time.

Tex agreed to drop our new friend off at the hospital then meet me afterwards. I found a napkin in my glove box and drew him a map to where I'd be, with a note at the bottom that read: "Follow the dirt trail into the clearing; where it all started. Same time, same place."

The drive from Benny's parking lot was a tense one. I took it slow, worried that turning too fast or hitting a pothole might jolt the suckers awake before I'd arrived at my desired location. Even going slow, it was only a few minutes 'till I pulled up by the side of the road on the edge of town. The spot was right by the old dirt trail, leading through the trees to where the carnival stays when it passes through town.

I killed the engine and stepped out of the car. The place was pretty secluded. Not another person in sight. Rapey and Roids were still out cold in the back seat. I popped the trunk and ran my eyes over the goods. The Sisters were all I really needed but I decided to take a few other things. I took the sack and filled it with some bullets, my hammer and a few other goodies. The duct tape could stay. I'd already used it to bind the suckers arms, legs and mouths.

[Track 40]

With a bunch of treats all wrapped up, I picked up the chains and nudged the trunk shut. The suckers didn't deserve a shred of dignity. Rather than carry them to the clearing, I pulled them from my car and dropped them to the ground. Fuck carrying them. I fastened my chains to their feet and dragged the fuckers through the dirt.

While pulling them along the ground I made sure to drag them over every rock, every tree root and every piece of shit I could find. When I finally came to a stop in the clearing, my heart was going bat-shit crazy. I was back. Everything had come full circle. The suckers were beginning to stir; finally regaining consciousness after Tex almost destroyed them with his car. Roids was the first to come around. He was confused, disorientated. It took about a minute or so for his head to clear. While I waited, I plopped my bag of tricks down and tipped the contents out on to the dirt.

367

"Mmmhhhpp" Roids mumbled through the duct tape, pushing himself into a sitting position.

I made my way to his side and tore the tape off his face. "Remember this place?" I said. "Remember me?"

"Who are y—"

I swung a fist into the side of his head. Being hit by Tex's car had already softened him up. My fist connected with his temple. I felt his skull give slightly under my knuckles. "Remember that?"

Roids crashed back down to the ground. Even though he was already a little beaten, I knew he was pretty damn strong. I didn't doubt that he could break out of the tape I'd tied around his wrists and ankles, so I picked up the hammer.

"What're you doing?" he said, rolling to his side, slightly dazed.

"Making sure you can't run. Making sure you watch. Just like you did to me."

He was about to speak when the glint of recognition crossed his eyes.

I raised my hammer, claw side facing him.

"Wait, no!" He yelled as he rolled on to his back and struggled to break free.

I aimed at his right knee and swung the hammer down hard. The claw tore through his skin and drove down deep behind his kneecap. I pulled a little, hooking the claw in there good. Roids squealed like a pig. His squeals grew louder as I gave the hammer another, harder tug. On the third tug, I put some muscle into it and tore the hammer out of his leg, bringing his kneecap right along with it. Blood and gristle burst from his leg as the little bone flew out and clattered off a nearby tree.

I took a look at my work. Where his knee had been, there was nothing but a ragged hole. What I assumed were his tendons hung from my hammer in gristly strings. A quick flick got rid of them.

Roids' screams had wound down to silence. He looked like he was screaming but there was no noise coming from his mouth. I took the moment of silence as an opportunity to repeat the procedure and remove his left knee, all with one smooth motion this time. Happy that he wouldn't be running off, I sat down beside him. He lay completely still; still and silent, most likely in shock.

"Don't you go passing out on me now," I said.

He stared up at the sky, silent.

Since he had decided to make it easy and wasn't putting up a fight, I stood and set about finishing my work. I took hold of his bound wrists, used a knee to pin them to the dirt above his head then took the hammer to his elbow. I mixed things up a little, though. Rather than hooking them out, I just smashed them repeatedly 'till they were nothing but pulp. In retrospect, all I needed to do was paralyse him. One well-placed hammer to the spine would have done, but I just got carried away. Taking his elbows and knees may have been unnecessary, but shit, it was fun. Either way, I knew he'd eventually heal. It'd take a long time, but he'd walk again.

For the final touch, I took out a pocket knife and helped myself to his eyelids. He needed to watch, just like I watched. By the time I was finished, Roids was wide eyed—literally—and tremoring violently. Snot and drool ran down his chin. He had essentially been turned into one of those wacky wavy-armed tube things you

369

see outside car dealerships, flailing their useless limbs around.

I pulled him across the dirt and propped him up against the tree so he had a good view of what I had in store for his friend. It was Rapey's turn, and he was just waking up.

"Hi there, sleeping beauty," I said as I positioned Roids' head for his viewing pleasure.

Rapey mumbled through the tape, clearly distressed. I wanted to see what he had to say, so off came the tape.

"What the fucking fuck? Who are you? What's this?" he yelled. He struggled for a second then caught sight of his friend. "Oh fuck. Fuck, fuck, fuck, what have you done?"

"Does this not ring a bell?" I said. "Neither of you have very good memories, do you?" It seemed like his memory needed jogging. Luckily, I had a picture of Suzie tucked into my wallet. I whipped it out and stuck it in his face. "Recognise her? The girl you murdered nine years ago?"

His face dropped. "Fuck. You're that kid? No, you're not him. I'm sure he's dead."

"Technically, I was dead. I died a few times, actually. But I was never as dead as you're gonna be." I finished with a smile.

He struggled against the tape around his wrists. "You've got no idea who you're messing with."

I picked my hammer up off the ground. "I know who you are, Wane Wachesky. You're a rapist, a murderer, a royal piece of shit, and a vampire."

His expression changed as soon as I finished the sentence, going from confusion to amusement. "You know huh? How long did it take to figure out?"

"I know everything, I remember everything," I said.

A smile crept across his face, and the corners of his mouth just kept on going. "So do you remember this?" he said.

I stood and watched as the sides of his mouth split and jagged teeth pushed their way out of his gums. His nose sank back and his eyes turned black. I simply shrugged. "I've seen it all before. It was creepy the first time you done it but now I think I've dropped scarier turds."

With one quick motion he snapped the tape around his wrists and used his yellow claw-like fingernails to rip the tape from his ankles. He snarled and stood up. Even at his full height he was about a head shorter than me. He was no longer intimidating. In fact, he looked kind of pathetic. To think this little cocksucker murdered Suzie.

"I do remember," he said, "yeah I fucked up your girl. I fucked up her real good didn't I? Shame I didn't get to give her the goods." He grabbed his crotch and thrust his hips as he spoke in his raspy vamp voice.

I gazed into his black, beady eyes and said, "Well, now my girls are gonna fuck you up."

Before my words even drilled into his thick skull, I whipped out both of the Sisters and bust out two bullets, right through each of his knees. Blood, bone and cartilage sprayed across the clearing behind him. He hadn't even registered what happened before his legs folded the wrong way underneath him and he gave the dirt a high speed inspection. He gave an almighty howl as he went down.

I let out a loud, boisterous laugh. "Ooh, man, you really should have seen that coming."

A whimpering sound babbled behind me. I turned to see Roids' lidless eyeballs ogling his friend. "W-w-wane," he stammered, "he pulled my knees out, Wane. He's gone cut my blinkers off, Wane. I can't move."

"Shut up you fucking retard," Rapey yelled, clutching his legs.

"But I ain't got no kneeeees, Wane."

"Can't you see he's fucking shot my knees out too, you idiot?"

Standing there watching them bicker, I noticed Roids did seem a little mentally challenged. For a second I felt bad for what I'd done to him, but only for a second.

I held up the Sisters. "This here's Maria," I jiggled my left hand, then my right, "and this is Sofia. And they're not done with you yet."

"Up yours, faggot," Rapey spat.

A quick squeeze of the triggers sent a bullet into each of his shoulders. He howled again, even louder this time.

"Oh, sorry, don't you like that? Does it hurt?" I crouched down and got right up in his twisted face. "Are you not enjoying it?"

Rapey made a move to bite at my face but he was too slow. "I'll fucking kill you," he growled.

"I don't think you will. Now, what was it you said to me all those years ago? Oh, wait, I remember." I gave him a couple of light slaps on the cheek. "Sit tight, sweet cheeks, show's not over yet."

He froze. Those were the words he used right before he murdered Suzie, and he knew it. I didn't give him any chances. A second after he froze up, I was on him, tugging at his pants and pulling them down to his ruined knees.

"What the fuck are you doing?" he said, sounding somewhat self-conscious now that his junk was exposed.

"What's wrong? You didn't have a problem whipping the ol' Johnson out last time we met." I got on one knee by his side, raised Maria high into the air then pointed the barrel straight down, slowly edging it closer and closer to Rapey's junk.

"No, please!" he cried.

The barrel crept closer. "Sorry, Maria's just having some fun. She's a little crazy, you know. She likes it rough."

The closer the barrel crept to his package, the more human his face shifted. By the time it was an inch away, he looked completely human again. As if that'd make me feel any sympathy. No, I had come this far. No chance of cutting my fun short. I closed the gap and pressed the gun directly on to Rapey's left testicle, pushing it down hard. His face turned grey.

"Please. I'm sorry about what I done. I can't help it, I swear. I can't control it."

"What a coincidence, I can't control Maria."

"I'm begging you, please! I'm sorry man, I'm SO sorry," he babbled.

I gave a shrug and lifted the gun away. "Well I suppose if you're sorry then that's okay. I forgive you."

Relief washed over his face. "You mean it? Oh, sweet Jesus, thank y—"

Nope. I turned my face away, swung the gun back down and BLAM! Blew his entire dick and balls clean off. Even through the noise of the gun, I heard it all splatter. After the splatter came the screams. Screams like I'd never heard.

"Did you really think I'd forgive you for what you did to her?" I roared, "For how you ruined my life? Huh, Wane? You took away what was most precious to me. I'm repaying in kind, with added interest, you fuck."

I holstered Maria and put my free hand on Wane's head, pushing my thumb hard into his eyeball as I held the barrel of Sofia under his chin.

"Night?" A voice said from behind me.

I turned to see Tex walking up the trail.

"Hey," I said, lowering my voice.

Tex took a look at my work and ran a hand over his face. "Jesus, Night. You're a pretty scary guy, you know that? Fuckin' chainsaws for arms, alright."

I shrugged. "Yeah, well, you know how it is."

"Revenge is a dish best served cold, huh?"

"I'd say revenge is a dish best served raw, bloody and screaming for mercy."

Tex cast his eyes to the floor and sighed. "So I guess this is it? This is the grand finale?"

"Just one more thing, for now," I said before holstering Sofia and flipping Rapey so he was face down in the dirt, whimpering, with his ass in the air.

"One more thing?" Tex said, raising an inquisitive eyebrow.

I nodded toward the bag on the ground. It had something green and spikey poking out of it.

"Is that what I think it is?"

"Yes, yes it is. Tex?"

"Yeah?"
"Pass the fuckin' cactus."

[Track 41]

B-MOVIE BLOODBATH

Writer
Isaac Nightingale
(But really, Liam Blaney)

Tea provider
Liam Blaney
Hannah (Sometimes)

Director of music
Liam Blaney

With a big, juicy **thank you** to the following:

Cassandra Chaput
For being a fantastic editor and catching the many mistakes I was sure didn't exist.

Hannah
For painstakingly designing the cover, all the everlasting support, being the best human in general, and for keeping me humble by falling asleep whenever I read her my work.

Kaitlyn, Tanya, Fardin, Toots, Kirsty, Kayleigh & Paine
For reading the early drafts and providing valuable feedback.

Joe, Paul & Steph
For the above, as well as being constant sources of
support and inspiration.

Marina
For being my first reader and encouraging me to start
writing in the first place.

And finally,
Thank you to anyone who's bought, read,
recommended, enjoyed, hated, reviewed, sniffed,
donated or borrowed this book.
But especially those who've bought it. Thank you for the
money.

Please don't forget to leave a review on the likes of
Goodreads, Amazon, Facebook, Waterstones, etc.
Each and every review is greatly appreciated and is a
big help towards any success this book may have in the
future. Even if you thought it was shit, let me know.

You can close the book now, there's no end credits scene
to set up **the sequel**…

Told you.

Made in United States
North Haven, CT
25 June 2024

54064025R00233